BLOODJEWELS

BLOOD JEWELS

BOOK ONE OF THE REALM BOUND TRILOGY

AMBER HANOPHY

ISBN: 979-8-88785-032-0 (Paperback)
ISBN: 979-8-88785-034-4 (Hardcover)

Library of Congress Control Number: 2024936664

Any references to historical events, real people, or real places are used fictitiously. Names, characters, and places are products of the author's imagination.

Book design by Allison Chernutan.
Edited by Alex Vicarel and Carol Kudeviz.
Pearls art by renata.s via Freepik.

Printed in the United States of America.

First printing edition 2024.

emily@fracturedmirrorpublishing.com
Fractured Mirror Publishing
Knoxville, Tennessee

www.fracturedmirrorpublishing.com

For all the untamable witches out there.

Skull
Uncliff
Crasmere
Eldon
Nexe
Neom
Wiverens

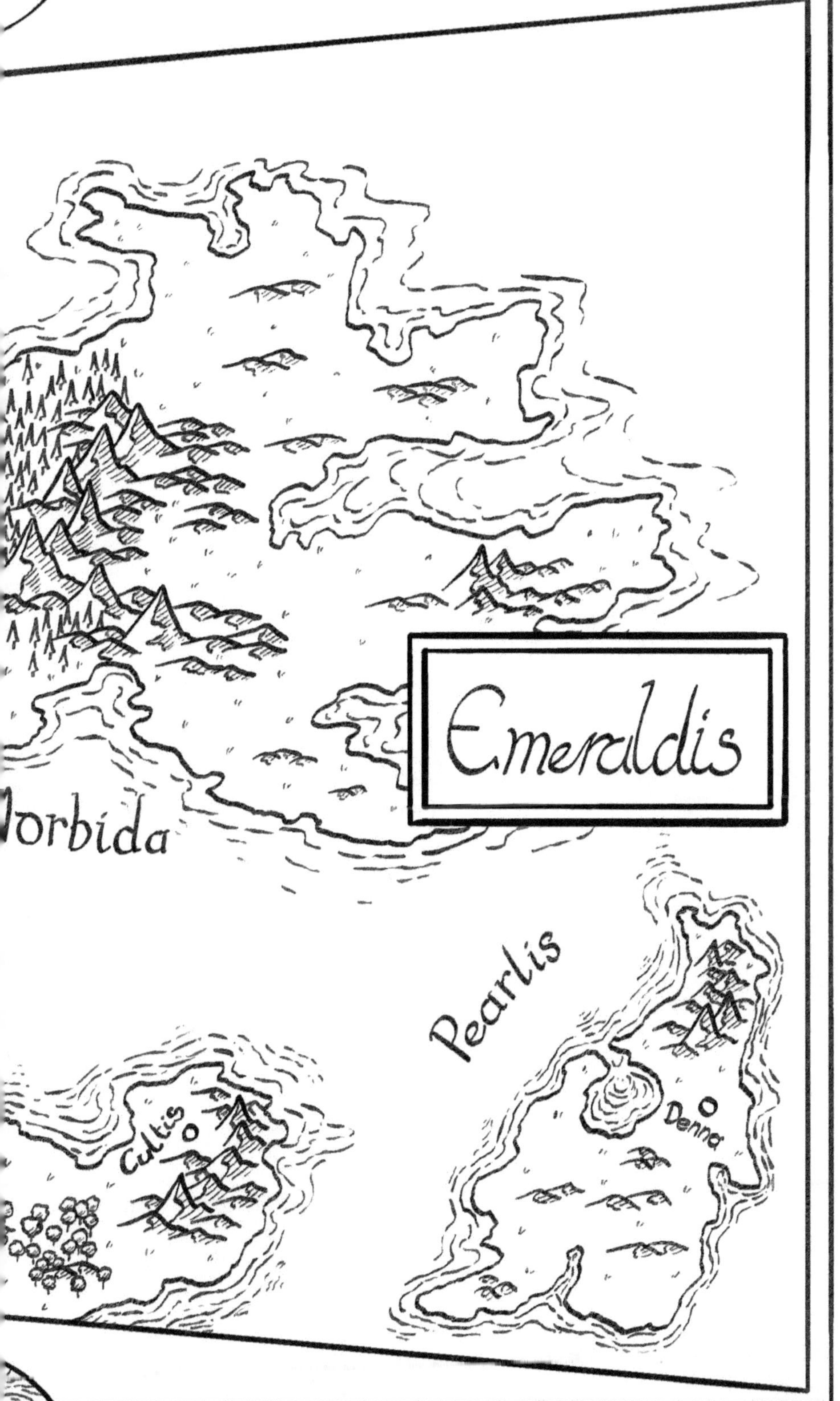

Emeraldis
orbida
Pearlis
Cultis
Denna

PART I

The Ruse

PROLOGUE

I don't consider myself an angry person, but nothing sours my mood like blood stains ruining a perfectly good tunic. Though I shouldn't be that upset; I do have a closet of them back home. But the damp and unsalvageable one clinging to me now *was* a favorite.

Before it was soaked in the smell of rotting iron.

In fact, everything is steeped in the stench of loss. It's filling every crevice of the wet stones around us, knotting my stomach as I push down feelings I'd rather not name.

Because I am the cause of this death and destruction. By my own hand—I am the chaos.

Dying witches lay around me, sputtering and spewing their last moments. My fingers are shaking in a violent chatter; I'm certain you can see the nausea on my face.

It's almost over.

I remind myself, not looking into their bleeding wounds or hazy eyes.

It's almost over. It's cost you everything, but it's finally almost over.

Truthfully, I've spent far too long tracking the rogue fledglings—nearly five days. Five days of trading my silk bedsheets for sleeping on branches and pine needles. Of swallowing down nuts or wild fruit instead of savoring my usual hot meals.

Don't get me wrong, I *love* the lush green forest. And alone time. A heap of alone time. As much of it as I can get.

BLOODJEWELS

But even a grumpy introvert grows restless in the isolation. Especially if you've been tasked with hunting down rogue witches by your lethal ruler.

Which I have been.

At first, I was eager to leave my coven and enjoy the solitude, despite the heinous task that came with it. *At first*, this didn't seem so bad.

But now—I'm just pissed. And wet. And willing to do just about anything to wash the grime down. Even if it means returning to my mother.

My mother.

Thinking of her sends a prickle through my neck. It's not like *she* would ever leave the comfort of her capital, *her cushy manor*, to deal with the traitors. Not when she could just send her own death incarnate heir in her place.

Doing Mother's dirty work is something I've grown used to. After a century, you stop asking questions. Especially when you know the Coven Crown would rather bite through her tongue than share anything important with her own daughter.

But even if she's ruthless, she's not impractical. Whatever the witches did, it must have been a heavy threat. Malvolia doesn't end her coven members' lives without reason. Not when our own numbers remain so low. And the magic remains diluted.

Ruthless, but not an idiot.

Unfortunately, I'll assure my mother that her traitors have been dealt with, though the slits opening their necks and their shaky fingers make my throat go bone dry.

Don't look.

I focus on my lungs instead. Filling them with air, releasing it back out. Again. And again.

With an even breath, I step over the tribe of bodies and

put their fading pleas in the back corner of my mind. I'm busy locking them in the dusty depths of everything bad as a chill trembles through the air. Rain lightly falls against my sleek hair.

The north part of the Isle is dark and uninhabited. I can't see much, despite my sharp vision. A split tree blocks part of the path ahead, blackened and splintered from some serious lightning. I doubt a rogue witch could get past the mangled tree. Hell, I don't know if I can get through the blocked path. The ground is slick, my hands are bloodied. Beyond that, I'm *tired*. For days I tore through the woods trying to retrace their movements. But Malvolia would skin me for the misstep; if they're beyond the tree, I need to know. Maybe I'm just out of practice, maybe I'm just fed up with blindly following orders.

I count the bodies around me. Maybe I don't need to go beyond the tree.

1. A boy with splotchy freckles—newly matured a decade ago. He stops moving first.
2. Dark raven hair that matches my father's. There's a gap between her two front teeth, smeared with blood.
3. Round twitching cheeks. Green eyes. I think she studied botany in her early years.
4. A crooked nose attached to our most trustworthy carpenter.
5. And worst of all…an original Elder. A graying man, old enough to look aged, with a few wrinkles around his mouth. Once, he'd been Malvolia's closest advisor. Now, he's croaking out his last breath.

But one's missing.
Damn.

BLOODJEWELS

There's supposed to be six dead traitors. Six lifeless bodies to report back to Mother so I don't meet a similar fate. Six graves etched with blood, on my hands. Although I am heir to the Coven Crown on this gods forsaken Isle, our leader won't hold back her wrath if I mess up. If I disobey.

I hear a crack and watch a streak of color dive behind the lightning-struck tree, pulling me back from every bad thought I've ever had.

I pick up my own pace just in time to see a flash of her blonde hair tangle in a leaf. I push the magic and she's down on the dirt fighting off sparks of silver that are gnawing at her leg. She does not scream, though I know how badly it hurts.

"Malvolia sent her most faithful hound for a group of teenagers?" the blonde witch asks baring her teeth. I hide the recognition that must be splattered all over my face the same way the blood is on my tunic.

The Isle is small, the witches almost extinct. I was lucky to not know the others she ran with. However, the fledging spitting before me has crossed my path many times. She sells herbs in the town square, tends to the children who live in the capital. She studies healing and has a mother and a sister and a small cat—

"Get on with it," she says, cutting off the thread of panic weaving through my mind. I'm surprised to see she wields no fear.

"You've upset the Coven Crown with your treason." My voice sounds sure, but my mouth feels heavy. The young witch laughs, a defeated sound that carries more bone than muscle. Her blue dress is torn, her knees dirty. I wonder how many times they had to pack up and run before I came after them like the dog she claims me to be.

"Treason," she says. Like it's a sick joke rather than the ugly truth.

I don't know exactly what these fledglings did to lose their lives; Mother only said they betrayed the crown and therefore the coven. That they need to die. I'm rarely in a position to ask questions or demand reasoning, so I don't.

"What do you think, Dove Seraphina?" she asks. "Is this any way to live?" I remember her name as she says mine. This is Clarissa Bow and she only matured last year, immortality setting into her bones early compared to some others. Early, like me.

I don't answer.

"I used to wonder if this was truly a punishment," Clarissa carries on.

She's looking at me. Maybe through me. Maybe above me. I can't tell, I'm still silently screaming at my fingers to *act! act! act!* instead of feeling like icicles attached to my hand. Gods, I just need to get on with it. There's no reason to turn Mother's wrath back on me. On Calix. Althea. The only reasons I haven't completely given up.

My fingers slightly thaw, my wrist twitches. Clarissa catches the movement, a sharp witch for someone so young. Something close to terror settles within her pupils, she swallows slowly. I try not to acknowledge how beautiful she is in the dark, how much she seems to know.

Things I clearly don't. Hell, I don't even know why she's a traitor.

"You could stop her. Don't…don't allow her to unlock the gods' magic. If the witches escape the Isle…if we're free to roam the realm again under her rule…" She looks away from me and into the distant trees, like she sees something that I can't. She's shaking. I might be, too. Her gaze makes me want to turn around, but I hear my mother's voice in my head chastening me.

Never turn your back on an enemy, a friend, or even your family. Expose nothing.

I stand perfectly still while the girl in front of me comes to terms with her impending death. She speaks once more, quieter this time.

"We deserve what the Realm Bound gods did to us."

I hear the words but I'm already moving, unable to listen for another second.

Don't prolong death or life. Never hesitate.

So I don't, and I slit her throat when she isn't expecting it, when her eyes are still lost in the trees. My hand is on my dagger and against her skin before she could register what had happened. I think I see a ghost of smile on her lips as she settles into the earth. The others clawed at their wounds, tried to keep the blood from leaving their body. Clarissa does no such thing, petting the grass below her with outstretched arms, staring into the stars.

I question if the witch is brave or spineless, wise or insane. I try to remember what it's like to believe in something worth dying for. To feel chosen by the energy of the realm. I look up at the stars, just as she is. Even though she's no longer breathing. And I am. I take my own unsteady inhale and I turn to start trekking towards Uncliff. Back to Mother.

Dread holds my hand the entire journey home.

CHAPTER 1

"I swear she laps at their silence like a bloodthirsty wolf!"

I roll my eyes, looking to my cousin nearly a week after returning home.

Althea's chuckle melts soft and sweet against the light wind.

"Malvolia definitely enjoys theatrics," Althea replies, laying in the grass beside me. "Half of that meeting was absolutely pointless."

The sun hits her golden hair, glistening against it. The rest of her features are just as warm—wild green eyes, a delicate nose, lightly bowed pink lips. Between the two of us, she's always resembled the sun.

I roll onto my side. "Just half?"

Althea's dimples deepen, unsaid words dancing around her freckled face. She debates risking treason for only a moment. "Don't test her patience, Dove."

Immediately, she gives a paranoid look around, though we're the only two souls on the hillside.

An hour ago, we'd been sitting at the head table amongst the other Seraphina witches—Malvolia's living relatives. Mother rattled off various tasks and assignments to the coven, urging everyone to stop slacking off if we're to have a good winter. Althea was staring at me the entire time, every so often jerking her head to the door, begging we find an excuse to leave. My aunt and uncle had listened with great intensity, hung on every word the Coven Crown said. My father only looked bored, matching my own mood.

Actually, I was surprised to see him there at all. While Malvolia holds weekly meetings for the coven, her husband can rarely be bothered to show up. Not that I blame him, I can't be around her for long periods of time either. Especially in public, where she's even more cruel than behind our closed door. Most days it's unbearable.

It was only when Mother started taking questions that opportunity struck. Althea and I slipped out of the stone-walled room, giggling like fledglings as we jogged to the hill behind Malvolia's manor. Once secure in our favorite location, Althea put a delicate finger to her lips before reaching inside her dress pocket. I choked back laughter when she produced a thinly rolled paper stuffed with our favorite herbs. *Very hard to grow herbs.* We'd spent ten summers experimenting with different weather and temperature to perfect it. It paid off though, even if we'd bickered like catty sisters during every attempt.

Now, we lay against the ground taking turns inhaling and coughing, watching the clouds move towards the continents beyond us.

"You two didn't think about sharing?" barks a familiar grumpy voice, trudging up the hill. Before he appears, Althea rolls her green eyes, but she's unable to hide the way her lips twitch up.

"That depends, would you have asked nicely?" She blows a perfect ring of smoke directly in his rough, unshaven face.

Calix uses his big arms to swat away the smoke, shooting her a glare under a mop of brown curls. "No, probably not."

The oversized hunter plops down between us, stretching his long legs and interlocking his fingers behind his head. I can smell his cracked leathers from here, his tan skin feels sticky, like he's spent the day in the woods. Which he probably has, knowing Calix. When he's not digging us out of messy situations, he's tracking game with his father. The pair of them are the reason we're well fed. I wait for Althea to pass him the paper, but she takes another huff and waves him off.

Calix ignores her lack of manners and turns to me. "Glad to see you're alive." I haven't seen him since my return to Uncliff. Though the three of us usually spend every spare second together, I've been…*busy.*

I mockingly smile. "Yeah, well, Malvolia hasn't pushed me off a cliff yet."

Though she has pushed others off the cliffside throughout the years. And a witch does not survive beyond the Isle. Not even for a second.

He gives me a cocky grin. "*Yet.*"

"What would she do without her prized possession?" I ask, tracing the clouds with a slender finger.

"Maybe smile every once in a while," Calix grumbles, earning him a whack on the shoulder from Althea. His cheeks redden and he tauntingly glares at her, pushing her buttons early for a weeknight. Usually, we can make it well into the evening before they start going back and forth.

"She could return at any moment!" Althea hisses, giving another paranoid look around. Gods, the girl is so nervous about Mother. It's not like Malvolia is going to burst down the hillside over a few sarcastic comments.

I mean, she might. My mother can be…unpredictable.

But it's unlikely. Not when we have bigger issues to deal with. Our "teenage angst," as she would call it, though we're all fully matured, is low on her radar as the coven grows restless.

Calix gives me a knowing stare, agreeing that Althea needs to loosen up.

"Thundering dragons, Thea. Relax," he grumbles.

With a pin, I twist my hair out of my face, letting the sunshine warm me. "You worry too much, cousin."

"You two idiots don't worry enough," she scoffs, pressing her pink lips together.

Calix was already waiting for my gaze. When I meet it, we're both choking down chuckles. Amusement lights up his rugged features; I'd forgotten how much I missed him while I was gone. I realize I don't think I saw him inside the meeting, but that doesn't surprise me—he likes to teeter the line of respect just as carefully (and frequently) as I do.

"Your journey was good? No folklore dragons or evil monsters?" the hunter teases, shifting the topic to keep my cousin from exploding into another dreaded safety speech. I think we'd both jump from atop the cliff if we have to hear Althea ramble on about keeping my mother off our backs one more time.

He playfully taps his foot against mine. His boots are caked in mud, the laces fraying. I make a mental note to get him another pair—he'll never ask on his own.

"The only thing to be afraid of out there was me," I joke, but my throat goes bone dry. I don't tell them about Clarissa and her dying words or the rotting smell that's still wedged between my nostrils. They know what I had to do, and they would never judge me for killing. My friends know just as well as I do that there isn't a way out of Malvolia's orders. But I keep it to myself, anyways. I don't need to remind them that I'm the real monster, not the extinct dragons or goblins we've read about.

We deserve what the Realm Bound gods did to us. Clarissa's dying words echo in the wind, playing over and over for only me to hear.

The first two nights of my return home I practically slept on the tavern floor. After I'd drunk away all my bitterness, all my guilt, I threw myself back into training so intensely that my palms were perpetually raw and blistered, despite our advanced immortal healing. Only then did I sulk back to the manor library where Mother finally found me, demanding details of my journey—of the spilt blood. I was lucky she didn't whip me for puttering around.

"I hope you spared them the extent of your temper," Althea says. I want to remind her that I'm not an angry person… sometimes. Just a girl who doesn't like to take any shit and can often get red with rage.

"I have no idea what you're talking about."

Calix snickers at my angelic voice, the one that is usually reserved for getting us out of terrible predicaments we managed to web ourselves into throughout our youth. Althea raises her eyebrows, unconvinced.

"Tomax Den would kindly disagree with you after losing his favorite finger," she points out. I roll my eyes at her and the memory. *Damn Tomax.*

"I would kindly remind Tomax that there are consequences for cheating in a card game. Especially with the Crown's heir." I scowl, thinking of the pervy man. Honestly, I really did enjoy butchering his hands. Not just because I like to win, though I do, but because Tomax has a nasty reputation around the female fledglings.

It's harder to be a creep when you're missing a few fingers.

Unsurprisingly, Malvolia wasn't pleased with my vigilante routine. She'd threatened to cut off my own fingers if I dared to act without her permission again.

So far, I haven't.

Althea pokes at me. "Sure, it has nothing to do with you being a sore loser."

I start my defense but settle for a nasty scowl shot directly at her.

Calix pushes himself up. "He's better off without those fingers, anyways." Standing, he towers over us both. He outstretches a hand to Althea. "Care for a drink?"

She grabs onto him, hoisting herself up and offering the same to me. Even though Althea is tall for a female, Calix has at least a foot on her, and a foot and a half on me. It's a shame he's awful with a sword or he'd be one hell of a warrior.

We start down the hill, the sun disappearing behind the Isle. The capital will soon be settling into the night.

And with the night comes young immortal antics.

Althea cuts me off sometime in the early hours of the morning. I scowl at her, so does Calix, but neither of us protest when she heaves us out of the tavern, *the only tavern in this damn place,* and onto the muddy street. I'm swaying around, having drunk one too many glasses of the bitter wine. My cousin's parental grip is the only thing keeping me upright, guiding us both to the manors where our mothers lurk. Calix lives near the tavern, veering off to the home he shares with his father after a quick and tipsy goodbye. Now, we're alone again, giggling and stumbling.

"You know, Thea. I hate a lot of things. The Isle. Myself. The way Mother always sneers and disregards me. Being heir. But I don't hate you," I slur. Gods, whatever was in this wine has me messed up. Everything spins, even Althea's long golden hair swirls into the green from her eyes and the light blue from her dress.

My cousin smiles, rolling her eyes. "Sure thing, Dove."

I don't remember making it up the hill or the stairs. I don't remember tripping through the stone hallways or navigating my rooms. I also don't remember the faces of the witches Malvolia ordered me to kill, or the way Clarissa's death gutted my insides. I can't feel the heavy chains of my life trapped on Skully, our wretched little Isle. I only taste the warmth in my chest from one too many glasses of bitter liquid and the ease of my linens under my head as I drift into sleep.

I try very, very hard not to hear her dying voice.

CHAPTER 2

"You have certainly smelt better," comes a shrill and judgmental tone, jolting me from a sleep that seems too short. Too shallow.

It comes with a hellish headache.

The incoming light through the now-opened curtains only intensifies the pounding. Instantly my mouth seems dry, and I crave a gallon of water so badly that it almost seems worth moving for. There's a familiar steady ache through my left thumb, I push down a wave of nausea.

"Is that any way to greet your only daughter?" I grumble, more of a croak than a sophisticated response, which causes Mother's smirk to deepen. When she has you in a vulnerable position, the game always begins—it's her favorite time to play with her prey. Now that we're on the battlefield, she's already scored a point.

Malvolia loves to have the upper hand. The mental superiority. And she often does.

"Good morning, Dovey. You're lucky I'm feeling pleasant today." She stands in the doorway, her red hair unbound and falling in sheets down to her waist. The same hair that inspired my own long locks—I've always been envious of her. Aren't all daughters in some weird, twisted way? It's the red of her hair that makes me feel insecure about the sheer white of my own. Instead of vibrant fire, my straight strands are pure snow. A colorless crater while she bleeds it.

24

Between her casual plum dress and that intrusive grin she wears, she seems relaxed enough to overlook my hangover and sharp tongue.

"Was there a witch to punish? A small child to obliterate?" I taunt, jumping on the tightrope that is conversing with her. One battle point to me, for wit despite my massive headache. Besides, today I'm feeling sour and can't blame the wine. I wait for her to strike. Some days these remarks earn me a pretty punishment. Others, a rare laugh.

My mother is constantly shifting from one version of herself to the next. I've spent years mastering the art of defusing her, learning the war tactic of being left alone. By now, I know the things I can say. But more importantly, I know the things I cannot.

She crosses her arms in boredom. "Funny, I thought *you'd* been tasked with killing the children." I flinch, letting the blow stick. It stings twice as sharp, so two more points for her.

Why do you keep engaging? I scold myself, choking down whatever smart retort I'd been thinking up. Malvolia does these things on purpose—haunting us with the skeletons she's shoved into our closets. She knows I didn't want to hurt the witches in the woods. Hell, I'd passed them on the paths, andsome had even grown up with me. But Mother's orders come first. The coven always comes first.

I pull on the duvet. "A reason for your early morning visit?" I mask the hurt she's expertly dug up. I try to ignore it, but all I can see is Clarissa's eyes behind my own. Suddenly, I'm thinking of her sister and her mother and that damn cat always outside their house. I've even thrown it scraps a few times. It sends another wave of nausea down my gut. Gods, she was so young. I can't remember what it's like to be as young as I look. Even though in immortal terms I'm practically a teenager, with only a century under my belt, I've been stuck in the same unageing skin. Nineteen in my physical body but one hundred and seven in my mental prison.

I naggingly rub my cursed left thumb.

"Today, I have use for you." She moves from the door to the edge of my bed. In response, I get out of it and creep towards the window. The more space between us, the better. Malvolia frowns but doesn't bite at my movements. Another battle point for me. The weight of my body forces my knees to buckle, my head pounds harder.

"How thoughtful," I mumble. *Really* super thoughtful.

I reach for a pin to hold my long hair back. "Do I get a say?" but I already know the answer. It wouldn't matter whether she asked or told me—there is no real choice. Either way, I would do whatever she wants of me. It's the best way to stay alive.

A shiver sweeps the room, unseasonably cold against the circular walls. My rooms are usually warm, the highest in the spiral tower of Malvolia's polished manor. The only polished thing in all of Skully.

Below, Uncliff looks even smaller than it feels. It's busy with life as the morning draws on. Witches are trading herbs and fish on small stands in the square. Fledgling children weave throughout the muddy paths and between their parent's legs. A man is grilling and bartering rabbits. After nearly five hundred years trapped on the Isle, it's honestly an impressive accomplishment to have such civility.

Unlike the continents around us, Skully is modest. The Realm Bound rulers have a flare for extravagance, a kindness never extended to the witches. Most of our homes are built from mountain rock or forest lumber. And we don't have countless towns or cities, just Uncliff, where most of us stay. A few live beyond the capital, in smaller outposts or communities away from the watchful eye of our Coven Crown. Sure, other parts of the Isle are livable, especially with the right magic.

But if you are a witch, you can't live beyond these shores.

Mother's voice pulls me back into the room. "Not really, no." She flattens the blanket on my bed. "But given the hideous state you're in and the stench dripping off you, I'm starting to doubt my own judgement."

I shrug. Can't argue with that. Another battle point to her.

But I'm feeling rebellious, so I raise my eyebrows. "Why can't Father do it?"

The mention of my father makes her frown further, if that's even possible. She still looks beautiful, in a cruel way. Beautiful, but lethal. Mother has always been different—sharper and more ruthless than the others. Everyone whispers that it was the darkest parts of her who made me; the silver-eyed heir who can wield too much magic.

It makes me a threat. Even to her.

"Roe," she spits his name, "is probably off in the woods frolicking or cowering away from his duties."

Sounds about right. Malvolia gave up on controlling my father years ago. Any love they might have once had is long gone, squashed to nothing. It's only her loyalty to tradition that keeps her from publicly shaming him. As long as the coven thinks we're united—*we're united.* But for all the hate she has, the coven actually adores my father. Probably for his kind words or willingness to defy Malvolia more than anything. To keep her hatred for him under wraps, she often sends Roe away on business, constantly making him trek to different parts of the Isle to deal with minor witches on the outskirts. Journeys that take him far too long to return from.

Can you really blame him?

She waves away the bad taste his name brings. "Bring your cousin along. She's always been the head between the two of you. And that common boy—the one you always drag around."

Her tone annoys me, meaning another damn point for Malvolia. She's always thought herself better than the coven. Better than anyone living below the manor lines. Or even those within it. She knows Calix's name. We've been friends since I was small, even sharing a birthday. He's been a part of my trio for the hundred years I've been around, an inseparable part of me.

She knows his name, she's just a bitch.

Malvolia moves into my space, making me meet her dark eyes. "Those pathetic witches on the Western front need someone to put them back in line. You'll go and do it. *Without* complaint." There's ice in her voice, a familiar contempt. Ah, there it is. Seeing this more expected version of her brings me a weird comfort. An ease now that I know who she'll be today.

I swallow down any of those unsaid complaints. When her eyes go violent, I usually shut up. The Western witches are harmless. If anything, it'll practically be a vacation. Especially with Calix and Althea along, if they can manage to stop bickering long enough to enjoy the view. I push down any hint of being content, unable to let Mother know it's not the *worst* job she's given me.

Mother crosses her arms. "And at least pretend like you're taking this seriously. Gods, Dove, you really are a handful."

A point for her. Or me. I can't tell anymore. I'm too busy repacking my knapsack, still half-full from the last task she'd sent me on. Two small daggers, a smutty book, and three hair pins all come tumbling out. *The essentials.* Malvolia is scowling and barking at me to stop wasting her time. I try my best to hang on every word, my packing becomes frantic under her sneering eyes. She doesn't tell me what I need to bring or why I'm going but that's not unusual. Information is currency around here and my mother prefers me broke.

Before long, I stop keeping score of the jabs or the insults. I forget any quick satisfaction I'd gotten from besting her earlier. Or the pang of hurt from her doing it back to me. I retreat back into the face I wore ten years ago, the girl she needs me to be. Whatever the score is, I'm sure as hell it's not even. And that after this round, she's won.

CHAPTER 3

I don't want to bring Calix. I know the capital will struggle without him for a few days—he's the best hunter we've got. And the reason we've made it through some harsh winters. I don't want to bring Althea either, though she's a proven expert at handling coven disputes. Logically, both of my friends could be very helpful on this trip.

Realistically, another moment of their bickering is going to send me into the deadly ocean below.

"You have no idea what you're talking about, Cal. You practically *slept* through the history lessons," Althea huffs, not as polite as usual. She's only half wrong. Calix loves lessons, he just prefers the ones on the woods or the realm, not the politics that landed us into this mess. She's just looking to jab—the hunter often unravels her sense of diplomacy, bringing out the wild in her green eyes.

We've been scaling the rocks for hours now, surrounded by the foliage and their arguments. It'll take us an entire night to reach the Western outpost—a small group of witches far from the capital and Malvolia's clutches. They're still her subjects, of course, but they prefer isolation and a quiet life. Most of them only have minor magic, anyways.

If Malvolia deems you useful, choice goes out the window. Lucky for them, she has enough magic at her disposal. We left shortly after my conversation with Mother, who reminded me thrice more not to mess up. When I found my friends in the square, Calix complained there are more important things for us to handle than a land dispute, but it was Althea who reminded him not to bother challenging a direct order from the Coven Crown. He bared his teeth at her and she back at him. It's been a battlefield ever since. My head still pounds as they argue, and I find myself wishing for comfort instead of the forest. A silk gown and diamond earrings rather than my hunting leathers and knives. Oils and soaps and perfumes—

"What do you think, Dove?" Althea asks, expectantly looking at me.

I glance between the two of them, both eager to be proven right in whatever argument they've been sparring in. "About what?"

"The gossip against our family. Your mother," she says with an edge. The heat and hike must be getting to her, unhinging the polite demeanor she's so good at projecting.

"Gossip!" sneers Calix. He steps ahead, cutting down a branch in our path.

He's right, gossip isn't the word for it. I've heard enough rumblings from my time at the tavern. The witches are growing tired of Malvolia's ruthless rule and her relentless work schedule. Time on the Isle has made them weak. Farmers and carpenters rather than warriors or conquerors. Mother's complained about it countless times.

"I cut down a group of teenagers last week, Thea. And an *Elder*. Someone who made the Isle what it is. We're beyond gossip and whispers surrounding Malvolia," I tell her. Calix nods in agreement, only upsetting Althea more.

My cousin is the family peacekeeper, constantly putting out fires amongst the Seraphina witches. Between my mother, my mother's sister, my aunt's husband, and my own father, Althea has her work cut out for her. And that's before considering all of my extra bullshit. She's a fierce protector of our kind, our name. More so than I ever am; something that Malvolia frequently notes. The Seraphina's have always been among the most powerful witches, even before our exiling to the Isle. My cousin is no exception.

Neither am I.

"She must have a reason," Althea protests.

Of course. Anything to make Malvolia seem innocent. "Fear is hardly a reason," I snap. My cousin looks alarmed at my outburst, but I'm not done. "I'm sure those witches posed a very serious threat to the oldest woman here. The *teenagers*, Thea. The ones who you taught to pick herbs. The very same we would see in the streets. Killing the Elder will have consequences with the coven. He knew something, I can feel it."

I keep walking, not meeting her eyes, which are probably filled with disappointment or concern or something else I just don't care to see. Althea didn't have to kill them. She didn't cut the throat of the Elder, the same man who watched us grow up. She doesn't have to break necks or end lives. She isn't responsible for the raw and nasty things that keep us alive. Keep us in power.

Calix looks smug when I throw him a glance. No surprise—they'd been sparring, and he just won. Year after year it seems as if he grows more resentful of my mother. Of her senseless bloody ways.

He isn't the only one.

Althea crosses her arms after wiping the sweat from her brow. "She isn't afraid. It was punishment for treason. You both know better than anyone how carefully our small Isle has to be run."

Calix stops in his tracks, turning on his heels to meet my

cousin's face. "Really, Thea? She's afraid and you know it." He sounds desperate, begging her to see the logic.

She opens her mouth to argue, strapping on her war boots for another battle.

Oh, gods. "He's right," I say before she has the chance. "Malvolia's scared of rebellion. Why else would she send me after that weird group of witches? An Elder mentoring newly matured witches isn't uncommon. They knew something, or did something, she didn't like. She's afraid." I just don't know what exactly it is she's afraid of, *yet*.

Althea doesn't look away from Calix, their argument unfolding nonverbally, now. Whatever victory they want to feel is nothing compared to my desire for some shade and a comfy cushion. The sun is setting into my eyes, sweat is pooling under my clothes. And I'm half convinced my only friends are going to rip each other's throats out right here.

Luckily, Althea solves one of my problems when she breaks Calix's stare and backs down. She starts walking, shoving branches out of the way as she stomps forward.

He hangs back for me. "Malvolia's wise to be fearful. The tides are shifting." Calix looks out into the ocean, his eyes glossed over in a daze as he pools into his magic.

There are many types of magic to wield and no two witches are alike. Magic comes from energy, *your* energy. The stronger the spirit, the stronger the magic. Or at least, that's what Mother says. You have to reach within yourself to find it, like diving into the ocean from a tall cliff. Often big bursts of power need preparation. Reaching the ocean floor takes time. So does the ascent back to the water's surface.

Some of us have small ponds of energy inside. Others, decent sized lakes. The rarest of us have vast seas. Everyone's power can show up differently, a few types of magic happen enough for us to categorize.

It's common for a witch to be a healer, like Mother. Though Mother doesn't actually heal anyone, instead using her ability to snap bones rather than mend them. Inflicting gashes more so than sealing them. Hurt, compared to heal.

Others are contortionists—sneaky little creeps who can alter their physical features, shifting into whatever suits their current needs. They're lucky the magic is almost always temporary, or Mother would deem them dangerous and slaughter them all.

From a young age, Calix showed mastery over the natural elements. Some witches can only harness one aspect, maybe a couple if they're lucky. We have a handful of elementalists. But Calix can wield them all.

His favorite? Lightning.

As a fledgling, he set the tips of Althea's hair on fire. He panicked so badly he almost drowned her trying to put it out. Althea couldn't muster a single spark in retaliation. Trust me, she tried.

It took Althea a couple more years to manifest her own power—having influence over other's emotions, compelling them to follow her commands. Compulsion is a rare magic, even for witches. When we were twelve, we convinced Calix to sneak into the tavern and steal some liquor. Obviously, he'd been an eager participant. When he was inevitably caught (twelve-year-olds aren't the best thieves) we thought we were done for it. Until Althea *very politely* asked the tavernkeeper to forget we'd been there. He did. She's the only compeller on the Isle.

Well…kind of.

We were thirteen when we found out I could do it, too. And like Calix, I can wield the elements. I'm even decent at contorting. And an almost passible healer. But there's more than that. A deeper part of me. Mother has always been taken aback by how much magic I can wield. It seems as if my power has a mind of its own, a living entity that can accomplish whatever it's seen, heard, felt. The silver sparks of my magic resemble no other witch.

The elements. Compulsion. A half decent healer. A shaky contortionist. My bizarre silver flames.

It makes me a threat.

A paradoxical threat, since I'm not the greatest at anything but throwing knives and winning fist fights. But a threat, none-theless.

And I feel it too, the way the sea is shifting.

"Well, I don't feel anything," Althea says with a raised chin. I bite back my smirk. My cousin will argue with Calix under any circumstance, any time. Sometimes, I'm convinced she takes the opposite stance just to be difficult. But she can't hear it—the humming from the realm. Not like Calix can. Not like I can.

Calix points ahead. "There. Like old times, yeah, Dove?"

The winding trail expands into a clearing as we near it. We must be close to the mountain peak; I can feel the air thinning. And if I remember correctly, this used to be our favorite view.

Calix was right, and as we hike higher we break from the trees and into the clearing. The same clearing we used to find as fledglings, giving us an exclusive view of our neighboring continent, Morbida. Gods, are we really that close?

Morbida is practically touching Skully, our wretched little Isle. It almost circles around us, under a watchful eye. *His* watchful eye. It makes perfect sense the witches would be trapped *here*, of all places. From the capital we usually just see a few twinkling lights and a ton of trees from Morbida. But from up here, you can see the tip of the dark castle that rests atop a daunting cliff.

BLOODJEWELS

There are ships in the water, swaying against the royal docks. You can make out a window in the castle's tower, see the clearing for the massive city unfolding beyond it.

A massive city we'll never be able to explore. Jealousy runs through me, poisonous and taut.

Althea stands between Calix and me, she's looking at Morbida like some forbidden candy, something she desperately wants but can't have. "What do you think it's like?"

Calix squints, as if it'll help him see the city better. "Filthy rich. Disgustingly clean. More books and magic than we've ever learned of in our lessons." Yeah, the outdated books we have don't make for a stellar education.

Althea touches his arm. "Imagine the taverns! Or the food! I wonder if they have different spices?"

Usually, I would join in on their daydream. The three of us have made a game out of hypothetical post-Isle life. What we would do. Where we would go. People we would meet. We've read every history book here, sat through every lesson with eager ears—all in hopes to perfect our coping fantasy. But it's been years since I've seen been this high up, seen Morbida from this angle.

And it makes my blood so hot I feel it sizzle into steam.

All around us, the realm grows. I can't even imagine all of the potential advancements it's made since our capture. It maddens me to know there is more within our world, things I can never afford to see or touch or experience. And just like Althea, I desperately want to. Honestly, we're lucky that Malvolia is such an efficient ruler. The coven can say what they want, but it was an impossible task making this land livable. At first, we'd barely survived at all. Mother's brutality was the only reason we aren't extinct like the dragons.

But there's more out there. More I can't feel. More I can't grasp. "Someday," I whisper, mostly to myself.

Someday, we will break the magic keeping us here. Cut the five-hundred-year-old chains leashing us to the Isle.

And the witches will reap their revenge.

CHAPTER 4

The western witches seem to bicker more than Calix and Althea,
which alarms me instantly because I didn't think it possible.

A day later, under the blazing summer sun, an older beady-eyed witch looks at me. "So, if it's the Seraphina will, I think you'll find the crops best kept under my watch."

His equally weird enemy scowls. "Please, Miss Seraphina. Rupert hasn't grown decent vegetables in *years*. The western farm needs a reliable owner!"

I'm barely listening as they throw jabs back and forth. My leathers are as stiff as my spine. My jaw refuses to unclench. My fingers are full of tension.

Something feels…off.

The wildlife is too loud, chirping and growling around us. The hot air flushes my cheeks, and every so often my vision seems hazy. It's been a while since I've been this far out, but the journey was nothing too awful. I'm not at all tired or groggy. It's as if my magic's whispering warnings in my bones. Frantically pinching me with caution.

At first, I was convinced I didn't get enough sleep. It took me a bit to close my eyes while I'd tossed and turned at our campsite, but I eventually found slumber and got a full eight hours. After that, a bath in the cold river Calix found. And a filling breakfast of oats and berries. No unpleasantries, no complications. Our journey here was quick enough. I didn't even have to slit any throats this time.

So, why the worry?

I can't shake it. Althea noticed right away, quickly after we entered the make-shift village gate. When we trekked through the muddy shacks bordering the farm, she'd offered to take the lead if it'd make me feel better.

I thought it might, but it doesn't.

There's no town square or makeshift market stands, no tavern or clusters of homes. Instead, the witches gather in the mud near the animal stalls. A pig grunts nearby, a chicken clucks in agreement. The opposing witches are shouting to be heard. Calix and Althea stand among them, look just as tense as I feel. Strangely, there's more of the coven living out here than I remember. A butcher hut is smoking, there's a well surrounded by damp and drying threads. Children are scrubbing clothes and pitching hay. It makes my stomach turn.

Malvolia would not be very pleased at their growing numbers.

Calix groans, leaning against the fence as the heat and argument continue. His eyes are tight as he looks at me. A man presses too closely against him, and I watch his fist close, the hunter prefers his personal space. Althea picks up on both our discomfort, politely offering the disputing witches a head-clearing walk, where she'll listen to their details. Both agree, taking her arms as they move away from the muddy path. The other arguing witches follow her. I fold my arms. "I know, Cal. I don't want to be here either."

He shakes his head. "Malvolia's wasting our time. And you're jumping around like someone's going to strike you."

Well, my mother isn't here so getting struck is unlikely. "Something feels wrong." My skin prickles, every nerve on edge inside my hunting leathers. He looks worried, touching my shoulder when I lean into the shade. "We'll go quickly."

Althea leads the witches into the middle of the field, where the argument picks back up so we can hear. I've never seen two people get so heated over vegetables before, but Althea handles it with grace. She's nodding along, consoling them both with her big green eyes. *Great.*

"Yeah, that's likely," I grumble.

Calix lets out an exasperated sigh, throwing his head back into it. "As if we don't have bigger problems! Like getting the hell off this Isle *before* Malvolia works us all to death." He kicks a pebble with his worn-down boot.

"They'll likely grow diamonds from the ground before that happens," I say.

The arguing gets louder. A child bumps into Calix as they pass by. How many fledglings is that? I wonder the last time Mother has been out here at all. There's no way she knows how many witches truly reside here.

"Malvolia didn't specify *how* we have to solve the land dispute. She never said we couldn't *politely ask them* to knock this shit off," Calix whispers, trying to seem nonchalant.

He's right. And it's not the first time we've used Althea to our advantage. Her magic might be the key to keeping us sane. Though she won't compel them on her own. She'll need a nudge of approval in order to do anything so drastic. I bounce up from the lumber fence, sloshing through the mud to get close enough for Althea to meet my eyes. The arguing witches are too busy with each other to notice her attention go to me. Behind her polite mask she looks tired, her blue dress growing dirty. She'd rather the fabric shred to ribbons than wear hunting leathers, arguing that she doesn't need to fight in order to battle. I give her a knowing nod. Instantly, she perks up.

There are some advantages to being around the same people

for a hundred years—like being able to communicate without words. Besides, I'm too anxious to handle this without magic. What's it for if we can't use it? Calix chuckles, dimples tan on his skin. "Poor guys."

I shrug my shoulders. Sometimes, I find it hard to feel bad for men.

Althea gets to work, her pupils going wide as she pools into her magic. The air shifts, but I doubt the others can feel it. Both men's eyes gloss over; they're in a daze, unable to move even if they wanted to. Which they don't—compulsion feels euphoric. That's why it's so easy to get someone under your influence; it's like a nasty drug with a heaven's high.

Calix and I lean back, bumping shoulders and laughing while Althea works her magic over the witches. The bustling *village* is too busy to notice the witches' sudden change of tone. Althea shines them a winning smile, whispering something, hopefully convincing enough to get us out of this place. Even from here, I can feel the tinge of magic she manifests like tiny lightning bolts against my skin.

The sun moves slow while she works for a few more minutes, the anxiety still prickling at me. A couple times I bite back waves of nausea, I'm picking and pulling at the skin around my fingers. I don't stop when I see blood. I can't seem to stand up straight enough. Hold my shoulders back enough.

Before long, the witches shake hands in the field, moving back towards us in hushed conversation with a triumphant Althea lingering behind them. A small trickle of relief fights to the front of my nerves. Calix instinctively moves to her side as she approaches. She smiles up at him and thanks the bickering men for their time. They shout their thanks and grab at her hand with spews of appreciation. They touch a strand of her hair before Calix guides her away with a stern look. I stay in the background, lurking and trying to find the source of my discomfort.

The coven men try to thank Calix, but warily look away. They're lucky he didn't break their fingers for touching Thea. The men don't bother to meet my gaze, instead just giving a quick bow from a distance.

They know they'll lose any hand they try to touch me with.

We leave quickly after this, eager to get back into Uncliff as we dash to the front entrance. No one says anything until we're well away from the other witches.

"Malvolia is going to flip if she finds out how many of them are gathered there," Calix whispers.

That's an understatement. Whatever nerves I'm feeling, this adds to it. Calix only said what we were all thinking—do we tell my mother?

Thea gives him a shaky nod. I swallow, looking at both of them. I know that they'll rely on me to make the final decision, as always.

"I guess we'll find out," I say, starting the journey back. We begin walking without another word, both of my friends sensing the growing nerves I can't shove down. I don't know if we should tell my mother, but not telling her could be worse. If she found out that we knew and didn't confess, the punishment for my friends could be extreme. She can hurt me all she wants, but I refuse to let her harm Calix or Althea. Whatever decision I make, it'll be for them.

Every decision I make is for them.

Even after another night under the stars and with Uncliff in sight, something is still wrong. I know I should be happy to return home—maybe I am, through it all, but I can't ignore the nipping nerves. My palms are damp, and I clench them tightly, feeling the tremors that course through my fingers. The sun has gone down again, the cool night taking over. We'd journeyed in mostly silence, working at double pace to give me some peace of mind. Even the bickering between Calix and Althea has stopped, as if they could sense my paranoia. My desperate need to get home.

After some time, we're close. So close.

I can smell the sour capital air and see the distant lights. We step along the beach, looking up at the capital business. But something is wrong. As it has been all night. All day. It's more than just my magic, it's a gnawing chaos deeply chewing my nerves, my sense. Althea halts to observe me. "Dove?"

I didn't realize I've stopped. A wave of nausea washes over me, threatening to spill my stomach's content. I press a hand against my abdomen, trying to quell the rising tide of discomfort. But the unease persists, twisting and turning like a knot in my core.

My mind races, thoughts colliding and tumbling in a chaotic frenzy. I try to grasp onto something solid, something tangible to ground me, but the threads slip through my fingers, slipping away into the abyss of my anxiety. It's a maze of uncertainties, a labyrinth of fears that trap me in its unforgiving grasp.

Something is screaming inside of me: *Wrong! Wrong! Wrong!* I can't shake it, can't smoke or drink it away. Hell, I can't even smile. My shoulders are tense, and my jaw consistently clenched.

Because something is wrong. Something is very, very wrong.

"Just another couple minutes. Anyone care for a drink?" Calix asks, far too casually.

I can't escape this weight pressing down on me, this suffocating heaviness that settles deep within my chest. It's an uninvited guest, lurking in the darkest corners of my consciousness, whispering doubts and insecurities.

BLOODJEWELS

Althea tries to speak but I hold up my hand, cutting her off. The air feels too thick…it smells darker. Metal lingers in it, seaweed, and something else I can't identify. Calix must smell it too because he stops. Dread tightens around me. I pick up the pace and the others follow behind in eerie silence, all of us hang on what we're about to stumble upon.

With every step, the smell is growing stronger and stronger. I see now that the shore is lit, unusual for a typical night. Figures crowd around it. *Oh, thundering dragons*, that's not normal.

When I hear someone shout, I break into a run.

Everything but the beach becomes blurry, and I am running so fast I don't remember taking off. Just forcing my legs to move! Move! Move! I push my body faster, kicking up sand into my moon-colored hair. Wind whips around me as I spring faster. Calix and Althea burst off behind me, but they can't match my pace.

Somehow, I manage to slow down as I approach the witches. I skirt to a halt when I land on the scene, pushing through the coven to find the origin. Most of them are taller than me, but I'm stronger, and swiftly shove my way to the front, despite my pounding heart. Everyone is whispering.

I can place the final scent now—fear.

There's a flash of red hair and something inside me twists. Only one woman has hair that red on this Isle: my mother.

Malvolia is kneeling before me, lightly shaking. *Mother? Of all witches?* And she looks…*terrified.* I start to ask her what we're doing on the sand in the middle of the night. I mean, shouldn't everyone be in bed? Summer is almost over, there's hard work to do in the morning. She knows this, or so I thought. Besides, Mother can barely be bothered to come near the water *ever*. Let alone in the middle of the night? I open my mouth to question her, but I'm stopped when she looks up.

Not by her hard, sad eyes, but by what she is clutching.

I think I am screaming. Or frozen. Or running away. The seconds stretch into eternities, while minutes slip away unnoticed. Reality blurs, and I struggle to discern between what is real and what is a creation of my restless mind.

The eyes are shut, and the mouth is slightly ajar. The skin is pruned and wrinkled.

My mother is gripping a severed head, muscle and skin still dangling from the chopped neck. The lips are so blue they rival the ocean and the hair on his head is so thick and so straight I've only seen it on one other person—

Me.

I wonder where my father's body is as Malvolia stands up.

CHAPTER 5

Mother and my teachers always answered any childish questions about the Isle growing up. Like any small fledgling, I wanted to know why we were *stuck* here when there was an entire realm around us to be explored. Mother would sneer but explain in a way a toddler could comprehend.

She told me that the gods beyond created every form of life and magic, silently watching over all the realms they'd forged, even the ones I couldn't see or touch myself. That some of these gods grew to love our realm—Emeraldis—where the roaming witches reigned over the continents, conquering and cutting down all forms of life.

"We were the rulers, Dove. For thousands of years," she had told me when I was five and stationed at a desk for lessons. *"The witches roamed so freely; we could have had a castle anywhere! We had so much more power than the other species, even the ancient fae. But the people prayed to the gods beyond for help. For guidance. And some of the gods beyond—the very ones we used to worship—found our bloodshed a little…unsettling. Those gods found favor with the people, convincing a handful of the gods to depart with a drop of their power, to create a new form of life. It was meant to* protect *Emeraldis. This is how the Realm Bound gods were born."*

I remember turning every word over in my head, careful not to mix up the details and displease my mother.

"Born like me?" I flinched as I asked, scared it sounded stupid and she would not be happy.

46

"Not like you. The Realm Bound did come to Emeraldis as newborns, just like you, but they were birthed from the sky, falling from it in a flash of stars and fire. The gods beyond gave them great power, greater than ours, but with a cost: they would be bound to this realm. Despite being created in their parents own image, they could never be with them. Only ever here, ruling over us."

I knew what bound meant, but that wasn't the part that concerned me. "How could they take care of themselves if they were babies?"

It was a rare moment to be awarded a smile from Mother, but when she flashed me one full of teeth, my insides leapt around with pride.

"Many people throughout the continents worship the gods beyond, Dove. A pair of devoted followers took the newborns in. All five of them," Malvolia said, still gentle with me then.

Siblings? I had always wanted a sibling, or for Althea to secretly be my sister.

"The Realm Bound grew up strong, wielding all kind of magic, giving them each special powers. That was what made them so much better than us, they had a gift from most of the gods! Once they'd matured, they started to civilize the continents, making room for large cities and permanent settlements. And the people of Emeraldis rejoiced, worshipping them for taming the witches. But we worked quietly against them, waiting to strike. To regain our rule of chaos. War was coming, us against the Realm Bound gods.

"I was only a little older than you were now when it happened. The war, I mean. My own mother wore the Coven Crown, I was her heir. Just like you are now. Five hundred years ago, when the fighting began, my mother sent all the children to Skully, the Isle we're on now. Every fledgling remained here, but every mature witch was sent to fight. The eldest of the Realm Bound siblings is the *strongest living being on Emeraldis and he was furious at our attack. He tore through the realm, slaughtering every last living witch." Her voice remained even, but my heart was pounding in my ears and through my throat.*

"When he finished killing everyone I knew and loved, he used his magic to seal the fledglings on the Isle, trapping us here. All that remained were us children—fledglings. My father and mother were both killed, so I was left to lead as the oldest and most powerful witch here. From that day on, I did. With my sister behind me and your father beside me. We built this Isle up for four hundred years before you came along. And it'll do, for now. The Realm Bound promised us an eternity of imprisonment. His magic is strong. So, we're stuck here. For now." Her gaze was distant, I couldn't catch her eye.

"What happens if someone tries to leave?" I asked.

Malvolia snapped her attention back to me. "They die."

CHAPTER 6

We burn our dead. Most immortals do. The fae have been practicing it since the dawn of time, with other folk following suit. Truthfully, it was the humans who took it up last—sending their dead out on flaming ships. We don't have any ships. We don't even have a body.

Just a severed head.

So, Mother put him in a box. A very flammable box. It's small enough to hold, but big enough to burn. While we stand in the square, the coven is completely silent and dressed in black. Malvolia is the only one to speak, like a black cloud rolling in an angry storm.

Too many pairs of eyes watch me, waiting for some sort of outburst or commotion. If I had something left to give, I would. They don't know that I'm too numb to move. Too still to give them anything but a void stare. I don't remember how I got here, and I won't remember how I got back home, either. I won't remember much at all, now.

Frozen on that image of a chopped head and shaking hands and my mother's eyes.

Malvolia bellows that our family should have a thousand more years together, that Roe deserved a natural descent into the death realm after a long immortal life.

Because, though all magic eventually fades, his was snuffed out.

"We will find who did this to Roe," my mother says and I choke hearing his name. "And they will pay with their life." She lights the box. Silent minutes past until it's engulfed in a blaze. He burns quickly and I hold my breath so I don't inhale the charred flesh. It's almost over now, and I can escape back to my bedsheets and my sleepless hours.

For once, I agree with my mother.

CHAPTER 7

There was a time when I was young that my father splinted my thumb after Malvolia snapped the bone. I think about it often, as I lay here and rot away.

I was eighteen, my immortality was rapidly settling into me. When I started to show real power, my mother was pissed.

Pissed.

Even now, part of our daily regimen is a dawn training session. Malvolia is an orderly mother, so we would stick to a strict schedule. Sparring with swords. Then hand to hand combat. Often times, her warriors would join us. Afterwards, a few hours in the library, either studying any useful information or decoding answers to get us off the Isle. I'd make my rounds in the capital. Gossip with Althea. Practice manifesting magic.

But something had changed between my mother and me during those years, shifting from measly affection to bitter competition. One morning, she took sparring too far and broke my thumb. I had already outmaneuvered her, so she swept me down and stepped pressure on the bone until it popped. I cried on the training mat for hours, refusing to get up for help. My face was so red and swollen, I barely knew how to retell the incident to my father when he found me hours later.

Roe winced and wrapped my bruising flesh that night. My poor, kind, sweet father. It was obvious that my mother maimed my finger beyond repair. And that she'd done it on purpose, though that part remained unspoken. The healers wouldn't touch it, wouldn't go near anything Malvolia did, so as not to incur her wrath. But Roe tended me. He came into my rooms with a cloth and salve and helped me organize my thoughts as I cried into my bedsheets.

He told me things could be easier for me, now that I'm older and on Malvolia's radar. He smiled, shining black hair and dark eyes, saying that there's a special trick he uses to get by. My father took my broken left thumb and told me to start making my own mental lists.

Lists can compartmentalize. They can separate the words pouring out of your head, sorting them into tamable beasts, each with their own separate stable. He said we could start right now, with my hand.

1. Malvolia wouldn't say sorry, even if she were. I shouldn't expect any apology, it won't come.
2. Sometimes magic can't heal everything. And my hand looked rough. So, I should prepare for some long-term effects. Think of the worst, maybe the truth will be easier.
3. Blaming Malvolia will only make it worse. She didn't mean it. She was just jealous of my power. I'm young and new and bold and bright.

Our list was right. My left hand has never been the same since. The tendons and ligaments between my bones are still gone, replaced with a constant grind. Some days it aches worse than others, but the pain has never bid me farewell. It chews at me or locks up on me. It almost always throbs. During my studies, I read that it's a common condition amongst older humans, as they age and wither.

Not so common for an immortal witch.

CHAPTER 8

"Your mother wants you up. She says it's time to stop sulking," Althea says as she moves to tidy my chambers.

She has two teacups, a romance novel, three empty raw spirit bottles, and an ash tray in her hands. I don't know how many days it's been since my father was found. Since the pressed image of his stringy muscles and chipped bone was forever implanted into my mind.

"I'm not sulking," I defend.

But I am sulking. And Althea knows it by the way she raises her eyebrow and puckers her lips. I'm sprawled out on the mattress, my sheets caked in night sweats and sadness. My hair feels stiff and my skin aches for hot water.

"It's been two weeks, Dove. I know it's hard, but it's time. We're all worried about you," she says, putting her hands on the curtains and forcing them open. The incoming light is blinding, it sends spots through my vision. I wasn't aware of the hour before but now I know the sun is up and bright. I hate it.

Because putting a clock to someone's grief seems unfair. There are no minutes or hours or days or years when I am standing still.

But Althea doesn't give up, it's not in her nature. The light hits her golden blonde hair, the blush pink of her dress shines.

"Just down the hill! It's barely outside!" She's practically beaming with desperation.

Growing up, I was always envious of Althea's features. While she shot up tall and generously filled out after we matured, I stayed slim. And short, though it drives me mad. I only look like a woman by the curve of my thighs and razor-sharp cheekbones. Althea has the height. The weight on her bones.

And she gets blonde hair. Golden, vibrant blonde. While I'm stuck with stark white.

White. Not even an extremely pale blonde, like she tried to convince me of as children. It's completely colorless—as white as the clouds or craters on the moon. Along with my big round, silver eyes. An angled jaw. A delicate nose, thick eyebrows darker than night and arched with authority. Full pink lips dramatically bowed against my pale skin.

"Fine. Only if you'll stop being so damn cheerful," I mutter, getting up. Althea takes an audible breath of what I can only assume is relief.

"Who do you think did it?" Calix asks, laying against the hill behind the manor.

Althea looks at him, softly. "A damn traitor, that's who."

It's been three hours since I've come outside. The sun doesn't feel pleasant and neither do I, but my cousin was right. The air in my tower was getting stale and my skin needed an exhale. I even managed to bathe.

"Are we sure it wasn't the western witches? Maybe the compulsion didn't work the way you thought it did, Thea."

Althea scoffs. "It *worked*, Cal. It always works."

Calix is wrong. It wasn't the western witches. That was the first place I looked the night we found my father's head. I tore through the woods in record time, landing on their doorstep. I grabbed the men so tightly around the neck they were barely able to choke out alibis.

It wasn't the western witches, my magic made sure. I dug compulsion through their minds, smelt their fear from my presence. They'd been too busy relocating assets and assigning new crop groups to even think about doing anything else.

"It wasn't the western witches," I say with conviction.

It wasn't any of Malvolia's lovers, either. I know she sleeps with her closest warriors, her favorite staff members. But they'd seen me coming and confirmed their location with my mother. I was *busy*—after we found Roe.

Calix gives me a knowing grimace. "So that's where you ran off to that night."

If he wasn't killed for love or power, what for? I lay back, running my hand against the grass. "I had to be sure."

He nods, understanding. I let the trickle of warmth seep into my sadness. The hunter has always been rough around the edges and raw on the inside, like me.

"It could be another rebellion. Perhaps they're growing stronger," Calix says.

It could be. But we haven't had serious trouble in years, since the last rebel tried to stand tall against my mother. Maybe it was a beast? Or a disgruntled lover? Roe kept to himself, but I know for damn sure he hasn't shared a bed with Malvolia in years.

"My mother says we'll find them soon. I mean, they can't possibly be far. We'll question every single witch on the Isle if we must," Althea says, grabbing my hand.

But finding the killer won't bring my father back. My kind, trapped father who ran from Malvolia just as often as I do. Who went away more times than he was home, who was lost in his own world. I push down the wave of nausea threatening to spill over. Steady the tremble of my fingers.

"This wouldn't have happened if we weren't caged here like wild animals," I spit, looking to the continents beyond. The one that's so close but so far. "If we could roam the realm again."

Althea looks weary but doesn't protest. She knows I'm right, and I know how badly she wishes to leave, too. The evening heat is still burning down, adding color to our skin. A shuffling comes from my right, and I jolt up, the sea breeze drifting into my nostrils.

And maybe I'm just on edge, but I almost swing on the staff member who appears from nowhere. Well, okay—maybe not nowhere. She came from the manor, dressed in a black working gown. She holds out an envelope as we sit up, a scared expression settles on her face, probably from my tense reaction. The cream-colored parchment has my name written on it in familiar fancy cursive.

Althea and Calix sit up beside me, leaning on their elbows to take in the sun. Calix apologizes for me as I take the letter. The scared girl scurries away without a word. I try to place her face, but I can't. She must be one of Malvolia's new younger staff members. Sometimes, the coven thinks it an honor to work within her house. Others do it out of fear. She seems like the latter.

I rip the envelope open, taking out a single card written in the same intricate writing. I'm hit with a wall of floral perfume, something so sweet it's almost sour. I steady my breath as I read it once over.

Dinner tonight in my private hall. Don't be late.
— M.

Ah, gods beyond. I feel my heart pound faster, my throat goes bone dry. Dinner with my mother is never pleasant. In fact, it almost always ends in disaster. The last time we dined we barely made it through the first course before she started throwing knives and insults.

Althea touches my shoulder, concern laced in her green eyes. "Is it Malvolia? What does she want?"

I don't get a chance to reply before Calix snatches the note from my hand. He reads it over, holding it close to his face. Then he lets out an angry sigh. "You don't have to go, Dove. She can wait until you're ready."

"Yeah, right. We all know this isn't a request. Nothing is ever a request," I snap. Immediately, I feel guilty for taking it out on Calix, who's just trying to help. My cheeks redden and I look at him with apology. He smiles, letting his dimples forgive me.

While I applaud my friends' protectiveness, I know they're no match for whatever Malvolia wants from me. Growing up with a mother like her, everything is a transaction, noting is said or done without purpose. We haven't had dinner since she asked me to hunt down those traitor witches almost a month ago.

A month? Already? Maybe this is my punishment. My karmic fate.

There is no saying no. There is no freedom or chances to stand up to the Coven Crown. I can only walk into whatever scheme she's cooking up and hope it leaves me unscathed.

Malvolia only requests a dinner when she has something important to say. A war to declare or a battle to win. And I am a *very* sore loser.

CHAPTER 9

I know Malvolia will be late, but that doesn't stop me from being early.

Think of it as a survival tactic—the more time I have to scope out what she wants from me, the longer I have to figure it out. I count down the moments, trying to think about anything other than my father. I tap my wooden chair in an anxious rhythm, drink down the wine our staff set out. As more minutes tick by, I wonder if Malvolia is late on purpose. A way to throw me off her game. The stone room is lit up with candles, the staff silently line the wall behind me, unable to move or converse without the okay from Malvolia.When the door creaks open, my eyes dart to it. Mother walks in, her red hair is bound up by golden pins, her long dress is a sleek black. I frown down at my own dark clothing, bland in comparison. We'll all wear the color until she's done mourning—a longstanding coven tradition. But the black looks good on her, making her features bold.

I swallow down any fear, diving into my mental list of questions I compiled for her. "Where was father when you first found him?" I ask.

The first strike. And by the cryptic look in her eyes, I know she's come to battle.

She sits down at the table setting closest to mine. "It's a good evening, don't you think? And *that* was a lovely way to greet your mother."

"You found no body?" I press, gulping my wine while she fills her own cup. I wonder if the servant will lose a finger for her empty chalice.

She slowly sips it. "No. And before you ask, I don't know what he was doing down on the beach so late, either." She waves a finger, signaling dinner. "Probably got into that drug garden you and your cousin grow."

I roll my eyes. A little bit of herbs didn't cause Roe to lose his life. It was obviously someone with access to a weapon. Or very sharp teeth. I shiver, thinking of the tales of dragons we've read over the years. When the door creaks open again, the staff bring in plates of food. Malvolia chooses every dinner, and tonight it's some sort of tender roast, with buttery potatoes and a carrot glaze. Even though it's one of my favorites, I'm still not hungry. Not until I can squeeze her for information.

"And you've learned nothing more of his death?" I question with more urgency. Malvolia keeps her features neutral, her thin lips in a straight line. She picks at her meat with a delicate fork.

"No more than you have. What were you thinking, tearing around the Isle and scaring half the coven with your rampage?" she scolds, as if I'm a thorn in her side.

The need to defend myself bubbles within. *Great, here we go.* Our words will begin to clash like swords, just as they do every time there's an offense or defense in our conversations. Besides, I didn't *scare* the coven, I simply demanded hard evidence from everyone I've come into contact with since his death. It's not my fault they started shutting their doors or packing up their stands when they saw me coming.

"I'm just trying to find some answers, Mother. It's not every day the Coven Crown's husband is found dead," I defend. She gets the first battle point, unhinging me before the first course is even finished.

It's true, though. Althea has been through all of Uncliff, compelling everyone she sees to tell the truth. Calix has also been frequenting the square. And the tavern. And every little nook or cranny where gossip could grow. There's just nothing to report, nothing to be uncovered.

"*I'm* maintaining order in the coven. *You're* supposed to be finding who did this," her eyes grow stormy as she stares into me. "I don't care how long it takes you. I don't care if it breaks you. Find the person who did this or else the coven will think we're all weak. A spill in the family will bring thirsty rebellion." She grabs her wine again, swirling it.

I hate to admit it, but Malvolia is right. A Seraphina's murder could bring uncertainty to us all. Change, if we aren't careful. And change doesn't usually pan out well for the oppressors. Especially with all the chatter of discomfort and displeasure I've heard recently.

Fine, she gets another battle point. I really hate when she's right.

But I've already planned on hunting down the witches who did this. I'll find them and kill them slowly. Not because my mother has asked me to. Not to show unity amongst the witches. But because my father deserves justice. And I deserve to fill this aching gape left burned through my chest.

"And you'll do what?" I spit, my body temperature rising with my temper. "Just wait for me to kill more teenagers? Maybe the entire western front, now?" I'm getting angry, but she brings out my inner beast. One point for me.

Malvolia stops swirling her wine. Another point for me— it's hard to throw her off and she looks taken aback. For a moment, she goes very still. Then, she gulps the remaining liquid down in a swift motion. Energy crackles in the air, on the brink of something potentially terrifying. Oh, *gods*. She pushes my dinner aside, but the look in her eye keeps me from protesting. I feel the atmosphere shift even darker when she glares into the glass she still holds, deciding what to do next. Malvolia turns, facing me before she dangles the now empty wine glass near my face. It doesn't hit me, but I can smell the bitter grapes from it. A remaining drop splashes on my dress.

I stay perfectly still and quiet, hoping it'll be enough to calm her down.

She throws the glass against the stone wall with remarkable force. It shatters, a pool of sparkling dust sprinkling the floor around us. I hear it over and over, knowing I pushed too far. The staff slyly exit, knowing their cue. My heart pounds as the shards settle. It's stupid, I should have known before this point I was treading dangerous waters. Roe just died, she's as unstable as I am. *Remember that late spring dinner eight years ago?* I almost lost a finger that night; a chalice against the wall is nothing.

Malvolia grabs my own glass from in front of me, emptying that down her throat, too. I watch the wine vacate, a blood red tear forming at the corner of her dark mouth. Instantly, I sit up even straighter in my chair and don't move again. It's easier to just take it, always. I think she's going to throw this glass, too, but she doesn't. Instead, she slams it back down on the table, directly in front of where my food should be. I manage to keep my shoulders steady as she gets up from her chair, heels clinking against the floor as she walks to the broken glass. Mother bends down, thoughtfully picking through the broken shards, comparing the more jagged edges while humming something that sounds like an eerie lullaby.

I can't take it any longer. My voice is a whisper. "What are you doing, Mother?"

She doesn't respond. She shifts through the pieces with concentration before finding one that seems to please her. I can tell by the way her face lights up a little, a wicked darkness behind her eyes. I clench my jaw. What's the battle score?

She casually walks back to the table, still humming. I get another whiff of her floral perfume as she takes her chair again. She's holding a large broken piece from the wine chalice, with a sharp jagged end. Her pale skin glows against her blackened eyes. And when she holds out her slender fingers, it's like she's waiting for me to hand her something. My stomach drops— I know she can only want one thing.

To punish me.

With a sigh, I give her my hand. Though I'm not exactly sure that's what she wants, I am sure she'll let me know right away if it isn't—probably with some brute force. Whatever is happening will only be worse if I try to protest or plea. I've seen that outcome too many times. Malvolia lightly drags the glass across my palm while I try to keep my arm from shaking. At first, she doesn't break the skin, but then she starts applying real pressure, digging into my wrists.

Pain follows.

Blood swells instantly, but she moves my hand over the chalice, collecting the crimson liquid. *Huh.* It's weird—Mother doesn't do blood magic. No one on the Isle can, anymore. The practice was lost with the war. Maybe she's just being sadistic, proving her ownership over me. Gods, what's the score, again?

I struggle to keep my face blank, but she drags the glass up towards my wrist, cutting the tendons in my thumb, digging it deeper and deeper inside my hand. I watch the glass disappear inside the wound, mentally moving into the corner of my mind I reserve for her harder punishments. She gets up to the tip of my thumb, before turning around and doing the same thing back down.

And then up again, severing all the working nerves in my hand for each and every finger. She's wielding it intentionally slow, deep enough that I can hear it scrape against my bones. The blood spills out into the cup, filling with color as I grow paler.

Deeper.

Deeper.

Deeper.

I feel a piece of glass break off and burrow inside my muscles. I have some healing magic, though it's not great. Even if I use my power, she'll only inflict worse. It's an unspoken rule we've had—*don't* heal her wounds. She put them there for a reason.

"If you're done whining," Malvolia says, unwedging the edge from my palm. Without the weight of the glass, my hand starts shaking. She wipes her fingers with a dinner napkin. "There is something you can *actually* do to help me. Something for Roe, too."

For my father? She has my attention, and the throbbing in my hand seems to lessen. Whatever she's leading up to—*this* is why she forced me to dine with her. I grab my napkin, wrapping my hand as I move to the edge of my seat. Already, I can feel the tendons start to mend. Immortality does have its perks.

"I'll do anything to help avenge my father," I say in a soft voice. I feel something tighten in my chest, the familiar high of my mother *finally* needing me. It's a rare feeling to have, a stupid drug. Her black eyes don't register any feelings, only war glory, but I stare into them anyways.

"Things have been hectic lately, even before Roe's death. The witches you killed weren't just unhappy with life here. They thought something impossible. Something they had to die for," Malvolia says.

"Thoughts of rebellion?" I ask, holding the napkin tight on my hand.

Malvolia shakes her head. "They thought they could leave."

Laughter bubbles inside my throat. Of course, they did. Sometimes, old enough witches can feel a little stir crazy, an itch to get off the Isle. They even convince themselves it's possible sometimes. The thought is absurd, but Malvolia's not laughing. She's still just peering into me.

"And?" I question.

"And I think they're right." Malvolia swallows, moving her chair closer to mine. "Well, maybe not exactly. There's no way those witches had the strength to leave the Isle. They were weak, untalented. But I think it might be possible. Something is shifting, Dove. I know you feel it. I think…I think the Realm Bound's magic might be fading. Or the spell is unraveling. I don't know for sure if it's the moon or the tides or just sheer luck. I think I've found something, or there's been a breakthrough," she says breathlessly.

Impossible. Not at all feasible. But there's conviction in her tone. A certainty that makes me wonder. "A breakthrough?" I ask, shuffling through the possibilities in my head.

Mother and I used to spend hours every day combing through ways to break the Realm Bound's magic. She thought that maybe combined, our power could overcome his own. Day after day we tried. Year after year we failed. Between spells and hexes, rituals and sacrifices, nothing ever budged it. Soon half a century passed, and we moved onto other things, like maintaining peace and order. But Malvolia has never stopped searching, she never will.

What did those dying witches know?

Malvolia nods. "We need to know for sure."

But she can't be serious. We know this outcome.

"You know what happens when someone leaves the Isle better than anyone," I snap. Her eyes narrow, recalling the same memory I am. The one where a rebellious witch threw himself off the tallest cliff nearly seventy years ago.

It was quite dramatic, even from the shadows where I watched it happen. Mother had been hunting him down for gathering forces against her. Honestly, it was the closest the witches have ever come to a rebellion. The man had been working for years in secret, meeting with like-minded witches to usurp my mother. It all came to a standstill when he'd been cornered by her loyal soldiers. Instead of facing the Coven Crown, the witch chose to jump into the choppy water below.

He knew what would happen. We all did.

And as soon as he hit the sea, he'd just…exploded. Blood sprayed those closest to the cliff. Gasps and screams were heard over the choppy water. But any trace of the witch had been wiped away, the Realm Bound's magic not allowing him even a moment away from the Isle.

"What if there's a way?" Malvolia grabs my hand and I instinctually jerk away. But she grips it tight, keeping hold of me. "You possess more power than any of us, Dove. It's as if your magic mimics what it sees, latches on to other forms around it. I've seen it adapt, the power behind you. It might rival *his.*" She spits the words but doesn't say his name—the Realm Bound god who trapped us here, the one who holds authority over his siblings and the realm.

The ruthless son.

The hand she's holding atop of mine warms with magic. She pulls at her power, sinking it into my bloody hand. I blink in surprise, putting the flawless skin up to my face. It's no longer throbbing, the wound completely gone. I wiggle my fingers. No pain.

I look at her. "You want me to try and leave the Isle."

It's crazy. Maybe the death of my father has affected her more than I thought. Witches have gone insane over less. I can't possibly leave the Isle, no matter the amount of power I have. Which is a lot, at its core. But it's not just about raw power. You have to be able to manifest it.

And sometimes, I suck.

Silver flames come easy; they always have. But there's a reason witches usually only manifest one or two forms of magic—having that much raw energy can be hard to wield. Impossible to grapple. And in immortal terms, I'm still young. I haven't mastered the ins and outs of what I can do. The power feels restless at times, a mirror image of myself.

"If there are beings powerful enough to cross in and out of the Isle, we need to know. What if this has something to do with your father? If we're able to confirm the theory…we can do something about it."

A chance to help Roe. I'm desperate, so I grab on to it. "You really think it's possible?"

Mother nods. "Magic can change over time. It can break down. It can unravel. Your energy is strong enough. I know it."

"You want me to go to Morbida?" I say the words very slowly, very carefully. She wants me to go to the continent that's so close some days I can smell the laughter. The humanity. The freshly cut grass.

"I want you to take this way out and use it for the witches' gain. If you can leave Skully, you can help the rest of us leave, too." She's looking into my eyes feverishly. "And there's something out there, something on Morbida. I think…I think it's the key to unlocking the Isle. I think it can free us."

I'm no longer breathing. I'm no longer on this realm or at this weird dinner with my mother. I'm not on the conversation battlefield or surrounded by bloodied napkins.

We have been stuck here for five hundred years. I don't know anything beyond the Isle. Hell, how many times can you read the same histories over and over?

"A way out," I say, deciding. Even if it means death, even if the magic will strike me down as I step off the cliff.

She nods again with approving eyes. "A way out."

I don't even pretend to think about it. I'll take the chance. A chance she's studied long enough, knows enough. A chance for a sliver of an escape from life here. Besides, is this really living, anyways? Most days, I don't think so. I raise my eyebrows, a small hopeful grin on my face as she watches me with importance.

"Tell me what I need to do."

CHAPTER 10

"Since when are the western witches such a threat? Didn't we *just* deal with them?" Calix asks, voice laced with skepticism. He's just come back from a hunt; a piece of moss hangs from his white shirt.

I try not to flinch as we stand near his father's game trading stand, Calix slicing off meat pieces from an oversized animal, Althea and I wrapping them in cloth. When he peers his brown eyes into me, I look away.

Mother was *very* specific—don't tell either of my friends what's happening or where I am going. It's too risky that they'll want to follow. Or want to see for themselves. And I won't let them watch me implode…should it come to that. Mother promised to explain my absence away if they grow too suspicious.

Judging now from their raised eyebrows, I bet that time will come soon.

A storm is rolling in. I secure the canvas around the meat with a tight knot, keeping it from the impending rain drops. "Malvolia doesn't think their timing adds up. She just wants to be sure that they're truly innocent from my father's death. You know that compulsion can have loopholes," I say.

Althea doesn't look convinced. She's staring into me like I'm a filthy, dirty liar. I tighten the knot, focusing on the twine instead of her accusatory features.

Calix grunts. "You're going to leave me alone with Thea?

Do you want to come back to one less friend?" he puts his still-bloodied hands behind his head.

The town square is full of activity, fledglings and witches are trading and shopping and prepping for meals. It's growing darker out, the overhead clouds matching my anxious mood. After I finished my dinner with Mother, we stayed up all night going through the details of her plan.

The first step? Jump.

It's a big job. A potentially life-ending job. And for once, Mother seems to be sympathetic of my need to say farewell. She told me to take the day and wrap up things with my friends, as long as I don't blab about my upcoming *trip*. I stayed up even longer than I should have, grappling with how to do it. At first, I thought of writing letters, explaining everything that Malvolia asked of me. I even considered saying nothing at all, deeming goodbye too big a task. But ultimately, I settled on building the narrative Mother started.

Calix and Althea think I'm spending a generous amount of time on the western front, where I'll oversee the growing population and prevent any further disputes.

"Only some days, Cal." I poke his arm. "Besides, you know I can't deny an order from Malvolia. I'm better off dead." *Though I might be, anyways.* I nervously swallow. "I couldn't lie when she asked me about their numbers."

Calix nods, but Althea doesn't bite. She hasn't said a word since I informed them I was going away. Her face went hard at my announcement, her silence is still icy. She's staring into me—*through me*—like she knows there's something I'm not telling her. My throat goes dry, I force a pleasant smile as I look at her, which probably doesn't help since I'm not known for pleasantries.

"Neither of you can come," I argue. "Mother says the meat isn't the same when you're away, Calix. And Thea, you need to keep our family in line."

She doesn't budge, dropping a severed deer leg and crossing her arms. Althea won't directly accuse me of lying, she knows whatever's happening is coming from my mother.

But she can sense the dishonesty. Or maybe she can feel my fear. Because I'm beyond terrified.

The sun is starting to set, and I know Mother is expecting me back soon. It's almost time to test her theory. To see if I can survive the fall off the Isle. The gray clouds help hide the fear that must be splattered across my face.

"She must have a reason," Althea mumbles. She grabs a bloody leg, strangling it under a piece of cloth.

"I'll be back before the cold weather," I lie. "And that deer is already dead."

My cousin narrows her eyes, giving up on her grumpy fold. Her stare hikes my body temperature, and I struggle to keep her gaze. I don't want her to be more suspicious. And usually I'm an excellent liar. I've perfected it throughout the years practicing *with* and *on* my mother. I keep my heart rate even, my face a blank mask, my intentions hidden. In fact, I spent the majority of last night going through the very specific details of the lie Mother has curated for me, even well after she told me to get some sleep. I couldn't, instead, I spent most of the night tossing around the lie that'll get me into Morbida and into their capital.

Amongst their king.

It'll come naturally then. But lying to my friends feels sticky and wrong, like a dark spider web. Althea and Calix and I *never* lie. You can't—if you want to have real friends here. This is the first time and it's eating at my insides.

BLOODJEWELS

The evening bell tolls, the summer sun disappearing. When Althea finally speaks, her words drip with hurt.

"Wherever the hell you're going—be safe."

Mother hands me a pack with leather straps, full of various items I might need. I'm wearing hunting leathers, a hard corset around my torso, and strings of knives and daggers throughout my thighs and waist. My boots are tied up, my hair sits in a simple braid down my back.

"Thank you," I say, taking it from her.

We're standing on the cliffside near the back of the manor, the waves violently crashing below us. From here, I can see the tip of Morbida's capital castle and the green of the continent around it. She hands me one final item, a dark cloak with imbedded silver stitching. It's thick, like it's made of an expensive fabric. And the stitching is well done, silver peeking through and weaving a little moon pattern at the bottom.

"To hide your weapons. Don't ever rid yourself of them, just keep them concealed," Malvolia says in a stern voice, strands of her red hair wisp around her face as the wind blows.

I nod, putting the cloak over my leathers. It'll be annoying to swim in, but that's a problem for future me.

If I even survive the jump at all.

I glance down into the sea, the water crashing against the rocks. We're high up enough that when a small pebble falls, it disappears into nothing. This type of fall would kill a human and probably bust up an immortal. Perhaps the jump itself won't kill me, but the magic might. My heart pounds through my ears, I repeatedly push down mountains of panic. Malvolia will stay and watch, getting her answer one way or the other. Either she'll witness her only daughter mist away into nothing, or she'll watch her deadly protégé slither into enemy territory.

And I suppose I'll be free, too, one way or another.

"I left letters for Calix and Althea. If I don't return…" I fold my arms.

Malvolia doesn't roll her eyes like I expect. Instead, she nods. And though she hasn't shown me genuine affection in years, she places her slender hand on my shoulder.

"You're strong enough for this," she says like she believes it. For a moment, she sounds like a mother, rather than someone whose made me into a beast. And then she steps back, leaving just myself and the cliff's edge.

The wind whips around, the smell of rain looms over us both. I turn to the water, inhaling only sea salt and my own sweat. Gods, was a hundred years enough? Do I want to do more? I won't find out if I explode into nothing. If I try to leave the only place I've ever known.

But Malvolia is watching, and if I break my promise… Jumping now would be a better fate. As the seconds tick on, I assume she's mentally sneering at me for being such a coward, but I refuse to look back. I just keep swallowing down the nerves.

Keep inching towards the edge.

The sun is long gone, the moonlight reflecting into the ocean. Mother was assertive that I leave during the night. We don't know if the king has guards watching the waters. Or if anyone keeps tabs on the Isle. So, if I'm going to swim the distance from Skully to Morbida, I need to do it soon. Because something tells me being a woman with bright white hair swimming from a long-forbidden Isle would land me right in front of the king.

And to play the game, I need to be the mastermind. Which

means when I meet him, it's going to be on my terms. If I don't jump soon, I'll have to sulk back to the manor and wait for whatever disappointment or punishment will come. Maybe I'm wrong, but waiting seems to always be the most dreadful part of it all.

Jump the cliff or turn and face my mother.

Death or death.

A bit of the rock crumbles beneath my boot, tumbling into the choppy water. I take a deep breath. It's time. Now or never.

I close my eyes, leaping from the edge. Before I can change my mind, wind is rushing around me. I wait for something to happen, for everything to go dark. But I'm sailing down the cliffside. And then, brisk salt water, stinging my eyes and pricking me like a million little pins. I shoot down deep near the ocean floor, the adrenaline pulling me back up. My ears pop and my heart thuds in my throat, but I'm still here.

I crash through the water surface, gasping for air. I hear roaring waves around me, birds gawk in the distance.

I'm alive. Oh gods, I'm alive.

It's not possible. I didn't do anything differently. But Mother was right, I didn't have to do anything at all. My magic was simply strong enough to slip right under his. I didn't implode. I didn't burst away to nothing. My shaky hands paddle against the icy water. From above, Malvolia peers down, a small, satisfied smirk on her face.

She's right to feel victory. I haven't been struck down. I didn't stop breathing and my heart stayed in motion. Mother was right—it worked.

It worked.

She nods, disappearing from the edge. A blur of red moves from the trees, and I know she's going back towards the manor.

I don't see her again, even as I move further out. Time for her coddling is over. Now, I have work to do. With her gone, it's up to me to free the other witches. And for the first time, I'm alone (despite whatever nasty beasts lurk below me, which I refuse to think about).

Paddling in place, I look at Skully, even smaller from afar. It looks…empty. Only little lights burn from Uncliff, a small portion of trees shaved out for our capital. It makes me burn with embarrassment. I've spent my entire life reading about other places, but I haven't been anywhere. I don't know what the hell is going to be out there.

Perhaps I'll choke on either my salty tears or the water, but I don't feel any remorse for leaving. No tug of guilt brings me back, despite not having my friends. Now that I've gotten this far, it's as if my blood is pulling me towards Morbida, to whatever new chaos awaits.

I start to swim.

CHAPTER 11

I read a lot.

That's how I've passed the time, all these years. It never hurts to know more than you should. Books saved my life more times than I can count, whether it be random knowledge or a thrilling escape from reality. And once, I read that the Realm Bound god named Morbida the art capital of the world. The continent is supposed to hold every ounce of history: sprawling castles and grand towers, culture and vibrant life.

A place for people who feel compelled by the arts. A learner's dream.

After the war, when the Realm Bound gods split up, the eldest god stayed there. Morbida was built mostly by him, and the capital—Crasmere—is supposedly wildly beautiful. The king's palace resides there, hugging a cliff near the edge of the ocean. It's a close enough watchful eye on the witches trapped nearby, the tip of the tallest tower mocked me throughout my youth. Interestingly enough, I've always obsessed over the Realm Bound and the gods beyond. Wouldn't you want to know your captors?

But for all I've read, I don't know much about the Realm Bound themselves. I at least expected to know what they look like. Or perhaps what their magical capabilities are. Hell, I'd take the slightest hint. I know none of it; I'm going into this completely blind.

76

A few years ago, a shipwreck washed onto our beach. It was still semi-intact, and some of the books and artifacts were pretty salvageable. It brought us loads of new information on the continents and the Realm Bound. Updated laws and traditions were found. Holidays had been laid out and the history of our realm post- and pre-war neatly organized. But I wasn't lucky enough to learn what they look like. *Who* exactly they are. If they have any strengths and weaknesses.

I did learn one thing—the Realm Bound are notorious for keeping their identities murky. Only those closest to the kingdoms or living amongst them could spot them in a crowd. So, I have no idea whether Mother's ruse will work, if it will get me in the palace undetected. I don't know if the eldest ruling god is a smart man who could find suspicion with a beautiful young woman.

Though, I guess I'll find out, because I'm on my way to Morbida. To scour his castle and take what I need. I mentally repeat my story again and again.

I am Dove Clepta (though Mother didn't think the irony of it as funny as I do), a traveling scholar. I've come to Morbida from across the sea—the southernmost continent. I am here to observe your traditions. I wish to study your culture and artifacts for my upcoming book "The History of Emeraldis."

I am not a threat. Actually, I'm just a girl. I couldn't cause any harm if I tried. I have glistening white teeth that match my hair and some deep dimples when I smile. A simple schoolgirl, just trying to start her career in the world of academia.

Nothing more. Nothing less.

Now if only I can do it—be conniving and convincing enough. How does someone become delightful and brave? I'm usually neither, and almost never pleasant. But I have to be, I'm the only one who can save the witches.

BLOODJEWELS

Mother says the majority of my time should be spent on the castle grounds—that's where she thinks the item is. The one thing on this very realm that could set us free, unleash us again.

The amulet.

She had no picture to show but gave a vivid description. Drilled it into my mind and made me repeat it back six separate times. A large dark gem attached to an ornate silver chain. The stone would be in the shape of a heart, and if I listened closely enough, I should hear it beating. It's the color of crimson blood. Once I find it, I'm to return home immediately. *Immediately.*

If I find it. If the kingdom does not think me a witch. If someone doesn't rip open my chest for standing outside my Isle.

I am Dove Seraphi—no, dammit. I am Dove Clepta and I am a traveling scholar from the southern continent. I am half fae, which is why my ears are round and my canines elongated. My father is a merchant, and my mother is a seamstress. I have siblings and a small family estate in the south. I possess minimal magic, though immortality has chosen to settle within me. Lucky, for someone only half fae. I enjoy reading and writing and painting and studying—

Well, at least the last part is true.

I'm walking, sopping footsteps squeaking a trail of water behind me. It's been an hour of being back on land. Different land. Right now, I'm barely sure of two things.

1. If I don't get to dry off soon, I'll lose my mind. Mother said no magic unless necessary, so I can't summon any wind or sizzle the water from my skin
2. This place is a lot bigger than Skully. A lot.

Thankfully, there are real roads here. Not like the small muddy paths we have back home. The cobblestone paths guide me through the woods, pointing me in the direction of Crasmere. That's the second thing I'm grateful for—the signs. Plus, I don't notice a change in the language, so it could technically be worse. It's the only thing keeping me sane.

Much like Skully, this continent is covered in green and sprouting with mountains. There's a hum from the river flowing nearby, wildlife buzzes beyond me. If Mother is correct, I should be nearing the capital gates. When we mapped out the route, she made sure I was swimming in far enough away from the capital, landing where she assumed it would be deserted.

So far, she's been right.

I have no reason to doubt her, she helped plan every small detail to increase my chance of survival. She told me everything she knew, laid out every potential scenario or my expected response. For once, it seemed like we were working *together*, compared to her usual authority. It rumbled something within my chest, a feeling long shoved down once I grew old enough.

So, I trek like a wet dog, alone under the moon hoping that something will come into sight. I start to whisper my story out loud, perfecting my polite tone and accent. *Gods*, how does Althea do this all the time? I'm exhausted from my pretend smile and gentle demeanor. And…I already miss her. I shake the feeling away. There's still no one else around, even as the signs start to point me closer and closer to Crasmere. I don't know if I'm relieved or terrified, but I am starting to really dry off. It's still seasonably warm, the night air is hot. And as I move, my cloak starts to swish; my leathers aren't wet.

My legs are sore from walking and my thumb aches from the stress. It comes and goes, but when Malvolia's name circles around my head, my thumb throbs constantly. At least the sun is starting to reemerge. That was a quick turnaround time. If my shoddy calculations are correct, it only took me a couple hours to swim here and hike towards the capital.

Good thing immortals don't need a ton of air. Or breaks.

As I approach a larger wooden sign, the craftmanship seems better than the rest along my way. It has *Crasmere* carved in large letters with small little vines chiseled around the edges of the rectangle oak. Excitement shoots throughout my body—I must be close. The stone path only has one route, straight ahead and into a small wall that gets taller and taller as I get closer. *Is the gate black?* I could never see it from Skully, the rocks around this area are too high.

It is black. I near the walls, and they're triple my size. But even more so, the wall doesn't look like a traditional wall to keep intruders out. Instead, it's made up of giant thick shards of black obsidian. *Crystals?* The jagged pieces remind me of an oversized version of the glass splinter Malvolia dug through my palm. I flex my fingers at the thought.

But unlike that, they're…beautiful. It's as if the obsidian springs from the ground to protect this very city. I step close enough to touch it, an electric hum emitting from it. It's caked in magic, strong magic, sleek and midnight onyx, reflecting rainbow now that the sun is out. It's the most interesting entrance I've ever seen—not that I have much to compare it to.

There's an open entry way, stacked pieces of obsidian form a giant arch. I can hear life beyond it, so I straighten my shoulders and prepare to walk through the gate. I try to remember everything my mother taught me about this place as I pass through, coming face to face with the city. Instantly, I'm in a sea of people coming to and from a thousand different places. A woman knocks my shoulder, followed by a hurried apology. A child weaves through my ankles, chasing after her. It's four times the size of our town square on the Isle. My heart pounds and I keep my eyes low to the ground, focusing on the stones. If I seem bewildered, I'll raise the attention of any potential guard. Though I don't spot any, so far. Just people laughing and shopping and eating and dancing, from what little I can see. I don't look up—I can hear Mother's voice in my head.

Don't stare at anything. Don't stand out at all. Pretend none of this is new to you and have a purpose. Look busy.

I dare a peek, taking in the sight of the city sprawling before me. Curiosity usually gets the best of me, and I pull off my hood to get a better look. No one stops and stares at my white hair, so that's a good start. With my cloak out of my face, I smell something exquisite, like cinnamon and warmed apples.

I try my best not to gawk. It's all too grand, too rich. I can't look away from every single direction. Everywhere there are folk of all kinds, laughing, and dancing, and selling, and shopping. A man puts fresh bread in the window of a bakery. A boy is pulling his mother inside it. A group of girls are giggling and drinking nearby. There's cobblestone everywhere, and townhouses and marbled structures as far as I can see. The morning sun is glowing and it's all vibrant with life. Distantly, I hear piano music from an open window, delicate playing of the keys.

I can't imagine seeing anything grander in my entire life. My bickering friends on the Isle were right; it's more than we could have ever dreamed up. There's an ache in my stomach from wanting to share it with them.

My feet keep me going, though I'm looking everywhere I can in small glances. If I stare at something too long, someone could notice. Mother went over this specific detail three times. She expected guards at every corner, but so far, I still don't see any. I'm pretending that this isn't the most exciting thing I've ever done as I come to a section of the city selling all different kinds of flowers. They're strung above the apartments, overflowing in buckets, resting on different colorful stands. Everything is clean and polished, kept and tidy. I walk on the far side of the cobblestone, following the general crowd as if I'm just a traveling scholar before bending down to inhale a flower. A simple girl who plans on writing a book, nothing more.

Right.

"Take it," an older woman says, lightly grabbing my wrist. She's behind the flower stand, pulling white lilies from her apron. "It matches your hair." She puts the lily in my hand, it glistens like an ocean pearl.

I smile at her, bringing the flower to my nose. Her face lights up, and her grin has a golden tooth. The crow's feet set into her dark skin deepen, she starts to nod. "Enjoy Crasmere."

"Thank you," I say.

She releases my wrist with a gentle pat, sending me on my way. Where I'm going—I still don't know. But the woman's kindness slapped me in the face; life is thriving here. People are…happy. It's nothing like what I know. In fact, I bet the kind lady would be *shocked* to know I've lived right beyond the ocean for the past hundred years. If someone grabbed me like that in Skully, I'd have them in the ground in a mere moment.

But this is nothing like home. The flower lady continues to hand out lilies behind me. I keep moving forward, looking for anything to help me get started. I don't want to be wandering the streets after dark, that means I have the day to figure out how to get from here to inside the castle.

I need to get my bearings, maybe do a lap of the city to take it all in. But maybe there are guards up ahead. It's all so big, I could spend days in just a small section. Mentally, I pull up the map Mother drew out. If I want to be near the king, my best bet is west. Or east. Hell, it could even be north.

I'm not really sure of anything, now that I've seen it.

I know what I need to do next, but one wrong move could gut my scheme before I even begin. And failure isn't an option. There is no plan B, there's not a single alternative. I have to succeed, so I must be careful. Really careful.

I lean against a marbled building, watching the people pass around me. In a twisted moment of fate, I suddenly wish for Mother's annoying guidance to pop into my head, telling me where to go or what to do. But nothing comes, I'm trapped with my own thoughts and my own resources. What's the best way to infiltrate a kingdom and get inside a castle? There was never a book on *that* in my little library.

All seems lost until I think of Althea and her excitement around Morbida on the mountain. Where my cousin had said something about this place and taverns.

CHAPTER 12

"Another?" the tavernkeeper asks.

I shake my head, though I do want another. He sways away, taking the pitcher of mouthwatering beer with him. My pickpocketing skills are amateur, and when I was nabbing some funds, I could only think of Mother telling me to keep a low profile. I replaced each coin with a rock, so they suspected nothing, and ended up with enough for approximately two beers. After I scoped out the city for a few hours, I landed on the barstool, discovering yet another delicious drink our Isle lacked. The beer is bitter, but still somehow tangy and sweet.

I could drink an entire pitcher.

Instead, I sip it slowly, trying to savor it and buy myself some more time. Calix would be howling over the thick bubbles and sour taste, and I wish I could give him some. It doesn't burn my nostrils like the hogwash we make back home, and I don't cough after every single swallow. The tavern is buzzing with life as it gets later, more and more people pooling in. Malvolia's advice comes to mind.

Someone within the capital walls can get you inside the palace. Find someone who can get you close to the king.

I've watched every patron come in and out, wondering if they're the right fit. Honestly, I can't tell who is helpful and who is just drunk. The lighting is low, exquisite interior marbled walls that match the shining exterior ones. The tables beyond the bar are all made from iron and full of people eating and drinking. There's a small group of people playing upbeat music in the corner, something on high-pitched string instruments.

Everyone here seems like they might fit the profile. They all look rich and well put together. Some are wearing oversized jewels or golden trinkets, but they're already surrounded by others, and they don't seem easy to get to. All my advice and confidence suddenly disappear now that I'm here. Surrounded by all of these people, I feel young and small. Everyone who smiles looks important, everyone who nods along seems relevant.

And I don't know shit. Mother told me to always assume everyone is a threat until they prove otherwise. I'm trying my damnedest to be careful.

I feel the stool next to me fill, so I turn my attention to its occupant.

"First time?" asks a sleazy-looking man with thinning grey hair and a crooked nose.

His eyes are rimmed with red and his mouth looks permanently open, like he struggles to breathe otherwise. The linens on him look expensive, a deep red. He's coated in arrogance, but he's wearing *gold*. And there's a circled medallion hanging around his neck.

Maybe he's important. It's not an impossible thought.

I lace my hands together on the bar. "It could be."

He looks human, but that doesn't mean much. He could still be half fae, *like I'm supposed to be,* or he could be mortal. Apparently, the king has lots of different folk in his court. I'm not as angry at the general male population as I was thirty seconds ago, especially once I see his hands are scrubbed clean and he looks well fed. When he leans closer, I make out a lion and a snake on the medallion.

A *royal crest*...I think.

He grins and there's a gap in his smile. "Mine too."

But he's lying. His posture is too relaxed, the tavernkeeper served him without asking his order. He's smirking like he's better than everyone else here. The music gets faster around us. He leans in further when I laugh. Gods, it really can be that easy sometimes. What wouldn't a creepy man do for a sliver of attention from a pretty girl?

"Do you have a name, first timer?" I touch his arm, batting my eyelashes like I've seen Althea do when she's homing in on a new boy.

"It's Sebastian," he coos, settling into his stool and drinking down the beer.

"Just Sebastian?" I press.

He rolls his beady eyes. "Sebastian Wattis, Lord of Valen."

Valen—that's not too far from here, if I'm remembering correctly. But more importantly, he's a lord. I've struck gold. Subtly, I start dipping into my magic. If I harness it softly enough, it won't raise any other magic user's attention.

"A lord, yeah?" I lean on my elbows, getting close enough to take in the stench of his overdone perfume. He reeks of the powder we use on infant fledglings.

"The king is generous," he shrugs his shoulders, but I see the glint of ego behind it. He motions the tavernkeeper for another drink. As I pull on my magic, I can feel my heartbeat pounding in my ribs. I have to steady my fingers and breathe deeply. This is the most tedious part. Mother warned me time and time again on it—compulsion can be finnicky.

I need him to look at me, but he's busy inhaling another beer. He slams the glass back down on the table after he drains it, wiping his mouth with a sleeve. I'm close enough to the door to watch it open, revealing a now setting sun. I don't know how long these places stay open, but I need to handle Sebastian before it empties out.

"Do you ever stay at the palace?" I ask, getting his attention.

Yes! He looks at me, and I feel my magic seep over to him, grabbing on. His weird eyes move into a daze, his opened mouth widens. I ease up on my power—don't want to fry his brain if he's useful. Plus, too much magic or an incoherent lord might raise suspicion. Even humans can possess minor magic, but too much can leave a permanent mark, on either the land or the person. He regains a little of himself, straightening up but still held tight by my magic.

"Oh, for sure. Whenever I come into Crasmere I stay with the king. Most lords do. Though the king is often away..." he trails off.

Perfect. He'll do just fine.

I've never compelled someone as deeply as I'm about to, not even to gain favor on the Isle. Like I said, having a lot of different outlets makes my magic unpredictable. And it's easy to mess someone up, though I have read extensively about compulsion from our own coven texts and what the realm has written on it. Before the near extinction of witches compulsion was a familiar magic amongst the stronger of us, so it's been well studied. The coven keeps excellent records, especially on power that can be used against other witches. I've learned about the dense layers of our minds; that there are some layers to peel back. Others, you melt into ash. If you're not careful, you'll take someone's memories. And if you're really careless you can take their whole mind.

Just as I aim to do right now.

I put my elbows on the table. Sebastian is deep under my spell. "You know the king, then? Does he trust you?"

He nods, the magic forces an overly honest answer. "I don't know him well. None of us nobles do. The king doesn't really take any counsel. But I'm respected here—I'll never be turned away."

It's as if he was sent into this tavern just for me. Mother was exact in her instructions—find an escort into the kingdom. He can't be too important, but he must be notable. If he's too close to the Realm Bound king, it won't work.

I can't have anyone looking too closely while I poke and prod, lie and steal.

The tavern music gets louder, and the air starts to lose its heat. Time is getting crucial. I need to have my claws into him before the tavern shuts its doors. I don't know how easy it will be to compel a lord in the middle of the capital street.

I tug on my magic. "Well, Sebastian!" my hands clap together. He looks excited at my own enthusiasm. "Aren't we so lucky to have run into each other?"

His brows furrow in confusion, but he says nothing. I touch his arm again.

"It's been so long, my dear old friend!"

The magic seizes him, a euphoric grin plastered on his features. Finally, he nods. "My sweet Dove!" he slurs.

I get to work.

The moon is high by the time I'm finished. My head throbs as hard as my left thumb. I feel the irritating pain up my wrist and biting between my muscles. Maybe it's gotten worse after Malvolia's dramatics during that dinner. I'm rubbing it again and again, but it doesn't help like it should. I feel my fingers lock up and I desperately wish for a new hand, one that won't pinch me with annoyance.

But Sebastian is smiling ear to ear as we wrap up at the tavern, like there isn't a problem in the realm. Like he hasn't a single worry.

Because he doesn't. I've compelled them all away.

They were measly worries, anyways. Awful human male behavior, like if his maid is actually carrying his child. Or if his wife will find them out. He wondered if the king would ever agree to renovate his summer estate, if he could hire new and younger staff to hit on. He's more concerned with betting on the right horses or wearing the biggest medallions than caring for his people.

Fickle problems, created out of necessity to complain rather than deeply inflicted wounds haunting him.

Sebastian holds the door open for me, his vacant smile lingering. "And of course, when the morning hits you must allow me to escort you to the palace!" he throws his hands up as we enter the street. "Have you seen the city yet? I'll get you a room at the bed and breakfast I'm staying in, now that it's gotten too late to burst in the castle. Your brother would *hate* me if I didn't escort you to the palace."

I nod along, agreeing that my totally fake brother would flip if Sebastian was rude to me. Said fake brother would also rage if Sebastian tried to flirt with me like he does his maids. And Sebastian knows it, my compulsion made sure.

"How exciting that you're finally going to publish a piece! My oldest and dearest family friend is writing a history!" he shouts, his dense cheek red from the alcohol. "Come, let's check in to the rooms." We walk down the street as he continues to rant. "This is the place to be if you're an artist, Dove! And writing is an art!"

I'm nodding, but not listening. I'm still mentally reeling over nailing this magic.

I *did it*. I compelled him—damn near perfect, too.

I left most of his memories alone, planting a few of my fake family doing fake things in his later years of travel. He's visited the southernmost continent, where Dove Clepta and her prestigious academic bloodline hail from. I didn't have much altering to do, just little ways to make me legit. Like hunting parties with my nonexistent brothers. Business deals with my not dead or decapitated father. A schoolboy crush on my fictional older sister. I made his heart swell with loyalty and love for his dear old family friend. And I was meticulously careful.

If anyone else, like a ruling god with rumored compulsion abilities, would ask Sebastian about me, they would have a lot of magic to undo. A lot of compulsion to dissect.

Layers.

So, it would take a lot of suspicion to unravel that magic. Which seems like an awful lot for a respected and trusted lord. I'm willing to take my chances, considering the alternative is the streets of Morbida. The lord seems like my best option, and I know Malvolia would kill me for wasting it.

We come upon a little stone house, wedged between two smaller buildings. It's strung with flowers and has a "B&B" sign hanging in the window. I can't believe I've managed to come this far. He holds open the door, but I have one final task to complete before I slip under the enemy's roof.

"Sebastian?" I ask.

He cocks his head. "Yes?"

"When the sun rises, will you show me to the nicest garment shop?"

CHAPTER 13

It's a good thing Sebastian is under too much compulsion to have a personality, because he seems to sneer at my new dress as we stand in the garment shop the following morning.

"My wife would never be allowed to wear something so *scandalous.* Where are the sleeves?" he snickers, crossing his lanky arms.

The seamstress is still pinning the bottom, and I catch a quick roll of her eyes after his comment. Hearing him talk spikes my irritation, too. So when the young girl steps away mumbling about needing more pins, I turn to the sordid man.

My magic starts to manifest. "Don't ever offer me your opinion," I command. The compulsion easily sweeps him. "In fact, don't speak to me at all until you're spoken to, *unless* it's incredibly helpful. Think carefully about it." It's something Mother used to tell me when I was getting on her nerves.

Sebastian nods along, still dazed from the rush of magic. Though I've never been compelled, Althea and I did once try it on Calix, who begged us to experiment on him. We were both weary from it, though we only made him jog to the lake and back. He said hearing the compulsion out of Althea's mouth was euphoric. Better than any herb we've ever grown.

After that, we stayed away from using it on our friends.

Sebastian doesn't count—he's annoying and immoral and thinks poorly of women. Disregarding him, I think my new gown is enchanting. The seamstress offered me a silky lilac colored fabric, an apparent favorite amongst the rich here. It flows near the ground, but clings to my waist and hips. The neck is low enough where I don't feel stiff and the material is still easy to run in. To fight in, if it comes to that. I mean, I couldn't show up to the palace wearing my leathers or tunics. Besides, I go feral over a new dress. The new look gives me a burst of energy, despite barely sleeping on the lumpy bed and breakfast mattress.

And through the wall, I could hear Sebastian struggling to snore all night long.

We woke up early enough to be the first customers at the garment shop, one that Sebastian deemed the "best in the city." He of course, offered to not only fund my spending here, but my entire stay. It's convenient to have found a long-lost family friend.

When the seamstress returns, she slides her needle through the dress, giving it some final touches. I stand still, not used to having a stranger so close to me. Especially with something sharp in their hands.

The girl steps back with a smile. "It's rumored to be the king's favorite color."

I blink in surprise. Lilac? It's pretty for sure, light enough purple with hues of white and pearl, but for a murderous king? It seems too…calm. I glance in the mirror. It does compliment my moon-colored hair, and the sleeves only fall halfway down my arm. There's a matching pearl colored corset over top of the plain lilac fabric—it shines in a certain light and is comfortable on my torso. The seamstress even embroidered some flowers along the hem of the skirt, the thin vines stitched with silver. Just like my eyes. For a second, I'm speechless. It's prettier than anything I've ever owned.

And she made it all in under a couple of hours.

I turn to the young seamstress. She can't be over seventeen, and she looks human.

"It's beautiful. How did you manage it so quickly?"

She shrugs her frail shoulders. Her dull brown hair matches her eyes and skin. "It's my parent's shop—I've been doing this for as long as I can remember."

It shows. Her slender fingers are steady, and the cream dress she's wearing is covered in stray pins. "Thank you," I say.

The girl flashes a shy smile, handing me my bag stuffed with my leathers and cloak inside. "Yeah, 'course. I'm Lucy, if you ever find yourself in need of a repair or another."

Sebastian groans from behind me, causing Lucy to roll her eyes once more. I choke back a laugh, slyly smiling at her as I hand over the coins to pay for her time and the garment. I throw in a few extra—the girl has talent. And when Sebastian makes another noise of protest, I toss in a handful more.

He can afford it.

Lucy beams as we leave, profusely thanking us and telling us to enjoy our time in Crasmere. The streets are busy for the early hour; it can't even be noon. When we start to walk, Sebastian leads us down a quieter street, and my panic starts to set in.

What if I'm found out? I don't think the king, or his people, will ask questions. They'll likely just kill me. What if I can't pull it off? The weight of the witches' fate is a heavy burden, crushing my shoulders and my ribs and my chest. I try not to be nervous as we walk, knowing the only destination from here on out is the castle. I'm pushing my fingernails into my palm, deep enough to bleed. When I feel the liquid, I use a tiny push of magic to seal the wound.

Bleed. Heal. Bleed. Heal.

BLOODJEWELS

The compelled Sebastian stays silent, which is good, because the road we're on is made up of homes, and I don't need him letting everyone on the street know we're here. There are townhouses and apartments, most with open windows and blowing curtains. Houses are on the corners and wedged on the sides, everything is completely polished and grand. A fae man plays violin on the porch of his townhouse. A woman kicks a ball to her daughter on their lawn. There's another flower stand for people to stop at.

It's so impressive, I can't help but wonder what it would have been like to grow up here. Everyone seems so…healthy. The children are well-fed, the adults look well-rested. Could I have been someone else, if the circumstances had been different? Maybe I could have grown up nicer, trusting, instead of constantly baring my teeth.

Or perhaps it wouldn't have made a difference at all, and I've always been dark at my core.

"Tell me about the king and the palace," I say to Sebastian.

"The king is the eldest Realm Bound, and of course, he's the strongest. No one knows exactly how their magic manifests, but he holds more of it than the others. Obviously, our continent reflects his rule and his strength," Sebastian brags. "The other Realm Bound siblings are good rulers, too! I would never speak ill of the gods. But our king is very meticulous. He can be… impulsive. Some would say he's even a little cruel. Not me, though! I would never speak poorly of our king. To manage an entire realm? Well, you must rule with an iron fist!"

It's little more than I already knew. Even the histories vaguely tell of the Realm Bound's ominous behavior. There seems to be an aura of chaos about him in the pages mentioned. And Sebastian says he's meticulous when he's around. Does that mean he looks closely at all his guests? A wave of disgust rolls through me.

I'm going to live inside his walls. *His* rooms. The sole person responsible for locking away my entire kind. The one who made my existence miserable by caging me to the Isle. He holds all my rage. All my misery.

I don't have time to soak in the feeling as we approach what I can only assume is the castle gate. It's a lower version of the same jagged obsidian that surrounds the capital, sticking out of the cobblestone in a somehow polished way. The castle is…nothing like I expected. I search for words as we pass through the open unguarded gates.

Thinking about it, I always assumed the palace would be made of marble. Aren't most grand palaces are made of it? Or maybe a nice, polished rock, some big slabs of stone.

Instead, it's made out of *obsidian*.

Just as the gate, just as the surrounding walls. But the castle crystal has an intense rainbow shimmer that changes with the sunlight, sparkling in the afternoon. It's unlike anything I've seen in books or sketches, so ominous, yet vibrant. The castle itself is grand, sprawling up the edge of a cliff overlooking the sea. The tip I could see from the Isle belongs to the sole tower attached to it, spiraling up. The roof looks colorful, but it's too high for me to see, and the window arches are big and bold.

It's surely made for a dark king.

There aren't any guards on our walk up, but I see plenty of seemingly endless gardens. Vines and petals climb up the entry stairs, the air is heavy with their sweet floral scent and a hint of…mint.

Sebastian stands up straighter as we climb the stairs and approach the massive doors—made of colorful stained glass. Thousands of different colored pieces are laid in a mosaic onto it, making up more vines, leaves, and flowers throughout. Each door is double my size, maybe even double Sebastian's six-foot frame. I could stare at them for hours if I wasn't so nervous about going inside. The compelled lord pulls open the handle. Still, not a single soldier or guard in sight. *Does the king invite trouble in?*

Inside, everything is sleek and colorful from the shining crystal walls, lit up by the incoming sunlight. I look up—*no way.* The entire ceiling, I think spanning the *entire* castle, is stained glass, just like the door. I can't see the details of it, but I'm sure it's covered in leaves and flowers and other beautiful images like the entrance. And I must admit, it's breathtaking against the sun; it makes the walls shimmer.

In front of us is a massive double staircase leading up, and two seemingly endless hallways. The same green thumb outside extends inside as well. Plants are nestled in corners or weaving through railings. Every so often, I see a mismatched patterned rug covering a part of the hall. Candles are lit with magic on open surfaces and in the overhanging chandeliers. Paintings are strung up with other displays of weapons or ornaments.

It's sleek and lived in. Dangerous and cozy. I can't stop staring at its beautiful paradox.

From the stairs, a fae woman descends. It's easy to tell she's fae, her ears come to a point and her canines are elongated. Plus, she's walking with perfected immortal grace for someone who looks maybe twenty, as if she's ready to either jump into battle or sway into a dance at any given moment. She's not wearing a gown, but leather pants and a long sword strapped behind her silky tunic. Her brown hair matches her eyes and sits in long coils, reaching her waist.

Sebastian turns to me before she approaches us. "That's Nemir Ironyield. She's the head of the king's armies—basically his right-hand man. Er—woman. Whatever. She controls the military. And she's ruthless on the battlefield, I've heard." *Oh, she's definitely on my list of people to avoid.*

She comes close enough that I can see a long scar stretching down her deep umber skin, running from the inner corner of her eye down to her sharp jaw. It somehow suits her, like it warns how dangerous she can be.

Nemir folds her arms. "You brought a guest?" she sounds displeased.

Sebastian claps his hands with an obnoxious grin. *Ugh.*

"Nemir!" he shouts. "My dearest family friend has come to town. This is Lady Dove Clepta. Her family is rooted in academics down on the southernmost continent. She'll be my honored guest during her visit."

I smile as friendly as I can manage when Sebastian puts a grubby hand on my shoulder. "It's an honor to be here, Nemir."

She doesn't return the smile. Instead, she's looking at me like she can't decide if I'm going to be trouble or not. I swallow down any fear. She can't *see* my nerves, and I certainly don't think she can feel them. I'll have to study up on common fae magic if I want to make sure she's not a threat.

"Dove is writing a history of Emeraldis for her first official traveling scholar task! I can't believe her brother approved it," Sebastian mutters. "But Morbida is the best place to start, isn't it, Nemir?"

Nemir looks like she would be more content ripping out his vocal cords rather than answer Sebastian's question. "I guess it is," she says. Her voice is thick with an ancient accent. One I can't quite place.

"Surely she can stay here and use our resources?" Sebastian asks.

My heart pounds as I wait for her to answer. I don't see anyone else around, but Nemir stands like she can make any decision she wants. And I can tell she hates Sebastian, but if I'm lucky she'll overlook that for a simple schola—

"Anyone of nobility is a guest of the palace," she says with annoyance. "You're welcomed to stay with us as long as you're here, Dove. You'll find lots of court members and their families reside here. You'll both stay in the guest wing, then."

Relief floods my body, but I stand motionless, a noble grin plastered on me. "Thank you, Nemir."

She's frowning, her slender cheekbones cutting sharp. Something tells me the king wouldn't pick a weak second-in-command.

"I'll walk you there to get settled," she motions us on. "What type of history do you plan on writing, Dove?" she asks as she leads us down a hallway. Fireplaces are lit and it still vaguely smells like mint.

She doesn't accuse me, but it sounds like it by the way she purses her lips. I keep my composure, not a single stumble in my rehearsed answer as we pass by people and doors.

"Mostly paintings and artifacts from the early years. I'm especially interested in realism." I don't recognize my voice, it's too polite.

She nods, stopping a door. "Lord Wattis, you'll be here for the duration of your stay."

Sebastian nods, grabbing the handle. "Grand! I'll rest until dinner. Does the dining hall still serve nightly? I'd like to arrange chicken and corn, or maybe a roast."

Nemir slowly blinks and I'm sure she's visualizing ways to strangle him.

"Yes, it serves nightly," she says through grit teeth.

Sebastian doesn't notice her anger—but that's *not* a result of the compulsion. That's just a horrid personality flaw. He clicks his tongue in approval, waving goodbye to me as he opens the door.

"You'll be down the hall," Nemir says, looking at me. "I'll take you there."

Oh, gods beyond.

I don't think being alone with Nemir would do me any favors. You can't get any closer to the king than second-in-command.

"Oh, Sebastian!" I say with sudden enthusiasm. "But I still haven't told you of my brother's latest travels. Walk to my room with me, I'll fill you in! What do you think?"

He's grinning at my newfound interest in him, but then his eyes gloss over and he enters a momentary daze. "I'm not to offer an opinion on it." He nods at Nemir, pushing his door and stepping inside the room.

I guess it's karma, or just bad luck—of course, this is what I get for muzzling the bastard earlier. From the side, I see Nemir's eyebrows raise in suspicion. *Great.* Just. Great. I turn to Nemir, offering her innocent smile, all crinkled eyes and dimples. She doesn't budge.

Is there a curse word strong enough for this?

"This way," Nemir decides.

I follow beside her, grateful she let it go. Mother would have skinned me for that slipup. As we go down the hall, I worry she'll question me more after my misstep, but she doesn't try to poke any holes in my story. It gives me time to gawk at the art. She stops at another door and pulls at the handle.

"Yours," she says curtly, nodding her head for me to go inside.

I step in, already admiring every direction. I thought it might rival Mother's chambers—the nicest our Isle has to offer—except it blows hers away. There are a few bookcases, all full. Instantly I want to run to them, but Nemir is still in the doorframe. It's not one room, but three. One for sitting or eating, one for sleeping, and a massive bathing chamber. I make my way to the bathing chamber, following the sound of a steady stream. It's a massive steaming pool *and* a running waterfall against smooth rocks.

It looks *magnificent*. My bones ache for it.

There's a fireplace in each room, eccentric rugs throughout it all. The bed is three times the size of mine back home, and so plush as I run my hand over it.

Like Clarissa did to the grass when she was dying.

It pulls me back to that night, and for a moment I can't breathe. I see her blood on the soil and her blonde hair sprawled as she looked at the sky. My mind is screaming at me, *killer, killer, killer.* Over and over again. My throat goes bone dry, I squeeze my eyes shut and will it away.

It's not real. It's not real and I have a job to do right now, for Mother. Yes, Mother. Think of her. If I do this, she might finally accept me and—

"You'll find the dining hall rarely closes, like Sebastian said. And maids will frequent your room should you have any needs," Nemir says, unphased by whatever she just witnessed. *Did I make a scene?* Hell, this is harder than I thought.

I forgot she was in the doorway at all. I nod along, looking for signs she watched me break down.

She just frowns. "Try not to need anything."

And with that, she shuts the door.

I do nothing for at least a minute, staring at the door trying to digest the last twenty-four hours. Even Malvolia would be forced to admit how impressive this is. Inside Crasmere and holed up within the king's castle all within forty-eight hours of being on the continent.

It's a damn good job. And an exhausting one.

I glance at the pillows as if they're actual clouds. A few hours rest wouldn't hurt, especially after the whirlwind week I've had. And strangely, without the looming presence of the Isle, I feel light enough to sleep.

I guess I'll need it—for what's to come.

CHAPTER 14

I once spent six months away from Uncliff, deep in the heart of Skully.

This wasn't on purpose—an isolating forest isn't my brand of insanity. My mother had taken me out there, leaving me alone with the trees and my hot tears. I'd matured a few years earlier and rebelled in the small ways I could. No matter how hard I tried, I wasn't ready to settle into life as the Coven Crown's heir. Instead, I could be found drinking with Calix until we were both dizzy. Or spending long nights at the lake with Althea, flirting with handsome witches we'd invite to join us. It was always harmless, idiotic fun.

Until it wasn't.

Because it's men who get me into trouble. Men who light a red fire inside of me until I burn with rage.

The night it happened, I'd been too busy taunting Calix by the water, clutching a bottle of raw spirits while he laughed and ran from my voice. We were well beyond sobriety, and I was starting to see double of him as he moved. I didn't see that Althea was missing. I didn't note her absence, though it had been hours.

But when I found her, face covered in bruises, I scorched the entire Isle.

It was the first time the coven saw what I was truly capable of. My silver flames grew bright, bold. Everyone was terrified—at least, that's what Malvolia says. I only killed three men. *The* three men who beat her senselessly. Later, I found out they were doing it to get back at me. Apparently, I'd bested them in swordplay earlier that week, and instead of trying to come at me, they'd just practically killed Althea. I didn't feel bad. Truthfully, I still don't. I'd enjoyed it and I'd do it again, too. They deserved it, so much so that I drew out their deaths, making them plea before wrapping their own insides around their necks.

Did they bleed out? Suffocate? Burn?

I don't know. I didn't care to know. I was red with rage.

When she'd gotten wind of it, Malvolia detained me immediately. She asked me if I was sorry. I wasn't. She asked if I had any sense about me, if I thought about the havoc this would wreak. I didn't. Mother asked if I was out of my mind.

I was.

But is it truly that bad to kill for those you love?

Mother dragged me by my hair from the lake, pulling on the braid while I flailed around and begged her to stop. She kept going without uttering a word, tugging harder every time my protests became too much. She marched me into the very heart of Skully, away from anything and everyone. She told me to survive—or die—until I calmed down. Only then would she be back for me. The top of my head was bleeding from her grip on my scalp, so I barely pleaded for her to stay.

Then it was just me and the woods.

I guess it'd taken awhile—for me to calm down. I was alone for six months, counting the seconds, hours, days.

I don't think Malvolia intended it beyond a cruel punishment, but I'd learned a few things in the isolating forest. It was either adapt or die, and I was too stubborn to die, so my only choice was to adapt. I taught myself tons of things. Things that helped me tremendously during my first week living in Crasmere, under the king's roof.

1. Befriend the shadows. Lurk among them if you want to survive. They're a constant informed companion to have.
2. Leave room for silence. Often, whatever's around you will fill it. *You* learn more from listening, anyways.
3. If you think you know the lay of the land, you're wrong. There's always another path, a hidden way, or something you haven't seen.

Ironically, it's the advice from the forest that's been aiding me the most as I grow comfortable in the palace. Maybe the king's court is more of a beast than I thought. There are daily comparisons to my time in the woods, ironic since I'm living in luxury instead of sleeping on soil. First, I'm better fed here. The food has been mouthwatering, well worth the hour I have to sit and mingle with Sebastian each morning and evening. Stews and pies versus soggy berries and skinned squirrels.

The clothing is obviously better, too. I was delivered more flowing gowns my first day, fine silks and leather corsets. Different shoes for every outfit, even another pair of boots. None are as flawless as the one Lucy made, but they're still stunning. The maids tended to each and every part of my room and my clothing.

There are people everywhere. The castle is massive, and I see new faces every single day. Mother never told me just how central the palace is to Morbida operations. It's not just for show, there are diplomats in and out constantly. I know because I've spent my spare time watching everything around me. Just like in the forest, the shadows are the best way to learn your surroundings.

I've acquired the names of everyone important, rounded up all the hottest gossip, and stumbled upon two secret tunnels, both seemingly leading nowhere.

I've been *busy*. But I haven't found anything tangible. And if I'm not snooping, I'm reading new things—the library is unbeatable.

Still, between all the hours alone, or the fake polite smiles I shoot around in the hallways, there's a pit of loneliness growing inside of me, the same one that grew during my isolation in the woods. These people aren't Calix or Althea. They aren't the witches I'm so used to. And I haven't seen the king.

Or at least I *think* I haven't seen the king. I still don't know what he actually looks like. Even with all the paintings on the wall, I haven't seen a single portrait. Nothing of him or the rest of the Realm Bound. Around the palace I haven't heard any gasps or witnessed anyone stop to bow and stare. So, I'm guessing he isn't here. Which is good, because I've been doing a lot of digging. However, I have seen Nemir.

A lot.

I'm assuming she's been told to keep tabs on me. Or maybe she's doing it of her own free will. But she appears everywhere that I am, more times than anyone could deem a coincidence. She's smart to be suspicious—*obviously*—so I can't decide if I want to applaud or strangle her. It's got to be exhausting being so vigilant of a shadow. When I'm in the library scouring for new books, looking for a trace of the word *amulet*, she shows up. In the dining hall as I eat with my dear old friend Sebastian, she pops up. As I walk the courtyard, listening for trails of gossip, she joins me.

And of course, right now, as I walk the garden eight days after my arrival, there she is.

"Another evening stroll?" Nemir asks, falling in step beside me. This time she's wearing a plain dress, though her sword is still strapped to her back. There's a dagger at her hip along with it.

I try not to roll my eyes. "I'm a creature of habit. And I love the outdoors." Plus, I can't exactly a hike a hill with my witch best friends while I'm here, so the flowers and fresh air will have to do. Not that I'll tell her this. I like to keep our interactions to a minimum.

"Do you have any gardens like this back home?" she asks, but she doesn't really care.

She's only trying to pry any bit of information out of me. It's our daily routine. She'll ask me a million questions, poking holes in everything I say, or don't say. And I dodge her like a knife aimed to kill. I don't have to see the king to know she could be telling him every move I make.

"Nothing this big. Your king must enjoy employing all these gardeners," I joke.

Nemir's lips twitch up. The scar across her cheek moves with it. "Actually, he does a lot of it himself."

Oh, shit. I definitely didn't expect that. How can he be tending to flowers when he hasn't been seen in over a week?

She pulls a yellow tulip from its stem. "Some say he's... painstakingly diligent."

I can only imagine, from the hundreds of flowers that need tending just in this garden alone. While she watches me, I pull out a small notepad from my pocket, followed by a pencil. I bend down to the flower in her hand, writing out details of its leaves and some bullshit on the season. Notes for my *research*. Mostly just to throw her off. And to keep up appearances, of course. I have pages of useless scribbles on various items and plants around us.

The notepad settles something within her, like she's been reminded that I'm here to study. But she also keeps glancing around as if she's looking for someone. She's usually more diligent with her questions. I'm actually shocked she didn't ask to see my notes today.

Instead of badgering me, she sees something in the distance and perks up. "I'll find you tomorrow."

"Looking forward to it," I mutter, but she's already off.

That night, I'm wandering the halls well after everyone should be asleep. Even though I've still been, strangely, sleeping well. It's funny how all the luxury has grown normal in a short amount of time. I can't imagine bathing without the waterfall or having the extra fireplace to read by. My shoulders fall easier with such a plush bed, and I'm no longer constantly grinding my teeth. Even my stupid left thumb hasn't been as sore.

It's kind of like a messed up vacation.

Except I'll never really be at ease. Mother's shrilling voice still echoes my thoughts.

If you feel as if you can relax, you're probably about to die. She snarled that once at me when I was twelve and lounging with a novel.

But no one's coming for me now, even as I wander around with a teacup in my hand. It's weird that I never see any guards, but when I asked Nemir about it, she said they don't *need* guards. The king deals with any trouble on his own. It sent a shiver down my spine and had me locked in my room the first two nights. At first, I was really hesitant to step out after everyone was asleep. But I just couldn't stop thinking about how the best kept secrets can be discovered in the dark. Curiosity got the best of me by night three.

No guards. No difficulties. It's as if they set themselves up for failure.

BLOODJEWELS

I feel a chill as I walk near the top of the castle, close to the spiral tower I could see from the Isle. A month ago, I was hiking the mountain with Calix and Althea, daydreaming about what life could be like on Morbida. Now, I'm in the palace itself.

And I can't waste this opportunity. So, each night, I sneak out and pretend to wander like a restless owl. I sip my tea and learn the layout of the castle. I pull on door handles and learn what each room consists of. Tonight, there's a wooden door with an iron handle. It's locked, but I jiggle it twice to be sure. Most doors here aren't locked, and this one looks different from the rest. When I touch the wood, I feel a hum of magic.

An important door.

I tuck the detail in the back of my mind but move on for now. Better to be more prepared when breaking through a magic door. And I heard rumors there are sketches of the palace structure somewhere in the library. *If only I could find them.*

Further down the hallway, my billowy nightgown moves with the breeze. The stained glass ceiling gives me a glimpse of the moon, a waning sliver tonight. I haven't been this far down yet, and at the end of the hall there's another door—one that matches the ceiling and the intricate entrance set on the palace.

Obviously, I pull on it. Every pretty door gets tried. You never know what's inside. The handle moves open at my gentle touch. Instantly, I'm swept with hot air and a fresh earthy smell.

Plants are high and low. It's not a room, but a globe of stained-glass entrapping what should be the roof. There are vines hanging from the top and spilling onto the floor. Spiky flowers and leaves grow wild everywhere I try to step. Hues of rainbow reflect on each surface, and different vegetation is stationed all around. The air is crisper, wetter, sweeter. Greenery I can name is everywhere—lilies and orchids and snapdragons and sunflowers.

There are a few I don't recognize, some that glow.

A greenhouse.

We have one back home, but nothing like this. The floor here is tiled and it smells more like flowers than manure. This one is big enough to walk about, overflowing with leaves but also cushions and candles. It's warmer than the hallway, but not sweltering like the caged deathtrap of a greenhouse on the Isle. I find a small table with a chess board atop it, near a couple stacks of books. Interestingly, there's a colorful couch in the corner, worn but cozy. It's practically begging to be sat on. And there's no one around.

Just me and the novels and this cup of tea that's growing cold.

It would be a shame to let this secret hideout go to waste. I haven't found anything this exciting since I started looking. And it's borderline tranquil in here. I convince myself to sit at the table, just so I can browse the books near the stack. I won't get *too* comfortable.

I run my finger over the book spines and pick a random one from the stack. It's a romance. One of my favorite romances. I'd first found it when I was seventeen and scouring Skully for new stories to read. You can only reread the same novels so many times before a restless energy sets in for new content. I think I'd harassed every single living witch on the Isle for their books. Back home, my own copy of this one is well worn.

It's a stroke of luck. I eagerly open it, diving it. I'm not going to get sleep, anyways, I might as well get in a few chapters while the moon is high. I scan chapter one. And then chapter two.

Three.

Four.

Seven.

Ten.

Fifteen.

Twenty-nine—

"That one has a nasty ending," a new voice says. It's low, rumbling, and thick with accent.

A shiver travels down my spine as my head jolts up. My loose hair falls in sheets around my arms as I find the source of sound and the sudden lavender scent, standing in the opened doorframe. I blink. Again. Maybe once more.

He's devastatingly, strikingly, achingly beautiful. Has the air always been *this* warm? It can't possibly be my blood temperature.

The stranger is smirking, a lazy expression on his full lips as he leans against the wall. His arms are folded over his expensive black shirt—silk and carelessly buttoned against his muscular frame. His head is titled back in chaotic ease. His presence is devilish for someone so young—he's probably not much older than I look. And he's tall. So very tall. At least a foot higher than me, possibly more. There's an otherworldly glow to his features—big, heavenly glowing eyes, soft wispy eyelashes, a delicate nose. And raven black curls, a ringlet hangs near his eyebrows, arched thickly with authority.

I try to remember my voice, or the language we speak, perhaps the place I'm in, before I open my mouth.

"Do they all die in the end?" I blurt out, forgetting the ending to my favorite story.

He shakes his head with a chuckle, bouncing the mop of black curls. He drips with sophistication as he strides over to me, golden rings adorning his tanned fingers. In a swift motion he pulls out the other chair and sinks down into it, cufflinks shining on his sleeves. Nemir did warn me that there are plenty of resident royals lurking around.

He looks pretty and rich and bored.

"Worse," he says. "They end up together." His husky voice sounds as ethereal as he looks, but is cynical. Up close, the angle of his jaw is sharp, and his eyes look light. Are they golden? Hazel? Amber brown? I can't make them out, but they shine.

I narrow my eyes. "Isn't that the point?" It is a romance novel, after all. It's practically a crime for the characters to end up alone. Maybe he doesn't see what I'm reading, or he's just *grumpy.*

He turns a chess piece over in his hand. "It's *boring,*" he claims, and rolls his eyes. *Rolls his eyes.* Clearly, he doesn't have a lick of sense about him if he's bashing the genre.

I scoff. "It is not."

His smirk deepens. Now I get it. He's some rich pretty party boy or something, maybe a nobleman's son or a young diplomat. It explains the taunting attitude and expensive clothes. He keeps turning the chess piece in his hand, pressing his bowed lips together like it's funny to mock romance novels. I'd like to see this *man* write something like this. I'm sure he couldn't if he actually tried.

"You're a fan?" he muses.

I cross my arms. "Well, I have a personality. And excellent taste. So, yeah, I'm a fan." I don't mean to sound as smug as I do, but I can already tell this boy will get on my nerves.

He holds up the knight in his hand. "Do you just read? Or do you have opinions on chess, as well?" The arrogant stranger pushes the board forward.

He wants to play a game of chess. His oversized hand puts the knight back down and moves a piece forward before sitting back, expectantly.

Screw it, I'm decent at chess. "Not often," I say, sliding a pawn on my side forward. It causes him to shift, settling into his chair now that I've accepted his offer. He pushes a black piece up.

I was right. His eyes are gold, bright metallic gold. They glow as he focuses on his next move. Something tells me he takes his chess matches very seriously. I slide a white queen. Him a black pawn. We don't speak for a moment, silently moving the game along. I think we're both invested in beating the other, a competitive energy hums in the air. He's good at the game, I can tell already. His moves are patient, strategy flickers behind the gold in his eyes.

I've never seen another being with the same metal in their irises, so similar yet different to my own.

"It's late. Everyone else is sleeping," he says before swiping my pawn. And then my bishop.

"You're awake," I counter. Two more moves and his knights are mine. Candles burn around us, I'm overly conscious of the ugly silky nightgown I wear.

"I don't sleep well," he frowns. "Or often." His attention is on the board, causing me to focus harder.

"Not even a *boring* romance novel to help you drift?" Sarcasm drips off me.

He rolls his golden eyes again, huffing at the board while he moves a piece. "I crave sleep, not torment."

I swipe his queen and he scoffs, furrowing his thick eyebrows and delicately scowling. I catch a flash of gleaming white teeth. He has my bishops. My knights. My rooks.

As if romance novels are torment. He sounds like a man who can't enjoy anything unless it has nothing to do with feelings or love. Bring on the action, or a man in charge, then they'll read it. Typical. Expected.

I knock down his queen. And another.

"I thought you didn't play often?" he asks with a pinch of frustration, looking up at me. For a moment, he stops scowling and stares. And then he blinks it away before shooting back to the board.

"Maybe you're not very good," I bite. His ruggish features perk back up, crinkling the corners of his eyes. He moves another chess piece as slowly as he blinked at me. We're neck in neck, it's anyone's game.

"Are you always this rude?" he asks, half-annoyed, half-amused.

I shrug. "Only sometimes." And if I feel like you deserve it, which this romance hater clearly does.

Before I can move my final queen, the brute who can read leans back. He's shifting through the stack of books as if he's making a very important decision. He pulls one from the middle, quick enough that the others don't fall. He turns it over just like the chess piece, considering his next move.

He extends the book out. "Try this." He uncrosses his legs, getting up and readjusting his shirt.

"I don't usually take recommendations," I sneer, but take it anyways.

He's shaking his head in amusement. "Strangely, I don't usually give them out." He turns to go, hands in his pockets. I think he might say something else, but instead he struts out the door like he owns the place.

His arrogance still fills the room. Probably some overly coddled court member or rich son. Another man with an ego bigger than the continent, denser than the sea. When I turn the novel over, my mouth drops open.

Another romance. One I haven't even heard of—an impressive feat. Would reading it be admitting defeat? The description looks thrilling. *Who the hell was that?* My heart races inside my chest, I sit in a daze watching the chess board. It takes me a while—long, hard minutes—to see that he would have beaten me in just a few more moves.

CHAPTER 15

I couldn't pick the lock on that wooden door I tested before finding the greenhouse. Trust me, I tried. I went back the following night, a long wood sculpting tool in hand. Obviously, at first, I tried magic, but it bounced right off the handle. Seems like the door rejects anything with magic. But I had no luck with the wooden tool either. Figures, it was made for wood, not getting shoved inside metal keyholes.

Naturally, the night after that I came back with a hammer. Don't ask me how I got it.

I wasn't loud or anything. Well—I probably was. But I used some magic to keep the sound contained to my immediate surroundings as I whacked at the door handle. I couldn't have Nemir randomly showing up after hearing any strange noises. Again, no luck. The door didn't have a single scratch on it, despite getting days' worth of my pent-up rage. Which was for the best, considering someone might have raised a few questions if they'd come across a beat-up door.

By the third night after meeting the mysterious stranger, I was curious enough to go back inside the greenhouse. Part of me was hoping I'd never see him again. The other part of me was secretly wishing he'd show up. He never did, and the unfinished chess game remained untouched.

While I explored the greenhouse, my restless nights caught up to me and I sat on the plush couch for just a moment, until I ended up with heavy eyes that fell shut. As I slept, I had a strange dream. Having strange dreams isn't uncommon for witches, sometimes they even serve as warnings or instructions.

This one felt like a warning.

I was standing in the woods back home, surrounded by the black night sky and the breeze. At first, I was alone. Until I heard a familiar branch crack and was greeted with messy blonde hair, dead looking eyes, and a bleeding, cut open throat.

Clarissa.

"Don't let her summon him," she said.

Now, you're probably thinking I'd ask a few standard questions back, like *who?* Or, *what?* Maybe even, *why?*

Instead, the only thing that came out of my mouth was, "I killed you."

Ghost Clarissa didn't look amused. She was still wearing the same clothes she died in, and if I had to guess, we were probably standing near the same spot where I slit her throat.

"You're the only one who can stop them," she pleaded.

I felt a chill down my spine. "Stop who?"

Apparently, manners don't improve in the afterlife. Clarissa ignored my question. "Stay with the king, it's our only hope."

I started to ask for clarification. Or to possibly tell her I'm sorry. I don't know which would have come out of my mouth first, but I never got the chance to find out. The dream dissolved just as quickly as it began, ending in a shimmering mist that felt like sparks against my skin.

When my eyes flew open, I was back on the couch inside of the greenhouse. My skin tingled and I felt all alone.

CHAPTER 16

The eldest Realm Bound holds the most power. No one knows why, no history book says—and believe me, I've looked. Along with any indication of what the gods might look like, or what to expect if I encounter one. When I found the library, those were the first books I tore through, hoping for a shred of information on my host. It seems that even after all these years, the Realm Bound have done a good job of keeping their magic under wraps, despite having rumors of intense power.

Beyond that, it's pretty much blank. The true depth of them remains unknown, even right here in Crasmere.

Not everything gets left out of the records, though. I may not know his face or his magic, but the books aren't completely useless. I know a few undisputed facts on the king, a few things I've picked up from the whispers or found in scattered documents.

1. He has a violent heart. Achingly black. There have been no wars since he defeated the witches, only examples. So many examples. Not many challenge his rule, but when they do, it seems his tolerance is low.

2. He's reckless and evasive. One text said he disappeared from castle grounds for *over five years*. Another time, he was gone for three more. Every so often, he vanishes. Rumors circle that he wanders the realm avoiding people. Or reality. Maybe he's mad.

3. His temper is boiling hot, and there is no leashing it. I know this personally, from what he did to the witches. All of us trapped on the Isle do. He left our children without fathers or mothers and brothers or sisters. But that's not the only account of his anger. He's ripped scales from disobedient sirens, cut down ancient shifters. I even read he somehow used a fae's own magic against the man. He snaps human necks with a click of his tongue. No remorse. No regret.

Needless to say, this has always been a dangerous task, even before I found all of this information. But I knew it wouldn't be easy. Hell, I was ready to die when I jumped off Skully. Mother didn't have to coach or remind me how important or impossible this might be.

I guess I got distracted with everything flowing so seamlessly. There aren't any guards around, I haven't even laid eyes on the king. I slithered into the castle in under twenty-four hours, becoming a credible member of the court's guests. I pretty much nailed it.

There wasn't any real danger biting at me, so I lost my edge. I grew soft. I haven't even used my magic in days.

So when Sebastian turned up at my door before our usual dreaded breakfast, trembling like a scared toddler, I learned I've always been a coward.

Because when he extended his hand and told me what was happening, my first reaction was to run.

"I didn't even know he was here." Sebastian said earlier this morning in a hollow voice. There was an envelope in his outstretched hand. "None of us knew, actually. It's not like he ever speaks to us, let alone sends word. Dove…I'm really sorry."

He was still in his nightgown. *Nightgown.* It was utterly terrible sight. I was already dressed, reading the last chapter of that romance novel the arrogant boy suggested.

"For what?" I asked idiotically. Densely. Stupidly.

A fool could have seen the fear on his face, smelt it on his pale skin.

He handed me a note written on crisp parchment, fingers shaking with terror. It was sealed, but I tore it open.

Send the scholar to the front balcony.

It wasn't signed, but it didn't need to be. It was stamped with the royal seal and held the royal crest—a lion entrapped by a snake.

The king.

I numbly walked there. Through the grand halls and atop the ornate rugs. While I came to terms with my impending death, I went over the details of my life—repeated my name, recalled my fake brother and not decapitated father, thought out more stories of my studies. I thought I was prepared for either outcome, even if it was slaughter or a handshake. In my own head, I decided if I smiled brightly enough or looked convincing enough it would all work out. Clearly, I'm just a girl who loves academics, a family scholar with weird silver eyes but a harmless demeanor.

So, now that I'm here, I need a minute to collect myself. Because I was prepared for a lot of outcomes, but not this one.

Please, I need a moment for my thoughts.

My anger.

My vile hatred.

Confusion.

Embarrassment.

Just give me a singular moment, now that I see him.

BLOODJEWELS

The balcony is massive in the morning light; it's bigger than my assigned room and littered with couches and tables. There are stray chairs and opened novels.

Romance novels.

I swallow, having followed the sound of swishing swords only to land in front of two people locked in a friendly duel. A sinking feeling sets into my stomach as I watch their massive frames come to a stop.

No. Way.

"Have you ever taken up swordplay?" asks the same set of golden eyes and loose raven curls I'd bickered with the a few nights ago. The same arrogant boy who crushed me in chess and recommended that toe-curling romance novel. It was him the entire time.

Axlan Nightfall, the Realm Bound god, king of Morbida, supposedly stands before me.

I say *supposedly* because he doesn't very much look like a king. Just as he hadn't that night. Everyone I've talked with says he's meticulous and cruel, but the man in front of me looks more like an overdressed party boy with permanent snark in his words. He still has that same ethereal smugness from the other night. The same expensive suit and perfect ringlet over his eyebrow.

And suddenly, I feel stupid. And pissed off. Really pissed off.

I cross my arms, meeting his metallic eyes and wishing I could smack that smirk right off his face. "Well, I'm no king." I keep my words sharp.

Axlan dismisses his training partner with a single finger. "No, just a traveling scholar, from what I've heard. One that Sebastian speaks very highly of."

He's wearing all black again, casual but sleek. It compliments his soft tanned skin. His hair is just as messy and ravished as it was against the candlelight. Only now he wears a titled crown in his curls. It's gold, matching his eyes, and wrapped with tiny vines. Everything about him is ageless, timeless—beyond the concept of decades and hours and years and seconds.

"I've dabbled in swordplay," I say, desperate to talk about anything but Sebastian. I should have been more thorough, asked the annoying noble more questions about himself. I'd been so worried making sure his compulsion was airtight, I'd forgotten the king might question *me* instead.

Still smirking, he throws me the sword from his hand without any warning. On instinct, I catch it with ease before remembering that Dove Clepta would be decent in sword wielding—*not* exceptional. Not deadly. I loosen my grip and drop my arm, pretending to be thrown off by the heaviness of the metal.

Axlan grabs another sword nearby, turning it over in his hands. "I thought you might."

Swiftly, he swings the blade at me. It forces our weapons to clash and my reflexes to show. I want to sidestep him, swipe low and throw off his center, but that might make me seem more suspicious. Instead I awkwardly thrust the sword towards him, hoping it seems novice. A lady would have taken lessons as a girl, but nothing beyond it.

The king's face is impossible to read, so I pry. "You didn't tell me who you were. The other night, I mean."

Axlan moves back with a shrug. "If I did, I figured you'd stop scolding me for my book preferences."

It connects the dots in my mind. "Those novels," I glance around, pointing my swords to the stacks of books. "And all of these ones. They're yours?" I narrow my eyes. "I thought you didn't like romance very much?"

There's a mischievous glint under his golden eyes. "Well, what's *much*?"

I scoff. "It seems you have plenty of your own copies here."

"You can borrow more, if you'd like," Axlan says.

"You called them boring!" I defend.

He nods. "And tortuous. But maybe I like a little self-inflicted pain. Did you like my recommendation?"

Okay, well clearly he's as mad as the books say. "A masochistic king."

His smirk deepens. "Please tell me you loved it, or even better—you loathed it. I'm convinced it's one or the other."

I raise my sword again, clashing his when he isn't expecting. "It was…fantastic," I mumble, not wanting to admit how much I enjoyed reading it.

He easily blocks my movements, taunting me with a white shining grin that irks me to my core. "Better than your sword-play."

Oh, now I'm moving to win. I tighten my grip, adjust my feet. It loosens whatever moves he was holding back, too. Axlan grins and widens his stance, ready to dive into the competition. Something tells me he's just as competitive as I am. The king throws himself back into the swords. For a moment, we clash weapons in a matter of moves and countermoves. I mostly block, but his comment has me on the occasional offense. I focus, but not too hard. I let him think the weapon is uncomfortable in my hand instead of natural. I hope he assumes that it's impossible I could be deadly with a blade.

He doesn't say anything for a few minutes. But after the sun rises further up into the sky, were both breathing heavy and I feel a bit of sweat trickle down my forehead.

"You shouldn't lock your knees," he says with a raspy voice.

I know. Obviously. But his comment pulls me back into reality, and I'm laced with annoyance. What am I *really* doing here? I doubt the king pulls all his guests on the balcony for sword fights. There has to be a purpose, I mean—he summoned me here. It can't be for nothing.

"Did you bring me out here to criticize my technique? Not all of us have won wars with our weapons." *Or our magic.*

He shifts, and I see a sliver of that violent king everyone talks about when the smirk turns into a thin line on his mouth. Axlan lightly points the sword at my heart, but I'm unable to move. His clothes are still as unkempt as his hair, but there's a storm of warning brewing around him. My heart pounds through my ribs. Maybe he just toys with his victims before slaughtering them.

"No," he says. Axlan steps closer to me, giving me another whiff of that sweet lavender smell. It's overlapped with mint— the same scent I've been inhaling all over the castle since my arrival. He continues, "To be honest, I don't like Sebastian very much." *Well, that makes two of us.* Axlan throws my weapon to the marbled ground. "He's off-putting and rude, but rarely brings any guests." The sword tip still points at my chest. "I don't like outsiders, especially from my least favorite nobleman. Gather your research and write your book, but if I find out you have any ill intentions by being here I'll rip your heart out and feed it to my dragons."

I nod, swallowing down any fear. "Good to know."

He's clutching the hilt with golden rings on his fingers, standing close enough I can see the sparkle in his hair, again. He's burning with anger, boredom, maybe even cruelty. I barely notice, *not* captivated by his handsome face, but by the power exuding off him once I take a moment to feel it. His magic is massive, enough to make me want to tremble. I swear there are golden sparks flying off him as he stands. Suddenly, I understand all the retellings I've read. All the stories of his rage and his cunning. But there's more, something underneath it all. I hold my breath, waiting for him to speak again.

He doesn't.

Instead, he stalks to the balcony doors, putting distance between us. I find myself missing the sweet smell that was just in front of me moments ago, along with the slight tremor rush his terrifying presence brings. But more than anything, I feel my gut start to bloom with anger. I can taste metal on my tongue, a bitter reminder of why I'm here as I bite it down. It takes my teeth clenching down to keep me from spewing all the wickedness I wish him. No matter how good he smells.

He's still the enemy.

But he glides to the door like he could take on any army with a snap of his fingers. Before he pulls it open, he stops.

"Oh, and ask for Fawn Avani in the library," he says. "You're a terrible notetaker."

Notes? He didn't look at—

My dress pocket feels lighter, and I pat down to find my notebook gone. *The jerk took my notebook.* My cheeks heat up and I open my mouth to shout something vulgar but that mischievous smirk is back on his annoying face. He reaches through his pockets, pulling out my small spiral notepad. Before I can protest, he throws it back over to me with ease. I catch it with a scowl as he steps out, leaving me alone in this massive space.

What. The. Hell.

I practically stomp to the library. Without anything else to do, I might as well see what he was talking about, though I'm still seething over the king and the way he tricked me. Axlan seems like he might screw with people out of boredom, so I can't help feeling cautious over our meeting.

And more than anything, fiercely embarrassed.

I scowl at everyone I pass. If a maid dares to look my way, she's met with an angry stare. A court member crosses my path and immediately looks down upon seeing the fire in my eyes. It's almost pleasant in its own way—to act like my angry self again. I shove through the wooden library doors, greeted by the smell of parchment pages. Suddenly surrounded by books, I momentarily forget Axlan and his scheme. Except to remember the name of the librarian he gave me. Which I can't remember, after getting irate thinking of his raven curls. And not to mention the *audacity* he had to go through my pockets. That stupid smirk against his angled jaw when he said my notes were terrible. Obviously, Nemir had been instructed to keep an eye on me, and he knew exactly who I was when I entered the greenhouse that night. Dammit—

Fawn. The librarian's name is Fawn.

I storm around the rows of books looking for Fawn. And as I walk, I find no one but noblemen, which only upsets me more. Often times, men do. Especially now that I know who they work for. *An arrogant, bored king.*

Up and down the aisles, I run my fingers over the book spines, my boots tapping against the marble ground. There are spiral stairs leading up to other floors, each a different section of something grand or historic. You could spend days in a single stack—I have.

But up the stairs and on the second floor I come across a desk stationed with a small ginger-haired woman, round rimmed glasses cover her deep brown eyes. She's scribbling on some pages, her big round lips pursed in concentration, freckles splatter across her dark skin. Underneath her desk I can see her dress skirt is layered in different pastel ruffles, each even more frilly than the previous. Her billowy shirt has a purple corset, though it has that same sheer look as my own. It's a bold choice, but somehow not incredibly hideous. Especially on her.

"You're the librarian, Fawn?" I ask as I approach.

She jolts up, dropping her pen at the sound of my voice. Her eyes grow wider than a doe in front of an arrow. "And you're the scholar, Dove. The king told me you may be visiting."

I try not to scowl at the mention of the king. And I came right from the balcony, so unless he has super speed, he must have told her I was coming before he met with me. I add it to the lengthy list of puzzle pieces surrounding him.

"I just came from my introduction with him," I flash her a smile. "I'm working on a history of Emeraldis. He said my notes could use some work." *And he pickpocketed my dress, but whose asking?*

Her dimples deepen. "He's a stubborn perfectionist. Probably just wants to make sure you make Morbida sound better than his sibling's continents!" her teeth gleam, perfectly straight.

"I have to admit, this library is massive, and I feel like I've barely made a dent," I say.

Fawn gets up from her desk, she's even shorter than I am and maybe eighteen or nineteen. She looks like she might be immortal, I just can't figure out what kind. "I think I can help with that. I assume Nemir mentioned the archives. Have you been yet?"

Archives? No, Nemir certainly didn't mention that. Not that I'm really surprised that she would be hesitant to help. But really, this could have been helpful a week ago, as I dug through rows of useless books. Nothing has given me a trace of the amulet. I wonder if the egotistical maniac wearing the crown waited this long to tell me for his own personal game.

I guess the confusion on my face is answer enough, because Fawn motions for me to follow her. We step down a spiral staircase, and then another, leading into what I can only assume is the equivalent of their underground cellars. The air gets drier the further down we go, making my skin feel a little warmer.

"We have so much history here," she says as we walk down a dingy hallway. "It's hard to keep track of it all, especially the older stuff. Axlan created the archives to keep it all organized."

We come to a halt in front of an oversized wooden door and Fawn pulls a skinny key from her dress pocket. She unlocks the big iron lock, pulling the entrance open. Inside, the room is lit with candles and full of items in every spare crevice. The librarian gives a ginger smile, stepping inside. Parchment and dust fill my nostrils, I can practically taste it.

Fawn looks around. "Anything you could think of, we have it here."

Every single place I look, there is history. Portraits and landscapes and colored paintings are hanging on the walls, propped up on easels, and stacked in the corners. Weapons are scattered throughout the display cases and wedged between the other wall mounts. Statues both taller than me and smaller than my hand are sprawled around, depicting various people, animals, and objects. There are journals, and pens, and perfumes. Jewelry, letters, and documents.

Jewelry.

The amulet. It could have been here the entire time. It must be. "It's massive," I tell her.

She nods. "You can come here as often as you'd like. If you're looking for firsthand history, this is your place. It still might take you a while, especially if you're thorough. But feel free to check out some of the smaller items through the front desk. You can take them with you for a change of scenery—it can get dusty down here," Fawn says, in a bright voice.

I try to push down my excitement, forcing my feet to stay in place rather than sprint to find the amulet. There are cases of jewels. Rows of necklaces. Could it really all be that easy? It gives me such hope, I forget how pissed Axlan made me. Whatever temporary victory he had on the balcony, I'm playing to win the long game. And he will lose. His first mistake was allowing me in here. Amongst his history.

Now, I can unravel him.

I smile at the librarian. She returns it.

"Welcome to the archives," Fawn says.

CHAPTER 17

The amulet isn't here.

I've gone through each and every display looking for it. The first hour I was hopeful. I'd walked the length of the room just a few times, homed in on the glass cases housing bracelets and earrings and necklaces and rings. The second hour I was pissed and started digging through the boxes with trinkets, flipping through paintings for any hint or clue. The third hour I was blinking rapidly just to keep my eyes focused. The librarian was right—there's so much to go through. And if it's under different crates or stacks of things, I haven't opened it yet.

I've lost track of time, consumed by one thought. There isn't a heart-shaped gem or a single blood-red jewel in this place. Trust me, because by hour four, I'd held everything that even remotely sparkled. None of them are the right fit. There are plenty of pieces I'd want for myself. A dramatic bracelet laced with pearls and diamonds. An amethyst ring with a thick silver band. I might have taken some—morals be damned—if I wasn't under the watchful eyes of Fawn.

Fawn, who every few moments launches into another history of any item I hold. The girl can *talk,* and she settled in beside me for the duration of my time down here. My head is pounding with facts; I have no idea how she retains it all and spews it all back in such a bubbly manner. It's as if she can't stand the silence, or can't bear to have me touch an object without sharing everything she knows about it. Worse, I think she's actually excited about the shit she's telling me.

"And our king's oldest sister, Viska, actually wrote this correspondence with the elder fae council before inheriting her land. She wanted to make sure their way of life wasn't lost."

I smile and nod like I appreciate what she's ranting on about.

"Oh! And the pen your holding is the very same one Axlan's younger brother held when he signed his first peace treaty. Thrilling, isn't it?"

I coo and agree.

"And the youngest Realm Bound wore these jewels on her coronation day," Fawn says matter of factly. I'm holding a chain of stones in my hand, but the shade of red isn't right, and the center gem is a sphere, not a heart. If it wasn't for my shadow, I'd have probably screamed with rage by now, or used my immortal strength to demolish some busts or these diamonds.

Not to mention I'm still a little worked up after my dream.

But Fawn is still watching. Actually, anyone could be watching. If I've learned anything after today, it's to remain on my feet. So, I take a couple deep breathes—I have to keep it together. This is only temporary, and I have a big task to complete, for the sake of everyone. I have to come back successful. I need to pull my emotions together for the ruse.

"There are so many things," I say with fake amazement. "Is this all of the collection?"

Fawn eagerly nods. "Yeah, almost everything. Everything in here has some connection to the formation of modern Emeraldis. Some items are dated before the Realm Bound existed, though. It just depends how far back you're willing to go."

As far back as it takes. But it could take months. A handful of them, at least. I lean a painting back against the wall, doing another lap of the room—for the hundredth time. I need to make sure that no matter what, I didn't overlook it. Or anything that could be deemed important. My mother would be besides herself with how close I am, so there's no room for a screw up.

So close, yet so far. Some things never change.

Sooner or later I have to accept that it might take weeks to find it under all this stuff. Besides, it's getting quite late, I'm sure I've already skipped dinner. A hundred and one laps around the room isn't going to manifest it from nothing. I round another already looked over corner, touching a display case that holds only one item, it looks empty compared to the others. There's a single booklet peeking through the glass, one I've come back to again and again.

A simple leather-bound journal, its dark brown hide matching the wood of the trees in my forest back on Skully. It's thick with pages and bound with a single dense cord.

I look to Fawn. "Can I take this back to my room?"

She cocks her head to the side in curiosity. "Of course—Tissinah's journal gives some great insight. I can mark it out for you."

Fawn turns to leave, and I grab up the journal, turning it over in my hands. Inside, the pages are scrawled full of lavish cursive, and the writing is so small each entry could take an hour to get through.

Great. Another time-consuming task. Just when I have so much of it to spare.

But I wonder who Tissinah is, and why the hell Fawn didn't explain her journal to me as she did with every other object I touched. I meet her up the stairs and at the main desk, where she signs a sheet and hands me a small card with the outtake number. Her smile painfully reminds me of Althea—both girls radiate warmth and energy, some serious nurturing bullshit. It makes me miss my cousin dearly. Under different circumstances—you know, ones where I'm not lying and stealing from her king—I might come to like Fawn.

I'm not very good at making friends. That's why, even after a hundred years, I've only managed two.

"Enjoy it!" Fawn leans over the table. "I'm here almost every day, so if you ever can't find me, check my office on the fourth floor. I have over thirty types of tea and am always happy to share!"

I find myself grinning back. "Fourth floor, got it."

By the time I'm out of the library and into the hall, I finally realize how late it is. Not only did I miss dinner, but it's practically time for bed. My shoulders dip with exhaustion, I can feel the bags weighing under my eyes. Even if there's still work to be done—with Nemir, and possibly Axlan himself watching—I can only think to stalk my room and hide inside. It's a good place to start tearing through this journal, or to finish another book from the looming shelves. I really wish to read something smutty, or caked in action, but my responsibility will only prevent me from enjoying it. So I settle for the faceless woman's journal. It had to be down there for a reason, right? Tucked away in its own case.

I bathe quickly in the chamber, undressing into a simple lace nightgown. Tonight, I smell like jasmine. Every time I go into the bathing chamber, there's a line of new soaps and oils to try, it's like nothing we have back on the Isle. They all smell divine, with leaves or flowers sticking out of the pastel-colored bars. I wrap myself in a blanket near the fireplace, unraveling the journal again. It still has a layer of dust over it but is otherwise well preserved. I can't imagine Axlan having his archives any other way, now that I've seen the organization of his castle.

Which is ironic, since he dresses like a crumpled party boy. The pages are overwhelming, well over a hundred of them. Mother would tell me to take my time and go chronologically, not to confuse the information. That way, I can turn over every clue in my mind, collecting them to complete the puzzle and find the amulet. Maybe there'll be a hint of some kind. I'll take anything, even if it's a weakness the Realm Bound could hold. Something. Anything. A long as it's useful.

None of the pages are dated, it's just endless untimed entries. I guess that makes sense, if the writer doesn't have a good concept of time, or just wanted this for their own eyes. Does it matter? I bet the context clues alone will help me date it. I smooth the first page, diving in.

The witches raided again. After this, we're up to three a month. This time, the baker didn't make it—one witch managed to bust right into the kitchen. Neither did Alicinda, or her husband.

It's getting easier to lose someone around here.

I can't remember if I even shed a tear. Perhaps I should have, they were my friends. My neighbors. But this is becoming a war—loss is inevitable. Just as civilization starts to come together and villages form, the coven swoops in and steals it away. I'm consumed with grief. With loss. We all are.

Jonas remains adamant that it's only a matter of time before the witches seize control of the entire realm. And that if you aren't a witch, you're pretty much dead. He's begging me to run away with him, into the mountains where we'll live off the land. He's better than okay with a bow and arrow. I can sew our clothes and slice up our meat. He says we can marry and start a family, a quiet life.

It sounds like my dreams pressed into flowers and ready for hanging. So, why do I refuse?

BLOODJEWELS

Maybe it's our measly village. We've built a community here, no matter what anyone has to say about it. These people rely on us. And we on them. Or perhaps it's the dreams. The ones of the gods beyond.

Jonas rolls his eyes whenever I wake up in a cold sweat, rambling about the messages they're sending. He says it's just my subconscious, considering how much I pray to them. After he mentioned that, I started praying for him, too. Whatever it takes to keep the gods' favor. They're the ones who provide. The reason we have Emeraldis at all—

Okay, crazy gods lady. I pull myself from the pages, taking a moment to gather my thoughts. This woman writes of the witches before the Isle. That means, whoever she is, she was alive before the war. Maybe this has absolutely no connection to the amulet, but I'm always desperate for another piece of my heritage.

Even if we are the villains in her story.

I flip to another entry.

Jonas and I fought again today. We're locking doors more frequently, going outside less. The witches burned our new library down last week. We found three dead children within the ashes. The stress of it is getting to him, I can tell. And I think he's at his wits end with my refusal to leave. Some of our other friends already have. They're not wrong—it's unsafe here, practically a slaughterhouse. The garden I grow feeds half the village children, there's no one else who can mend dresses. I can't leave. Not yet, anyways.

Not when the dreams are becoming more frequent.

Last night, I received a message from the gods. I couldn't see exactly which ones; everything was a little hazy. But they told me to stay here and wait. That they had a gift coming for me. The entire time, I had a deep feeling in my stomach, like their voices were music I'd forgotten, a book I'd read but couldn't quite recall.

More so, they said there's a darkness coming. An evil that sides with the witches. And that everyone around us is right to feel afraid. That I should feel afraid. Only faith can save me now, can save us all. If I'm strong enough to survive this, I swear I'll devote myself to the gods forever. Jonas, too. Oh, gods, please save Jonas—

His eyes were wide when I told him about the potential gift. Now, I must rest in the shade and drink all kinds of teas, "for the nerves" he says. I know he thinks I'm mental, but he just cares, and I can't fault him for that. I think the gods will bless him, too. Neither of our magic has ever been strong, but perhaps the gods have a plan. Perhaps I play a role in it.

I look up. A darkness that sides with the witches? I knew we were powerful, but was it more than just our own magic? Tissinah seems a little unhinged, and diaries can be really biased. But something about her words…

Instead of solving portions of my puzzle, the journal just added on more pieces.

I flip through a handful of other pages, but they're not as interesting since Tissinah had to start drinking Jonas' special 'tea' which I'm half convinced is just some sort of sedative. There are recipes for soup, sketches of dress patterns she could sew together, and pages of poetry.

Eventually, it becomes harder to keep my eyes open. Whoever the hell Tissinah is, she's nothing compared to the cozy warmth of my fireplace. Suddenly, sleep is pulling me into its wave.

And I'm okay with drowning in it.

CHAPTER 18

Breakfast with Sebastian is more brutal than usual. He goes on and on about the king and how he's still rattled from my summoning yesterday. The man is pleasantly surprised to find me still alive and walking about. He's been rambling about it for twenty minutes.

It's easy to block out his annoyance, I'm still trying to figure out who Tissinah is and if taking her journal was worth it. Not to mention, there's still the archives to explore.

I eat quickly, inhaling my oats and fruits. Partly because I don't want to spend any more time with Sebastian than necessary, but mostly because I want to get back to the archives or dive back into the journal.

After I fell asleep last night, I awoke in the early morning to keep at the journal pages. Tissinah must have had a lot of down time. I find entries with poems and songs, details of the scar on Jonas' shoulder, potential play and novel ideas. But still, no other mention of the witches. No scribbles on the dream she had or the gods she worshipped.

I wonder where she is now. It seems she's fae by the mention of magic and immortality. That would make it likely she's still alive. Unless she was already old and descended into death after a few thousand years, like the witches do. I wrap my mind in theories as I make my way back to the library, not even saying goodbye to Sebastian on my way out.

I don't see Fawn, but the archive door is unlocked this time. When I enter the cave-like room, I find a small chair and a desk now stationed in the corner. This wasn't here yesterday, so I approach with caution, though no one is around. There's a note laying on top of the smooth wood.

Figured it might be more comfortable to work sitting down. Happy hunting!
– Fawn.

I sigh. She seems like such a kind girl, gentle. Like the type of person who helps simply to help, because it brings them their own joy.

I pull my focus back to my task at hand. Where do I start? Now that the jewelry has been eliminated, I feel utterly lost again. There's a stack of documents in the corner opposite my new desk, atop a display case holding a shiny sword. I remember Fawn mentioning something about the ship logs. Something about gems and transportation. It's as good of a place as any to start.

Now I'm in a wrestling match with sleep. I guess that's what happens when you ruin your eyes over documents all day. I swear I'd been using the papers as a pillow. The afternoon was spent inside the shipping logs, only to come up empty handed again. After that, it was city blueprints, then histories of magic. I've spent the entire day inside this room, sitting in this chair. My muscles are stiff and my head is pounding, so is my thumb.

On top of all this, I read more of Tissinah's entries, whoever the hell she is. I'd brought the journal with me this morning, just in case. But there's nothing giving her away, to tell me her history. Fawn never came down to see me either, so I had no chance to ask about the journal. I feel lost, again. I realize the hour must be late, given how much colder the air has gotten. I trek through the halls and approach my chambers, where everything is empty except a few passing servants. Another wasted day with no new information. Another twenty-four hours Malvolia can deem me worthless for.

But it was nice to read about the witches, even though Tissinah had good reason to dislike them.

Sure, the witches are a brutal species. Heartless, devious. But I also know that we did what we had to do to survive, to rule the realm. It was no more savage than the gods among us now. There is only one way of life: survival. The other folk would have taken us out first if we hadn't exerted such force. It was a necessary action.

I know what it's like to be fed cruelty from a soft spoon and love from a sharpened knife. I know it's easier to slit throats than to hold hands. And apparently, I'm not the only one here battling with that darkness. But I'm thinking of the books, the art, the culture. Of all the things that have been able to grow since the witches have been tamed. All the things that, even from afar, I've depended on for my own existence.

Malvolia was right, time on the Isle has made us weak. Or something like it.

Weak? Or gentle? Is the latter so despicable?

I shove that down and lock it up with the other apprehensive thoughts I have about Mother, our kind, and our way of life. Standing in front of my door, I feel restless again. Maybe it's because I slept through the evening, or perhaps it's feeling caged within the castle.

Instead of opening the door and settling in for the night, I turn away from my rooms and start back down the hall. Honestly, I've been too exhausted the last couple nights to wander, so I hold my breath for the first few seconds. No one jumps out, stops me, or pins me down, so I deem it safe. Besides, I'm suddenly feeling reckless enough to not care about getting caught.

The candles are still lit with magic, but there isn't a soul around as I sneak, and tiptoe, and whisper about. I don't go near the greenhouse or the tower. I debate the library as my destination again before turning my heels and deciding the garden will do just fine. I could use the fresh air, the crisp smell of flowers. Even if it's just a few steps outside these damn obsidian walls.

When I arrive, the moon shines down on the flowers, giving them all an ethereal glow that somehow reminds me of Axlan's skin. I shake the thought away and pinch myself for it. Lock it back up with the others.

Instead, I think of Althea. And Calix.

I wonder if my cousin has managed to strangle the hunter. Or if they've been peaceful. If they've been able to avoid Malvolia and maintain tranquility on the Isle. I hope, and hope, and hope Althea hasn't been tasked with something as brutal as I often am. Or that, if she has, Calix will protect her from it. Carry it out for her.

I ache for my family; the chosen one I've made. I don't mean to take it out on the snapdragons or the lilies, but I do, plucking each from the soil they grow in. Inhaling the fresh scent does nothing for this pit inside me. I've gotten nowhere since coming here, found nothing. Mother will think I'm a fool and the coven will never be free.

Maybe they shouldn't be free. Or maybe I'm just bitter.

Damn it all, this place is making me go mad. The Isle will remain entrapped, and no witch will get to breathe in any other air. Never have a chance to see this snapdragon or smell these lilies. And what about me? Now that we know I can leave the Isle? Will I still be bound to it by Mother's orders? The thought sickens me.

What if I never go back? If I just—*Whack.*

The sound pulls me away from my anxious thoughts. My eyes scan the area. The garden is empty.

Whack.

I can tell the noise is distant, maybe coming from the castle or the hill beyond.

Whack.

Whack.

Whack.

Curiosity gets the better of me. Besides, whatever it is, it's better than drowning inside my own mind. As I get closer, I can tell the noises come from the training yard. The one I've been longing to use every day I've been here. Even thinking about it makes me feel out of shape and out of practice. But scholars do not wield swords and spar. So instead, I've watched the other soldiers during my down time. I've picked up on their blind spots while they duel and their weaknesses while they spar. I've laughed at the thought of who must be training them, and how I could cut them down with half a smile.

There are no soldiers in the yard now, no drills being run. Only the strong smell of vodka and one pathetic looking Realm Bound god.

He's clutching a bottle in one hand, a throwing knife in the other. Scattered on the ground around him there are swords, daggers, and a bow and arrows. He's stumbling a little, not planting his feet right before launching the knife into a target nearly a hundred yards away.

Axlan misses, by a lot.

"You have shit aim," I find myself saying.

He turns around, still dizzy on his feet. The king is wearing all black and I'm beginning to wonder if he owns any other color. The buttons on his shirt are undone, revealing his bare chest. I try very hard not to look at it as my cheeks redden. When he turns and meets my gaze, his eyes match the knives. I worry that he'll use me for target practice instead, but he takes another swig from the bottle and seems to settle into amusement. A goofy grin appears on his face. It's so polar opposite from the god spitting threats at me a day ago.

He's drunk, very drunk.

"And yours is better?" he's slurring the words.

Yes. I want to say. Instead, I walk closer him, my head slightly tilted in curiosity. His golden irises follow my every move, waiting for an attack. I know I should turn around and head back to my rooms. Being here, close to him, is a mistake.

"It wouldn't take much to upstage you," I say nonchalantly.

His hair is ravished, a chain hangs from his neck.

"Go on, then," he says. And hands me a bow.

My heart expands and contracts in rapid fire. Is this smart? To reveal I can shoot. He's such a pretentious prick I feel almost obligated to show him up. To remind him not everyone worships the gods or their stupid bratty children. But he's already suspicious of me. And I shouldn't tempt fate when I know what he's capable of. However, he's also very intoxicated. And I have a very deep desire to prove myself right.

I take the bow from his hands and bend down to grab the arrows. He doesn't move, watching me steady myself between swigs from his bottle. He's so broad and tall that he blocks my target. I want to snap at him for being in my way, but instead I just lean a little to the left, taking a breath in.

I'm not distracted. I am *not* distracted.

But he doesn't have to be such a stubborn ass, not even stepping aside so I can have proper aim. As if he knows I can show him up. He's so close I can smell the lavender and the mint and the sweat from his neck—

Inhale.

Hold.

Exhale.

Release.

And the arrow hits the center of its target, a perfect bullseye. Axlan sneers at me, rolling his metallic eyes. I know I look smug, smirking with satisfaction.

"Yeah, well. You're standing too close. Even for a young scholar," he points out. I suddenly remember why he's a thorn in my side.

I've seen ten lifetimes, I have years. Though I don't know if I've ever really lived. Not that I'll tell him this.

"I've been alive for over a hundred years, you idiot. I've had time." Besides, I can tell his immortality set in young, too. He doesn't look a day over twenty, if that.

He stumbles back laughing, taking big steps until he's colliding with the wall. The impact surprises him, and he rolls up his sleeves, as if he's suddenly warm. When he does, he reveals another entirely unexpected piece of himself.

Golden tattoos. All up and down his right arm. Metallic vines wrap around his skin, flowers popping up from various leaves. It takes up almost all of his tanned skin, different plants and leaves swirling around that I couldn't identify if I tried. The art looks intricate, well planned out and shining with a golden ink

I've never seen before. It only defines his muscle, despite looking so feminine. The smallest of vines comes all the way down his wrist, wrapping around his middle finger. I guess I didn't notice it before while he was wearing his rings, but now…It's beautiful enough to make me want my own.

Slowly, Axlan falls down the wall until he's sitting on the dirt. He tilts his head up and takes another swig.

"Ah, the early years of a mundane fae."

I am neither mundane nor fae, but it's better that he believes I am. It actually settles something within me; I'd been thinking I was coming close to getting caught. But he's drunker than Calix on our seventeenth birthday right now and I have a feeling he's only interested in the truths he knows. So, he must at least buy my heritage. I cross my arms and roll my eyes, biting down any retort. Mother would be proud. Or disgusted that I can even stand his presence. I don't know.

I look at the king, deep in whatever sorrow he's drowning. He seems incredibly human when he's drunk and gazing at the sky. He's perfectly normal sitting under the moonlight, despite his golden tattoos. Which look loaded with magic.

"Doves are peaceful birds, you know," Axlan slurs.

I sigh, having given up on making an escape from the conversation. Might as well have some company if I'm going to avoid sleep. I move to the wall and sit beside him, resting my aching hands on my knees.

His raven hair is still messy, I doubt he even owns a comb from what I've seen. There's some scruff on his angled jaw. And drunk like this, he's almost roguish. A kept rage. Another paradox, like his castle, his own history.

"And?" I grab one of the blades he discarded. Flip it around in my hands.

He's chuckling, dimples shining against the moon. I wonder how much he's had to drink, if it's late evening or early morning for him. There's really no telling.

His words are only half coherent. "They're a sign of hope. Peace. A peaceful, hopeful bird."

"You already said that." I snap.

This amuses him more. Lazily, he looks over at me. "So, how the hell did someone like you end up with that name?"

I throw the knife and it wedges into the dirt.

"You're a real dick, you know that?"

He shrugs. "I just say what I'm thinking. Often letting the darkness win and whatnot."

My blood stops moving for a moment. He's joking, but it hits home. I look away, unwilling to acknowledge that I get it. Because he's not wrong. Darkness can coax us all, anyone at any time. It feels alive, like a living breathing entity.

And mine hums and thrums inside my ear, throughout my skull, flushing my bones.

It's thrilling, consuming even, to give into it. To slice open throats and spy and lie and steal. To eat plates of bitterness and hatred and allow everyone else to expect the worst from you. The ugliest you can offer. I'm comfortable in my murky morals—no expectations, no standards. The king feels the same way? It almost makes him...tolerable.

I look up at the stars. "My mother named me. I guess it's because of my hair, it's always been this white. I've never even seen a dove in person, just through book pages. When I was younger, she would laugh at her private joke, like I was being funny when I'd look for them in the sky. I hated it so much I put rocks under her pillows."

I realize I didn't lie to him. But I don't know if I'd planned it or not. Mother really did always seem sly about my name. About a lot of things, actually.

He clicks his tongue, takes another swig. "Rocks, huh? I'm not surprised that you've always been like this."

I whip my head at him. "Like what?"

Axlan shrugs again. "Mean."

"I'm not mean," I defend.

The king shrinks down, bending himself to whisper in my ear. His wet lips stick to my loose colorless strands. So close I can feel his warm breath mix with mine.

"Oh, come on now. Let's not lie to one another. You won't embrace it? I thought you were so unlike your name."

I roll my eyes. "Maybe you're just a spoiled prick—"

He cuts me off. "Why are you rubbing your thumb?"

I look down and find my right hand soothing my left, massaging the bones. I didn't even realize I've been doing it. I've dealt with the ache for so long, sometimes it becomes subconscious. And shooting that arrow must have prickled the pain.

"I, uh, broke it. A long time ago. It'll never properly mend. Healers already tried." I don't know why I tell him, it's a weakness. And showing your cards can mean life or death.

"And wielding weapons worsens the pain?" he sounds curious.

I shrug. "Sometimes."

A breeze blows between us, and I shiver. It's gotten colder, later.

"I wish it at least messed with your impeccable aim," decides Axlan.

"Maybe then you'd have a chance," I bite back.

He's still sitting next to me, so close our shoulders are brushing. When he looks down, our eyelashes might be touching now, too. "No, most likely not."

I wonder if it's the alcohol making him this brave, this stupid. And if that drunkenness somehow has an adverse effect on me. Because the next question out of my mouth could get me killed. Pinned to the target board next to my knife and arrow.

"Who is Tissinah?" I go still, so still.

Axlan just takes another drink to hide the flinch that came with her name. "You found the archives, then?"

I nod.

He sighs but is no longer slurring. "She's my mother."

His mother?

I've been reading about the gods' mom this entire time? Out of all the things Fawn lectured on about, and she couldn't explain who this journal belonged to?

I rack my brain. "But you came fallen from the stars. Hence, your dramatic name and whatnot. A son of all the gods beyond."

"Not all the gods." The ends of his lips tug up. "Tissinah raised me. She raised all of us as her own children. She helped us survive. Taught us how to listen to the gods beyond."

The journal is his mother's. But where's the mention of the Realm Bound? Maybe I just didn't flip far enough through, maybe I missed a hint.

And I'm thinking of the conversation I had with my own mother as a fledging, about the gods and our Isle. She had mentioned a pair of devotees who took in the newborns, raised them. This must be her. Tissinah.

"Where is she now?" I ask him.

Axlan takes another gulp from the bottle. He chuckles, but it's not pleasant. It's a desperate, sad sound.

"She's dead."

He's taking another drink. I don't want to admit it, but I can see the god is covered in invisible wounds. The kind that are so raw and different from the gashes on flesh. The brand of hurt that carves its grief onto your ribcage before cleaving your chest cavity wide open. I often feel it, too. Under the stars, he's not the same king who spit threats at me on the balcony. He's merely a man with a bottle and waves of regret.

"I'm sorry," I say. I don't know why. But I think I do feel sorry for him. Or I just relate to him. Loss can make anyone a monster. Does this make me a fool? Mother would think so.

Axlan leans back, close enough our thighs touch. "Yeah, me too. My mother was all that is good in this realm. She bled kindness, seriously. And she took all of mine with her when she died."

It's so honest I almost flinch.

I swallow hard, not thinking of my next words. "I think my father took mine, too."

"He's dead?" Axlan asks.

I see his severed neck, the chipped bone, his blue lips and greyish skin.

I nod.

"And your mother?" he asks again.

Thinking about her tastes like rusted iron. It sends a prickle down my body. I whisper, "I think I wish she was dead."

I can't believe I've said it, especially out loud. I'm a pathetic daughter. A traitor and a coward. Unlocking these thoughts only brings harm and chaos. But Axlan just nods. There's something in his golden eyes, but I'm too busy yelling at my insides for revealing my truth to a lethal enemy. Even a divine looking one.

The king smirks, brushing my shoulder with his. "Parents, huh?"

I find myself smiling back. "Torturous."

It's a moment before he speaks again. And when he does, it sounds painful. "Do you know what we're to do, Dove? With the dead things we carry?"

I lean back, looking up at the stars with him. "Perhaps we just survive."

CHAPTER 19

The next day. I find myself eager to be free from the castle
walls. Maybe it was the time I spent in the training lawn that
made me almost *guilty* for being here and knowing the king.
All I know is I need a break. I rise and dress earlier than usual,
hoping to evade Sebastian for the morning.

Because right now, I would rather out myself as an espionage
or a witch than have another dreaded meal with that ugly human
man.

The sun is barely up before I'm out my door and heading
down the shiny palace halls. I hustle through the courtyard and
past the ballrooms. Servants smile at me as I go, court members
who dare to be up this early nod their heads in a sleepy hello.
Despite the dawn, I'm not the only one who wanted to get a
head start on the day, the castle is bustling with life. And of
course, there's that spicy mint smell always in the air, which I
now assume is just Axlan's annoying presence.

But thinking of Axlan and our most recent conversation,
I feel…good. Maybe I shouldn't have told him all that stuff about
my mother or missing my father, but I'm pretty certain he doesn't
suspect me more than he would an average guest. And he did help
me learn who Tissinah really is, even if the answer wasn't what I
expected. Beyond that, even the weather is brilliant today. There's
nothing that can sour my mood, not when I have a nice list of
tasks and good weather to accompany me into the capital—

Until I spot Nemir, standing at the gate with her arms crossed. Looking pissed. Very pissed.

I'm half convinced that's just always how her face looks. Her brown hair falls in small braids down to her waist. Her leather jacket almost matches her hair, and her signature sword is still strapped between her shoulder blades. She looks like an iron wall, unmoving and unfaltering. The scar on her face screams lethal, and her narrow dark eyes are shooting knives.

Great.

I swallow down my pride, beaming a pretend smile I'm sure we can both see right through as I walk to the gate.

"Going somewhere?" she accuses. No—she asks, it just sounds like a damn accusation already.

Nemir is taller than I am, not that it's hard to do. But she'd be taller than Althea, too. Maybe near six feet, but not quite. Despite her size, I bet I could get a few good shots in during a fight. With magic, I could take her down in seconds. But without it, we might have a pretty fair brawl. Based on the way her feet are planted and the way her posture is ready to jump— she's probably good.

"I'm going to do some reading in the capital today. Crasmere supposedly has the best bakeries in the realm," I say.

She doesn't buy it. I knew she wouldn't.

"You don't think the most helpful information is inside the castle walls?" There's skepticism in her tone.

I keep my composure. "Oh, absolutely. So much that it's overwhelming." I lift the bag of books I've been carrying with me. "That's why I'm taking a piece and getting a change of scenery. Fresh eyes and all." *And I need to get the hell away from you.* My smile probably seems insane, but it's hard to fake mediocre polite with her.

She doesn't say anything, so I try to move past her. Nemir sidesteps me, blocking my path again. Though I keep my face blank, I'm growing more and more frustrated. Can she just find someone else to look after today? For once, I'm actually going to do what I said I was...kind of.

Nemir grabs my arm. "I don't believe you." *Shocker.*

It might risk the entire operation, but I don't have a very good temper. And she *touched me.*

I pull my arm from her grip. "Doesn't Axlan have more important things for you to be doing?"

She sneers. "I'm flattered you've taken a liking to my schedule, but I don't care what you think of me. I don't believe you. At all. Whatever you've done to fool the king into thinking you're innocent, you haven't tricked me." She steps aside, motioning I can go through the gate.

My first instinct is to let my flared-up magic destroy her. I have to shove it back down, along with that desperate need to shut her the hell up. Why did she decide to hate me so much, so quickly? I mean, I know she's right to distrust me. Maybe her intuition is just strong. But to have her constantly breathing down my neck is maddening. And it reminds me of the Isle— the very place I'm trying my best not to think of.

"I don't care what you think of me, either." I move through the gate, brushing her shoulder as I go. "So, enjoy the view," I narrow my eyes and point between us. "*We're* going to the bakery."

She narrows her brown eyes right back, like she knows this is a challenge. If she accepts and comes with me, she's proving that I'm not to be trusted and need to be watched. But that also prevents her from doing whatever she actually had planned for her day. Unless this is all a big ploy to come along with me, anyways.

I'm hoping she'll call my bluff. That she'll turn around and remind me to be present for dinner. Because having her by my side all day sounds like its own version of a twisted hell.

She takes a step—*toward me.* "Fine."

Shit. Walked right into that one, didn't I?

I can't compel her—Mother was very clear. Too much compulsion, especially on the wrong person, could raise alarm bells. Any real magic would raise alarm bells. Especially if what I suspect is true and Axlan can also compel. It's dangerous. Risky. I mean, kicking her ass would be too noticeable. Not many fae have the strength I do. The speed. The lethal magic. I'm forced to swallow all my pride—*which is a lot.*

The only choice is to accept her company.

I mask my shock. "Fine."

We start walking. But not talking. She doesn't speak again as we take the path from the palace into the crowded capital street. This time, I do see guards as we slip in with the people. But only two, stationed on either side of the outer castle gate.

"Where are the rest of the guards?" I ask Nemir. Sure, pretty boy seems to have the castle under control, but Axlan can't manage the entire capital.

Nemir debates if I can be trusted before grudgingly telling me, "We don't really have a need for them in the capital. There isn't a lot of crime or contempt. If the locals have a concern, they can take it to the guard on duty, who will most likely take it to me," she says.

I can only imagine Nemir dealing with a land dispute or disgruntled neighbors, but the citizens who pass her seem to recognize her. They smile and wave like she's friendly. And for once, she doesn't scowl back. She flashes them each a smile and reveals her perfectly straight white teeth.

As if this morning couldn't get any weirder.

"Is it because they fear the king?" I suggest, thinking it's the only reason these people would be so tame.

Nemir contemplates. "Maybe a little. But mostly it's respect. Life is fair here, why would anyone want to mess it up?"

Heat floods my cheeks, but Nemir doesn't notice. Life may be fair for them, but it's never been for us. Do they even think of the species they locked away, merely a hundred miles across the sea? Music plays from around us, another distraction from the real task at hand.

She points a finger. "The bakery."

It's a small storefront with at least seven types of bread in the window. Everything here is tidy and glistening, the same marbled brick is used throughout the architecture—especially the popular businesses. We've managed to come all the way to the middle of Crasmere, where all types of beings are busy going about their days. There's a human boy kicking a ball to a fae child. A siren lounges by the fountain. I try not to stare at her, specifically—I've never seen a siren in real life. She's as beautiful as a graceful fae, until she opens her mouth and reveals a row of razor-sharp teeth. It knots my stomach. Brutal little creatures.

Nemir pulls open the door and we trek inside. Bricks cover interior walls and sweet cinnamon fills the air. My stomach growls from missing breakfast, and an eager human girl takes my order.

Two slices of lemon cake, a pot of earl grey tea, and a plain croissant with extra butter. Nemir chokes when I order but I ignore the jab, paying the girl with an additional tip. When it's Nemir's turn, she gets a cup of black tea and a plain muffin.

"Flavorful," I mumble.

Nemir shoots me a haughty look.

And then we sit. It's excruciatingly awkward. But neither of us lack the pride to give in and go home. Or to talk like civilized adults. Instead, she picks at her muffin, and I pull out the journal. If she's going to intrude on my day, I won't let her derail it.

I have information to uncover, now that I know what could be inside. The Realm Bound's own mother wrote this—Axlan's adoptive parent. This time, I flip to the later entries. I try to begin—

"What's that?" Nemir asks.

I scramble for an answer. Which is dumb, because I should have expected she'd ask. Of course, she would. "It's research for my book. I'm going as far back as I can with as many primary sources I find. This is Tissinah's journal."

Nemir raises her eyebrows. "Axlan's mother."

I perk up, nodding. Maybe she could be useful, after all. I forgot how much she must know of the king, and maybe even his siblings. Serving someone for however many years must mean you come to know them at least a little, right?

"How long have you served the king?" I ask. Nemir glares like I shouldn't be asking. "For my book," I defend.

She backs down, settling into agreement to answer the question. "Since the first war. My parents were fae warriors and after their deaths I joined the ranks in Morbida—to honor them. Axlan saw my potential and took me in." Nemir grabs the muffin, taking a mouthful. "Now leave me alone and read your damn book," she mumbles.

That's a long time to be beside someone. And how old is she? She must be powerful to look so young. With most species, immortality sets in earlier for those with more power. She's barely twenty. Maybe I need to investigate her more, too.

But first, I go back to the journal.

It's been a week with the gods' children. A grand, terrifying week.

None can speak yet, but I see the silent communication happening. I swear they're mentally linked, or at least incredibly in sync. They all look to Axlan, maybe because he's bigger than the others. I can't tell. Jonas says nothing is impossible and that now I need to look to my dreams for further answers.

The same dreams he's been dismissing for years. Funny how that works.

I can overlook that now, because he's right—nothing is impossible.

I found them after another dream. A goddess—I'm unsure which one—told me it was time to receive her gift. Jonas says I was practically in a trance when I sprang from our bed in the middle of the night, walking out the door and into the woods without any shoes. I didn't know where I was going or what was waiting for me, but when I got close enough, I knew it was them. Laying in the middle of the forest, inside a giant crater where the earth was once flat, were five small babies.

When Axlan stared into me (I knew their names, just by looking at them), those little black curls soaked on his forehead, I knew who they were. And what they would do. That these children are incredible beings—so we should expect the very most from them. We've been chosen, blessed by the gods just by being able to care for them.

And now, I'm a mother.

I pull from the pages and glance at Nemir. "Do the Realm Bound speak telepathically?"

She burrows her brows. "I don't think so. I mean, don't know. They're not really…forthcoming about their abilities." Nemir crosses her arms. "Why?"

I dismiss her. "Something Tissinah wrote, that's all."

BLOODJEWELS

No offense, Nemir, but I need something *useful*. Something I can bring back to Mother or use to rip Axlan's own heart out. I keep flipping, looking further.

It doesn't matter what I do, the girls will not stop fighting. I knew these middle years would be hard, but the gods are testing me. There is one consolation, though. The witches haven't attacked once since the siblings turned five. It's been years. The children's strength must have scared them off. Good. I hope they know, that even at twelve, the children of the gods are a force to be reckoned with. It's giving me room to gather the folk, all kinds of us.

Jonas has been laying out buildings, planning a city. Morbida could finally have a chance. If the girls don't end up murdering each other before their own maturity…

Mother had already told me this much. When the witches learned of the newborn gods, they retreated to commence a plan. None of this was helpful, none of it new. I flip the page again.

Today Axlan told me that sometimes he and his siblings hear whispers inside them. I asked him what he meant. I was terrified. He explained he knows it's the gods, his real parents. Something inside me hurt from his comment.

"Real parents."

But I told him it's okay and they're probably just trying to help him grow. He cried and cried into my lap, begging me to make them stop. Between heaping sobs, he said something that broke me.

He claims the gods spoke to him last night and told him his purpose. That he's cursed and wicked and wretched. He wouldn't tell me why or how, though I asked and asked.

It was Viska who consoled him better than I. And then she told me the reason for his tears. They're not to ever leave this realm. Any one of them. They're tethered to it. Gods forsaken from their own family; realm bound to this measly place. Only then did I understand his sadness, then: Axlan hoped he could eventually return to the gods.

I didn't know how to tell him I already think this is his home.

I shut the journal in a panic. I don't want to think about Axlan crying. Or as a pre-teen, burdened with normalcy like family fights and a consoling mother. I think I hate him more, now. For having the things I don't. But I never considered how the Realm Bound came to be what they are. The gods were only twelve in this entry, they were just children. And that's a lot of responsibility for a child.

Is this why he's so angry? So cruel and conniving? Because he thinks the gods have forsaken him?

"What is it?" Nemir scowls.

Her voice makes me jump; I'd honestly forgotten she was there. "Nothing," I mutter, going back into the pages.

It is wrong to have a favorite? Because I think I do. Axlan knows it's near my birthday, though I begged them all to keep it quiet. Who needs a birthday when you're immortal? I know that sounds silly since we celebrate the Realm Bound's every year. But for myself, the idea seems ridiculous.

I have everything I could ever want and need.

Axlan couldn't resist, though, and shocked me again when he wrapped a small box in beautiful shining paper. I was cutting carrots when he asked me to sit in front of the fire with him. Gods, he's so kind, so sweet at eighteen.

Oh, how I'm still crying! He got me a necklace, the most beautiful one I've ever seen. Attached is a heart, carved from a jewel so red I thought it had to be made from real blood. The color is so rich that it looks as if it's…beating. How on earth did he manage this? He told me he spent three weeks scouring Morbida for something so beautiful. And that it still doesn't do justice to the kindness of my own heart.

What did I do to deserve them? The gods have truly blessed me with the raising of their children. I haven't taken it off, I refuse. I don't think I ever will. Even though the gem is big and the wealth shows. I do not care. I only know that my son loves me, and I love him.

It'll happen soon, now.
I'm sure his immortality is close.
And I hope it does not change him, though I fear it might.

Holy. Gods.

The amulet belonged to Tissinah.

Nemir picks at her muffin. I contemplate how to ask something like this without being suspicious.

"Do the archives have anymore of Tissinah's personal items?" I decide on, hoping it's obscure enough.

Nemir shrugs. "Ask Fawn, that little librarian knows *every-thing.*"

It's the first thing I plan on doing when I see her again, obviously. My heart beats in a fast motion, I'm reeling at the idea of being so close to the amulet. But how is this connected to the magic on the Isle?

It has to be. Mother was very specific; the amulet is a heart. A beating heart. Something in my own tells me there is only one like that in the entire realm. And it's close.

So close.

I steady my hands, though my body is now filled with adrenaline.

I want to stand up on the table, shouting that I'm closer than ever. If only I could scream:

I've got you now! You're nearly done for it!

Unfortunately, it's important to keep calm and not let the excitement consume me. The amulet is simply mentioned, not found. I have a long way to go. For all I know, it could still be on her body. It could be at the bottom of the sea, floating against her rotting corpse.

Mother would demand I gather enough information before leaving this semi-uncomfortable metal chair. Like most of my time here, I find nothing else useful. And Nemir is growing restless as I read more entries of the two youngest Realm Bound fighting each other. Axlan learning how to control his magic. His sister Viska stirring their drama and egging them all on. Tissinah's alone time with Jonas and the woes of raising five magically gifted children.

There are still pages and pages to comb through, but Nemir makes it obvious that we need to leave. She's tapping her foot and giving an extravagant sigh every few minutes. I wasn't wrong when I'd guessed it would take me quite some time to go through every entry. I didn't even realize how much of the day's wasted away. Finally, I tell Nemir we can pack up and go. She doesn't hesitate, mumbling something about having better things to do than sit around reading some musty journal.

Excitement shoots through me as we walk back to the castle grounds.

The amulet exists. This little journal could actually be useful, if I keep it long enough. Which I plan on doing. For once, Mother might be proud of me if I come back with intimate knowledge on the gods and their magic. If I hand her the bloodred jewel that can free the witches.

Strangely, I'm feeling light as we enter the gates.

A smile plays on my lip. I'm relaxed enough to hear the cardinals sing, to enjoy the striking landscape art on the wall. I even stare at the light of the candles and the tall ceilings covered in stained glass. I'm finally at ease enough to make out the pattern on the glass above me.

It mirrors a forest, with branches and vines reaching in every direction, clutching onto flowers and clouds. It almost looks like a bigger version of Axlan's tattoos. I wonder how it got there, whose idea it was for a ceiling to be so pretty. Maybe Tissinah had a hand in it. When I open the door of my rooms, I feel energy sizzling around me. I'm hit with a wave of lavender, much like the soaps in my bathing pool. Perhaps I'll take another shower under the rocks—

"What are you doing here?" I ask in confusion. Because someone is in my room.

Not just someone—*Axlan* is in my room.

He's sitting on the armchair I've pulled close to the fireplace, combing through a book that *was* resting on it. Resting on it and holding my damn page. He's flipping the page, clearly not concerned about my bookmark. Honestly, he looks like an oversized cat curled up into the seat. There's a lazy grin on his face as he reads, his long legs dangle over the left arm.

And he's smoking something laced with tobacco, burning the nasty smell into my clothing, and probably every other fabric here.

He snaps the book shut. "I didn't hear you come in." Axlan waves the book around enough for me to catch the title, and though it's technically a suspense novel, there's plenty of romance. "Do you want to know how it ends?"

I raise my eyebrows. *Oh, really?* After all the shit he's given me on reading such awful books, I keep catching them in his hands.

"Did I scare you in *my* rooms? Is this your usual smoking spot?" And what the hell is he doing here.

Axlan can't be here, not when I have to find Fawn and uncover more about the amulet. Asking him directly would be too risky, and I can't raise any suspicion. I need time to think, time to plot out my next move.

He shrugs. "Sometimes, I think I'd rather know the plot before it concludes." He brushes a raven curl from his face with a smirk. "And yeah, you did scare me."

I sigh, putting my pack on the table and binding my hair up. "I'd rather be surprised—by an ending."

He clears his throat and stands but the movement is almost… awkward. And I didn't think Axlan had the capacity to be awkward. Something is off, Axlan is cracking his fingers and shifting his weight. It looks utterly ridiculous for someone with so much power. "I, uh—" he exhales, "I brought you something." He fishes inside his pocket.

No way. *He's nervous.*

"You brought me something?" I ask with suspicion. I don't exactly think of us as friends, so his motive isn't particularly clear. He did threaten to tear me apart. And I guess I've also picked at him with insults. Not to mention, I'm here to lie, cheat, and steal. Maybe take down his empire. So, definitely not friends.

Axlan pulls out a circular tin from his pants. It's the size of his palm, which is still much bigger than mine. The pot is a plain silver, nothing out of the ordinary. I think I've seen some in the healer's wing before.

He extends it out to me. "Here. It might help."

I take it from his hands, turning it over in my own. It smells strongly like herbs and medicine. I open the top with a hesitant motion. Inside there's a creamy colored salve, sticky and dense.

"What is it?" I stick a finger inside and feel the medicine work, both cooling and hot. My bones tinge where the salve has touched it.

He won't meet my eyes. Now I'm really convinced he's tense and anxious. "For your thumb. I had my healers check the work, so it'll do the trick—the salve might help with your pain." He puts a hand behind his head, like he doesn't know what else to say or do.

My heart is pounding. Something is rising to the surface. "You made this for me?"

"Yeah, well your aim is shit without a working thumb," he says casually, a little jumbled. There is a red tint to his cheeks, highlighting his sharp angled face.

"Why?" it's not exactly a thank you, not quite nice.

I seem to have said the wrong thing, because his nerves replace with anger. He snaps back into himself, almost sneering. "What do you mean, why?"

Is he dense? I raise my eyebrows. "I mean why did you make this for me?" I shoot him a haughty look.

He whips one back. "Can't you just say thank you? It's not a trick, it's an ointment. It'll help," he says, flustered.

I cross my arms but don't release the salve. "I never asked for your help."

He's decided to argue, prepping himself for battle by the look in his metallic eyes. "I was just trying to—"

"Trying to what?" I cut him off. "Days ago, you were down my throat with threats. You have your lapdog watching my every move. You tricked me into a chess game without telling me who you are. So, what? Now you want to help? I have a hard time seeing the truth in that." The words felt strange coming out of my mouth, maybe I even feel a little *bad* talking about truth knowing why I'm here.

His eyes are swords and knives and daggers. He presses his lips into a thin line. It's familiar. It is who I want him to be. "Fine. Never mind."

When he turns to leave, he grazes my shoulder, staring those golden weapon eyes into mine. I hold my breath, thinking that if I don't, I might stop him. I could just thank him, maybe offer another game of chess. How easy would it be to drop the façade and give in to his kindness?

Because that's what this is—kindness. I don't want to admit it, I almost can't, but Axlan just did something *kind*. Very unlike the image Mother painted of him in my head. I hold out a hand to stop him, but he's already shutting the door with a vibrating push, leaving me with its echo.

Maybe I should have just said thank you. Or something else. Anything else. It's like I can't even try to imagine he could do something to be a good person, as if I can't see him with anything but a blackened heart. But it's better this way—what can we be, other than enemies? Because, even if I did so without telling him the truth, accepting his salve peace offering would be bad news. I'd be forced to see him as the sobbing boy inside Tissinah's journal rather than my soulless opponent. I'd have to confront something inside myself, something that I'd rather just shove down.

Down.

Down.

But the room is maddingly empty now. The castle is suffocating me with its secrets and its watchful eye and its pressure to please my mother.

Gods, I just want to please my mother. Be worthy of her. Collect any scraps of love she's willing to throw my starving way.

Honestly, maybe I'm not cut out for the job. Perhaps the king with golden flower tattoos would do better to remain the villain in my story. I have to keep him cold-hearted, until I cut it out of him. It's the only way.

And I have a lead.

I'd be a fool not to take it. There's one person in this whole damn place who might be willing to give me some answers. Nemir even *told* me to go ask Fawn what she knows. Pocketing the salve, I gather myself. Force my feet to move. To start my search.

But she's so hard to find. I check the usual spots—the main desk, her fourth-floor office, even the archives as a last resort. She must be here, so I'm scouring the first floor and then the second. All the way up to the third. I check the top level with the poetry, and the loft with the non-fiction. I'm at the main desk again and lingering near the archive door for her to appear. I almost give up. Run to the greenhouse and sulk in the plants. It'd be better than—wait.

"Fawn!" I shout after finally catching a glimpse of her fiery orange hair.

She jumps high in the air. Well, okay, maybe not high in the air, but she's clearly startled. Her doe eyes look around in confusion before locking my gaze. Fawn smiles, but it's apprehensive. I imagine I look a little deranged, a little unhinged.

I did just kick the king out of my room. Maybe I am a little… off.

"Y-yes?" she asks with a flinch. We are near the only stairwell I hadn't checked. She's sitting with her own novel, well beyond the middle of the book.

"You said 'almost all' of your history was stored in the archives. Where is the rest?" I ask. She stands up, brushing the non-existent dirt off her pastel-colored dress. This one has massive bell sleeves and a belt of crystals.

"Oh," she sounds relieved, pushing her glasses up. "Axlan has the rest in his personal collection. Some family items, specifically."

Family items. That sounds like where I need to be. Tissinah was his mother, after all. Maybe he keeps her amulet there. I could kiss the petite redhead on the lips for the information, though she's looking at me like I'm crazy.

"Where does he keep his personal collection?" *Please say nearby, please say nearby.*

"In the tower. It's his own private section of the castle. All of his rooms are there, including his personal chambers and study," Fawn tells me.

Of course, it is. Under lock and key, I'm sure. And the brute's watchful eye. It wouldn't be this simple, this easy, with him involved.

"The same tower near the greenhouse?" I urge.

She chuckles. "There's only one tower, Dove. But it is by the greenhouse! Isn't it lovely up there? It was one of the last renovations to the castle nearly thr—"

I don't have time for this. "Fawn?"

She doesn't seem to mind I cut her off, remaining pleasant and light. "Yes, Dove?"

"How did the Realm Bound's mother die?" my tone is even but my center is shaking.

Fawn frowns. "Oh, it's tragic. Not many know, only those of us who study the history. The king doesn't like to speak about it. She was murdered during the Witch War. At the very end."

Time stops. For a moment there isn't air for my lungs or moving blood inside me. Everything is frozen. But then time starts up again. Because it was all in my head, and even this explosive reveal can't stop the clock.

I don't think it's me who whispers the words. I think I no longer know our language. "Thank you, Fawn," I say, apparently.

Her brown eyes are full of concern. "Can I help you with your studies? I'm not really that busy."

I shake my head with pressed lips. My heels are turned and I'm out the door down the staircase before she can say another word. Thankfully, the stairway is empty. My breathing is labored, thoughts are flinging at me like sharp edged throwing stars.

Does Mother know who Tissinah is? Does she know that the amulet belonged to Axlan's mother?

No, she would have told me. Malvolia wouldn't send me into a situation without giving me every possible detail, right?

Or would she?

I'm leaning against the wall—my bones are liquid. I refuse to let my vision blur and my panic take hold. I refuse, but the panic doesn't listen. I squeeze my eyes shut. *It doesn't matter what Malvolia knows.* It's too late to think that way. I'm already here. I've been here for weeks. But…what if she sent me into danger without giving me all the knowledge she has?

There is only one way to know for certain if Mother knows or not. One thing I can do to find out the truth.

I can go home.

CHAPTER 20

I've never been a thief, a liar, or an idiot.

Okay, well—that was a lie. I've already said I took liquor from the tavern when I was seventeen. Well, Calix did. But Althea and I both convinced him. And I've taken things from Mother, too. A gown here and there, gems to put in my hair or on my wrists. Even my cousin and I snatch each other's kohl lingers and red lip stains from time to time.

But I am not an idiot. *Mostly.*

Even though I was stealing liquor as an early teen and pilfering dresses from a ruthless Coven Crown, that's beside the point. Now, I'm not an idiot because I know that I need to go home. And I can't do so without the item I desire most.

Here's the truth: I've never stolen from a god. From a cruel king. An entire kingdom.

Until tonight.

I don't have much time if I want to do it before dawn. The dead of night is usually the best time to take things—Malvolia taught me that. And even though I've been trained for something like this, I'm pushing down panic and pacing the floor of my room. Mentally, I go over my plan. And again. I think up every scenario, pull on every loose thread. Gods, I must be mental. Dripping with insanity. Even my own intuition is shouting *she's crazy! Dead by morning! A damn fool!*

But it must be done. There's a good chance the amulet's here, and I need to know if he has it. It'll be a simple heist—I'll break into his tower, search all of the rooms within it, and find the bloody jewel. My mother would expect me to go through it all, no matter how guilty I'm feeling. If it's there, I need it. And the sooner, the better. Morbida is grand and massive, but I'm still suffocating. I miss my friends, my routine. Being able to wield a sword or run for miles.

I miss using my magic.

And soon, I can again. Once I unscramble my thoughts and collect what I've come for.

1. Breathe in and out. Again. Do it again. Keep doing it. Seriously.
2. Gather the weapons I've *borrowed* during my time here. There are two daggers, and that cutlass I had to steal from the throne room on my first night out. See, there's that word again—steal. Apparently, I steal a lot. This shouldn't be any trouble.
3. Remember that it *could* be trouble. And I need to prepare for that trouble. Oh, and strap the knives to my thighs. My upper arms, my ankles.
4. Put on my hunting leathers. They're black as night. Black as Axlan's curls. The clothing he always wears, hiding those golden tattoos.
5. Forget about Axlan.
6. No—don't be stupid. Remember Axlan. He's the king I'm going to heist. Don't forget he's a threat.
7. Wait until the dead of night. And then a bit longer. The god likes to stray from sleep. Or maybe he's not even here. Maybe he's holed up somewhere drinking heavily or mocking fiction.

The list doesn't help. I'm still thinking of Axlan and *why* this almost feels like a betrayal. I push it down, pacing again as the night marches on. Maybe I expect his vapid lapdog Nemir to kick down the door and drag me out. Perhaps I assume Axlan will show up again with another jarring act of kindness and his golden eyes. *What the hell was that, anyways?* He isn't known for being kind, it's…maddening. I watch the clock tick. I wait for someone to come take me away. The night grows darker, but no one comes cutting me down. And then it's time.

To steal from the king.

So, I unlock my door and step outside it. Empty, like all the other usual nights. *This* is *a usual night,* I remind myself. I'm the only one causing chaos. I'm the sole person up to no good. Still, I stick to the walls, blending into the crystal as best I can. Without the crowds, I can once again admire the vast echoing halls. The moon glows through the stained-glass ceiling but there is no other light.

With feathers for feet, I cross the castle and approach his private wing in minutes. Simple enough, so far. There's tremble in my fingers, but not from my weak bones. My heart pounds, my vision borderline blurry. *Don't be an idiot,* I grumble to myself, shaking the anxiety away.

The greenhouse is to my left and a sleek wooden door on my right. I know which one I need to open.

The locked one, obviously. And it doesn't budge with my forceful turning of the knob. But this time, I'm prepared, and I take out a small blade to stick inside the keyhole. Not a hammer or a wood sculpting tool, and definitely not more magic. I'd learned my lesson the last time. I jiggle it around, pick it with precision. It's an easy maneuver, something I'd perfected in my youth. And the lock clicks open. I sigh with relief as I creep through it. Already, I smell him. Without thinking, I inhale it deeply—the lavender and the mint. *Damn it.*

I don't know what I expected behind the door, but a massive staircase leading up to more stairs wasn't it. Sure, I'd thought I'd have to climb a few more steps, but it will take me minutes just to get near the top of these. No wonder he's in such fine shape. It must be maddening to trek every single day. I haul the steps, greeted by a wide arched hallway. It's smaller than I'd expected, more modest. Much like the castle below, there are worn decorative rugs and candles everywhere. On the marbled tile floor, on the shiny walls. He's decorated every open space, overflowing with papers and pictures and ornate items. It's a damn fire hazard.

There are four doorways, two on each side of the hall. Luckily, I hear nothing and see no one. So far, I've been fortunate. That doesn't help my lack of knowing what's behind the doors. I don't have a guess for the right one, or if he's up here at all, so I pick the closest entrance to me.

Slowly, I open it. There aren't weapons or a torture chamber or something gruesome. Instead, it's cluttered with different paints, pallets, and canvases. There's a splattered sheet attempting to keep the floors clean, but I note specks of blue and yellow smeared on the hardwood anyways. Jars of murky water and hundreds of paintbrushes touch the easels and the floor and any open surface.

It's an art studio.

I can smell the drying ink. The wood of the pencils and parchment paper. There's a breeze coming in through an open window frame, tall enough to bring in such beautiful light from the outside during the day. The view itself is inspiring, choppy waves and bright blue water below.

Axlan has an art studio.

And the paintings are all beautiful, delicate, and precise. There's a landscape of snow and glowing pink glaciers, twinkling in the night sky. The details are sharp and the linework is clean. It's the work of someone who spends hours on even the smallest corner of the canvas. He's been painting for ages, it seems. It's so lifelike, I almost touch the snow with my fingers and feel the icy chill.

I've never seen something so perfect.

Axlan has an art studio…because he's a *talented* artist.

And not just a ruthless king.

I move to another painting, curious to see what he can do, though I don't have the time. This one is of the castle right before the break of dawn. It's in such detail I forget I'm standing in the tower and not just in front of the gates looking up at it. The exterior sparkles, a snapshot of something I'm sure he's seen with his own golden eyes. I blink twice when I see the next one, really trying to come to terms with Axlan as a painter. It's a full moon, reflecting in the waves. And it's stunning.

But the one beside it quickens my heartbeat.

Silver eyes, so close you cannot see the person they belong to, only the metallic shine and glimmer of mischief. I touch the shining paint, admire the time it must have taken to create. My throat goes bone dry; my thoughts wild. *No bloody way.* I'm not willing to acknowledge they resemble my own.

But the lashes are delicate and the eye wide, tilted just slightly inward. The silver is like a pool and the pupil is full. Very much like my own.

No—I shove it down. Bury it again. Take a breath. The amulet isn't here, in his intimate art space. And thankfully, neither is Axlan. I linger at the window, a fool's move. The tower is directly overlooking the sea, below thrash choppy waves and a glimpse of the cliff this castle rests on. But inside, in this strange piece of the king, there is still no amulet. So even though I want to stare at his paintings and memorize their details, I slide back out the door, shutting it like no one was ever here. *Shake it the hell off.*

I drag myself to the next door directly across from his studio. Cautiously, I creak open the entrance.

Oh gods, it's his bedroom.

A simple one, too. Beyond all the junk he has inside. I expected more—something theatrical, but only a small bathing chamber is attached, and a tiny walk-in closet. Everything inside the room is dark and mismatched in pattern or color, including the quilt on his bed. He has just as many bookcases as I'd assume, and the shelves are lined with romance. *Lined with them.* He's so damn irritating.

Otherwise, it's *ordinary*…if you're a grandmother. There's no sign of an egotistical maniac living in these quarters. Cross stitch flowers are hung on walls, a standard four post bed with drying herbs and smears of paint. An organized mess, much like the art studio. But beyond that—it's so incredibly full of things. Vases and flowers, drawings and plants. Books and bottles. Everything has a place, not a speck of dust within the disorganization. It's maddening, I can't decide who he is.

I go through the dresser, finding the contents all crisp and folded. Color coded. (Black, black, and blacker. I'm kidding, only half of it is black.) Same with the closet, itself. Not a single stray item, contrasting to the mess out here, *and* not a wrinkle in the clothing.

It's utterly psychotic.

But the amulet isn't in here either. I spend some time picking the room apart and putting it back together. *Nothing.* So, I move to the door next to this one. This time, it's his study. It's just as big as the other rooms, enough to fit a hefty desk with a very important looking chair, a couple of brown leather couches, and a few thousand books. It looks more lived in than the others; a blanket on the sofa, a half-full mug of something still on the table. Maybe he doesn't even leave the castle when he goes missing, maybe he's just hiding somewhere cozy within. There's an opened novel and another ajar window.

I go through the drawers, the shelves, and every small hiding place I can find. No gemstone. Just letters, dozens of them. Most are addressed to Viska, who I know is his sister in the south. There's no time to go through their contents, but I find myself curious. Until I remember point number six on my list—Axlan is a threat and I need to move.

No amulet, again. And since there's only one room left now, I hope I've saved the best for last.

I did, because behind this door is a room that looks very much like the archives, flushing with history. It's not as grand as the library downstairs, of course. But there are glass cases around the walls, statues in the open corners. Paintings are on full display. Now that I've seen his talent, I wonder if Axlan himself created any of them.

This must be it.

It must be here. I take one step at a time and maybe pray to the gods I don't want to believe in.

In the very center display case, I see the red that's been haunting my dreams. The crimson that's been begging me to find it. The stone is carved into a heart, the tip of it a little bit sharp. The silver is linked chain, but it's made of tiny leaves and vines. Much like the other items I've seen on the king himself.

BLOODJEWELS

But more than anything, if you look hard enough, close enough, the jewel is beating.

Tissinah's amulet.

Her journal didn't do it justice. It's a beautiful gem, hauntingly so. Maybe she was just more petite than I, but it's not as big as she described. The jewel looks like it will only take up a small portion of my palm. I open the case and grab it out, clutching the cool metal between my fingers.

It's real. I found it.

I tuck the amulet into my pocket, deep enough that I know it's secure. I can't believe it's been this easy. Not a whisper from another person. No sign of Axlan. Maybe I've gained some luck after a hundred years of bad parenting.

Now that it's mine, I shouldn't linger. I make my way towards the door and exit the room, taking a deep breath in the hallway. I'm almost done, it's almost time to go home. Back to Calix and Althea, a mother who might be proud, a coven who might be free.

For a moment, I breathe easy, soaking in my victory. Of course, the brute king wouldn't be smart enough to stop me. Until I hear the faintest of footsteps, the lightest of sounds. Accompanied by a hint of lavender.

A flash of black and gold has me off my feet and against the rocky wall before I celebrate any victory. The wind has been taken from my insides, and I'm gasping for air. My vision is blurred, I can only see a pair of straight white teeth snarling at me.

Get up! Get up! Up! Up! Up! I'm screaming at myself, but my body doesn't move, at least not well enough to have any defense. Not yet. And he has me pinned against the wall; both wrists bound by his own.

"All that talk about truth, huh?" It's supposed to be a question, but Axlan spits it with pure hatred that it seems more like a death warrant.

Our act has ended, the ruse slaughtered. I don't know what kind of game we've been playing, but I'm sure it's just turned to war.

"It's not my fault you let in a witch," I hiss back, fighting against his grip.

Axlan's eyes are wide, his handsome features cross with shock. Maybe he'd been expecting a thief, but he hasn't been expecting a witch. I try to pull on my magic the same way I'm pulling against him, but my surroundings and head are still fuzzy from the impact.

"No," he says in disbelief.

"Maybe you should get better security," I taunt. And then kick him as hard as I can. Which is pretty hard, considering my immortality and my feminine rage. It's enough to break from his grip as he staggers back. I sprint to the door leading down the stairs, but it swooshes shut with a gust of wind from Axlan's magic. Before I can pull on the handle again, he's whipped something sharp and shiny at me. And missed.

His knife lodges itself in the door. He's aiming to kill.

I dodge the second one. And the third, but narrowly. Good thing he's just as bad a shot sober as he is drunk. The king is across the room in an instant, and I have to leap out of his way to avoid collision. He's clumsy with anger, clouded with it.

"You're able to leave the Isle?" he demands as he steadies his feet.

But I am no fool and do not answer him. I pull open the door in front of me and stumble into the art studio. There's a blade flying past me. Not past me, *through me*. I gasp out as it wedges inside my leg, ruining my hamstring.

Shit.

I knock over an easel and splatter paint on my face and down my arms. Axlan crashes in behind me. He's pulling out another knife and I tip over some canvas, blocking his path from mine. Somewhere inside my pathetic heart I hope it's not the painting of my silver eyes. *No time.* The room isn't big enough for us both to dance around in, something will have to give. Blood is seeping through my pantleg.

"Does that scare you, Axlan?" I smirk. I should have added *don't taunt the angry god* to my mental list earlier. Maybe then he wouldn't be seething.

To prove a point, he's on me in an instant. I knee him in the stomach, which he clearly wasn't expecting. His eyes widen in shock, and he staggers back before launching again in my direction. I'm just as fast to scramble out of his way. He manages to hastily grab my shoulder, throwing us both to the floor below the center open window. I'm reaching for my own knife, but he knocks it from my hand, sending it skidding across the room. He straddles my stomach to keep me pinned down. We are tangled on the floor like some twisted dance without any music, only the melody of defense and a humming offense. I'm kicking and fighting with all my strength, trying to break his hold. He takes his free hand to grab my thigh, sending a shiver through me. But he's only going for my other knife, pulling it out of the sheath.

Shit, again.

If I don't act soon, he'll use that blade to carve me up. The grip he has isn't secure, he's too busy fending me off to grasp the knife tightly. I'm acting on impulse now, out of sheer survival. I push my neck forward and bare my teeth, ripping away a small piece of flesh from his upper cheek. Red blood flecked with gold drips down his face.

Good, I guess the gods can bleed.

The bite throws him off, he instinctually moves to touch the wound. It's my opening and I twist free, punching him in the jaw so hard I fear my own hand breaks. Even so, my fingers grab the sill of the window and I swiftly hoist myself up onto it, thankful it's larger than even the king I'm fighting. I ignore the pain in my legs, my hands, my heart. Once I'm solidly in the window frame, I thrust out my leg and kick him back. Because there's no glass in this window, nothing separates me from the violent sea and the crashing waves as I stagger to keep my balance.

I have a clear view of the door, a clean shot at running. Axlan is too busy gasping for breath and stumbling forward. I prepare my weight to move from the window as I watch him bolt up. That extra second on his golden eyes cost me. Something sharp and cold is under my chin and someone achingly beautiful is wielding it. Axlan is huffing and I'm utterly still under his knife. Any movement at all could cause his blade to press into my throat. It seems we are at a momentary stand still, both of our chests rising and falling rapidly. He with a dagger at my throat and I with an amulet in my pocket.

"I will fucking kill you," Axlan huffs and hisses. There are wars to be had behind his words.

I can feel his breath, hot and rapid. He has one hand on his knife, placed directly under my chin. His other on my thigh, keeping me sitting steady in the window frame. I can't move if I want to, but I'm not that stupid. I won't move. I don't doubt he'll stab me.

"Then do it," I spit back.

He doesn't move the dagger and the metal becomes warm from the contact with my skin. I notice he's also splashed with blue and gold paint across his face. He's gripping the blade so hard there's a slight tremble to his hand. I wonder where he came from before finding me, and what he thought when he saw me in his rooms.

He says nothing.

"Go on, then," I tell him. "It's the only chance you'll ever have."

For a moment, I think he might. His eyes shift from rage to something else and then back to rage. The pressure he's applying to my throat grows and I think any second there will be blood streaming down my neck. I'm convincing myself that this is the end—and it's a fitting one considering what I did to Clarissa. Even though, despite my unconventional life, I don't want to die. Except those brief moments when I do. But those are waves, choppy and thrashing like the storm outside. I fear death, I always have. Maybe that's why I decided to do what I do.

A reckless, suicidal, uncanny decision.

My lips meet his in a desperate collision. There's nothing gentle about the way he kisses me back, dropping the knife and snaking his hands behind my spine, through my hair, around my jaw. His breath is sweet, skin flushed with warmth from our fight. The dagger at my throat moments ago is replaced by his lips, his tongue. I'm running my fingers through the raven curls that have been haunting my dreams, they're softer than I even imagined. My thighs are wrapping around his waist, and I am thanking the gods for this window that allows him to pull me closer.

We are kissing and kissing and kissing.

He lets out a small growl, dropping his defenses and losing himself in the rush. I try to focus on anything else, but I'm drowning in the air he breathes, the lavender clinging to his glistening skin, his cheek rubbing against my collarbone, my neck, my breasts.

Kissing and kissing and kissing.

I've never known divinity like this golden god.

"Dove," Axlan rasps my name against my neck in his thick accent, a new religion. A sacred worship, or a damning prayer.

Kissing and kissing, desperate and ravenous.

Until we're not.

When I pull away it drowns the fire that was burning in my chest. Burning *through* my chest, smoldering the person I was before. A feverish part of me wants to stay here in this room and keep my lips locked with his. To whisper in his ear and hear him laugh against my hair between frenzied kisses. To know him, explore him. But a bigger part of me wants to live beyond today.

Or maybe not.

Because what I do next is more dangerous than his lips.

I am diving downwards, out of the tower. It's foolish, I know. And it wasn't on my damn list. But Axlan surprised me tonight, first by putting up a fight and then by kissing me back. I can't stick around for questions. Or *feelings*.

I smell salt and it burns my eyes while I listen to the waves come closer and closer. I'm falling fast enough to hurt, but I know I'll barely feel it. Not through the trace of the king on my lips. Maybe the impact will be enough to end me. Perhaps I'll drown in the sea. But if I didn't jump, I would surely be dead. Whether by his dagger or his golden eyes. At least now I'll have a chance at survival, if the choppy waters accept my sins. I hit the surface in a splash and get pulled under.

Down,

Down,

Down.

PART II

The Reveal

CHAPTER 21

Men are very easy to trick. At least, I've never had trouble fooling them. I credit this to Malvolia, who muddled my brain young. Who taught me how to smile and gaze like I was trustworthy and honest. Taught me to reveal nothing, yet gather everything. Who praised me for collecting secrets and took pleasure in helping exploit them. I used to feel bad, like I was sour on the inside. But if you cut the same finger over and over, the skin eventually becomes calloused.

So maybe I know I should feel guilty. Althea would. Hell, even Calix might. But I find no glimmer of remorse for the ruse I played with the god. For lying and stealing and kissing. I wonder if there is something inherently wrong with me, if my bones were boiled in poison and I was breastfed bitterness. But it's not my fault that I was born to my mother—into darkness. You cannot blame me for mistaking it as love and devouring it.

Dancing in it.

Becoming it.

Besides, if you learn to lick love off knives, could you even accept if it was spoon-fed? It should come as no surprise that I end up before her study door—sopping, and dripping, and bleeding. No, it shouldn't be a shock at all; I am my mother's daughter. My leg is so badly cut that magic still won't heal it. I can't remember how I got here, just that there was a lot of swimming and delirious hope that I would survive. Because there is nothing more important than returning with the amulet. Nothing bigger than freeing the witches. Than learning if Mother sent me into a death trap and what the hell I'm supposed to do if she did.

I've checked for the amulet over a dozen times since I swam back to Skully's shore and crept inside Mother's stone manor. It's still there, every time, nestled deep within my pocket. Along with the feeling of Axlan's lips on mine. The impossible idea that he kissed me back. A fact that would send Mother into a blind rage. I've already decided to leave that part out when I explain my journey.

I've decided to leave a lot of things out. Unimportant things, of course. She doesn't need to know that Axlan is good at chess. That he maybe both loathes and loves romance novels. She doesn't need to hear how I spent most of my evenings chatting with Fawn or listening to the distant ballroom music. That I'd confessed and confided in our enemy while we taunted each other over knives.

These things aren't important compared to the beating jewel I hold in my hand as I stand huffing outside Malvolia's door. It's dawn, somehow the night passed and the sun rose during my swim home. Only Mother will be awake this early, she spends her mornings in the study. I know she's behind the door. I know I should open it.

But I don't. Not yet.

Because I'm bleeding. Heavily. All over the carved stone floor.

I've lost enough blood to make me feel lightheaded. My mouth is dry and my fingers are shaking. I didn't realize how deeply Axlan managed to wedge his blade into my thigh. My ankle. My arm. Malvolia will think I'm weak for coming to her so badly wounded. Minutes pass while I struggle with the decision. Just as the night of my father's murder—something feels inherently wrong. I've come all this way to bring this stupid necklace back to her. Lied and stolen and mangled my emotions for it. And now I can't even face her? As if my nerves are screaming at me: *Turn around! Don't open the door! Run away!*

But where would I go? Fear creeps into my thoughts. I have this sneaking suspicion Axlan would hunt every crevice of Emeraldis to find me.

It makes the decision easier, as if I'm a wild animal backed into a corner. My own survival wins out and I turn the knob. Instantly, I'm met with the wilting floral smell of her perfume and freshly washed hair.

She looks up, probably to sneer at whoever interrupted her personal time. When she realizes it's me, her blackened eyes go wide in surprise. She blinks at me. I'm holding my breath.

"Well?" Malvolia questions. "Did you find the amulet?"

Not so much as a sigh of relief. Though she has papers scattered throughout her desk, I dig through my pocket and drop the amulet in front of her. The water droplets bleed through the ink, reminding me of my own open wounds bleeding on her floor. Usually, she would scowl at me for ruining her pages. Instead, she just stares at the crimson heart like she can't truly believe it's finally in her possession. *Only thanks to me.*

"Barely," I tell her.

She scoffs. "You seem just fine to me." As if on cue, a wave of dizziness washes over me. How much blood can an immortal witch lose before dying? I've never had to find out, but my skin is becoming colder.

"What do you know about the amulet, Mother?" I ask, with balled fists and an edge.

Malvolia shrugs as if I'm bothering her, uncaring of the growing red puddle beneath my feet. "I know enough." She pushes away her soggy papers.

BLOODJEWELS

I step forward and pick up the jewel, watching it beat in my hand. "Do you know who it belongs to?"

A curt nod, her eyes never leave it. "Yes."

"You knew I was going to have to steal the amulet out from under Axlan. And that it was a suicide mission. You sent me to die," I decide.

It confirms what my bones already felt to be true—no heart, neither the necklace in my hand or the one between my ribs would make my mother love me how I wish it. And I've been delirious from blood loss or seasickness to ever hope otherwise.

Mother rolls her black eyes. "That's a bit dramatic, don't you think? You're standing right here."

My grip on the amulet tightens. "By the skin of my teeth, Malvolia."

She gets up from the desk, still wearing a black gown that matches her eyes. Gods, have they always been this dark? I could have sworn they were lighter growing up. Maybe not much, but a deep brown compared to these pools of onyx. Or maybe I'm just hallucinating from the blood loss. She looks older. How long have I been gone? I can't count the days; I can't even stand without swaying. It's become certain that I'll faint soon—not a matter of *if* but *when.*

"But you got it. Just as I knew you would," she soothes.

I place the amulet back on the desk, using both of my arms to steady myself against the surface. "I think I deserve to know why I stole it. Clearly, you didn't risk everything to take something that's solely sentimental."

She snatches the jewel up as soon as I set it back down, her slender fingers protecting it. "No, it's not just that it belonged to Tissinah." She holds it to a burning candle, the rhymical beating jumps in shadows across the wall. "It's a bloodjewel."

"Which is?" I prod. I already know it's something magical, *it's bloody beating* for realm's sake.

"It's…powerful. A source of magic itself. Used to tether things together or open new doors. Axlan used this one to seal the witches within the Isle. His mother died while wearing it, near the end of the war. It was her death that triggered his rage and when he tore it from her neck, power exploded along with him."

Of course, even a god might need help wielding such a heavy spell. I meet Mother's stare, my vision becoming fuzzy. "The amulet is a talisman." It tethers magic together, amplifying one's own abilities. Something rare to come upon, even for witches.

She pockets the jewel. "Yes."

"And you're going to destroy it," I assume. Every piece of magic has a loophole. A way to unravel even the nastiest spells.

She nods again. "It'll undo the spell."

I burrow my eyebrows. "How?" a talisman is strong. Really, intensely strong. So rare and permanent that I don't know of history recording more than a handful of them, let alone knowing how to destroy them. Even the witches have only dealt with a few, *ever*. I've only seen one in my lifetime and even that was an explosive force of magic.

In fact, the only account I read of beyond the witches was in Axlan's library. Some years ago, a human who could wield minor magic took down a powerful fae. Something happened during the fae's death, and the human was able to take the fae's teeth as a talisman. Supposedly, she wears them in a string around her neck, and as long as she does, she remains immortal, wandering the forests of Morbida.

It read more like a children's tale, but even that folklore knew how indestructible a talisman can be.

Malvolia moves out from behind the desk, stepping into the pool of blood still slowly expanding around me. Suddenly, she's sweet. "The thing is Dovey—I haven't necessarily been honest with you."

"Beyond sending me to a certain death?" I snap.

"I do need the amulet if I want the witches free. But I also need something else. Something strong enough to obliterate the Bloodjewel."

I can't imagine such a thing exists.

"Another errand?" I groan. Can't she just accept that I've done enough? Or that I don't have enough blood to perform in another one of her ruses. I'll quite literally *bleed out* before I could help.

"Listen, girl. I know you've had it easy here, frolicking around with your little friends. But we're at *war*, Dove. We've been in one for five hundred years. And now, for the first time, we get to go on the offensive. We get to reap revenge against the god who did this to us. This type of vengeance requires sacrifice. And I've always been willing to do whatever it takes," Malvolia says.

My knees start to buckle. I swallow hard again. "As have I."

She raises an eyebrow. "Really? All that time in Morbida getting coddled at the castle didn't change your mind?"

"The Realm Bound exiled us," I defend.

Mother reaches for my arm, which is still supporting my weight against her desk. Even her perfect black heels are getting seeped in blood. "And they're powerful beings, Dove. Powerful enough to fight back."

"They will fight back, Mother. The king has armies. He has siblings." Who are probably just as strong as he is. It was only the kiss that saved me from Axlan. Otherwise, I'd surely be dead.

"Of course, they'll fight back. Which is why we need blood."

She runs her sharpest fingernail down my arm, slashing it and creating another dripple of red through my leathers. There's mania in her blackened eyes, it turns my stomach.

Blood? Blood magic? That died out with the war. No one's been able to wield any on the Isle, at all. Even Malvolia. Even me.

I pull my arm away from her. "You know it's not possible. Even if it was, *which it's not,* how could any blood rival a talisman?"

She holds up her finger, still covered in my blood. Malvolia's tongue snakes out and she licks it. "Perhaps if it was from a powerful young witch?"

She's looking at me. *I'm the powerful young witch.* Her only daughter.

Now, it's not my clammy skin or decreasing body temperate that sends a chill down my spine. It's my mother—and her big, black eyes.

"You would need too much," I whisper.

Another shrug. She reaches her hand out again, pushing a stray piece of my hair out of my face and behind my ear. "Only all of it."

A bead of sweat drips down my forehead. "No," I protest. I refuse to believe it.

She clicks her tongue. "Don't neglect your duties, Dovey. It always had to be you."

It doesn't make any sense. My blood is just…blood. I look to my mother, the woman who's raised me into *this* for the last hundred years. Who I've bent over backwards for just to please.

Who now wants to kill me.

"Mother, no," I plead. I don't want to die, not really. Not now, when there's an entire realm to explore. It's as if I've barely come alive. I didn't know a fire could bloom in your chest from a kiss or a touch or a meaningful look. I couldn't see all the continents or sail every ocean. I've just learned to laugh and mean it. I've just grown to patch my carved ribcage and beating heart with molding clay.

Her face is unreadable, her expression cold. "Why do you think you were able to leave the Isle, Dove? You've always been different. Stronger. It's the only way."

Did she lose weight, too? I can see her entire collarbone, much more than usual.

No. "It doesn't have—"

I don't see Malvolia move, but no one else could knock me out so efficiently.

CHAPTER 22

I always suspected my mother would kill me, even from a young age. It's always been her twisted way—to kill first and ask questions later. Without remorse or hesitation to get what she wants.

But something feeble inside of me always grasped at hope. That between her cold shoulders and lashings, she still felt *something* like love for me. Maybe it was stupid to wish for anything at all. Ah, hell—now I know it is. Maybe I've always known. She cut my hair to an angled bob when I was seven, after I sneered at her in public. When I was nine, she burned my dolls for asking if there were any gods willing to listen my prayers. By my maturing, it was clear I'm different from the others. And the jealousy consumed her.

A mother with a daughter stronger than her.

Well, usually.

I've been stabbed a lot lately. And concussed. I still have a damaged thumb. And apparently, intense mommy issues to unpack.

Issues or not, she needs my blood. All of it, apparently. Maybe my blood is a stream of steady power that can unravel the talisman keeping witches here—the Bloodjewel, she called it.

Whatever the *hell* that is. Talismans can be weirdly anything, what makes this one so special? Nothing in my time as a fake scholar or a real one has given me any information on what a bloodjewel is. Mother says it's a source of power, much like a living thing. That it can link magic together or enhance your own. A tether or even a door. And that my blood has the strength to undo it.

It's a lot to take in.

And that's before thinking of her betrayal. She essentially sent me to retrieve flowers for my own funeral. But I'm foolish and went willingly, even if she did force me off the edge. And threaten to kill me otherwise. Honestly, it's all a little screwed up. It makes me wonder how willing the other coven witches will be to accept my death. A lot of them respect me more than Malvolia wishes to admit. They dislike her constant demand of them. On top of her ridiculous rules, I can't blame them. Some have accepted life on the Isle and see no need for her obsessive revenge. But that's not everyone.

She has followers. *Very* loyal followers.

Witches who will gladly rush into war, no matter the circumstances or outcome.

The pounding in my skull is intense. Worse than when Axlan slammed me against the wall. Worse than the times Mother would get too harsh during training. And as I start grasp at consciousness, I smell something damp. Like moist soil and rusting iron. *I know this smell.* Just like I can identify the floral perfume mixed within it.

I force my eyelids open, squinting to see. It's dark, no windows—just a dirt floor and mossy stone walls. My hair is tangled and I'm still wearing the leathers I swam here in. My lips are dry and starting to crack, despite the moist air. I take in a steadying breath. *Oh, gods.* I know where we are. A familiar place Malvolia's taken me throughout the years, whenever I displease her. Fear creeps through me.

Malvolia sits in a simple chair, filing her nails with crossed legs. When I stir, her thin lips perk up in a wicked smirk. My limbs feel weighed down but I'm no longer bleeding. Which is weird, considering she wants all of my blood to destroy the Bloodjewel.

I have to hand it to Malvolia, though. Making your own daughter do all of your dirty work before luring her back to her impending death does have some sort of sick poetic nature to it. All this time I've been licking love off the sword she would ultimately plunge through my chest.

I pull forward, leashed by a heavy chain latched to the wall behind me. *Of course, she has me chained.* "The crypt, Mother?" I question through gritted teeth.

We're well underground, deep below Mother's manor. The torches aren't lit with either magic or fire, so even immortal vision is useless. There's an extra chill in the moldy air, the tomb eerily quiet. Everything is covered in dust and cobwebs, a distant drip of water echoes.

Malvolia ignores me, not looking up from her nails. I jingle the shackle with a sneer. It doesn't send any pain through my body; my wounds are gone. I breathe out a sigh of relief. The gashes from Axlan were deep. And though Mother is supposed to be a healer, she'd never use her magic to help me. *Or anyone.* Has it been days? The king knows how to cut.

"You know, you were right earlier." She's no longer wearing black, but a red flowing dress that matches her hair.

"Well, you certainly have my attention," I mock. There's another set of chains, smaller than these ones. Probably from my last visit down here. Moments and memories I've mentally covered over with thick black paint.

This isn't the first time she's locked me in the crypt. In fact, this isn't even the first time I've been convinced she's going to kill me. Our laundry list of back and forth is longer than most families. But this time is different—there's more on the line. Now, she can use me to blight the Bloodjewel and untether the witches.

The tides have shifted.

"When you said the Realm Bound will fight back—you were right. They will fight back. And we don't have the numbers or strength to defeat them," she reminds me.

"You've chosen now to see reason?" I shout.

Malvolia doesn't move, sculpting her left pointer finger. "Alone, the witches will get slaughtered by those insufferable siblings. Again. And who knows what Axlan has up his sleeve after all these years of advancement? I doubt you had your eyes on anything other than him, no help at all. But with the war—the outcome will be no different, even with the youngest fighting."

No. She wouldn't. Even revenge has rules. Ambitions has limits. Surely, she couldn't. Except, she would. I swallow, blinking at her. "You'll make the fledglings fight?"

"Of course," she says, like it's obvious. "I wanted to be out there helping my own parents during the first war, they won't have to want. We need the numbers."

My stomach churns, heat consumes my chest. I rummage through my memories, wondering how long I've been oblivious to her unreasonable cruelty. If the tide that's shifted is me.

"They're just kids," I protest.

Malvolia rolls her black eyes. "You know, you asked me a lot of questions about the Realm Bound when you were a fledgling. You wanted to know about the gods beyond. How the Realm Bound grew up and survived. How it was possible to have all that power—what it felt like. What it looked like," Malvolia sighs. "It was maddening."

I swear that if I stare at her, she's shaking. Not from conversing with me. She's never had a problem with almost ending my life. A shake, like Calix had after taking too much opium for three days once during a brush with death. A slight, desperate vibration.

It makes me want to flee but my feet are shackled, too. There's no use trying to get out of them—trust me, I've tried. Instead, I lean back against the moss and try to avoid the tender spot on my head.

"Is it a crime to desire an understanding of the enemy?" I defend.

She looks up, staring into me. "It's a crime to desire the enemy." My blood freezes as she throws her file to the ground. "But that's a complication for another day, wouldn't you agree? My point is, we were cursed by the gods beyond. They sent their own children as a punishment."

I scoff. "I've sat through lessons."

She sneers, crossing her arms. "Don't interrupt me when I'm speaking. Your lessons were exactly what I wanted them to be— you don't know nearly as much as you think. Not all the gods cursed us. There's one who didn't agree with the others. A god who didn't contribute his magic to their creation, not willing to lose a flicker of his power. Not when he had his own realm to govern. A powerful god that's full of spite, refusing to parent the Realm Bound."

Only one god has a realm of his own, as far as we know. A place where souls go after their immortality fades and they start to descend into something else. The keeper of afterlife.

"The death god is against the Realm Bound?" I whisper.

She nods. "He has been from the very beginning."

It sends a shiver down my neck. He's the darkest god of them all. Chaos himself, all the worst nightmare sagas are written about him. The god who slithers away with your soul and stores it within his collection.

I can't help it—I flinch. The witches have never worshipped any gods or goddesses, maybe landing us in this mess in the first place. It's not as if we don't acknowledge their existence—the Realm Bound are proof of the gods beyond, amongst more otherworldly things. But I don't have to worship him to know how terrifying the death god is.

Malvolia gets up from the chair, stalking closer to where I sit. I try very hard to remain still. "And with his help," she whispers, in a light dreamy voice. "I'm going to tear this realm apart, leaving only cities of bone for him to feast on."

I hold my breath, listening to the rapid beating of my own heart. "You've been channeling the death god," I realize. Shock fills my silver eyes. "Have you been conversing with him?"

It is possible, but it *changes* you. A dark unnatural form of magic. That kind of power can sicken someone, alter their mind. "Are you mad? He'll slaughter us all and drag our souls through the floors of hell out of boredom. *For fun.* You'll kill everyone. Not just the Realm Bound. Not just their cities. All of us, including the coven!"

She comes to my side, towering over me and causing a ripple of panic in my chest. My heart is beating faster the longer she stays near. Malvolia takes the chain and starts to unlock it. "He can dance on our ashes if he wishes. As long as the Realm Bound pay for what they've done to us. I serve him now, Dove. The coven means nothing to me. He'll treat them well in the death realm for their sacrifice. Just as he will you. He wants you there, he's waiting. He's been waiting." There's a twitch under her eye, a flash of black behind her veins.

One of my chains falls to the floor. Malvolia bends down

and takes my other arm. I resist, but she tugs harder and slides the key into the shackle. Once the other chain falls, she keeps a tight grip on me like she's scared I'll run. Yeah right, as if I could get away. She'd break my legs with a snap of her fingers before I'd take ten steps. Cool air rushes around my wrist as I watch her with caution. Slowly, she unlocks my feet. The entire time, I hold my breath. There's insanity rumbling around her, lurking around us both now.

"You'll really do it?" my voice cracks. "You'll kill your own daughter?" Gods, there must be something wrong with me—the way I can still, even after all of this, wish to doubt that she'll hurt me. There's a reason I don't fight back. I'm too heavy with false hope—too pathetic and embarrassed to be anything but frozen.

Malvolia pauses at my desperation before furiously digging into my arms. In an instant, she pushes me back down to the ground. I cough once, spraying blood on the dirt.

"You've made a mistake, Dove. You thought that I could love you. That I could give you something other than this life. Love is a weakness and to wear it is a noose. It'll only tighten until you suffocate. Perhaps if you weren't foolish enough to chase it, you'd see me for what I am," Malvolia argues, poisonous.

And what does that make me? I scramble back to my feet. "You can't do this, Mother. What's the use if we all die in the process of victory?" I plead. "Besides, you can't just summon the death god."

Communicating with a god beyond isn't the same as making one appear. Our realm belongs to the Realm Bound, no one can get in or out. Moreso, the gods beyond barely interfere. Even to stop one of their own. Though the death god has been known to be wild and full of tricks, he's powerful.

Malvolia bends down and digs her fingers into my arm with a hiss. "You're just a foolish girl." She pushes me again. "It's not impossible to let the death god in. His army will make even Axlan tremble with fear. His Olcar will dismember his siblings as an afternoon treat. My god will have shown the others just how foolish it was to send those *invasive* children."

Oh. Shit.

My cousin used to read me tales of the gods beyond, seeking out books older than our exile on the Isle. Books that were here when this was a sanctuary, rather than a prison. We'd find them in Malvolia's closet, back when there wasn't a severe consequence to scare us off. We read a lot of the gods' supposed adventures, centuries of stories and lore before the Realm Bound were created. It's how I know so much about the death god. How I know to be absolutely terrified by Mother's plan with him.

A few stories in her books center around the never-ending battle between the death god and light goddess. Two of the most powerful gods beyond. I mean, they were stark opposites, the goddess governing life, light, love. And the death god ruling over darkness, dismay, chaos. They'd vowed not to exist together, dividing the other gods and creating loads of disfunction.

In my favorite lore, the death god sought to outsmart the light goddess by creating a secret army of condemned souls. Beast-like monsters, blind with rage and power. *The Olcar.* They were once human, maybe even fae or witches. But after eons suffering in his realm, they walked on all fours, triple the size of our men, most covered in wings and fangs, extra limbs or eyes or horns. He named them Olcar, his loyal servants. The death god commanded his army after the goddess—a covert coup of her estate in the god realm one still night.

The goddess, smarter than she was vengeful, had already

cleared her estate, leaving behind a curse for the Olcar—she'd blinded them from light. Since then, the beastly creatures frantically roam their realm during the night, causing chaos in the name of their creator. Apparently, they're hard to manage, and I assume that they've created a serious problem for the gods beyond. I mean, imagine having a tea party and a nasty beast shows up to ruin your fun. No other god or goddess has been able to create an equal army to take down his Olcar. It gave the death god *power.* Freedom to disregard the other gods beyond. If the gods couldn't even stop the Olcar, their Realm Bound children would surely be no match.

But I know the coven. I fight Malvolia's grip once again on my forearm. "The witches will not serve the death god. You can't force them."

Malvolia doesn't budge, dragging me away from the chains and near a sliver of light. *The door.* "This is why you'd never be a good leader. I'm doing you a favor, Dove. You aren't cut out for the Crown."

I dig my heels into the dirt. "Think rationally. We can find another way to gain freedom."

She spits, warm saliva landing on my face. "You're weak. *So pathetically weak.*" She can't make up her mind and throws me down again, cracking my head on the wall. *Again.* It's not enough to knock me out, just blur my vision.

Malvolia chuckles, her hands on my shoulders, blood dripping down my tattered hunting leathers. She takes a needle from her hair, causing it to fall in sleek sheets down her back. The tip is covered in something sticky and green, but she presses it through my skin. "Just like your father, when I cleaved his head off."

Everything goes red.

I don't think, I just react. Much like with Axlan, my instincts take over. I reach into my magic, obsessively grabbing at it throwing the silver power out. There's no concentration, just a blind rage that's slowly tattooing every part of my body. She staggers back to avoid getting hit, a smart choice.

I've endured a lot of shit being Malvolia's daughter. I've traded in laughter and bedtime songs for training and humiliation. I didn't cry when she would hit me or ridicule me. I never questioned her inability to choke out the words 'I love you.' Instead, I accepted that my mother was different. Harder. Crueler. Someone who must wear a mask. How could she not? It's not her fault that she just happened to be the oldest fledgling on the Isle all those years ago, during the war. Just like me, she's been messed up by her environment.

But this—this is different. I have endured isolated years, nasty wounds, irreparable damage. I sat down and I took it from her because what else was I to do? What other life was around the corner, waiting for me to claim? Some people aren't given a choice, just a set of survival skills. Malvolia violated every rule of nature by killing my father. Even beasts have a sense of loyalty. Family. Protection.

And now I see that she has nothing in that void heart of hers—I'm going to rip it from her poisonous chest.

"You killed my father?" it's a calm, deadly question. I'm waiting for my eyes to focus, but they still don't. My tongue feels overweight.

She doesn't respond, her eyes somehow becoming blacker. Or maybe it's all the spots consuming my vision. *Hell.*

I step forward, but gravity refuses to respond. Instead, my cheek smacks the floor and pain shoots throughout my face. Malvolia's distant chuckle is fluttering away. It takes every ounce of my being to roll onto my back.

"I'm-going-to-kill-you," my weighted lips slur.

I can't tell whether it's the rage or drugs that consume me.

CHAPTER 23

When I wake up again, I smell only the sea and feel only fury.
It's a stark contrast to the mildew and rotting soil I was inhaling underground. Even as I try to open my eyes, something is off. No irons could be as heavy as my bones right now, I attempt to wiggle my fingers but barely muster a twitch.

She's stuck me with drugs.

The only thing I can really tell is that we're away from the crypt. And I can't decide whether that's good or bad. I use all my will to open my eyes, but even when I'm sure I do, everything is black. Malvolia blindfolded me. I try to twitch again, hearing a faint *clink* of chains.

Drugs. A blindfold. Shackles. Unfortunately, I expect nothing less from my mother.

She'll do whatever it takes, including killing me.

I force my muscles to work, but I'm still too groggy. With running out of the question, I focus on trying to figure out where I am, while *staying alive.* There's no trace of my magic—her cute little concoction keeps me from scorching her. With the drugs still flooding through my system, I won't be able to use my magic. Drinking and drugs can dull someone's power, but it usually takes a lot. I've only felt mine slip away a few times, despite my constant reckless behavior.

Whatever was on the tip of her hairpin was potent. I can barely move or string together my surroundings.

I strain my arm, begging it to move. My hands. My fingers. Nothing responds as it should. The cloth over my eyes is sheer enough to make out a massive fire burning, with something hanging over it. The smoke is close enough to burn my lungs, the smell smoldering throughout the air. But between whiffs of fire there's something faintly sweet.

A familiar, smoldering smoke that distinctly reminds me of the coven.

A smell that has panic creeping down my spine and resting in my hips.

Because if she's taken me to where I think she has, my chances of surviving just dwindled. I lash out, trying to move *something*. I twist every movable part of my upper body, thinking of all the ways I used to slip out of blindfolds in the past. My neck convulses enough to loosen the fabric, giving me something to work with. I shake my head furiously until it's over my eyebrows.

Ah, gods.

I'm lying on the altar, exactly in the middle of the coven's poppy field. The worst possible location for my survival.

Sitting on the highest jagged point in the Isle, the poppy field overlooks the distant sea, surrounded by either a deadly drop or a dense forest. We don't come here often—this altar is saved for spells and rituals that require extensive concentration, strength, or time. And in recent years, there hasn't been a need. Occasionally, something would come up and we would gather on the slab of stone. Like when a wild cat clawed out Tobias Flinnick's eyes and the healers worked to create new sight for the boy.

It was complex magic—the heavy stuff usually is. They'd needed a talisman. Nothing compared to the Bloodjewel, but something to replace his loss. Calix hunted the cat and extracted its teeth. A healer, *a real one—not a demented one like Mother—* carved out the cat's eyes while the boy's mother burned its tongue to ash, sparking the carcass ablaze after.

The head healer's daughter is a contortionist, a bright young girl who could alter someone's features. They worked together, adapting the cats' eyes for the maimed boy while they hoped he would see again. Unbalancing and rebalancing acts of nature. Finding the symmetry in cruelty. Creatively using our magic to bend the will of survival.

That's the witches' way.

It had been a grueling process, but it worked. The boy lived through the ritual, even though his eyes now look more feline than witch. He'd even strung the extracted teeth on a necklace, wearing it with pride to keep the magic in place. It was twenty years ago, and the poppy altar has been untouched since. Until now, as I struggle against my chains. How did I just evade death in Crasmere only to find it again here on Skully? Distantly, I hear a voice that sounds like Malvolia. And another gentler one, but I still can't really see through the haze of being drugged.

Minutes pass and nothing happens, just faint chatter. I'm in the center of the stone slab, a few feet away from the cauldron and fire blazing besides me. I don't recognize the cauldron atop the fire now that I've stared at it long enough to digest. It's a smaller pot made of moonstone. It looks nothing like the typical large bronze one we use, to withstand the heat, and I wonder where the hell she could have gotten it from.

I run out of time to wonder. Suddenly, the coven starts pooling around me, standing out in dark cloaks against the vibrant flowers. They say nothing, walking swiftly with no hesitation.

A quick glance up confirms the moon is full above us. *Great. That's so good for me.* Malvolia emerges from the side, keeping her back to me and facing the coven. She's wearing the same red dress and I'm guessing only a few hours have passed since our last encounter. Two other witches flank my side, standing where the chains are bolted into the stone. Everyone is silent, eagerly waiting for the Coven Crown to speak.

"Tonight, we escape the Isle that's held us prisoner for the last five hundred years," Malvolia bellows. "It starts with a sacrifice from our heir and ends with victory over the Realm Bound and our *freedom.*" Interestingly, she doesn't mention the part about their imminent death or my lack of willingness to participate.

And I'm still too far gone for any protest.

The witches roar with excitement in response. Finally, the Coven Crown has given them what she's promised. It's been centuries of wishing, of endless rants from Malvolia on life beyond. To them, it seems like all her demands are finally paying off. I open my mouth to say *anything* but the drugs pull me back down—my tongue's more like liquid than muscle.

Malvolia motions to one of the witches at my side. Who just happens to be on the list of people who probably want me dead.

"Tomax, proceed."

Tomax, the witch whose hand I butchered five springs ago, grabs the latch with his three remaining fingers.

They never could reattach his other two fingers. It was a *damn* shame.

He yanks the chain, dangerously outstretching my arm. On my opposite side, one of Malvolia's other favorite lackeys does the same thing. They force me to stand, keeping me upright only by the strain on my shackles. I *really* wish I would have taken Tomax's entire hand. And maybe his beating heart. My legs still won't work, my upper body is just as useless.

BLOODJEWELS

The Coven Crown moves in front to the edge of the altar, looming over the cauldron and overlooking the witches. Malvolia picks up a shining red object, and if I blink, it looks like the Bloodjewel. With the drugs, it's impossible to tell.

What else could it be? The drugs haven't taken all my intelligence.

She throws the Bloodjewel inside of the empty cauldron. It clanks and clangs at the bottom, and even the sky seems to grow darker. From beneath her cloak, she produces a long, sharp dagger.

"Cut deeply, we need it all."

Every witch standing around us reaches inside their cloak, mimicking Malvolia and bringing out a knife. The brutes with my chains heave me over to Mother's side, positioning me directly beside the burning fire. Then, they bend me over so that the upper half of my body is looming over the empty cauldron. The movement jolts my vision into another blurry haze—*just* as it was starting to grow steady.

Malvolia grabs my cheek with force, making me meet her black gaze. She says nothing, just stares into me. I stare right back, channeling every vile ounce of hatred I have for her into it. *I will kill you*, I hope it says. And her eyes dare me to try. But we both know who has the upper hand today.

She takes the knife and drags it through my cheek, ironically in the same spot I bit Axlan before jumping from his tower. The cool metal is sharp enough to make it sting, but the drugs take away any real pain. My blood drips down my jaw and into the cauldron below, sizzling from the heat of the fire. I'm blissfully numb and wearily unaware of how much blood I could be losing, especially as the witches continue to cut.

They circle around me, moving in closer until there's a solid ring of coven members close enough to lash their blades. I still can't see their faces, but I'm avoiding looking. I don't want to know who's stabbing me. It'll hurt worse than the wounds.

Malvolia does away with the last of my ragged hunting leathers in a single swoop of her knife, leaving me exposed in tight shorts and a slim strapped tank top. When a young member of the coven slashes my arm, I gasp. So much blood seeps out, instantly paling me. Even the drugs can't keep me from feeling it.

Another witch cuts me. And then another. I lose track of the minutes, both my arms and my face are soaked in red. By high moon, my neck and chest are covered in gashes, too. I lose count after a hundred—even the corners of my face and ears have been sliced.

The witches keep coming. After a while, I'm almost grateful for the drugs Mother fed me. I can't imagine what I'd be feeling without them. *Almost grateful.* If she hadn't killed my father. And wasn't currently killing me, too.

There are some things you can't come back from. Things that even a messed-up daughter who just wants to please her mother can't turn away from.

The cauldron is getting full, and the Bloodjewel is completely immersed under the fluid. But the witches keep cutting, a new one appearing from behind the last. Everyone is eager to get in their turn. *Let them.* I've killed their sons. Daughters. Neighbors. And I've allowed Malvolia to do the same. I've helped her kill them all.

I block it out until I see a flash of golden blonde hair and familiar freckles.

The rush of adrenaline finally allows me to croak something out. "Thea."

She's not holding a knife and her green eyes are ringed with red, as if she's been crying. Her full face is puffy, and her wild waves are unkept. No one stops her when she throws her arms around me, drenching her tunic and training pants in blood. She sobs into my hair, and I can smell the sage stuck to her skin.

Malvolia, still watching from the edge of the circle, clicks her tongue. "That's enough, Althea."

But Althea doesn't move, wailing into my collarbone. I try to tell her it's okay. To find Calix and run when the magic is lifted. To find some obscure part of the realm to hide in until it's all over. I try and try, except nothing comes out. I'm tapered down, sluggish.

"Althea. I said that's enough," Malvolia threatens. "Unless you'd like to join her."

And then, in barely a whisper, Althea utters two words into my ear. "South woods."

Before I have time to question if I hallucinated it, she untangles herself and backs up. Althea wipes her wet eyes and shoots Malvolia a glare that promises revenge, before melting back into the crowd. The witches start to murmur about her disobedience, but Malvolia silences them with a deadly look. *It had to be real.* The south woods. What of the south woods?

The cauldron is starting to spill over, and my breathing becomes shallow. The pearly white is so stained with blood it looks like it's meant to be red. It's full, full enough that I know I'll be dead in minutes. And the fire roaring below it has my blood warm enough to boil. Everything is quiet, every knife in the coven bloodied. Until we start to hear a rhythmic beating.

The same steady sound of the amulet inside.

The pulsating grows louder and faster. Black spots enter my vision. If it's not the drugs, it's the lack of blood, but something is taking me under again. The sizzling blood inside the cauldron starts to bubble, followed by quick *pops* and splatters of crimson showering anyone nearby. It's hot against my skin. No one moves or looks away from the cauldron, despite the increased *splats* and *pops*. The cauldron beats faster.

Faster. Like after a sword fight.

And then faster, like a brush with death.

And even faster than that, as my heart was while my lips crushed against Axlan's.

Faster.

Faster.

The cauldron fractures, red liquid leaking from the cracks. The hissing and sizzling grow louder, matching the increased intensity of the beating amulet inside. Dread works up my spine. I've never studied a human sacrifice before, but I'm pretty sure this isn't supposed to happen. A broken cauldron is always bad news. Maybe Mother messed up. Maybe there was too much blood magic involved in this spell. Magic she didn't know and couldn't truly understand. I told her to—

The cauldron cracks again, splitting open and breaking into two separate pieces. A collective gasp comes from the coven as all of the blood it was collecting comes rushing out, crushing the flowers under the liquid when it drips off the side of the stone. Every pair of eyes is on the broken moonstone and the pool of blood now seeping into the soil.

And oh, is there blood. Lots and lots of blood. Probably close to every ounce within me. But there is no amulet. The Blood-jewel is gone.

Not a trace of it remains.

Where did it go? It's a talisman *and* some magical object bullshit. Those things don't just evaporate into thin air. They're damn near impossible to destroy. Even if the fire melted it down, or my weird blood managed to break it, there would still be something. *Right?*

BLOODJEWELS

I can see the question linger on Malvolia's sharp features as she blinks in confusion. My heart is beating through my chest, my legs tingling with some feeling. I'm not the only one patiently staring at her. She's promised the coven freedom— a chance to escape their fate. Now, with her hand empty and her cauldron cracked, the witches are looking at her like starving wolves.

A *CRACK* through the air saves my evil mother. I'm not quick enough to see what's happening beyond a flash, but the electric tinge gives it away.

Lightning strikes down, hitting the altar. The stone beneath us breaks in response, the force of its impact sends me flying backwards, along with everyone else around the cauldron. My guards are no exception, they let go of my chains the instant the lightning hits. For a moment, I'm hanging in the air, my shackles clinking as I soar. But the ground I hit is unforgiving and I gasp for breath. A high pitch sound and more black spots consume me. I can't feel my body quite yet. There's a cry and screams from beyond as I roll onto my side.

The fire beneath the cauldron pops, and suddenly triples in size. It engulfs a witch standing too close, his ghastly plea quickly done away with. The flames grow taller than a castle tower, climbing up past the trees. Is this the work of the amulet? It seems elemental—

Then it explodes.

Bright embers are floating in every direction. The ringing in my ear doubles, it's so intense I move my hands to cover them. I smell burning flesh and more blood—gallons of it. It takes both my hands to push myself upright, swaying with gravity before settling into my legs. At least I'm good enough to stand—all around me, witches are crying out. Some are pinned down under boulders from the broken altar. Others are so badly burned you can see their white bones. No one is left completely untouched; the explosion was big enough to reach the cliff's edge. *So, you have a few second head start.*

I need to move.

My head is not keeping up with my eyes. Thankfully, I was flung a decent distance but didn't manage to break or bruise anything. Either that or the drugs are still keeping me deluded. And I still have to manage my extensive open cuts. Even standing here for a split moment has a new pool of blood below my feet. I'm bleeding out.

Fast.

The witches that aren't trapped beneath the boulders start to scatter. A woman is clutching her *empty* shoulder socket with her remaining arm. Some with limbs remaining flee to the woods. Others move amongst the wounded offering help. A few are screaming for Malvolia. My knees buckle when I take a step, sending me back on all fours. *Damn it.*

From the ground, I see Tomax. Somehow, the bastard was lucky enough to be completely unscathed from whatever the hell is happening. He's walking towards the edge of the field near the cliff.

Tomax grabs a small fledgling girl with big blue eyes who looks no older than ten. The girl begins kicking and screaming, fighting Tomax off with her fists. I'm pushing myself up, but everything is shaky. I can't move.

He's too big to care or notice that the girl is screaming, keeping her at an arm's length when he lifts her up. He dangles the fledgling over the cliff, threating to release her into the choppy sea below. The sea that will tear through her the moment she hits the water. She's yelling but it's no use, the coven is still scrambling around us. No one can hear her cries, and if they can, they're trapped like me.

Tomax lets go of the girl with a huff, sending her falling to the waves below. Her young screams fade as she drops lower and lower, echoing until I hear a splash. I strain my ears to listen. Even the witches who were moaning in pain or wrapped up in one another's injuries are staring at him now. Her shrieking was louder than any alarm. All eyes are on the bastard who just murdered a small child. One witch runs to the cliff's edge, shoving Tomax to the side and peering down with curious eyes. More follow, running and stumbling to overlook the commotion.

"She's not dead!"

"She's alive! She's swimming!"

"Malvolia did it! The magic is broken!"

The witches are shouting all over each other. Some are jumping with joy. Others are stoic as they process their freedom.

The girl is not dead. And Malvolia has done it. The witches are…*free.*

Another witch jumps into the water, gleefully cheering. And then another. We hear them splash and yelp from the ocean. A part of me deliriously smiles before I remember. Maybe it'll take me time to realize these people who tried to kill me are no longer my allies. I shouldn't be happy; I should be running. Either way, this moment has been my life's purpose. A hundred years of working tirelessly with my mother to escape life on the Isle. The victory I feel can be excused as an automatic response.

Just the drugs and the chaos and the adrenaline.

"Dove! Do not run, Dove! This isn't over yet!" a voice pulls me back into reality, squashing any fleeting joy I felt moments ago. I knew it. She'd find me no matter what, even now. Freedom or not, she wasn't going to let me live. I'm a loose end.

I find Malvolia's voice pinned and helpless under a massive rock. She's badly injured and trapped in place. *She's stuck*, I realize as she twists and pulls herself to no avail. Stuck gives me another head start.

I don't hesitate to run. I'm off the ground and scrambling on my feet as quickly can be. Even with Malvolia down, the witches will have order restored in minutes. I've seen coven emergency plans—I helped create them. In fact, now that she's yelling, members of the coven rush to her aide. My muscles are sluggish as I take off, but I push my body further and further, refusing to die at her hands.

The tree line is close, leading back down the cliff and into the south woods.

I push my legs, my lungs. My open wounds are gushing, marking my steps. The south woods—where Althea instructed me to go. She must have known about the explosion. Or maybe the lightning. She must have planned for this all. Despite the pressure in my body and the blood still leaking down my frame, I feel relieved she came for me. I have one person on my side.

Not every member of my family betrayed me.

The red of the flowers blur around me until I no longer see anything but the dusk of the woods. I feel the pine needles crunching under my feet as I sprint. Even as I clear the field and enter the trees, I don't slow down. I have no idea if Mother is on my trail or if she sent anyone after me. I haven't a clue if I can make it much further. If my body will run out of blood before it reaches the south woods.

Even immortals can die from blood loss.

So, I try not to think about how cold I am as the tree branches scrape against my face. I feel warm liquid down my chest, inside my tattered top, seeping through my exposed shorts. I drag my mind from the pain, pleading with myself for a distraction. I don't focus on the chattering of my teeth or how my lips must be blue. Instead, I think of all the ways I can kill my mother.

Poison.

A knife through the heart.

Her fiery red hair perched on a stick.

Her crown, melted down to scrap metal.

If my mother will not love me or find pride in me, she will learn to fear me. I'll show Malvolia her own wicked reflection as I take her coven and bury her legacy. I'll take her head, just as she did my father's. I'll remind her just how deadly I can become. How deadly she made me.I can envision the plan circling together inside my maddening head—the moves and countermoves.

My thoughts fly as fast as my legs, pushing me forward and hoping I'm somehow on track for the woods. Fear creeps inside me—it smells more like salt here than tree sap. Each branch I break sounds too thin for the southern forest.

Shit.

It wouldn't surprise me if I've gotten lost in my half-dead state. There's no time to stop or turn around. If I adjust course, she'll find me. Even if I'm wrong, I just have to keep running. Until I fall over or there's no more blood left to bleed.

Big hands grab my shoulders, stopping me dead in my tracks. I scramble, ready to face my attacker. Never will I go down without a fight. Even though I didn't hear them coming, whoever my attacker is. Even though black spots are engulfing my vision and I've let someone sneak up on me.

It seems that everything is blurry, and I can no longer see. My legs are trapped in this dirt and my head is caged in the clouds.

Because you're dying, reason whispers within me.

"Gods, Dove! I said *south* woods. Are you trying to get us killed? Or is Thea just that bad at remembering instructions?" a familiar grumpy voice barks.

My smile must be delirious because the hunter looks more concerned than I've ever seen him.

"Calix, I think I've landed us all in some trouble," I say, before I pass out.

CHAPTER 24

"She's not going to leave us, you big dumb idiot," a familiar sweet voice says.

As my senses gradually return, I feel as if I'm emerging from a deep abyss, slowly clawing my way back to consciousness. The world around me is hazy and disoriented, most likely the drugs still pulling at my system. Sounds faintly echo, distant and indistinct, snippets of bickering and cracking branches. My body feels heavy, as if anchored to the ground, but a glimmer of awareness begins to awaken within me.

"I'm just sayin—"

"When has she *ever* followed our plan? She's practically immune to any advice!"

"This is about keeping her safe and—"

With a labored breath, I feel the cool rush of air filling my lungs, invigorating and cleansing. The scent of damp earth and foliage mingles together, permeating the air around me. A dull ache pulses through my temples, throbbing in tandem with my returning awareness. Gradually, my eyelids flutter, struggling to lift the weight that holds them shut.

Everything hurts.

"She's going to want *us* safe—"

"Will you please let me finish a sent—"

"I would if you had any good ideas!"

As the world swims into focus, I see blurred shapes slowly

216

taking form. Flashes of blonde and brown, pink lips and hazel eyes. A looming figure, who, even with no distinct features, looks grumpy. Colors bleed into one another before solidifying into permanent hues. Shadows dance and play across my vision, as if the very fabric of reality is shifting and weaving before my eyes. The details sharpen gradually, like one of Axlan's paintings coming into focus.

"For once in your life, Althea, I need you to think rationally."

The whispering voices, once an echo, transform into murmurs, forming recognizable words. My name is carried on the gentle currents of sound, beckoning me back from the abyss. It's a familiar voice, tinged with concern and relief, a lifeline pulling me back to the realm of the living.

A surge of awareness courses through me, like a flickering flame being reignited. My surroundings solidify, revealing the towering lumber. I'm no longer bleeding, my wounds bandaged. I gasp for air, dragging their attention away from the argument. My back is against a tree, keeping me in a sitting position.

"Dove!" Althea exclaims.

She's standing over me, next to an equally concerned Calix. The pair of them look like they've fought their own war tonight, dirt's smeared against their faces, there's a twig in Calix's hair. I try to stand, forcing my feet down. I don't make it very far, grabbing the tree for support only to snake back down to the damp ground. Everything's still too hazy.

"Careful," Calix warns. "You've lost a lot of blood."

The corners of my lip twitch up. "Just a bit."

Calix smiles back at me, forcing his own anxiety back down. I can only imagine how messed up this is for them, too. For a moment, all I can do is let the savory feeling of escape wash over me. I didn't die. Malvolia was moments away from slaughtering me back there. It was only a stroke of luck—*or lightning*—that saved me. I only know one elementalist willing to piss off the Coven Crown, a hunter brave enough to risk it all for his friend.

I keep my eyes on Calix. "You set the poppy field on fire."

He crosses his big arms. "The bugs were unseasonably bad this year, anyways."

My grin becomes goofy, and I can't tell if it's the drug or his awful joke. Either way, *my friends saved me.*

Althea scoops something up from the ground. "We don't have a lot of time." She's right. Gods, how long have I been out? The moon is still high, everything still hurts. "Malvolia will come for you when she restores order. Whatever happened back there, she won. *We can leave the Isle, Dove.* And she won't risk it being some sort of fluke by keeping you alive. You need to go."

I swallow, looking into the dark woods around me. We're far enough away from the poppy field to have seclusion. But the Isle is only so big and my mother will come for me, no matter what. Though my blood somehow broke the magic *before* killing me—it just makes me a living breathing loophole. A piece of the puzzle that could unbalance and rebalance her acts of nature.

Malvolia doesn't like loopholes.

"Here," Althea says. "Put these on." She hands me a pair of— *oh gods, I could squeeze her right now*—hunting leathers. They're midnight black, meaning she must have snatched them from my own closet. I dress quickly, covering my bloody bandages with a black tight-fitting shirt and curve-hugging leather pants. Every muscle I move is accompanied by a shooting pain, so bad I whimper a few times. Althea has to help lace me into a vested corset over the shirt. Calix kicks me a pair of matching boots before gently tying them up. Each of my friends takes an arm, hoisting me up with delicate hands. At first, I'm sure the ground is going to cave in again. But their grips steady me until my own feet can hold my weight.

Mother really did it—the witches can leave. I bet she'll waste no time. Althea says I have to go. *But where?* I can't just hide while Mother ignites a war. I have to do something.

"She'll kill you for helping me," I whisper.

Althea wears no trace of her usual polite smile, instead smirking like she's been playing a ruse of her own. "She won't know. A handful of witches *swear* they saw both Calix and me pinned under a couple rocks. We'll have the injuries to prove it."

Calix sighs. "Not looking forward to that part."

Althea rolls her eyes, lightly touching his arm. " Neither am I. But don't worry about us, Dove. The lightning can be explained away. I mean, it did *just so happen* to strike at the exact moment the cauldron cracked open. Maybe instead of an insubordinate witch, it was just some stray crazy magic leftover from the spell. It's not the craziest thing to happen around here—our heir did go missing for a month. But that's a story for another day, when you're not bleeding or being manically hunted."

So, the lightning was Calix.

And Althea had been lurking nearby during the ritual, ready to feed me information the moment there was an opening. It was…brilliant.

I stare at them both in bewilderment—the diplomat and the wildling. Althea comes up to his shoulders, like she could nuzzle into his collarbone at any given moment. Calix stands in old, cracked leathers, hovering over us both like he's waiting for a threat to pounce. He's rugged and wild, reasons I've always loved him. She's delicate, poised, and gentle.

But together the two of them burned an entire poppy field. Crumbled an ancient altar. Staged a daring escape and managed to drag me through the woods, alive. *They're badass.*

I shake my head. "Malvolia's lost it, you guys. She isn't just planning a war. She's planning on handing the realm *and* the witches over to the death god on a silver platter. She's going to summon the death god. She's going to kill us all."

Calix's golden skin loses some color. "How?"

I pause. "That's a really good question, Cal. I have no bloody idea."

Althea looks weary. "I'm sure she has a plan. Wasn't that amulet important to her?"

I furrow my brows. *How much did they piece together?* If we had more time, I'd ask her every question racing through my brain.

"The Bloodjewel, yeah. She needed it to break the Isle seal, along with my blood." I think back to my chained conversation with mother. "She also said it was a source of magic itself. Maybe she was planning on using it for something else, too." But now the amulet's gone. Either it disintegrated from my boiling blood or it just…vanished.

Althea's blonde hair bounces when she nods. "That gives us some time to stop her."

"Unless she has another plan," Calix grumbles. *She very well could.* And I have no clue what it could be. But with over five hundred years to plan, I suppose there's probably a back up.

"We can't waste time speculating on her plans," Althea asserts. "Now that the magic is broken she'll never stay on the Isle. I'm sure the witches will be gathered and ready to move before the sun rises." My cousin's eyes go wide. "Dove, what about the others? There are fledglings here. And witches who really don't mind the Isle—content, happy people. Calix's father?" she doesn't mention her own parents, who are surely flanking Malvolia's side. "We have to help them. She's going to take them all!"

Calix stares at Althea like he's desperate to think his way out of this. A flash of despair moves through his brown eyes. But just when he looks sadder than a landbound siren, there's a spark of something behind his face—a plan unfolding. A look that's gotten us into various amounts of trouble throughout our youth.

"And we're going with her," Calix says.

Althea whips her head around, glaring at Calix with such intensity I'm surprised he doesn't step back. "What?"

"Hear me out, Thea. For once." Calix breaks her gaze to look at me. Between the two of us, I've always been more receptive. "We go with her—Althea and I. Malvolia doesn't know we're helping you. I mean, even if she does, she can't prove it. And she's not stupid. She won't murder her best hunter or the *only* other compulsion witch in existence. Not when she can use us."

Thundering dragons. He's not suggesting what I think he is. It could work, but it'll be a tightrope walk hung high above a pit of snakes.

"You want to play her."

His mop of curls nod. "I want to stop her from killing us all. And an inside man is the best way. We can find out how she plans to summon the death god. Think back to lessons—it's not impossible. We'll learn her war plans and dismantle them however we can. Figure out how she plans on doing it all. You saw what we accomplished to get you back. We can stop her."

It could be a death sentence. She could find them out and slaughter them for the betrayal. But...it could also save the remaining coven. It could give them a chance, even if that chance is still just a simple life here.

Was it really that bad?

I want to say no. It's too dangerous—and they're the only two people I really love in this entire realm. I can't handle losing someone else, not after Father. After Mother. But if we don't try, *everyone* will die. Including us. It's suicide, but it's genius.

I look up. "Calix, find the witches who are against the war or against Malvolia. Witches that you can trust. Divide her army with the truth." I turn to my cousin. "Thea, compel the hell out of everyone else. Convince them that she's lost touch with reality and that only *you* are to be trusted."

Althea sucks in a breath. "But what about you?"

Unfortunately, I know what I have to do now. "Don't worry about me. The important thing is staying alive. And stopping Malvolia before she ruins us all."

My cousin looks at me. "We can handle it." *I sure hope so.*

Calix moves to say something else, but there faint shouts echoing around us. Mother's first hunting party, probably hyper-focused on retrieving me, dead or alive. My bones still ache and my head pounds, but a few steps don't kill me.

I turn back to them with more urgency in my tone. "Remember to grieve me. Don't forgive her too easily or she'll know something is off. Keep your patterns normal. Wait for her to reach out to you."

Calix nods. Althea grabs my hand, her silky fingers tremble slightly. I clutch her hand back.

A shaky breath in. "I'm going to do something stupid. More reckless than our worst night at the tavern. Than our decision to swim midwinter after smoking six of Althea's herb rolls. If it works, I'll find you."

Neither of them asks what happens if it doesn't work. Or what comes after. They don't have a chance to ask anything at all, because the shouting is growing closer. I hear a branch break nearby. My heartbeat kicks back up—we'll have to split up if it's to work.

"We *will* meet again," I tell them. Althea wraps her gentle arms around me in a hug. I embrace her back, tight enough to restrict her breathing. I take an extra moment to inhale her hair—lilac and cherries.

Calix grabs me next, though he smells like leather and fresh rain. "Don't die."

There's shouting between witches to check the south woods. We're out of seconds to spare, tears well within my silver eyes.

Althea sniffles. "Yeah, that would be tragic."

"And the entire realm might be dependent on our success," Calix adds.

Even our enemies.

I smirk, hugging them both once more. "No pressure."

The voice is getting close enough to sound distinctly male, and almost like Tomax. While I would *love* to take his arms, right now I don't stand a chance. Malvolia knows I'm running out of time.

But leaving feels like another knife in my stomach. And my destination could very well earn me another one.

"Go," Thea urges.

With one final look, I dart off into the woods.

PART III

The Return

CHAPTER 25

I thought he'd improve security. In fact, I vividly remember suggesting it to him on my way out. Not that I think he'd take any advice from me. It's just that there's *supposedly* a crazy witch on the loose with a knack for stealing family heirlooms.

The very same witch who now sits atop his desk stationed in his empty study. My legs are crossed, swinging in a delicate motion after I grew tired of rustling through his personal belongings. I can't exactly say how long I've been lounging here—waiting. Long enough to think of every possible thing I could say to the king when he eventually walks through the door. To consider every possible tactic to get what I need. Something tells me Axlan won't respond well to any approach. Not after our hasty departure last time. After I kissed him enough to distract him, almost forgetting my entire plan in his lips.

What could I possibly say now?

Sorry for stealing your talisman and giving it to a powerful witch who wants to burn your continent to the ground. But hey, she wants me dead now, too, so…allies? Oh, by the way, if we don't stop her from summoning the death god, we're all going to die, anyways. He would gut me before I could finish the statement.

However, the king isn't stupid, even if he is a little arrogant and irrational. He must know of the witches' freedom by now. And I'm his best shot of gaining the upper hand. Of stopping Malvolia before she starts. Working together churns my stomach, and he could very well laugh in my face (really that's almost my best-case scenario).

All the possibilities for mistrust and betrayal, the inerasable history between my coven and his family. The wars and the murders and the lines crossed. But this isn't about loyalties, it's about survival. An allyship doesn't need trust, just dependency. *And we need each other.*

I've run out of time to practice my pitch, and now that I'm thinking about it—he'll likely lose his mind over seeing me casually on his desk. When the door creaks open, I know it's him by the lavender and the…charcoal?

Axlan walks in and I can tell he's been up for quite some time. His hands are stained with black as dark as his hair, explaining the smell and the crazed artist look behind his golden eyes. Bags are under his usually smooth divine skin, the scruff on his face growing. His black clothing is wrinkled, the suit vest he wears is coming undone. Shockingly, there's still an angry red line cupping his cheekbone from where I bit him. I'm surprised it hasn't healed yet, but even more surprised that it looks as if it might…*scar.*

It makes him look rugged, edged with violence.

Which is exactly how I should have expected he'd react to a thief atop his desk—with violence. If he's surprised or confused by my being here, he doesn't show it, though I see some paint mixed on his fingertips, still wet. Like he's quickly come to grab something before returning to the studio. He wasn't expecting me, but the Realm Bound doesn't hesitate. Instantly, his face shifts into fury and he's whipping *another* blade across the room, narrowly missing my ear. How many weapons does he have on him at all times?

I can't help rolling my eyes. *Dramatic.* He's too close to miss, even for someone with bad aim. If he wanted to hit me, he would have. Maybe this is a good sign; he hasn't obliterated me, yet. I don't move, instead holding my hands up in surrender. "We've already thrown knives at each other. I didn't come back to fight."

One minute, I'm sitting on his desk. But before I can blink, Axlan is across the room in a blur of wrath, pinning me against the wall, wrapping his paint-stained fingers around my neck. Maybe I've underestimated just how angry I've made him; my vision blurs, and my airway closes.

"Then die without a fight. It makes no difference to me," he seethes, baring his white teeth.

Internally, my body's screaming in protest. But I remain still and try not to struggle under his grasp. I won't fight him like this; I have to show that I come in peace. This is my *only* solution to save Calix and Althea. The only way to save the coven from the Olcar. From the death god. From my own damn mother.

I grab Axlan's wrist, forcing myself to look into his golden eyes. "My mother wishes to see your downfall. She wants to destroy the realm and everyone in it. *I* wish to stay alive. We can help each other."

He tightens his grip, making me swallow down a whimper. My throat is on fire, bone dry. Maybe it was a mistake coming back here. "I don't want your help," says Axlan in a growl.

"I don't want your help either. But I need it. And you'll need mine if you care about your kingdom. I've been her heir for a hundred years. I know the ins and outs of her coven. I know what she's planning next." *Well, kind of.*

"Working together is the only way to keep us all breathing," I choke out.

Axlan's lethal eyes narrow at me in consideration. "And you've come back here out of what? The kindness of your heart? After a delusional moment *you* orchestrated?" he snaps.

I pretend not to feel a pang of hurt at his covert mention of our kiss. I certainly hadn't *orchestrated* the moment. I'd just acted on survival and sheer determination to live. Or maybe I knew I could die, and it was a reckless last-minute thrill.

Either way, I shove it down and shoot him a bitter look. "This isn't about *you,* despite your enormous ego. I need to save my coven, my friends. I want to kill my mother and avenge my father. I'll tell you everything I know. Every spell, every ritual. Every small detail Malvolia confided in me throughout the years. She's planning a war and if we combine our knowledge, we can stop her."

Axlan loosens his big hand, giving me a little breathing room. I can't move, and I'm still against the stone wall under the weight of him, at least now I won't pass out before I convince him to join me.

"But what do you want? I won't allow the coven back in the realm. I won't even allow them to live," Axlan says.

"There are witches against the Coven Crown. Not everyone wants this…not everyone can fight. Allow them to live on the Isle *unharmed* once we eliminate her. Pardon them. Everyone else can be dealt with however you wish," I say. "But leave the innocent out of it." It sounds cold but I know the king wouldn't let any known traitors survive. At least I can save part of the coven. At least Calix and Althea will live.

"Is that what you think of me? That I'll slaughter anyone for the hell of it?" Axlan spits, bringing his face close to mine. It sends shockwaves through my body, and his loose raven curl brushes my white strands.

"I always let the innocent live." His stare gets dark, I see the lethal king they claim. "But I'll burn everyone else to ash."

There's no doubt he means it, and the power vibrating off

him is enough to affirm it. I refuse to flinch away, meeting his gaze in a stern plea to see the logic of my argument. His words were terrifying, and a reminder that I'm completely at his mercy.

"Please, Axlan," I beg. "I wouldn't have come back if I saw another way."

Axlan's eyes hold mine, uncertainty flickering within them. I can see the battle waging in his mind, torn between pride and the faint spark of truth. With a resolute expression, he slowly removes his hands from my neck, allowing my feet to touch the floor. Once I'm standing on my own and he's backed away, I can still smell lavender in my hair and on my skin. And I can still feel the fireworks in my stomach from how close he was.

"Fine," he decides. I practically sag in relief, audibly exhaling. "After Malvolia is gone, I'll allow the remaining witches a pardon if they denounce her." It's the first time I've felt hopeful about saving my friends, maybe even the coven. I'll tell him whatever he wants, say whatever I need to—

"All of the witches," the king continues. He puts a hand in his vest and pulls out another small blade. *How many knives does the man carry?* Nearly as many as I do. It feels faintly familiar when he sulks forward and places the tip of his dagger under my chin. He doesn't apply much pressure, more theatrical than anything. I say nothing, waiting for the rest of his point.

"Except for you."

I blink. Allow the closeness of his skin to send a shiver down my spine. Process *another* death warrant being added to my list.

I don't see a trace of the boy who brought me the salve or laughed with me under the stars. The fireworks in my stomach are replaced with acid.

"When the witches are tamed and your mother is gone, I will tear apart the realm hunting you down." He leans closer, bringing his mouth to my ear, allowing the blade to gently pierce my skin. I don't feel it. "And I will kill you."

I turn my head to meet his eyes, making the welted blood drip down my collarbone. "Maybe you'll get it right the second time. Or maybe I'll get to you first."

Could it really come to that? The god and the witch chasing each other around the realm, hoping the other will either give in.

It's something to worry about later. I can tell Axlan's thinking the same by the slow nod of his head and the way he drags his eyes from my lips to my neck, lost in something questionable before he snaps back into himself and pulls the blade away.

He sits on the worn couch, throwing a leg over his knee. "Tell me what you know."

So, I do.

It's taken hours, the moon is well gone by the time we've come to an agreement. It was slow at first, both of us accusing the other of ulterior motives and withholding information. At one point, knives came out again and we took turns baring our teeth or throwing petty insults. Axlan would interrupt everything I say, asking a dozen unnecessary questions and getting his stupid curls all ruffled up. When I'd told him about the death god's help and my mother's need to summon the Olcar, he'd grown pale and serious. Asked a dozen more questions.

And though I don't trust him, I trust that he wants to save his kingdom, which is enough for now. The king doesn't know how Mother plans on summoning the death god's creatures, but he's convinced it's possible. I try not to focus too heavily on the how, especially since he says it with sheer accusation, convinced I know more than I'm letting on. Maybe I'd been assuming Mother was half mad and had unreachable goals. Knowing that she can actually do it reignites my fear for my cousin. For Calix.

According to Axlan, the best thing I can do for them right now is nothing. Part of our agreement is that I stay here under constant supervision, confined to the castle grounds. He's not convinced I won't try to contact Malvolia and double cross him. So, for the sake of our truce, I'll abide. The idea is as stupid as he is, but the most sensible part of me can see why. I wouldn't want him unsupervised in my home, either. He might mock my bookshelf.

Pure exhaustion wears us down more than our need to outdo the other.

I can't remember the last time I've slept, other than the black abyss of unconsciousness after getting knocked out. By my own mother. Fortunately, I could just go back to my old rooms and resume my old persona. That's the final part of Axlan's deal—do not raise any suspicion. He doesn't want the public to panic and plans to keep the witches' escape under wraps. I'm simply to resume my "studies" and commit back into the role of Dove Clepta while we plan out our next move.

When I get up to go, I'm somewhat satisfied by the outcome. And Axlan doesn't whip a blade after me, indicating our partnership is off to a halfway decent start. He follows me into the hallway, going to his own bedroom right across the hall. Before he opens the door, he stops, turning around to face me once more. Any trace of sarcastic jabs or arrogant wit are gone, replaced with his deadly golden stare.

Incandescent power hums around him. "And one more thing. If you *ever* get that close to me again—ever *kiss* me like that— our deal is off, and I'll rip your heart out."

It's not an idle threat, it's a promise. One that refuels my fury.

"Don't kiss me back and you might get to keep yours," I snap. Blindly, I throw open the door and stomp halfway down.

BLOODJEWELS

Kissing him is the *last* thing on my mind. Being here at all isn't exactly how I wanted to fill my social calendar. My cheeks heat as I get to the bottom step. Somehow, I know he's still listening.

"Something like that will *never* happen again," I shout.

I wait for him to bite back, to call me reckless or troublesome. Instead, I hear his own door slam.

CHAPTER 26

 nobleman, and steal an all-powerful talisman to unleash his immortal enemy back into the realm." Fawn doesn't look up, turning the page of her book.

"How could I forget with you constantly around to remind me?" I grumble, leaning into the plush couch. The cushions smells like the head librarian they belong to—sweet honey vanilla.

In fact, everything inside this damn office reeks of Fawn. The shelves are all painted different colors, varying from a deep plum to a wild green. Her furniture is mismatched, a maroon floral pattern armchair, a teal loveseat. She has an entire cabinet dedicated solely to tea. Her desk is a disaster, more lived in than probably her bed. Candles are burnt down from our recent late nights, the running wax long since hardened. Really, it's not a bad place to spend most hours of the day.

Fawn's big brown eyes scan the chapter. Her lip twitches up into a smirk. "Don't worry, I'll be right here when you forget again." *Oh, don't I know it.*

Which, while this is still very much technically a punishment, isn't a bad one. Fawn isn't the worst company to keep by a long shot. For the grief Axlan gave me, I half expected him to throw me in a dark jail cell or feed me to those dragons I've heard whispers about. Instead, he'd pushed me back into my original persona of Dove Clepta, equipped with my old room and unlimited library access. Under a *very* watchful eye, of course. He'd demanded a constant, always at my hip, Axlan-approved watchguard as part of our agreement. Fawn makes the most sense, given I'm supposed to be a scholar and we're trying to keep things inconspicuous. Plus, we're about the same age and she seems to be someone Axlan trusts.

So, she's been given the secretive task of keeping me in line. We actually have a lot in common, despite her overbearing optimism and disgustingly massive heart. If the circumstances weren't a little screwed up—I might consider us friends. Though she can be pretty ruthless in cards, swindling me with an angelic smile on afternoons when we sprawl against the floor and play.

"It's been *weeks,* Fawn. He must have found something!" I sit up, staring at her. She's snuggled inside the flowered armchair.

Two weeks. Two weeks since I switched sides and agreed to join the king. I've given up coven secrets, told and retold every minor detail of my departure from the Isle. Anything he needed to know, I forfeited. After our initial agreement—which was off to a very civil start with all the slamming doors and insults— Axlan met with me once, sitting across the table intently listening to anything I had to offer. He barely spoke beyond the countless invasive questions asked. After that, he disappeared. His silence has left me scorching, all those secrets spilt, for him to give me absolutely nothing. I've even laid out our politics, survival, our magic, and what kind of wielders we have right now. All of it. I gave him every grueling detail he asked for.

Mother would slaughter me for it. Even Calix might cringe. Hell, even I have to keep reminding myself I'm only doing it because it's life or death. Because Malvolia still has Calix and Althea. Which brings on the guilt—card games, earthy tea, a petite librarian for a chaperone. I'm not exactly doing much from here.

Fawn pushes up her round wired glasses. Another delicate page turns. "Axlan said he would find you when there's more to know. He hasn't found you, therefore there's nothing more to know."

I take in a deep aggravated breath. "I don't believe him."

Though she's still engrossed in the novel, Fawn rolls her eyes. "*I know.* You made that very clear when you stole his schedule from my desk and tried to *harass* him." Well, she hadn't given me much choice. It's not like she's willing to tell me where the moody king is always hiding.

"He's up to something," I protest. "Why else would he always be gone? And when he is here, he's evasive. We're supposed to be allies. It wouldn't kill him to admit that a witch is on his side."

"Well, you certainly don't help your case with constant insults," she says.

I cross my arms over my dress—one Fawn picked out to make me appear like a more legitimate member of Axlan's court. After gleefully accepting responsibility for me, she'd brought ruffles and giant heaps of ribbon, bows and pearls, and hideously big gowns. I'd protested almost every choice and we compromised on a simple ivory silk and leather laced corset. Still movable, still fightable. Slightly protective. But not the hunting leathers she had to practically tear from my hands.

"It's not constant!" I defend, but we both know it is.

Finally, Fawn looks up from her book with an accusatory glare and raised eyebrows. "Really? When he came to tell you he was leaving for a couple days and to remain put, you shouted that he's an 'oversized brute who cares more about his curls than his word.' And before that an 'egotistical ass.' Besides, we're helping now!" she gestures to the massive stacks of historical texts. "Someone must go through every ounce of research we have. What if there's a clue? The key to stopping Malvolia could very well be on these pages."

Okay, so maybe I am a little mean to the king. Well…a lot mean. I sink back into the couch, unable to argue. Something about him just infuriates me. And not just because I was raised to hate the Realm Bound. Not because he's responsible for my century-long isolation. He has a unique ability to get under my skin. To be both achingly hot and terrifying. *Difficult.* But I can't tell Fawn that.

"I know more about my mother than the books here do! I should be going with him, wherever he lurks off to," I grumble.

She sighs. "History didn't just start with the Realm Bound, you know that. Witches make an appearance in almost every ancient civilization. Others might have known something we don't."

Surprise crosses my features. "I thought attacks from the witches kept villages small and constantly moving?" At least, that's what Malvolia had always taught me. Except, obviously her record with trust and my best interest is particularly hazy.

"Yeah, in this part of the Realm for sure. But there were areas they left alone. Mostly because the terrain was too rough, or the locals knew it too well and would fight back."

I stare. "I didn't know that. I thought it was everywhere." Figures that Malvolia was dishonest. My stomach turns thinking of what else she could be lying about.

Fawn smiles. "Of course, your mother would want you to think that. Kinda goes against her scary reputation to admit the witches couldn't conquer everything. Lots of areas were developed enough to have history. The Realm Bound didn't just waltz into ruling. They were accepted into the positions by the kings and queens before them." She turns her delicate head. "Maybe Malvolia didn't know. Wasn't she just a teenager when the war broke out?"

I shrug. "Yeah, and she's full of secrets."

Fawn only smiles deeper, provoking her dimples. "Even more reason to keep looking."

"But we've read through everything! I can't take another scroll on the death god or military report on the witches. Even you've given up!" I point to the book she's been reading, still opened in her lap—an adventure saga. Not a dull historical document.

Her cheeks turn as red as her hair before she snaps it shut. Slowly, Fawn untangles herself from the chair, stretching out like an orange housecat. Her skirt is layers of pink and rustles as she slinks over to shelve her book. "Fine. I have to post the staff schedule before dinner. If we leave now, I bet there'll still be chocolate cake in the dining hall. And I will *not* miss it again just so you can throw daggers at inanimate objects."

I follow her out the door and into the fourth-floor library hall, overwhelmed with the smell of parchment and drying ink. "Better than at Axlan's head," I mumble.

She shoots me a sour look as we descend the stairs. "I will not dignify that with a response."

The librarian posts her schedule near the exit, while I think about dinner possibilities. The food here is way better than the Isle and the kitchen only closes late into the night. There's endless amounts of fruits and tender meat, creamy oats and fluffy muffins. I start to tell Fawn the chocolate cake is bland compared to the iced lemon bread, but I'm stopped.

By a flash of gold and black, so tall and broad and distinctly handsome that it can only be him.

BLOODJEWELS

Axlan is furiously walking in hushed conversation with the reemerged Nemir, who seems just as out of sorts. His white shirt (yeah—white and *not* black, which is cause enough for alarm) is wrinkled and rolled at his sleeves, his golden eyes tense. And he looks furious. Flecks of gold are sizzling around him, the power threatening to spill over. Nemir's hollow expression says she screwed up, given there's no trace of her usual snarl. They're clearly heading to his private meeting room, wedged behind a grand stained-glass door.

I hear Fawn make a noise of protest, coming to a halt on my heels. Across the way, Axlan's voice is getting louder and he's pointing at Nemir to leave. Whatever she's done, he's not happy about it. There's an angry blush to his tanned skin, his full lips poised in a nasty frown. Nemir doesn't argue back, slouching away in defeat. She sulks down the stairs and leaves Axlan contemplating in the door frame, hand hesitantly on the handle and utterly alone. Alone enough to answer some questions.

"That," I tell Fawn, "seemed important." And if it has anything to do with the witches, I want to know.

"Listen, Dove—" Fawn begins to say, attempting to reason with me. It's no use, I squeeze her hand before taking off after him. Distantly, she groans something about getting fired but makes no move to follow me, probably knowing it'll be useless. Instead, she heads toward the dining hall, shouting, "I'm not saving you any cake!"

I'll get an earful tomorrow, for sure, but that's a worry for later.

There's no possible way I can believe Malvolia hasn't done anything since my escape. She's always been more than a few steps ahead; I can't imagine her sitting around without some sort of plan. Though it is strange she's hidden. Maybe killing me was more important than I thought. Or maybe she needs me dead as some weird way to summon her lovely death god.

Or maybe she's just waiting for the perfect moment to strike. It sends a shiver down my spine. Because when she strikes, she intends to kill. Getting away from her once was lucky, and only possible with the help of my friends. I know I won't be able to do it again, no matter how much magic I have. Not when she has the coven on her side. And my friends in her pocket.

The thought only makes me angrier. Angry at my mother. Angry at Axlan. At my disowned coven. I mean, how can you get exiled from a group already exiled? It's a new low. By the time I watch him disappear inside the room, I'm boiling with bitterness. So much so that a minute later, when I'm upon the door myself, I fling it open.

Blind with rage and already speaking, I burst inside. "I don't care how busy you are looking in the mirror or counting your eyelashes, I will not be—"

He's not alone.

Three chairs are occupied and each three have very different reactions to my arrival. Axlan's sitting in the first, seething even more than he was moments ago. Whatever they've been talking about—it's tense. And my arrival was clearly not on their agenda. My stomach twists into intricate knots. Immediately, I know I've messed up.

In the second chair, she looks…just like him.

The woman has thick eyebrows, arched with authority. She can't be older than me, maybe matured at twenty-one or twenty-two. There's a splattering of freckles across her light, otherwise flawless skin. She has the same golden eyes as Axlan. Her hair is the same shining black. Only instead of having wild curls, her strands fall in thick waves with braids of brightly colored purple streaking through. Her lips aren't as full either, a thin set line, making her look serious. Seriously angry.

Gods beyond.

The chair beside her erupts into laughter, his voice deep and his hair cropped short. "This is the witch who outsmarted you, brother?"

Brother.

The Realm Bound siblings. Well—two of them.

Axlan, never missing an opportunity to scowl, crosses his arms. "She's supposed to be in her rooms."

I scoff. *My rooms.* "Maybe you shouldn't have a scrawny librarian for security if you want me confined to my room." Besides, he can't just order me away while we're allies. "And you're supposed to tell me when something important happens."

"I didn't know they were here," Axlan says through gritted teeth. Oh. So that would explain his heated exchange with Nemir. She must have contacted them without his knowing. She ambushed him into a meeting with his powerful ruling siblings.

The deep laughter continues, like he hasn't been this entertained by his brother's distemper in a long time. "Viska! Are you seeing this?! She's nearly half his size and she still got away!"

Viska doesn't look amused. "Oh, I see her, Kier. Isn't this the same king who ripped the jaw from a false prophet?" Her calm, lethal tone matches the intensity of her stare, now burning a hole into me. "The same brother who slaughtered an entire species because he didn't feel like negotiating?" It sounds like she's *defending* the witches. Axlan's stare burns a hole through her, but she doesn't seem to notice.

She glances at Kier, her other brother. "So, why hasn't he fed her to the dragons?"

Kier shoots her a weary look. "Ah, come on Viska. Not everyone can be dragon food."

Agreed. Already, I like him above the rest, though he looks a lot like his brother. Except he has a lopsided, goofy grin and isn't constantly brooding. They're both well over six feet, maybe even close to seven, like their bodies were built for war. He has the same ethereal features, the same divine eyes and bold cheekbones. Only his golden hair makes him stand out from the others, like he's a warm afternoon while they're the dead of night.

Viska scrunches her noses, adjusting the satin sleeve of her purple dress. "You're right. I don't think they'd even take her." She drags her eyes across me, not hiding her disgust. "She's just bones and shiny white hair. This is all it takes to undo you, Ax? A colorless girl with an aspiring criminal career?"

Axlan, *Ax,* doesn't answer her. He's still staring at the doorway, fury directed at me. If he hadn't promised to keep me alive for now, I think I'd be dead from the stunt I just pulled.

"Sit down." It's an order. A dark one, that sends a shiver down my neck. I don't like taking orders, room full of gods or not.

I cross my arms. He raises his eyebrows, questioning if I'm really going to fight with him over this. I raise mine right back. *Yeah, I am.*

It's enough to make him stand, leaning over the table in a barely kept rage. "You want to be included? Well, here's your chance. Sit. The hell. Down. Dove." Power rumbles off him. It's a losing battle—especially when I do want to know what they've been talking about.

Fine. I sit in the first open chair. Unfortunately, it's directly across from Axlan. He drags his eyes from me to stare at his siblings, silently debating what exactly he should tell them.

Kier raises himself on his elbows, eagerly listening with a ridiculous grin.

"Everything," Viska says with a frown, reading her brother's thoughts. "You'll tell us everything.

Interesting enough, he does, leaving only one thing out—our kiss.

Everything else is exact, and I learn he knew that Isle magic broke the instant it happened. That he suspected something was amiss with the witches months ago but brushed it off as paranoia, thinking the magic was secure. And worst of all…he hasn't been able to find the coven anywhere. At first, he sent a few trusted scouts to find any trace of them. But when they came back empty handed again and again, he started going himself. It explains all his recent disappearances, making me feel bad for constantly complaining to Fawn. Maybe even for calling him all those names.

Despite his efforts, it's as if my coven vanished just like the amulet did during the ritual. When he tells his siblings about my theft, he simply says I jumped from the window before he could stop me. He doesn't mention the daggers thrown or the way it felt to have my legs wrapped around his waist.

Viska raises her eyebrows on hearing my escape but says nothing. After Axlan finishes retelling the entire story, both of his siblings stare with bewildered expressions.

Kier speaks first. "Well, I guess the witches are still upset."

You could say that again. Imprisonment for five hundred years can do that to people, especially someone as unhinged as my mother. Viska narrows her golden eyes at her brothers. "Upset and coming for our people. You didn't think to tell us sooner?" she gestures to Kier and back to herself with a slender finger. "Are you forgetting how we won the last war? Together. I get leaving the youngest out for everyone's sake, but us?"

Axlan runs an exasperated hand through his hair. "I had it under control."

The goddess slams her hand on the table, baring her teeth at her older brother. "Does this seem under control to you?" she points another accusatory finger—directly at me.

I swallow, meeting her stormy glare. "Look, I know this isn't ideal. But I'm here to help. Everything Axlan said is true." Besides my exit out the tower window, which replays in my mind on a constant, lusty loop.

She crosses her arms, showing off the violet rings on her fingers—Viska really likes purple. And sharing her opinion, apparently. "As if anything you say should be believed. You're the reason we're in this mess."

Kier touches his sister's arm. "Whoa, Viska. We've had unlikely allies before. Ax says the witch is on our side and it seems like we need her help. We have to trust our brother, especially now."

She's unconvinced, brushing his hand off her shoulder. "What if she's lying?"

"I'm not," I say. "My mother wants me dead and she has my friends. Whatever history we all have, I'm on your side." And for the first time, I actually believe it. This may not be at all how I thought my life would play out, but there's no turning back now.

Kier claps his hands together, still wearing a goofy grin. "Great! See, Viska? We're all on the same team. Dove is, uh, here to help!"

She glares at Kier. And then at Axlan, before landing on me. "Prove it."

CHAPTER 27

Dawn, earlier than the birds. A thick wool jacket and leather
boots. A sleepless night with an endless interrogation. Eyes
so tired they can barely stay open. A smug king, with his arms
crossed at the palace gates.

An unknown destination.

This is what Viska apparently meant when she said "prove it"
nearly twelve hours ago. We sat restlessly in that meeting hall,
hashing and rehashing every detail I had on the coven. On my
mother. On the amulet's final moments.

Anything that could have possibly been thought of—Viska
asked. The sibling's left nothing to the imagination, and when
Viska would feel satisfied with her interrogating, her brother
Kier would pipe up something, unraveling an entirely new string
of questions from them all. Luckily, I wasn't the only one under
fire; they'd been prying Axlan open, who sat with a scowl and
mumbled through his answers. We both shot dagger stares at
the other from across the table, and it was likely the siblings'
agreement on working together that kept me alive.

By the time Kier finally convinced everyone to stand down,
I'd lost track of the hours and walked back to my room in a daze
before slinking into a deep slumber.

But that was before I'd been jolted awake at an unspeakable
hour by the king's personal maid. She'd forced me out of bed and
pointed a frail finger at me to dress. I didn't get the chance to ask

her the time, she was too busy scolding me for being a sluggish fool. Within thirty minutes, and along with a handful of threats, I was ready to meet the siblings. I couldn't have gotten more than a couple hours of sleep, but pointing that out seemed useless, though I regret not slamming the door in her old face now.

Regardless, I knew I had to meet the siblings, though I don't want to. There aren't a lot of options, and I'm pretty sure I'm the last person the Realm Bound want to trust. That Axlan wants to trust. But like me, it seems he put his feelings aside as he stands near the castle gate.And his face is so damn annoying.

"Where are the others?" I snap.

Axlan fixes the cuff of his sleeve. "Sleeping, I'd assume. It's pretty early."

The knives attached to my hunting leathers swish when I cross my arms. Gods, what time is it, actually? Did he even go to bed? I can't tell, reluctantly taking in his stupid, impeccable style.

He wears a well-crafted leather jacket, rich midnight material adorned with silver buttons. Despite my frustration, I can't help but admit that it fits him perfectly, enhancing his rugged allure. It's still strange to see a king in something other than a cape or puffed sleeves—Axlan's nothing like the fairytales we had of him growing up. He's not frilly, he's dangerous.

And to say the least—it's infuriating to feel both drawn to and repelled by someone, especially at the same time.

We lock eyes, a simmering tension between us. His golden irises move all over me, like he can't decide if he's willing to risk revealing his cards. The conflicting emotions entwine in a delicate dance, making my heart pound.

"We're going alone," Axlan says.

I look around at the empty lawn. The sun isn't even fully up yet, there's probably not even a bird awake. Half of me is curious, now that he's finally willing to work together, but the sleepier half of me just wants to go back to bed.

"Now?" I ask.

Axlan opens the gate, rolling his ethereal eyes. "I'm sorry if my schedule agitates you." His words are dripping with sarcasm. "I don't know if you remember this, but we happen to be a on a time crunch. You know—since you freed the witches and ignited a war." He holds it open, motioning for me to go first with a gigantic and devious smirk.

I want to slap it off his stupid face.

"Where are we going?" I ask but walk through anyways.

Axlan shuts the latch behind us. "To learn to trust each other." And he turns to go before I can argue.

He leads us away from the main road into the capital, instead bringing us through a small dirt path near the edge of the castle not towering over the sea. I reluctantly follow him through the tree line and into the woods. With each step, his silence bothers me more. It's not like I necessarily want to talk to him, but I would like to know where we might be heading.

The trees loom overhead, their branches intertwining like bony fingers, adding an eerie atmosphere to my mounting irritation. It's almost identical to the nightmares I used to create each night after reading Morbida folklore. I shiver when the temperature drops under the giant leaves. Axlan seems to take delight in luring me away from civilization, plunging us into a narrow pathway that winds through the forest.

I open my mouth to protest, but Axlan senses it, turning around and breaking the silence.

"Viska was right, in her own annoying way," Axlan begrudgingly admits it. "If we're going to stop Malvolia, we need to trust each other."

I step over a branch, looking up to meet his gaze. Gods, how the hell can someone so big and broad and deadly still look so… delicate. Like a work of art. An angelic painting.

"So, what?" I snip. "You're dragging me through the woods so we can pick berries and shake hands?"

He runs a frustrated hand through his hair. "I'm *trying* to make this work."

I hold up my chin. "Or you're just luring me to a secluded location where no one would hear my dying screams."

He's inches away from me, bending down close enough that I can smell the leather from his jacket lingering against that sweet lavender always clinging to his tan skin. There's something swirling in the air around us, chaos or something like it.

"If I wanted to make you scream," he says, dark and playful, "I wouldn't need to do it out here." His accent is husky, eyes lingering on my lips longer than they should.

My cheeks flush, and I push down any allure. Any romantic thought I could ever have about him. Whatever Axlan is, even if he's not what Mother claimed, it's an impossible thought, based on that one reckless time our lips crashed together…

"Keep going," I look away.

Hurt flickers across his face, but he grabs another branch and walks behind me.

"Look," Axlan says. "I know this isn't an ideal partnership. You don't trust me. I don't trust you. We have unfinished business and every reason to hate each other." He's not wrong— or making a very good argument for working together. Either way, he catches up to me and takes the lead, putting an arm on my bicep to show me his serious gaze.

"But you said it yourself," Axlan reminds me. "We need each other just as much as we hate each other."

"I'm not the problem here—I've told you everything I know." I point a finger into his chest. "*You're* the one who keeps leaving the palace. And then never telling me what you've been doing. The witches could be anywhere, and we can't even be in the same room without throwing knives."

It's true, he needs to let me in. Even if he's arrogant and rude…and tried to kill me, I shared everything I had. It's the golden-eyed king who won't participate.

I smirk. "So, tell me."

A dangerous ask.

He furrows his brow. "What?"

"Where you've been going every day," I urge.

Axlan scoffs, mocking my earlier words, "Keep going."

I cross my arms. "I could just compel you to honor our deal. It worked fine on your dull nobleman."

Axlan rolls his golden eyes, sneering, "You can't compel other compulsion users, but nice try. I spent days picking his brain apart and putting it back together after your scheme."

"My *scheme*," I spit, "was good enough to trick the likes of you."

He raises an eyebrow. "And it's the last time I allow a pretty face to distract me."

That sends another pang through my chest, but I ignore it. When I meet his eyes again, they're hardened with betrayal. It turns my blood to ice and my stomach to mush.

"A pretty face? Or was it how easily I could outshoot you in arrows," I taunt.

He groans, masking the pain from before. Axlan takes another step, sending us back on our way. "You're a good shot, I'll give you that. But I'm sure you have some elemental magic, and some steady wind can really make a difference."

His features darken, he begins to grumble.

"I've always sucked at the elements."

I blink in surprise. "Really? I thought you were good at… well, *all* magic." It's what I've read and what I've heard. The Realm Bound are a product of multiple gods, giving them ability in every aspect of magic.

Axlan whacks a branch. "Technically, yes. But there are some things I'm better that than others. Viska is a master elementalist. She could cause realm-wide natural disasters if she really wanted to. I prefer dark matter, like shadows at my beck and call."

To emphasize his point, he holds out a hand and little specks of gold start to swirl from his palm. It shimmers pure light for a second, until wisps of black start to blend within it. When Axlan snaps his fingers, the dark and golden shadows swirl around his entire body, pulling the energy from the air. I feel it crackle against my skin, against my own magic.

His eyes get brighter, glowing with gold. I can feel the power seeping through him. So can the king, because his half smile turns into a full-on dangerous smirk. I stare without a word, wondering if he's going to use this as his opportunity to show me how powerful he is. But a second later, he snaps his fingers again, and the magic is gone.

"You have shadows?" I blurt out.

Axlan shrugs again. "Shadows. Tethers. Manifestation of magical energy." He keeps down the path. "Whatever you want to call it. I can do almost any magic…well enough."

I smirk. "Just not like Viska."

He shoots me a sour look.

Our pathway narrows further, hemming us between gnarled roots and dense moss. The damp scent of soil and decaying leaves fills the air, sending another shiver down my spine.

BLOODJEWELS

Morbida really does have the eeriest folklore I've ever read, most of it based on some sort of truth—there are countless creatures lurking within the woods. None that would brave getting close enough to the castle, I'm sure.

We don't speak for a mile or longer. Until I can't stand the silence anymore, until the urge to accuse him of dragging us nowhere becomes too hard to ignore. He's up to something, and I'd rather know than end up stranded. My annoyance with him transforms into a simmering anger; he's enjoying this.

"Really, Axlan?" I accuse. "You can't possibly be taking us somewhere important right now."

He doesn't turn around, and the path swings right. We emerge from the thick foliage in front of a…cliff?

A towering, soaring cliff. So high up, so massive, that you can't see the water below. Only a thick misty fog. Faintly, I can hear the rumbling waves, and I taste the salt-tinged air.

Hell no. Not again.

Please, no more jumping. No more swimming through the night or fighting choppy water. I can't bear another moment practically drowning, swallowing down gallons of salt water or inhaling my own soppy hair. Not after I barely escaped Malvolia—I can't think of the ocean without thinking of her. Actually, I'd be good with never going near the sea ever again.

The sun comes up, reflecting on Axlan's dark hair. The vast expanse below stretches endlessly as the dawn colors of pink and orange begin swirling together. Air that was once cool is now warm against my cheek. Honestly, it's really breathtaking. Though I won't admit it out loud, to him.

But it's written all over my face. I'm staring in awe, watching the rising birds start to fly over the foggy ocean. It gives him a smacked look of satisfaction; probably proud he was able to shut me up. But a pretty view doesn't automatically mean we'll be able to work together. He knows that, so why are we here?

I shoot Axlan a dry look. "I'm not participating in your screwed up trust fall."

Axlan turns, facing me with his back against the open-ended cliff edge. A halo of emerging sunrise clings to his black attire, making him look more like a god than I've ever seen. He lingers near the crumbling rock, half a step away from falling backwards into the sea.

"What's the matter?" he taunts. "Too familiar? We both know you love a quick exit."

My ears turn red. "Congratulations." It's muttered with dripping sarcasm. I'm showing my annoyance. "You've successfully led us to the edge of the realm. You've been *so* very helping in stopping a war!"

My words hang in the air, a direct challenge for him to bite back. But to my surprise, he remains silent with a slightly cocked head and a mischievous look. His wicked lips twitch into a lopsided grin, forcing his dimples to deepen. Before I can process whatever mind game he's playing, Axlan cups his fingers, bringing them to his mouth and shrieking out a high-pitched whistle.

It rings in my ears. He's got to be losing his mind.

"Ax—" I start to say.

But my word mangles into a scream. A shocked, grueling scream.

Because he jumps.

CHAPTER 28

Yes—jumps. From a cliff even higher than the tower I leapt out of. High enough to hurt anyone, even a god.

My vision blurs for a moment, panic makes my tongue bone dry. I only hear my heartbeat and nothing more.

But he doesn't give me time to process his reckless decision, not even a minute to look over the edge for his mangled body, because there's a deep huff and a growl, followed by flapping of heavy wings. It only takes a second for the impetuous king to rise, and he's not splattered on the rocks or drowning in the sea below. Instead, he's sitting atop the most majestic creature I've ever seen.

A massive, hot breathing, deadly dragon.

Unlike the folktales I spent my childhood rummaging through, this dragon looks at me with deep eyes, like it knows exactly who I am and why we're here. But even stranger, it's letting the king ride it.

A real dragon.

I admit, I thought they'd gone extinct. I mean, that's what the books say. If they still existed after the war, historians put Skully right through their migration path—and we never saw any. But before they became lost, tons were written on them— wild, untamed, and impulsive creatures. Before Axlan, no one had gotten close enough to one and lived to tell the tale. One roar of fire could burn down an entire village. It was rumored for a while that he won the war with the help of the dragons. I never believed it—not a single credible source documented it. It was a rumor, of course. But seeing him now, I'm not so sure.

The dragon is slender, like it can fit between narrow rocks, made to fly long distances. Its scales are ragged, almost glowing, and it's the deepest black I've ever seen. In the night sky, the beast would be nearly undetectable until it's far too late. Its eyes on are a violent grey, and the massive teeth come to a sharp point over its jaws. Axlan has a saddle fitted on, keeping him steady on the back. From atop the beast, I can see how he could have won the war. How he's been able to remain in unchallenged power for so long.

Together they look…lethal.

The flapping wings are enough to blow my shining white hair from my face. Axlan points a finger down, raising his eyebrows at me to look below. I lean over the side and see a rickety set of stairs leading down to a drop off point against the rocks. Once I see it and nod to him, he guides the dragon back down, landing out of sight. At least it's better than jumping.

The staircase, like the king's ego, seems endless, snaking its way down the rocky cliff face. The steps are uneven, worn down by the relentless march of time, as if mocking my own faltering journey. Loose pebbles threaten to send me sprawling, but my pride refuses to grant them the satisfaction.

As if I'd let Axlan watch me die.

I reluctantly step down the worn stone stairs, watching Axlan and the dragon come into view on the cliffside cave. I shoot him a glare when he smirks up at me, filled with equal parts annoyance and resignation. His self-assured smile, leaning against the dragon, only fuels my contempt. My desire to punch him in the face for keeping things from me soars.

The cliff's jagged edges loom overhead, casting an ominous gloom that shrouds the descent. I'm focused solely on making it down without killing myself. Distantly, I hear dragon mumblings and sharp claws against the stone. When I get near the bottom, I'm a great deal closer to the beach below, but still high enough to do some damage. A bead of sweat drips down my face as I step onto solid ground. Relief floods my system, even my magic seems to exhale. I didn't realize how focused I'd been, how long I'd been holding my breath.

The clearing in front of me is blocked by an egomaniac and a beautiful dragon.

I raise my eyebrows. "And I thought Viska was being dramatic when she said you should've fed me to the dragons."

Axlan huffs. "She was. Saoirse prefers goats. Or the occasional whale."

I approach them both, shoving down the fear from standing next to a ghastly beast. Or two.

But Saoirse is curled against the king in what I can only assume is affection. She's watching me with one large slitted pupil, but more out of curiosity than anything. The tip of her tail sits on Axlan's muscular shoulder, her skull resting on the cave floor. She looks almost like a house pet, even if there's a swirl of smoke coming from her nostril.

"I didn't think the legends were true," I admit.

He shrugs his shoulders. "Most aren't. Dragons aren't what most anyone would expect. They're...like us. But they aren't bound by our laws, they don't follow our rules of nature. They make one hell of a story, though."

"But you managed to tame one," I say.

"I didn't tame her. We have a mutual understanding of each other." Axlan runs his fingers across her black scales. "Growing up there were times when I needed some distance from my family. I was hiking the woods near Morbida's heart. Usually, I avoid the woods there all together, some nasty creatures can lurk inside. But Viska had just chewed me out about claiming our thrones and moving into maturity—something I wasn't a fan of—so, I was feeling…reckless. There was a shriek from a pit of rocks, she was stuck between the boulders. Once I got close enough, I saw a hole burned right through her wing."

As if intently listening, Saoirse extends her massive wing, revealing a patch of black that's lighter from the rest. A place where her scaly smooth leather grew back rugged. Her grey eyes dart from Axlan to me, making sure I've looked.

Axlan nods, Saoirse re-tucks her wing.

"I couldn't just leave her there to starve. Especially after I looked into her eyes and saw something so human. More so than I could ever be," he admits. "And I really didn't want to go home. So, we went back and forth for a few weeks. I've got some nasty scars to prove it. Eventually though, she realized I was going to keep bringing her fish, and if she wanted food delivered, she'd have to keep me alive."

Saoirse *rolls her eyes.*

Axlan clicks his tongue at her. "Oh, don't. We both know I'm a better fisherman."

The dragon grumbles, nestling her head against the ground.

"As you can see," he goes on. "She isn't tame by any means. But she allowed me to ride her. And then I just knew—that we were going to care for each other. She can come and go as she pleases. Not that I could prevent it—Saoirse does whatever the hell she wants. But she likes this cliffside, it's her favorite spot. So, we keep her saddle at Dragoncliff," he motions around us. "And I hope to the gods she's here when I need her."

I blink at him. "You're afraid of the woods in your own kingdom?"

He groans. "That's the part you're hung up on?"

"I just didn't think you were scared of anything," I say.

Axlan shakes his head. "Everyone is scared of something, Dove."

I can't imagine the six-foot seven king having much to fear. Especially when the only other people who could come close to challenging him are his siblings, who, despite their tough love, do care for their brother. My heart pounds, I take a step closer to him, the heat of Saoirse and the tension between us making me red.

"What are you afraid of?" I whisper.

Axlan turns from the dragon, gently grabbing my wrist. My heart pounds harder from his closeness.

I don't pull away. He puts my hand on Saoirse's rough side, allowing my fingers to glide down her scales. She makes a rumbling noise, bending back for a better pet. My heart is going a million miles an hour from the dragon and the giant looming king inches away.

"The point is," Axlan evades. "Dragons don't give out their trust very easily. It takes time to earn it."

I snicker, pulling my hand from her scales. "You're not making a very good point for our partnership."

He sighs. "I'm *saying* that trust takes time. Time we don't have. Not if we want to win this war before the next century."

I narrow my eyes. "Really shedding a bright light on things, Axlan."

He runs a hand through his curls. "I brought you to Saoirse for two reasons. First, because I want you to see that you can trust me. I'll honor our deal."

I nod. He can say whatever he wants. It's action that I'm interested in. "And?"

"And," Axlan buckles the saddle down. "She's our ride."

I blink. "*Our* ride?"

He can't expect me to get on her. He just said it took him weeks to build up any sort of relationship with her. Maybe she won't burn him alive, but I'm not convinced she would leave me unscathed. Will she even let me on her? Axlan's adamant that they chose each other, and clearly there's some sort of rider bond. Something tells me she won't want his natural sworn enemy atop her back.

Axlan sees my hesitation. "We can't build trust in the time it'll take to stop Malvolia. I didn't bring Saoirse to lecture you or convince you to trust me. But I know someone who can help us. And Saoirse is the fastest way there."

I weigh my options, glancing around like there's a way out of this entire mess. "Tell me where we're going first."

If I'm going to risk my life flying through the open air on a creature who hasn't been recorded in over five hundred years, I'd like to know where we're heading. Axlan flinches, like he knows that his answer won't make me happy.

"If I tell you," he says hesitantly, "you have to promise not to whip any daggers at me."

I glare into him. "Fine."

Even Saoirse makes an apprehensive noise.

The king swallows. "We're going to see a blood witch."

CHAPTER 29

"A blood witch?" *I sneer at him.*

It can't be possible. In fact, it's so unbelievable I think I've heard him wrong. But he says nothing, and his cheeks are tinted with red, and his face is telling me he knows this is information he should have shared earlier.

Axlan has a blood witch.

I've never seen one in my life, of course. Blood witches were among the most powerful of us in the old days. They're everything a demented healer like Mother wishes she could be. Blood witches source their magic from blood, any blood. They were lethal witches, able to control anyone they pleased so long as they had a heart to stop. A clot could explode in your brain. Your eyes could inexplicably bleed tears. They could rise your organs to skin's surface, pulling them right out of your body. The magic is so intimate, sometimes it was used to bind promises or seal spells.

They were deadly.

And rare. Really, really rare. Even in the height of the witches, when our numbers were larger than any other species, blood witches were few and far between. Mother says it's because they were practically infertile, so pregnancy was almost unheard of. When the living blood witches went to war with the coven, none had any children to store on the Isle. They'd gone extinct when Axlan slaughtered them all.

All, it seems, except for one.

"A blood witch?" I ask again.

Axlan nods. "I could explain every part of it to you, and I will, if you want it. But the story isn't what you think, and there will be time for questions later."

I cross my arms. "Well, I have quite a few of them right now."

"I know," Axlan assures. "But Saoirse loves the sunrise—she'll be *pissed* if we don't let her soak up the morning light. It's only dark for bit longer where we're going. And I don't know about you, but I'd prefer if the dragon didn't disintegrate me to ash."

Saoirse grumbles in response, agreeing with the king. A perfectly timed swirl of smoke emerges from her nose.

Can I ride the dragon? I have a feeling she would have already protested if she didn't want me to, but it still seems…risky. My body isn't quite ready for another adrenaline rush, not so soon after the Isle.

Axlan puts his foot in the saddle, hoisting himself onto Saoirse's back. He makes it look effortless, but that's because he's twice my size. From the saddle, he holds out his hand, a daring look in his golden eyes. My heart pounds at a doubled speed.

He sees my hesitation. "You've leapt from towers and escaped a magically sealed Isle. Twice. Not to mention all the daring stories you've told me over chess or in the training yard, which I'm sure have some truth to them, even under your ruse," Axlan says, craning his neck and letting a raven curl fall into his face.

He's not wrong. The stories I told him while we passed the time during my first visit were about my time on the Isle and completely true, besides the location. I've done crazier things than get on top of a dragon. Besides, this dragon rolled its eyes and is wearing a saddle. She looks smarter than me. Than him. What's the worst that could happen? The realm may already be ending.

I meet the king's eyes with determination. "If I do this, we're actually going to work together. No more secrets, no more withholding information. I trust you, and you trust me." It feels like sandpaper coming out of my mouth, like it's a bigger price than I'll ever be able to pay.

Axlan stares into me, nodding like he means it. "No more secrets. I'll drop my weapons if you do."

Heat stirs in my stomach. With a begrudging sigh, I take his hand. His touch sends a jolt of awareness through my fingertips. His eyes meet mine, a smug glint dancing within them. I fight the urge to roll my eyes, instead forcing a snarky smile that barely masks the tension crackling between us.

"No more secrets and no more knives," I say.

I put my foot in the strap and Axlan pulls me up. It's clumsy compared to him, and I fall into his shoulder, forcing his other hand to grab my waist. I'm practically sideways on the saddle, but the king keeps his grip on me. I can feel the air heat up between us, a prickling sensation eats my skin where we connect.

He leans into me, lips close enough to touch the hair covering my ear. "No more knives," Axlan whispers in a rugged voice. I can almost taste the lavender clinging to him, there's a shine through his sleek curls. This is the closest we've been since I kissed him in the tower.

Axlan lifts my weight again, swinging me behind him in a single motion. I straddle the leather, quickly realizing there's nothing to grab on to.

Except for him.

"And you'll need to hang on," he grins.

I snake my hands around his waist, ignoring the way it makes me feel. The proximity between us feels suffocating, and I can't help but suppress an exasperated sigh. Our bodies are pressed together, his broad shoulders brushing against mine, and the closeness sends a flurry of conflicting emotions coursing through me.

Saoirse grunts, letting us know she's nearing take off. She begins walking towards the cliff edge, sending us shifting around her back. I grab at Axlan hard enough I think he's going to laugh at me, but instead, he presses his arms into mine. It's warm and comforting, especially as we're hit with the warm air. Any moment now we'll be off the ground and sailing with the clouds. I can't decide if I'm going to throw up or pass out.

As the dragon takes off, her powerful wings beating against the air, I grip the saddle tightly, trying to steady myself. The rush of wind tousles my hair, and I can feel Axlan's presence, solid and unyielding. There's an undeniable allure to the forbidden proximity, a magnetic pull that defies reason. I squeeze my eyes shut, as if it'll prevent whatever's about to come. We move around her saddle for a second more, until everything feels light, like we're barely on Saoirse at all. Everything's quiet, even Axlan. When my heart rate evens, I risk opening my eyes.

Holy. Thundering. Dragons…Literally.

I've never seen anything like it. Felt anything like it. Well, maybe one other time in my life, but that's not something I care to acknowledge.

The sky is orange and pink, purple and blue. We're high above anything else, and even the tallest mountains look like mere specks. Saoirse, for a couple ton dragon, soars weightlessly, moving us into a place where the sun has barely risen.

Axlan's grip on her back is firm and assured, his focus is sharp ahead, as if he's completely unfazed by our proximity or the jaw-dropping sunrise. When Saoirse lowers us near another cloud, I steal a glance at the side of his face, his angled jawline looks relaxed. Interesting. I've never seen Axlan without tension

in his muscles. Maybe this is exactly where he goes each day—
to fly. Honestly, I wouldn't blame him. Now that I've felt it.

I think he's about to say something, but instead he makes
another high-pitched whistle, just as he did before he jumped
off the cliff earlier. Saoirse responds instantly, jolting us to the
left. The landscape transforms into a blur of colors and shapes.
Everything on the ground gets even smaller, including my own
troubles. With each stroke of the dragon's wings, something
escapes from inside me. Up here, I'm no longer fatherless or
hunting my own mother. I'm not the girl who's just trying to
save her friends, her coven, maybe even the entire realm. I don't
have to be one constant wrong move away from cracking beyond
repair. From breaking down and giving up, letting out that final
breath of defeat.

Instead in the clouds, my moon-colored hair glides against the
wind and I find myself grabbing Axlan closer, tighter. Saoirse's
wings beat on, I become acutely aware of the rise and fall of
Axlan's chest in front of me. The deep rhythmic movement that
matches my own breath. It's both irritating and exhilarating this
unspoken thing that binds us together.

I try to shake off the unexpected warmth spreading through
me, deciding it's just delirium from the thin oxygen or adrenaline.
This is nothing more than a temporary alliance born out of
necessity. I need him to stop a war, and he needs me to prevent
one. But Axlan's presence consumes me—that damn crisp scent
and thick accent that coils every word. For a moment, I wonder
if Mother was right about desiring the enemy.

We fly like this for another twenty minutes, which seems
like an impressive time considering Axlan says we're flying to
the middle of the continent. But dragon travel is different from
other travel—faster. I don't speak, and neither does he, but the

silence isn't awkward. Instead, it's almost as if, for the first time in months, I can breathe again.

But the specks eventually turn to shapes, which eventually hold solid colors and grow into detail. Saoirse flies us over a clearing, where a big grey rectangle morphs into a tower if I squint.

"Hang tight," Axlan tells me.

I grip him harder, just in time for Saoirse to nosedive, sending a gush of air pulling me backwards. The wind is so heavy that I gasp for breath, feeling my heart rate rise. Perfectly timed, my bad left thumb starts to throb, locking up and loosening my grip on the king. Axlan grabs my wrist, sending shockwaves through my arm. It keeps me steady, and he tugs enough to secure me back down to the seat.

Another thump moves me again and I yelp, but it's just Saoirse putting us on the ground. I can't tell if my heart is in my stomach or my throat, if I'm shaking from excitement or fear. And in a second, I realize it.

I just flew on a dragon. A real, live dragon.

With the Realm Bound king. Who I'm still feverishly gripping. It reddens my cheeks even more, especially when I realize I like it. Immediately, I untangle myself, catching a smug smile on his face while I scoot backwards.

Axlan takes the opportunity to swing himself around, straddling the saddle and facing me, his face just inches away from my own. There's mischief in his golden eyes, but his face reads worry, like he can't decide if what's happening could be good or bad.

And that, I can understand.

"When we go inside..." Axlan trails off, trying to decide. "It's best if you stay quiet." I begin to protest, but he raises a defensive hand to explain himself further. "*I know* it's not one of your strong suits, believe me. But Mavis is very old and very clever. She'll use whatever you say to her own advantage. And she doesn't particularly like me. So, getting her help at all might be near impossible. But if she does ask something of you—do what she says."

I furrow my brows, ignoring the heat crackling between us. "Why? And why do you have a blood witch out here?"

He can't expect me to walk into another situation where I don't know everything I should. It's dangerous enough to encounter a blood witch at all—she's not a part of the coven, she could slaughter me merely for existing.

His leg is pressed up against mine. "I told you—I'll answer all your questions later." Axlan's dimple deepens as he smiles, and he puts a hand over his heart. "Scout's honor."

I roll my eyes, thinking up something sarcastic to shoot back when his words seep into me. Suddenly, I no longer need him to explain why he brought me out here at all. *Of course.* It's been obvious since he mentioned the blood witch at all.

"You're going to ask the blood witch to seal our agreement," I say.

Blood promises used to be common magic for the witches and anyone else who they would work for. *Blood binds blood.* It means all blood is connected. Marriages would use it to ensure fidelity, with the spouses promising to be faithful. Business partners would seal their arrangements with a blood promise, making them unable to work with competitors. It's a safety net, a loophole around trust.

And it's the perfect way for mortal enemies to ensure allegiance.

Axlan slowly nods, impressed that I figured it out. "If we can get her to blood promise our partnership, we can finally work together."

I stare into him. "It's…smart." And maybe it'll allow him to finally tell me how we can stop my mother.

He's halfway between a chuckle and a grumble. "I have *some* good ideas."

I find myself smiling back, fighting the urge to lean further into his chest. For a distraction, I glance into our surroundings. I've been too wrapped up with Axlan to even notice where we actually are.

The clearing is surrounded by woods and not much of anything else. It's big enough that it might take a few minutes to walk through, but it doesn't seem overly used. There's a small garden, a wagon, and even a table—all scattered near the looming stone tower hugging the edge of the field.

"She doesn't leave the tower," Axlan says.

He swings himself over the saddle and jumps, landing solidly on the ground. Saoirse is laying on her stomach with her eyes closed, already lightly snoring.

He holds out a hand for me to take.

"Did you trap her here, too?" I ask with an edge.

His hand falters, but he keeps it extended. When disappointment crosses his face, I pretend it doesn't send a pang in my stomach.

"No," Axlan says with certainty. "She just prefers the solitude." I almost feel guilty for asking, shaking off the accusation.

I stand up on top of the saddle, praying that Saoirse doesn't decide to move. Axlan looks at me in question, but I ignore his outstretched hand and jump from the dragon's back, planting my feet solidly next to him.

Now I'm wearing a smug smile, and he's left looking at me like he's finally met some competition. Axlan puts both hands in his pockets.

"We'd better go. In my experience, witches are rather impatient." He steps in front of me, turning his head back in amusement as I follow. "And mean."

CHAPTER 30

"This *is* a blood witch?" I ask, severely underwhelmed.

She's sitting in a rocking chair, humming something with an eerie tune while her wrinkled hands repeatedly clink two knitting needles together. Her hands aren't the only wrinkled part of her. She has lines around her eyes, mouth, cheeks—she's *really* old. Practically ancient. With this type of aging, she's probably close to her descent into death. That would make her alive during the war. Before the war. And the only witch in the realm who just happens to be free from a prison sentence on the Isle. I blink in shock, expecting something more…terrifying.

Axlan shoots me a violent glare, ignoring the remark that this woman probably can't even hear. Maybe once, centuries ago, she'd been deadly. But now, she looks like she barely knows someone has entered her tower. *Her very lived-in tower.* Full of writings and trinkets and drying herbs. The clutter stacks over tables, on the floor, on top of the chairs and the desk. Some look older than I am. Others…even older than Axlan.

"This is Mavis," he tells me.

Mavis doesn't move as Axlan steps around her clutter and approaches the rocker. He takes small awkward steps that look unnatural on his broad frame, unable to avoid squishing a few papers. Instead of responding, her wrinkled fingers are just clicking and clacking, furiously creating rows of yarn that spill down her legs.

BLOODJEWELS

Mavis, the deadly blood witch, is making a…blanket.

I shoot him a sideways glance. "Does Mavis…speak?"

She doesn't seem like it. Her hair is even longer than mine, completely grey and wildly curly. She's slender, borderline frail and best of all—I think she's blind. Both of her eyes are filled with cloudy liquid, her pupils smeared into streaks instead of circles. Surprisingly, the books I've read are true, and her irises are a bright blood red.

My father used to tell me bedtime stories to keep me from leaving my room—warnings that a red-eyed witch would come drain me of my blood if I were out beyond dark. It worked well into my teenage years; I never stepped a toe out of line. Until I realized the monster was my mother who would go for my heart *and* my blood. Even so, I've never lost my fear of the blood witch.

But Mavis looks senile, she stares at nothing—not even acknowledging our presence.

Axlan's stare becomes more violent than before, like he can't believe I'm already disobeying his order. The witch says nothing. Just as I suspected, we've wasted our time coming out here. I turn to the king with a quip, but before I can gloat, Axlan takes a small blade from his pocket.

But he said— "No knives." I cross my arms with assertion.

The king *rolls his eyes* and takes the blade to his own palm in a dramatic motion, showing me that we won't be sparring today. He slashes the skin quickly, blood leaking down his hand in a steady stream. Only then does Mavis whip her head around, inhaling the metallic smell like a hungry lion. Axlan holds out his hand with cupped fingers to keep the crimson from spilling. The witch takes his wrist with a shaky grip. And just when I think it can't get any weirder, she laps the blood from his hand, using her slimy tongue to lick it clean. A drop of red drizzles down her chin, she tilts her head back to savor it.

What the fu—

Mavis shoves his hand away. "What do you want, boy?" her voice crackles and echoes, split with age. Okay, so Mavis does speak.

The *boy* sifts through his pocket, materializing a small cloth to wipe his palm. "The witches escaped the Isle."

Mavis smiles, revealing rotted teeth, lined with grime and visibly black. "Good."

He pretends she said something else but my lip twitches up. So, Mavis speaks *and* has some loyalty to the witches. I wonder what she'll think about me, a witch who betrayed the coven. A knot forms in my gut. Maybe Axlan made a mistake bringing me here.

Mavis stares straight ahead. "But why has Malvolia's daughter left her coven?"

I'm wondering how the hell she got that information, but Axlan isn't. He glances back at me. "She switched sides."

Mavis cackles, an eerie sound that feels like spiders crawling over my entire body. "So much for the loyal heir."

I step forward, unable to bite my tongue. "Malvolia tried to kill me. And she's going to destroy the coven."

Axlan sighs in frustration, something that sounds like *I told you to stay quiet.* But I can't help it—I didn't want to betray the witches. I had no choice. And even I need the reminder. The blood witch turns her neck, staring near, but not at, me. She holds out a wobbly finger. "Come here, girl."

She doesn't look like she could lurch out and hurt me, but I still look to Axlan with hesitation. He nods, telling me to do it. I approach her with caution, getting close enough to see the small hairs on her chin and smell the metallic blood on her breath. Axlan finds the blade inside his jacket, shoving it into my hands. I raise my eyebrows. *He cannot be serious.*

The metal tingles against my skin, still warm from his chest. I turn the dagger over, filled with hesitancy. Who knows what can happen with my blood in her system. Not a chance. I shake my head.

"Do it," he barks, spiking my irritation. I think back to the conversation we had on Saoirse's back, where he told me to do what she says if we want any answers at all. I just didn't think submission would require my blood. Fine. I slice open my palm. The knife is sharp enough that it only stings for a moment. The blood drips against the stone floor, reminding me of the sound in Malvolia's office. I hold my hand out to the demented witch and she takes it with a chilling touch. Her tongue is sharp on my skin, like a mountain cat's. It's warm and uncomfortable, her salvia almost burns. When she's thoroughly licked my palm, she slowly swallows it down and drops my wrist.

Mavis leans back and starts rocking her chair. "Malvolia is looking for something."

"What is it?" urges Axlan.

"You already know what it is," Mavis bites back, picking up her knitting needles again.

Something shifts behind his rugged features, like the witch just confirmed his fears. He runs a hand through his dark curls, his lips are tight. There's no mischief in his eyes, he's no longer the king laughing and soaring on his dragon.

It makes my stomach drop. "What's she looking for, Axlan?" I question.

He begins to respond, but Mavis cuts him off. She raises her hand before turning a blank gaze to me. "The gods were bleeding when they fell, wouldn't you agree?"

"Uh, I don't know," I mumble.

"Didn't your mother teach you of the Falling, *Hexen*?" Mavis sneers.

The witch slang effortlessly falls off her tongue, self-consciously making my cheeks red. The nickname flickers both embracement and nostalgia, instantly sending me back to my youth on the Isle. Hexen is what we call untamed fledglings. Those who don't take well to the rules, the young witches who drip with stubbornness and immaturity. Malvolia used to call me it all the time, practically daily.

Beyond that, my only history lesson on the Realm Bound came from my mother. And we all know how inaccurate that could have been. I know almost nothing of the Falling, besides what the name so obviously states.

"Vaguely," I decide. I won't give her another reason to call me a Hexen, not when I can see the amusement dancing behind Axlan's eyes at it.

Mavis goes back to her knitting, looping the yarn. "They still have skin, do they not? Still hold a beating heart and breakable bones?" she looks at Axlan with a hunger in her cloudy eyes. "Still flowing with blood. Even if they fell with the stars."

Axlan tries to stop her. "Mav—"

She ignores him. "Do you know what happens when a shooting star meets the realm soil, girl?"

I shake my head. "No."

Mavis scoffs. "It burns through the land, cooling down until it hardens. The stars become stones. Incandescent, gleaming stones."

Okay. That sounds pretty and all, but Malvolia has a box full of jewelry back home. I can't image her digging around in the dirt for a couple of shiny crystals.

"Malvolia wants…rocks?" I'm confused.

Mavis snaps her jaw at me in annoyance. "Were you listening, girl? The gods were bleeding when they fell. Bleeding all over the stars they crashed with."

Maybe it's how much she sounds like Malvolia, perhaps it's the way she chastised me, but something within clicks. Holy gods. Realization swirls throughout me. "The Bloodjewel," I confirm.

That's why Malvolia said it was powerful enough to open doors and tether realms. It was infused with blood from the gods. And I handed it to her on a silver platter, bleeding and eager to please.

With a smug grin, Mavis turns to Axlan. "*The* bloodjewel? Even after all these years you've only managed to find one."

One? My eyes widen. "There are more?"

That certainly doesn't bode well for us. Not if Malvolia can get her hands on another. Vanished into thin air is one thing, a pretty even shot that she can't get it. But more than one? The knot in my stomach tightens.

Axlan meets my wary eyes. "Bloodjewels are the most powerful items in the realm. They're not just a talisman—though they make a pretty good one. They mirror the magic of my siblings and me, a potent source of power. And they're damn finnicky little things, lost deep underground when we collided with the realm during our, uh, birth."

"But your mother's amulet," I counter. They aren't *all* lost.

"Was the only one I ever found," Axlan sighs. "Despite the years I spent searching. We've looked everywhere—my entire family has. The one I found for Tissinah is a random fluke, there isn't another anywhere near it. Trust me, I've looked."

I tuck my white hair behind my ear as I process. "Malvolia's looking for the spot you and your siblings collided with the realm."

She's looking for another bloodjewel. That's why she hasn't attacked yet. She doesn't have a way to bring over the death god or the Olcar. There isn't an open door for her to use, or even a window to crack out. She needs the death god, and to get him, she needs a bloodjewel. She knows she can't beat the Realm Bound without it.

My mother is buying herself time.

Axlan nods. "I suspected it when you said she plans to summon the death god. Your mother probably thought that once she untethered my magic from the bloodjewel you stole, it could be used to tie the death realm with ours. She assumed she could use it to open a door. She didn't expect the bloodjewel to vanish." He grumbles. "Neither did I."

"And the land you and your siblings crashed into is just… gone? You're bound to the realm, it couldn't just disappear. Don't you know where it is?" I ask.

And an even bigger question: where did the found Bloodjewel go? I've been so wrapped up in forging new alliances and not dying that I've almost forgotten how strange it was for the amulet to just vanish inside the cauldron.

A flicker of vulnerability crosses his face, exposing the consideration beneath his clenched jaw. He takes a cleansing breath, deciding. "When we fell from the sky—the Falling, our world was dark for days. The gods may have abandoned us down here, but they didn't leave us helpless. We fell into a forest—an enchanted forest, to keep us out of harm's way. Any bloodjewels will be within it. Except, the forest…it moves, roaming the realm and shifting with the tides. We could have ended up anywhere, and I couldn't tell you the spot where we crashed with the earth.

But the forest cared for my silbings and me. Until she came for us." He swallows to keep his voice from cracking. "My mother."

I blink in bewilderment. "And now if Malvolia finds a bloodjewel before we do…"

"She'll destroy the realm," Axlan finishes. "And the Fallen Forest hasn't been located in centuries.""Tick tock," Mavis coos. Her needles are still clinking together, her chair swaying.

Yeah, tick tock is right. Does Malvolia have any leads? She can't possibly know where a bloodjewel is, especially if Axlan doesn't. The information only makes me restless.

Is she dragging Calix and Althea across the realm? How did she learn any of this at all? It's not like we had resources on the Isle. I feel my heart rate rising as the questions weigh me down.

What have I gotten myself into? How did the fate of the entire realm fall on a moody king and young witch caked in mommy issues? Our chances aren't looking so hot.

Mavis waves her wrinkled arm. "Now get on with it. You flew that deformed lizard all the way here. Ask me what you came here for."

Right, our alliance. Hopefully, the witch will seal it and ease both our anxieties.

Axlan doesn't look pleased at Mavis calling his dragon a deformed lizard, but he bites down any nasty retort. He crosses his muscular arms, debating how the hell to breach the subject.

"The witch and I are working together. But there are… complications." Well, that's one way to put it. Axlan sighs. "Dove doesn't trust that I'll spare the remaining witches. I don't trust she'll truly kill Malvolia."

Wait, what? He doesn't trust that I'll kill my mother? After everything she's done to me, the choice is easy. Is that what's holding him back from confiding in me? I make a mental note to correct him later. It's not me he should be worried about. Axlan is so infuriating.

"Have you tried having a conversation instead of violently glaring at each other all day?" Mavis nags.

He ignores that, too. "Dove and I have a deal. Now, I need you to bind it with blood. That way we're both forced to honor our word."

Mavis smirks, making me wary. "Blood is an unpredictable magic."

Axlan grits his teeth. "You've done it before."

She raises her chin. "Yes, alliances are easy to bind. But I don't like you very much."

I choke back a laugh. I've never seen anyone talk to him this way before. A crinkled old witch going up against the ruthless immortal king. She's likely the only person in the realm who would challenge him. Well, maybe besides Viska. But she doesn't seem like the type to be nice to *anyone*—much like her brother, in that regard. Hearing him beg for the witch's help would be almost ironic if the situation wasn't so dire.

There's a depth to the king's voice when he speaks, swirling with reverence and regret that sinks my gut. Fine, I guess I feel a little bad when he says, "Please, Mavis."

Her milky red eyes soften ever so slightly as she meets the king's plea. It's clear they have some sort of history. Why else would he leave her in a tower here instead of the Isle? There's a connection. A connection that transcends time, a bond forged in the fires of their past. Mavis hesitates, as if battling the loyalty she must still have to the coven, before finally relenting with a wobbly sigh.

Mavis hops out of her rocking chair with surprising speed, standing before Axlan and me with a curved spine and deformed fingers.

BLOODJEWELS

She takes his hand first, using her needle to reopen the wound on his palm. The point is dull, he clenches his jaw but makes no protest. I silently watch until Mavis spins to me, dragging the needle down my hand, eerily reminding me of my final dinner with Malvolia. Before I'd known she'd betray me. When I was still someone else. Someone who hoped for a mother. That if I lied and stole enough, I could please her. I could find my place among the witches.

That girl died when the lightning struck the altar.

As the blood drips from our palms and onto the stone floor, Mavis takes the end of her ratty gown, ripping off a slice of the fabric. She tears it into thin strips, the tattered material sheering with ease. Her cloudy red eyes stare straight ahead into nothing, but she reaches out her hands to take ours.

She presses our hands togethers. Axlan's skin feels tense against my warm and soft flesh. His palm is the size of my entire hand, wrist to fingertips. There's some color encrusted into the crevices of his nails, making me think he'd spent the remainder of last night painting instead of sleeping. He's staring at me, fluttering something in my stomach. He moves his fingers around mine, intertwining them. There's a flush on my cheeks from the contact, electricity crackles in the air. Mavis doesn't notice the tension, working the strips of cloth delicately around our tangled fingers.

When Mavis is satisfied by her knot, she steps back, letting the crimson flow down our arms, gliding down our elbows and onto the ground.

I feel her magic fill the air; the smell of metal hits my nostrils. My own power responds, rumbling throughout my body. "Blood binds blood. *Rex vinculum maga*," she says. Her voice deepens with the second part, sending tingles down my neck.

Instantly, my body temperature climbs, and my skin feels as if it's on fire. Axlan is wearing the same panic I'm feeling, and my vision blurs with black patches taking over. I've been knocked out or passed out enough times recently to know when I'm on the brink of losing consciousness. My knees buckle and I'm prepared to fall. A bead of sweat rolls down my forehead. I can't see and there's ringing in my ears. Axlan said she was clever, he warned me she was tricky—

I clutch my chest, feeling a searing agony surge through every fiber of my being. It's as if a thousand fiery tendrils are wrapping around my heart, squeezing it mercilessly. I pull my hand free from the bond, grasping the pulsating tendons. I hear Axlan smack to the floor beside me, I didn't realize I'd been holding him steady. A metallic taste floods my mouth, the air grows thick with a noxious odor, suffocating me.

She's killing us. After everything I've survived, after every escape from death, this is going to be what takes me out? I struggle for air.

Collapsing to the floor, I convulse uncontrollably, my body betraying me with violent tremors. *Stop. Stop. Stop. Get up!* I command myself to no avail. Each spasm intensifies the pain, sending shockwaves of torment coursing through my veins. I claw at the cool stones, desperate for something, anything, to anchor me to reality.

My vision blurs, colors bleeding into a distorted kaleidoscope of chaos. The room spins, and I struggle to focus on anything beyond the excruciating torment consuming me. Shadows dance around me, mocking my feeble attempts to find strength.

The pain pulses with a malevolent rhythm, hammering against my temples like a relentless drumbeat. My mind races, searching for answers. *Poison.* The word echoes in my thoughts, the chilling realization taking hold. She's poisoned our blood.

BLOODJEWELS

The witch poisoned our blood.

Bile rises in my throat as waves of nausea crash over me. The room tilts sideways, and I clutch my stomach, gasping for air. Each breath feels like swallowing shards of glass, the mere act of respiration a torturous ordeal.

A cold sweat breaks out across my forehead, my skin feels clammy and pales. Drops of perspiration drip down my brow, mingling with tears of anguish that stream down my cheeks. The agony is unrelenting, a constant companion in this nightmarish dance.

I strain to call for Axlan, but my voice fails me, reduced to a feeble whimper. He's on his back in surrender, already passed out from the magic. My words dissolve into a garbled symphony of pain, lost in the vast emptiness that surrounds me. The world dims, the edges fading to blackness as my consciousness teeters on the precipice.

I feel that thing again. The same thing I felt when my lips crashed against his before I leapt from the tower.

And then, in a final, desperate struggle, I succumb. The darkness engulfs me, swallowing me whole. My body goes limp, and the pain vanishes into a void of nothingness as I surrender to unconsciousness, the poisoned tendrils of agony releasing their grip on my shattered form.

Damn blood witch.

CHAPTER 31

Being on the other side of consciousness so much lately, you would think that I'd grown used to that limbo of being alive and asleep. Unfortunately, I could black out a hundred more times before I would expect to feel the king of Morbida shaking me awake, desperately calling my name again and again.

"Damn it, Dove."

He's distant, but something is pulling me back. A strange, unfamiliar tether. I follow it, clinging to the grumpy sound of Axlan saying my name. I don't feel anything yet, I certainly can't recall why I'm on the blood witch's floor. Just that despite his muscles, Axlan's arms are warm and soft, a great place to lay my head.

"Mavis! I'll rip you apart!" he sounds angry, but still so divine. Like he belongs to the heavens realm. I almost follow the sound into the sky, but I can feel his worried grip keeping me here. Reminding me something important is happening. Someone is full of laughter, practically hysterics.

The blood witch.

The blood promise.

Axlan.

It all comes rushing back, along with my ability to move. And when I open my eyes, I'm staring into his frenzied face, his curls are hanging into my eyelashes. He blinks, letting out a sigh of relief. But I don't say anything, I'm still looking into his golden eyes. His bright, shining golden eyes.

Which are no longer completely gold.

A wild heat stirs in my chest, along with an electric buzz humming throughout my skin. I'll wait for him to blink again— maybe my vision is still blurred. A second passes, and he does blink again, like he's waiting for me to say something. But I can't, I'm still too busy looking into his eyes. Particularly, his left eye. And if I see it right—all has gone terribly wrong.

"What?" Axlan barks, still holding me in his arms.

I can't focus on our proximity. Or how good he smells. Because a jagged strike of silver shoots from his pupil to the tip of his iris, swirling against the glowing gold.

And it's not just any silver—it's soft and celestial, like it belongs amongst the stars.

The same silver I stare into anytime I face a mirror.

My silver.

Something tells me this isn't what we've asked for. That we've been played. *Hard.*

I try to sit up and Axlan loosens his grip on my shoulders. At first, I think it's the fall, but I feel...different. Not from hitting the stone ground or getting my palm cut. Different like some unoccupied and forgotten corner of my mind has been filled by something new, taken up by something wild.

Axlan waves a hand in front of me. "Say something, Dove."

I can sense his frantic fear, his annoyance from being tricked by Mavis. It's layering on top of my own emotions, causing a hurricane in my chest. He's desperate for me to say something, to tell him I'm okay. In fact, I have about twenty seconds before he picks me up and drags me out to Saoirse and right back to the castle healers—

"I'm okay," I tell him.

When I speak, his anxiety shifts into shock. It's as if he was too clouded with worry to feel it, to sense me. But his handsome face wears bewilderment, and I can feel his mind shuffling through the different possibilities. I take a second to stare at his new eye—the left one.

Honestly, the silver doesn't look bad, slithering across his shining gold color. It's subtle enough to go undetected unless you're standing close to the king, which doesn't happen very often. Except for right now, when I'm still tangled in his arms. *Again.* He reaches for my jaw, grabbing my cheeks and looking at my face.

Despite his warm fingers, I start to snap at him for touching me. He's the one who said if I ever got this close to him again, he'd kill me. And now he's had his hands all over me, more than once today. *Not happening.* But I stop when I read his expression, because he's looking at me the same bewildered way I've been looking at him.

And I know he's scared—not from his grave expression—but because I can *feel* it.

Just when I think his eyes can't go any wider, they do.

And somehow, I know he's seeing something new in me, too. Something different.

Mavis is cackling from her chair, enjoying the witch and the god tangled on her floor, mouths agape and minds twisted.

Axlan drops his hand from my face, stands up, and walks to a table filled with trinkets. He starts digging around before grabbing a mirrored tray. With a shaking arm, he holds it up and stares into his reflection. It only takes a moment for him to see it.

The king stifles a gasp before glancing down at me, like he's worried I'll do the same thing. He's debating how I'll respond, rapidly looking between his own eye in the mirror and me. But Axlan must deem me tame enough because he stalks back and hands me the tray. It's cool against my shaky fingers; I hold it to my features, just as he did.

And though Axlan and I are sworn enemies, we might just agree on *killing this bloody witch.*

Wedged in my right eye, there's a bolt of gold. A shining, bright streak of it, like from a stroke of Axlan's paintbrush, delicate but bold. It's identical to the king's color, a mirror of his gold.

"Mavis," Axlan growls. "What the *hell* did you do?"

Mavis takes another moment of laughter before composing herself into a response. All the while, my mind is shooting a million different ways.

"Blood is unpredictable, boy." She says, waving him off, but I've never seen his cheeks his red, his eyes this angry.

And I've never felt this red, or this angry, either.

Before Axlan has the chance to move, I'm off the ground and on my feet. My heart pounds with rage, my face is a snarl. Shaky legs be damned, any potential concussion can screw off. Whatever Mavis just did, *she connected me with Axlan.* I feel it the same way I feel myself.

And I'm done letting others control my own body. My own mind.

I dart across the room, pulling a concealed knife from my boot. It's one of the dagger's Althea slipped into my belongings before I left—a blade that's very familiar with death. I push the knife against Mavis's wrinkled throat, standing directly in front of her rocking chair. Her earlier mocking laugh is gone, replaced with her chilling silence and blank stare. She doesn't move, but she also keeps that smug grin plastered on her rotting teeth, even as I press down deep enough to almost draw blood.

"Undo it," I growl. It's a low and dangerous sound, soaked

in promise. If she doesn't reverse the magic she just cast, I won't need Axlan's help with killing her.

"Stupid Hexen," Mavis says, laced with entertainment and loathing. "Your mother really taught you nothing of the blood witches?" She leans forward, engulfing me in the smell of her rotting teeth, her unwashed hair. Without knowing why, I ease up my knife so she doesn't bleed.

"Blood is forever. It is not a key or a knot. It's flowing, a combining of eternity." She lifts a hand to my knife, gripping the hilt. She pushes it down, bringing her lips close to my ears. Her voice becomes a raspy whisper. "Now, he is yours. And you are his."

My eyes must go wide because Mavis leans back and begins cackling again. She's clapping her old hands together, thrilled with her scheme. I hear my weapon clank against the floor. I take an unwilling step back.

I think the hell not. There's no way I can be attached to the king forever. No. Way. And he is *not* mine. I try to say it out loud, to tell her that she's wrong. But I can't form the words. My heart is moving faster than it should, I hear ringing in my eyes. The panic floods me, weighing me down and taking me from this world. *Blood is forever. Forever.*

"Damn it, Mavis!" Axlan booms, allowing a strand of those golden shadows to peek out. The temperature drops low enough that I instantly go cold. His energy becomes darker, seizing the power of the room.

Of the realm.

Axlan steps forward, shoving up the sleeve to his jacket. He looks dangerous, but that's nothing new. It pulls me from my panic, shifting my focus to the ethereal god.

Whose just as pissed as I am—trust me, I know.

"Oh, don't glare at me, boy." Mavis scolds him, grabbing her needles and her yarn. She seems to ignore the quaking power, forgetting who she's just fooled. "I told you that blood was unpredictable. I taught you better than sloppy magic, if you've forgotten. And your desire for the girl is written throughout your blood. You should have known not to mix emotions and agreements—your blood will never lie. Neither will the Hexen's." Her lips curl up, revealing a rotting grin. "A powerful little *witch,* isn't she? You ought to be careful with a Hexen like that."

"Enough," Axlan demands.

He walks to her chair, less aggressive than I was moments ago when I lunged at her with a knife. Instead, he takes powerful and deliberate steps, adjusting his sleeve as he walks until meeting her chair. Axlan grabs the rocking chair arms, stopping the motion before leaning down over Mavis. His gold and black shadows are slithering around him, making everything look dark as nightfall.

"Is it what I think it is?" he asks, low and serious. "Is it a blood bond?"

A blood bond? It vaguely rings a bell in my mind, but I can't remember where I've heard it. Certainly not in the Isle, I'd gone through everything we have.

"What is it?" I ask. "A blood bond?"

Mavis loops her yarn, knitting another row. "Ancient magic, Hexen. The binding of blood intertwines two souls, connecting their selves and their magic. And gods, is it *rare.* Comes less often than a gift from the gods." She points a needle to Axlan's nose, his stare is lethal. "A piece of the king lives within the Hexen. And a piece of your Hexen lives inside of you, Realm Bound *boy.*" Mavis snickers. "I wish I could see this—the joining of Nightfall and Seraphina. The gods are surely mocking us now."

"I should kill you for this," Axlan whispers. And he might, from the sound of it. His shadows still rumble around us.

"So, do it." Mavis waves a hand. "Wouldn't that be ironic."

Axlan blinks like he's been struck, as if she's reminded him of something important. Something important enough to change his mind, judging by his face. He wavers for a second, but pushes off her rocking chair, glowering towards the door.

Oh, shit. Axlan owes the blood witch something. We won't kill her. No wonder he's stashed her away in a tower, she'd be walking chaos.

The king looks at me. "We need to go, Dove. Now."

Though I have a million questions, *and a glaring new problem*, this isn't the place to get any answers. Axlan seems sure that Mavis won't be of any help, and he's decided not to kill her. Now, I can't decide if that's a good or a bad thing. But I want to leave just as badly.

I nod, meeting him near the door. All the while, Mavis has resumed clinking her needles together, working away at another row of her blanket. Axlan pulls the handle open, greeting us with the sun and a grumbling dragon.

The clinking stops.

"One more thing," Mavis warns.

We halt in in the doorframe, Axlan looming over me as we turn to Mavis. He props an elbow on the wall to run a stressful hand through his curls. I swallow, praying she won't say something insane.

"Malvolia knows things that you don't, *Realm Bound god*. Things that your Hexen doesn't know either. Ancient practices she's kept hidden from every living soul. Ways that can upset the balance of our realm, secrets that could change everything. Don't underestimate her darkness—she's had nothing but time and a blood for revenge."

Her words suck the heat from my bones, making me cold and cut with hurt. My mother has more secrets than truths, enemies than friends. And a traitorous daughter, bound by blood and magic to the king.

To Axlan.

Mavis is still staring straight ahead, starting her knitting back up. "Now get out. I have a blanket to finish."

CHAPTER 32

We don't speak on the ride back. We don't have to.

Whatever Axlan is feeling seems to trickle throughout me, intertwining within my own emotions. It's a constant invasive stream of…*him*. I can feel his rage at Mavis for binding us together. And his exhilaration from flying atop of Saoirse's back. I can even sense his fear, his utter panic at the thought of our blood bond.

So, yeah, we don't talk while we fly. In fact, it's the quietest I've ever seen Axlan. That is, up until we land back on Dragoncliff a few hours later. And when he finally does speak, I immediately wish he hadn't.

"What's a Hexen?" he asks, unbuckling the dragon from her harness. She slips out of it with ease, giving Axlan a heartfelt nudge before trotting away to bask in the afternoon sun.

I can't help the groan escaping my mouth. Of course, *this* would be the piece of information he's held onto from that experience. Not the permanent bond. Not Mavis' warning of my mother's coming. Not even the scheming blood witch who just screwed him—us—over. Instead, he's fixated on the ridiculous nickname given to untamable witches.

"None of your business," I grumble, starting up the stairs. A prickle of amusement floods my chest, warm and inviting.

And it's *not* my amusement.

"Ah, come on." Axlan jogs to catch up, smirking like an idiot begging to get pushed into the choppy water.

I shoot him a nasty look. "That's the least exciting part about today."

He shrugs, taking two steps at a time. "To you, maybe. But I've never heard Mavis use that name before. And you get all… threatening when it gets brought up."

I scoff. *Threatening.* Over a nickname rather than the Bloodjewel. Opposed to my list of kills and years practicing magic.

Axlan climbs the last stair before I do, reaching out a hand to help me up. We're moving faster than before, eager to get back. He smirks. "Is it a curse?"

"Old witch language," I say, ignoring his hand and taking my own step. I can almost hear his eyes roll.

"It means troublemaker," I tell him, heading down the path to the castle. "If a young witch seems too rebellious, they'll get taunted with the name." It immediately reminds me of the times Malvolia would scold me with the nickname. More times than not, I was convinced Hexen was my actual name.

Axlan's eyes go wide with possibilities, his grin turns feline. I can feel the wheels of his mind turning, thrilled to pocket another way to drive me mad. Which, of course, *is driving me mad.* I hope he can sense my anger, but he's stifling a chuckle behind me.

"Naturally, you're familiar with the term," he taunts. I can spot the tip of his tower, and the air turns more pine from the forest than salt from the sea.

I narrow my eyes. "I'm sure your siblings are waiting."

The king nods, remembering that they agreed to spend the day hunting down any clues for my mother.

"After you, *Hexen.*" Axlan's practically beaming with amusement. It takes all of my patience not to turn around and whack him while we make our way through the gates and back inside the palace.

And though Axlan is quiet, his mind is running circles over a solution for our bond. But for all of his mental somersaults, he's gathered nothing...I think. I'm not really sure how this whole bond thing works yet.

He sighs. "Me either."

I look up. "What?"

"I don't know how the bond works, either. But you keep popping into my mind...like I can almost hear you at times." He pushes open the library door. "I imagine it'll get maddening."

I scowl. "You don't say."

We find Viska and Kier stretched over a table with an array of books and scrolls scattered around them. Beyond the Realm Bound, the library is almost empty, making me wonder if Fawn cleared it out for them. Or if Viska really is just that scary.

Our steps echo, but they don't look up until we sit down. Kier gives us a quick once over and a smile before returning to his book. Only a moment later does he stop, shooting his head back up and looking at us in bewilderment.

Kier swallows. "Did Mavis—"

Axlan dryly cuts him off. "What do you think, brother?"

Viska slams her book shut. "Can you guys shu—"

She stares into Axlan's silver and gold eye. And then to my golden streaked one. Viska blinks—speechless, before bursting out into laughter.

Her laugh—more of a vicious cackle—fills the library. Axlan's irritation spikes, sending a wave of anger throughout me. For a moment, I'm so angry I could hit Viska for not taking this seriously. To contain the energy, I dig my nails into my palms, steadying my breath. *This could get difficult.* Feeling Axlan's emotions only enhances my own, almost making me a ticking time bomb.

A very dangerous ticking time bomb.

Viska leans back, still in a snicker. "I told you not to trust that old hag!"

Kier winces. "By the gods, Ax. What did Mavis do to your eye?"

Axlan crosses his arms. "I don't think Mavis heard me correctly this morning. Pull everything we have on blood bonds."

I scoff, "Oh, she heard you. She just didn't listen."

Kier shakes his head. "She never listens. And she never will. The witch has her own agenda." He smiles, nodding in his brother's direction. "The majority of it is dedicated to pissing you off."

Axlan rolls his golden eyes. "Well, she's succeeded."

I cross my arms. "Now seems like a perfect time to explain why you have one blood witch stowed away. Why didn't you condemn her to the Isle with the rest of us?"

His divine face flinches. "I knew Mavis before the war. Back when I was still maturing. She's just…upset. And old. And bitter."

Viska snickers, shooting accusatory daggers at her brother. "Sounds like someone else I know."

Axlan scowls in her general direction. "Regardless of her antics, Mavis confirmed what we've already known. Malvolia is searching for the Fallen Forest. She needs to find a bloodjewel."

Kier clicks his tongue, leaning into the table. "She can get in line."

Viska scrunches her nose. "Yeah, right behind you two idiots. At least we have a head start." She sighs, pointing a painted purple finger at Axlan. "Malvolia's only been looking for a few weeks. You have…five centuries on her, Ax."

The goddess leans back, crossing her arms like she's satisfied with her math. Her statement eases some of the tension for the others, but it only puts my stomach in knots. They didn't grow up with my mother. They don't know how resourceful she can be. How determined she is. Hell, she managed to unleash the witches without stepping foot off the Isle.

She's smart. Smart enough to hunt down the one item she needs for revenge.

"We'll send out scouts first thing tomorrow," Kier says. "I'll send word for my best trackers. Any lead we once had on the Fallen Forest, any crazy potential theories—our people will be on it."

"I want them across the realm by first light," Axlan says with crippling authority.

"Send them out in small groups throughout the day," I tell them. "Who knows if my mother has witches watching the castle." And she likely does. But I don't say that out loud, not with Viska and her colorful daggers for eyes, still likely blaming this entire thing on me.

Kier gives a curt nod. "Smart thinking. I'll meet up with my best scouting party. They could use an extra pair of eyes. Not to mention my guys have a little bet going." Kier's porcelain cheeks turn a shade of red. He runs his fingers through his thick cropped hair. "First one to find a bloodjewel gets to be king of Pearlis for a day."

"You're going to let a tracker run your continent over a bet?" Viska seethes.

"It's just a day!" Kier defends. "Besides, I trust my men. And we've been looking longer than most of them have been alive. It's practically legend at this point. No real harm. Back me up, Ax?"

Axlan pats his brother's shoulder. "Let's hope our luck changes. Something tells me that Malvolia can be quite resourceful."

"That *something* is just the new bond you share with your witch," Viska argues.

Okay, she really does have a problem with me. Granted, I did steal from them and unleash the witches. But I thought we were past that. Or at the very least, she'd see how useful I can be.

"It's more than that," I say. "Axlan is right. My mother will stop at nothing to get what she wants. And I have no idea what she knows or how far she's gotten. I wouldn't doubt that she has just as many bloodjewel leads as we do."

Upon hearing that he's right, Axlan immediately straightens, and I feel a wave of warmth spread through the bond. Our eyes meet for a moment, but he looks away. He must have felt how hesitant I was earlier when they mentioned Malvolia. He knows that I think she's capable of more. That, or he's taking Mavis' warning very seriously.

Either way, I'm surprised that he's on my side. Even if he should've been all along.

"What about Wailing Moon?" Viska asks. She puts her hair back into a long braid, strands of purple are peeking out of it. "Kier can't attend from the middle of the woods. Imagine how suspicious that will look."

"Wailing Moon?" I question. "Is that the ridiculous ball Fawn's been babbling about?"

"The ball is part of it," Kier says. "It's a tradition even older than us, honoring the Light Goddess' journey across the sky. Every year—on the same day—rays of blue and green dance through the night. Before the sky goes dark again, it rains. For hours, it's a torrential downpour."

"Supposedly, it's the goddess' release after her long journey." Axlan turns to look at me, putting his big arm across the back of my chair. "She weeps for the year ending, only to begin again."

"And I won't miss a chance to get drunk in the rain," Kier

says. "I'll be back for the party. That way the old bastards won't question our competency."

Viska puts a hand on the table. "Enough, Kier. Not in front of the witch."

It sends a prickle of anger through my gut to hear her speak about me as if I'm not in the same room, but I bite it down. As if I'm going to what? Use the information against them? Viska is so worried about my own loyalties, I wonder if I'll ever be able to convince her what side I'm really on. *The old bastards?* Fawn did say that there were rulers before the Realm Bound, and that some are still involved with the courts today. Are the Realm Bound…worried about their reputation?

Axlan rolls his eyes. "The witch has unfiltered access to my thoughts and emotions. I think she can handle our court drama." Axlan's eyes meet my own, silver and gold shining against one another. "Your mother isn't a serious threat without a blood-jewel. It's safe to move forward with our celebration. Besides, the people might become suspicious if we cancel."

I turn my head. "And you're worried about their opinion?"

"Just the fae court," Axlan says. "They hold power throughout Emeraldis. Honestly, they started what we eventually finished with their early civilizations. We need to keep up our appearances if we want to keep them away."

Kier glares at Axlan. "Them and the youngest. Getting them involved would complicate things even more. Only the gods beyond know what their spies have reported back already!"

"The youngest?" I ask.

Kier's glare turns on me, lightening into a smile. "Our other siblings—Sterling and Celeste. They're practically identical and can be *way* wicked. Attached at the hip, sneaky little bastards."

Viska groans. "And they're always up to no good."

Axlan winces, putting his elbows on the table. "The siblings don't need to know more than they already do." The king shakes his head. "Which could either be everything or nothing. Either way, I can't handle them sabotaging us out of boredom."

"You're right, Ax." Kier gets up from the table, shelving a book nearby. Even though the library is empty, he keeps his voice to a whisper. "We'll only involve them if we have to. Otherwise, we continue on like normal."

Viska nods, turning to Axlan. "Just keep people away from your face." She points to me. "Both of you. Anyone with a lick of knowledge will see the bond if they spot your eyes. Just be your usual unpleasant selves and we shouldn't have any problems."

Axlan raises his dark eyebrows. "And you're the picture of pleasant?"

Viska waves him away. "Mavis really did a number on your mood with her little…mistake."

The king scowls, brushing a dark ringlet from his forehead. "It's done something to my magic. Everything feels…different."

I nod. "Mine, too. I almost feel newly matured again. Everything is so intense, the power feels uncontrollable."

Kier looks wary. "I don't know much about blood bonds, but I do know that you two are sharing magic now. It makes sense that you both feel off. You have double the power and none of the communication to back it up."

Axlan scoffs. "Helpful, brother. Very helpful."

"I'll pull every bit of knowledge I can on the bond," Viska says. "Believe it or not, some of the books in this library are older than we are. If Fawn didn't screw with my organization system, I know where to look."

Kier's grin turns cheeky at the mention of Fawn, and Viska immediately reddens. She whacks Kier on his oversized arm, prompting him to make a small noise of protest. Before things can get any weirder, she gets up from the table and makes her way to the books.

Now *that* is definitely something I'll need to ask about later. I would now, except I think Viska has killed people for less.

I look back at Axlan, whose surprisingly calm while the siblings bicker.

"And in the meantime? The ball is weeks away," I say.

He leans down in his chair, bringing his lips close to my ear. I can't tell if it's his emotions or mine, but my stomach flutters and my blood feels hot from his proximity. I breathe in the lavender clinging to his neck while trying to keep my face straight. Gods, why does he have this effect on me?

"In the meantime," he whispers. "You'll be on your best behavior, *especially* at the ball. The perfect picture of an innocent scholar, humbly working on her book and her court image."

I blink. *He wants me at the ball?* "You want me to go?"

"Of course." Axlan's grin is feline. "You're my honored guest in their eyes. It would be scandalous if you didn't go."

Frankly, I think I would rather break my own leg than attend the ball on purpose. Not when I don't know the culture. The music. The social rules.

"I don't know how to dance," I protest.

Axlan shrugs. "We'll teach you."

Thundering dragons, I really thought that would work. "I've never been to a ball before. In case you forgot, someone had me trapped on an Isle my entire life. Balls weren't exactly on our survival agenda." I cross my arms in victory. *Take that, Axlan.* Can't argue with me now.

"Fawn will prep you," Axlan says with ease. There's a smug satisfaction creeping through our bond. Immediately, I want to whack him harder than Viska got Kier.

Viska returns from the shelf, blinking in surprise. "You've let Fawn take her in?"

The eldest king shrugs again. "They get along. And she needs to be with someone we all trust."

Kier nods. "Fawn will have you ready to go in no time."

"Great idea, brother!" Viska shouts, full of fury. "Put the violent and traitorous witch with the *meek librarian.*"

Viska looks redder than the late evening sun, and madder than even Axlan on his worst day. In fact, she seems so angry, I'm worried she's going to leap across the table and pull out her brother's hair. Kier seems to be thinking the same thing as he watches Viska move. Only Axlan seems unconcerned.

"Settle down, Viska." Axlan crosses his arms. "You don't get a say anymore, remember?"

Viska doesn't respond. Instead, she slams her fist against the table before storming out the door, leaving me alone with the two brothers. I don't know what has Viska so upset, but clearly these siblings have issues.

Axlan sighs, "Lovely."

"Ah, Ax. Just ignore her. We'll prepare for Wailing Moon and find information on the blood bond," Kier says.

"Don't forget about the bloodjewels, or finding the Fallen Forest," I add.

Kier chuckles. "Is that all?"

Axlan shakes his head. "You forgot about the death god attempting to overtake our realm."

Easy.

CHAPTER 33

If you've ever wondered whether an immortal witch can get
blisters up and down her feet from heinous shoes—she can.
Besides my will to live, Fawn has also taken my leather boots.
After meeting with the Realm Bound, Fawn took mere hours
to seek me out. The librarian became dedicated to the cause,
turning into a drill sergeant, forcing me through ballroom
bootcamp.

And she's taking her job very seriously.

It started with ruffles; Fawn had me try on seventeen dresses.
Don't get me wrong—I love dresses. I have a closet full of them
on the Isle. But these things are not dresses—they're a crime.

And that was just our first tailor. She'd lined our afternoon
with them. Just as she had yesterday, and the day before. Since
discussing the plan with the Realm Bound, my life has consisted
of strenuous dance lessons and hideous dresses.

So. Many. Dresses.

If I wasn't tripping over Fawn's feet during ballroom dance,
I was stumbling over the manners and politics of court life. My
lack of…everything became clear to her early on, and somewhere
within that second day, she realized that *my* failing is *her* failing.
Needless to say, she's become my babysitter and my tutor. And
she takes no funny business from either role.

Who knew librarians could be so multifaceted?

But even Fawn has her limits. And so do I, balling my

fists into my palm deep enough for my fingernails to leave a mark. She's humming below me, fussing with the giant skirt of another hideous dress. Moments ago, she poked me *yet again* with another pin. Three days of being prodded, three days of drinking tea and learning to courtesy. Agonizing hours learning the backward ways of curtsy.

I've been busy. But only with my new life, here. I haven't thought much of the witches, or of my mother. Kier and the scouts still can't find the Fallen Forest. Neither Ax nor Viska can get the blood witch to say anything more, frustrations have been high enough to send the king into seclusion.

"I wish you would go for something…brighter." Fawn sighs, holding a string of pearls against the ugliest yellow gown I've ever seen. "It's almost criminal to keep that white hair washed out with those dark colors."

I take a breath in, careful not to move the protruding pins. "I like dark colors. Almost as much as I like to breathe, which I can't in this dress."

Fawn waves a delicate hand. "If you would just allow yourself some time to get used to it, rather than complaining over every single outfit, we'd have a much easier time."

"I've tried on more dresses in the last three days than I have over my entire life!" I step off the pedestal and away from the mirrors, pulling at the gods-awful tulle on my shoulder. "It's not like anyone will even notice me. Can't I just wear something simple?"

She's shooting daggers into me, the very same stare Viska likes to throw around. To keep her from exploding, I grin the widest smile I can muster. But even my perfectly straight teeth can't keep her from launching into another dreaded court speech.

"The court notices everyone and everything." Fawn pulls out

another dress from the rack, shoving it into my hands. "And they will most certainly be interested in the newcomer who somehow manages to spend most of her time with the most powerful creature in the entire realm." Here we go again.

Every day, Fawn explains the importance of putting on a good show. She runs through every rule, every social cue, every important name, like I'll be tested on it.

Knowing her, I might be. I don't doubt the librarian somehow gets off on making flashcards or conducting handwriting quizzes.

I pull off the scratchy dress she forced me into, avoiding the sequins which are sharp enough to cut my neck. And they say that knives are dangerous.

But her mention of Axlan tugs on something inside me. "If we spend that much time together, explain how he completely dipped out and hasn't been seen in three days."

Three days. Three days of dresses. Three days of not knowing where Axlan disappeared to. It's not like he's responded to any messages I've sent down the bond. Neither Viska or Kier seem concerned with his absence. Kier figures he's off begging Mavis to reverse the magic. Viska doesn't care what he's doing, as long as he's back in time for the ball. And that was before she told me to get used to it, because the eldest king tends to live by his own rules.

If Fawn knows where he is, she won't say. Believe me, I've asked.

"He'll be back," Fawn assures. "He may skip out on planning the ball, but he won't miss it."

She pushes me back onto the pedestal, forcing me to glare at my reflection. At first, I try not to look at myself. But when I do, something looks different. Older, maybe. The cut of my cheekbones seems sharper, my eyes almost deeper with Axlan's strike of gold. My hair goes past my waist in long white sheets, almost double the length from before. Before my mother betrayed me. Before I had to abandon my friends. Before something inside me changed, permanently. Even my face looks slimmer—meaner. Along with the rest of my frame. The stress is wearing me down.

Getting stabbed in the back, front, thigh, and even arm, by your own mother will do that to someone.

"Viska seems to be doing a fine job in his place," I say. "I think I even saw her storming around with a clipboard this morning."

"Arms up," Fawn demands. Her face turns as red as her hair and her usually perky eyes grow darker. Not wanting to bring out her bad side, I comply. She throws the gown over my head and pulls it down my body. Immediately, I feel constricted by the fabric, but at least it's not as horrid as the last one. I brave another look in the mirror—orange. And rounder than the previous one. With more…ruffles.

"You're right about Viska," she continues. "The goddess is more…meticulous than her brothers. With her in charge, everything will be more extravagant." She takes a step back, assessing my *orange* dress. *Orange.* It takes every ounce of my new power to keep from sprinting out of the castle. Or the city. Or the continent.

Fawn doesn't acknowledge my discomfort. Instead, she places pins in the waist and chest of the wretched gown until her face grows worried. "Which means we need a bigger skirt. Or a smaller one. Or perhaps some sleeves. Maybe no sleeves?"

I start to tell her that we might as well burn the dress, just to be safe, but it's clear she's no longer interested in my opinion on it. Her eyes are distant, plotting a way to prove her questionable taste. Right, it's not like I'm the one wearing it.

She turns away, grabbing at a notepad with one hand and a piece of fabric in the other. On her way out, she runs into the doorframe, which only makes her face even more red.

"I'll be right back," she huffs. "Don't move." Her brown eyes promise consequences if I step even a toe out of line.

"I don't think I could if I wanted to," I say. "Which I do, to be clear! But I refuse to let a corset impale me to death."

Fawn mumbles something about complaining and witches, bolting out the door in a small fury. Whatever she's going to retrieve, it can't be good for me. A shiver creeps down my spine imagining her rummaging through her closet. And though she told me not to move, I'm seconds away from ripping this gown to ribbons. A wave of anger boils over, intensifying the need to get this ugly thing off.

I reach behind my back, tugging on the lace of my corset. It's no use, it ties too far up, and no amount of senseless grabbing will undo it. That's what I get for giving Fawn free rein…she's even banned my personal corset. She claims it's built for combat rather than a party, though it's better than anything she has here. In fact, I plan on wearing it regardless of the dress she chooses. I don't care how much she pleads or argues, the librarian can't physically stop me. It's probably the only perk of having the king's magic.

"Only?" asks an annoyingly familiar voice, raspy and full of bad intentions.

I can see his reflection in the mirror, leaning against the doorframe with his arms crossed and his hair ravished. He wears his usual attire–a black suit dark enough to match his hair, with just a trace of a billowy poet's shirt peeking underneath. His hands are full of golden rings and the amusement behind his eyes tells me he's thoroughly enjoying this.

Of course. Axlan wouldn't miss a chance to see how furious this bright dress makes me.

I turn from the mirror to face him, crossing my arms in displeasure. "Well, it certainly has nothing to do with your sparkling personality."

He smirks, moving from the door further into the room. "Or my dashing good looks?"

The closer he gets, the clearer I can sense what's going on in his head. It's just as jumbled as my own, full of spasms of different emotions. One second, I'm convinced he's angry, the next, I think he's scared. Before he can blink he almost feels… happy. And then an instant later he's back to anger. It's worse than puberty. Than maturing. It's…maddening.

"It's worse when you're here," I grumble.

"You're telling me." Axlan scoffs, stalking the room and coming up behind me. He's close enough to touch my shoulder, and I can see his frame in the oversized mirror. He's almost double my height. But his dark hair and shining eyes somehow compliment my own—opposites of each other.

"Behind these walls I feel you everywhere. But in the sky—oceans away—sweet, simple emptiness."

He looks tired, dark bags cover his smooth skin, and a weary look is wedged in his golden eyes. I should have known by the ravished hair or the wrinkled shirt. Just when I think he can't lose his mind any more, he lifts a hand and touches the lace of my corset. My heart is in my throat, I don't move a muscle, as he slowly pulls the ribbon out. Axlan hardly moves either. He's so intently focused on my back, my waist, that I'm sure he isn't breathing. He moves slowly, deliberately, until I feel some of the pressure ease up enough to take a full breath. It does nothing for the spinning in my head caused by his hands on my back, his skin close to mine.

Axlan is becoming unraveled.

"You've been avoiding me," I accuse.

He won't meet my eyes despite that smug smirk. "I was testing a theory."

I raise my eyebrows. "And?"

He throws his head back, dripping in irony. "And it turns out, I can track you down from any place, anytime." He pulls the ribbon again, loosening it further. Is he going to take it…off? It scrambles my brain further, takes any sense of logic from my mind. And his sultry sarcasm sends a chill down my arms. Either that, or the itchy tulle.

I click my tongue. "How convenient for you. When it's time to kill me, I mean." It's something I mentally hear over and over again—how he promised to free every witch other than myself. How he glared at me with pure anger. Hatred. Vengeance.

Now he does meet my eyes, and they're full of passion. Full of restraint. Full of silver and gold. "Yes, how very convenient." Another pull on the corset, and more breathing room for my stomach. The entire time he stands there, he doesn't take his eyes off the corset, or my shoulder blades. I can feel frenzied energy pour out of him and into me. Something desperate, something dangerous.

My heart beats against my ribcage as I take him in. Whatever magnetic pull is happening between us can only be blamed on the bond. Because looking at him now, he's…different. Maybe it's the way the light hits his raven curls, or perhaps I've just grown used to his egotistical ways. Regardless, I understand him more. He's not just a tyrant king with no regard for his people. He's an eldest brother, bearing the weight of his siblings. A leader, chosen by his own kingdom. A bad shot and a scheming chess player who may or may not loathe romance novels.

I swallow, staring him down through the reflection. "Did you come here to watch me try on dresses?"

His eyes grow mischievous, his smirk deepening. "No, but I should have." My cheeks turn red as he looks me up and down. "I didn't realize you liked orange so much."

"Not nearly as much as your librarian," I say. In fact, I don't think there's a single color that Fawn dislikes. "I'm worried she'll send me to the ball looking like a pastry.

"Take it off," he says, like a dark dare. He pauses for a moment, watching my face go from collected to panicked. "And put on your leathers."

At least he doesn't want me naked. Maybe he wasn't even considering it at all. "My leathers?"

"Whatever weird torture Fawn has for you will have to wait," Axlan says. "You and I are spending the day together."

I blink. "We are?"

He bends down, moving his hand from my loosened corset to my hair. With a delicate touch, he brushes my long white hair off my shoulder, revealing only skin and sparkling orange fabric. Every alarm bell is ringing inside me, every nerve ending is screaming for help. Or release.

I can't decide.

He's watching my collarbone with hungry eyes. "It's about time we get this blood bond under control, before it kills us both."

"What if I don't want to spend the day with you?" I question, heart pounding.

His mouth flickers a smirk. "We have to learn to control the magic, whether you want to or not. So we can either do this the easy way, or the hard way."

I keep my face even as I say, "I pick the hard way."

This time he does look up, meeting my gaze in the mirror. "We're going to need a dragon." He smiles so wide I can see all of his gleaming teeth. "And some space. Well, a lot of space."

CHAPTER 34

"I highly doubt we'll master the blood blond if you keep scorching me with those silver flames," Axlan grits through his teeth.

I grab at my magic, trying to reel it in. "I can't help it. You're irritating me."

A ball of silver explodes into a golden fire, so hot on my fingers I yelp and frantically shake it off.

Axlan stalks the distance between us, the heavy trees cloak our constant bickering. "I'm irritating? I haven't had a coherent thought that isn't imbedded with *you* in days. You're constantly in my head. It's maddening." Oh, he doesn't even know maddening.

Maddening is getting jolted awake at three in the morning because he's viciously swinging around swords or splattering a canvas with a high heart rate. Maddening is knowing where he is at any given time, simply by the way my blood warms and cools in his presence. It's the strike of gold infiltrating my reflection. It's the pent-up power pleading for release.

I ball my fists, staring up into him. "And you're in mine! So, focus. If Mavis won't help us, we'll have to figure this out without her." Stupid old blood witch. That's where we started our morning after he dragged me from the dresses—at her tower door. She practically threw us back out, shouting that a god's heart is still stoppable if we bother her again with our childish problems.

Can't really argue with that.

After she shamefully kicked us out and we remounted Saoirse, Axlan asked her to fly us somewhere discrete. With enough room to practice magic. Explosive magic.

We need to learn how to control these outbursts, at the very least.

Saoirse dropped us in an open clearing, a wide enough space between the thick foliage and tall trees. But even the dragon flew off after the first few dozen silver and gold spectacles, growing tired of our insults or the singeing of her scales.

"Just try again," Axlan suggests, running a hand through his raven curls. He's wearing his riding leathers, his angled jaw rough with scruff. "Maybe slower this time."

I was going slow. I've *been* going slow all morning.

"Fine," I grumble, closing my eyes to focus.

Hesitantly, I reach for all the extra magic, Axlan's magic—now stored within me. I pull on it slowly—just like he said. It seeps through my skin, flickering in both gold and silver under the seasonably warm sun. I keep pulling, unraveling it knot by knot. Just like there's a beginning, there must be an end. But it's too much. The air vibrates around me, there's a prickle of panic coming through the bond. I ignore it, focusing on getting the magic *out*. Axlan clears his throat. My eye snaps open.

"Dove," he warns, interrupting my concentration. I brush him off, digging again and throwing the wild power out. He can shut up for a few minutes, I'm sure it won't kill him. My body feels lighter as the magic exits, like I'm close to heaving it all out. I keep digging—

"Dove!" Axlan commands, his deep voice rumbles. Magic snakes around us both, threatening and ominous. I lose the thread, his inane power slipping back inside of me. I was so close.

Rage boils my bones. I push against his chest. "Gods! Could you be quiet for three seconds? I almost had it."

He grabs my wrist, stopping any further attempts. "No, you didn't. It was too much; I could feel it. You'll get yourself killed. Maybe even both of us killed. Who knows what the blood bond actually entails. Damn blood witch," he spits.

Finally, something we can agree on.

"Let me try again," I say, desperate to get rid of this feeling inside me. I'm jumping out of my own skin with an energized edge I've never had. It's maddening. Like I'm always seconds away from exploding with anger or laughter.

Axlan shakes his head. "No."

"Stop it, Axlan!" I shout, pulling my hand from his and stepping back. "I could strangle you right now."

Another flaming ball—all silver this time— flings against the trees. My fingertips sizzle. Axlan looks at the tree (now on fire), raising an eyebrow.

He takes off his jacket, revealing a black tight-fitting shirt under his leathers. "Fine. You want to fight?" he throws the jacket down on some rocks, cracking his neck. "Let's fight."

As if. I scoff. The last time we went up against each other, things got...out of hand. Though, it doesn't seem like a bad idea now. Fighting with Axlan was the last time I felt really focused on something, even if it was just my own survival. Maybe if we're both distracted with combat, we can get a moment of peace from one another. And if there's one thing we know how to do, it's brawl.

I meet his golden eyes in reconsideration. "Alright. Let's fight."

"No knives," he asserts.

I pull the blades from my leathers, throwing them into the ground. "No knives."

Without warning, Axlan strikes quickly, kicking my legs out from under me. I don't have time to catch myself, but I manage to protect my face with my hands as I hit the ground. I spring back up a moment later. I barely feel the pain in my cheek, energized by the sudden movement. As I turn, I catch the king toying with golden embers, deviously smirking before throwing them my direction. I dive out of the way before they land and fling my own wave of power at him as I roll against the ground.

Desperate to get ahead of him, I whip a silver tether out. I'm breathing heavy as it snakes his way, pulling his feet out from under him. Axlan smacks the dirt beside me, reopening the bite mark on his cheek that just won't heal. He moves and I scramble backwards to avoid the magic he whips. Axlan's on all fours, lurching after me. He grabs my foot and yanks me back. As we engage, our limbs become a blur of motion. The sound of our hands meeting in strikes and blocks echoes through the ancient trees. Leaves rustle and twigs snap under our feet, our surroundings watching the god and the witch battle it out. Axlan's attacks are forceful, his movements fueled by power and precision. I, in turn, rely on my agility and finesse to counter his every move. I mean, he's almost seven feet tall. I'm not exactly at an angle to break his nose at a whopping five foot three. I have to be quicker, stealthier.

With a swift dodge, I narrowly evade his sweeping strike, retaliating with a calculated jab towards his chest. Axlan anticipates my move, deflecting my attack with a fluid motion. He grabs my wrist, and we lock eyes before I pull back and hit him square in the torso. The dance continues, our bodies weaving and twisting in a deadly harmony.

I flip on my back, trying to use my free foot to whack him as I flail blindly. My heel smashes his shoulder, sending him flat on his back. Before he goes down, he fumbles the grip on my ankle. I hastily stand up, steadying myself.

Axlan's up a moment later, lunging for me. We grapple, muscles straining against each other, locked in a fierce struggle for dominance. The scent of sweat and lavender fills the forest, mingling with the underlying fire that crackles between us. It's a dangerous combination, a potent blend of hatred and undeniable attraction.

In a swift, unexpected blow, I manage to bring Axlan off balance. With a surge of adrenaline, I seize the opportunity, pushing him to the ground. He yanks my calf, sending me tumbling on top of him. As we grapple, our bodies twist and turn in a flurry of motion. and before I know it, I find my legs wrapped around Axlan's sculpted frame, our gazes locked in a momentary mixture of surprise and…something more. He's on his back in forfeit, gripping my thighs as I lean over him.

My heart skips a beat as I feel the warmth of his body beneath me, the rise and fall of his chest mirroring my own rapid breaths. The weight of the situation suddenly dawns on me, the realization of the compromising position we find ourselves in.

For a split second, time freezes, and our eyes connect in silent understanding. His dark, intense gaze holds a hint of amusement, as if he appreciates the irony of our predicament. My cheeks flush with a blush that I will away.

Gods, it would be so easy to close the distance between our lips. He must be thinking the same thing, I can *feel* it. As I gaze into his eyes, the air thickens with an undeniable tension that electrifies the space between us. The desire pulsates within me, an insistent drumbeat that drowns out any rational thought. The allure of his lips, so tantalizingly close, tempts me to abandon all caution.

In a synchronized motion, he raises himself up, his hand gently pressing against my lower back, ensuring our bodies remain intimately intertwined. His touch sends a shiver down my spine, igniting a swirling fire within my chest. The intoxicating scent of ethereal mint envelops me, invading my senses and fueling my longing.

We both feel it—the magnetic pull, the unspoken understanding that lingers in the charged air. It's as if a forest fire rages between us—*not* the one I set off moments ago with my magic—impossible to ignore or extinguish. His fingers graze my face, sweeping aside the tendrils of hair that veil my features. With each delicate movement, the mask of restraint on his face crumbles, revealing the raw desire that mirrors my own.

The soft caress of his lips on my neck sets off a cascade of sensations, a breathtaking symphony of pleasure that surges through my body. It's as if a thousand sparks ignite inside of me, spreading like wildfire, consuming any remnants of self-control. I yearn to pull him closer, to lose myself in the depths of his embrace.

But his words echo in my mind, a haunting reminder of the consequences that await us. He warned me, forbade me from ever touching him like this again. Chaos, he said, would be the result. An uncontrollable storm that could shatter everything we're working towards.

Conflicting emotions wrestle within me, the temptation to surrender to the passion battling against the fear of the unknown. The gravity of our connection is undeniable, an indomitable force that defies reason. And yet, the stakes are high, the risks incalculable.

The only thing under control seems to be our magic.

"Dove," he says it like a prayer against the nape of my neck.

BLOODJEWELS

Do you need trust when you have lust? What difference do a few letters make? It's stripping away my final grasp of reason. If I could crush my lips against his, snake my fingers through his hair. He would move his hands from my back to my thighs, feverishly gripping them as he kisses me back. I replay it in my mind, over and over as I stare into his golden eyes.

His breath brushes against my cheek, warm and enticing, as his eyes search for an answer in mine. I am spellbound, my defenses momentarily forgotten. His lips hover just inches away from my own, the magic or the blood bond luring us in.

"Are you going to kiss me?" he says, his accent thick with desire.

I'm staring at his divine lips. "Are you going to kill me?"

He hesitates.

It snaps something inside of me. I pull away, scrambling to my feet without his help. Confusion and guilt wrestle within me, their struggle threatening to consume my every thought. What am I doing? He's my enemy, an alliance born out of necessity. There's no room for romance, no time for distractions.

I swallow hard, trying to regain my composure.

I take a step back, the weight of my actions pressing heavily against my chest. "I need some air," I manage to say, my voice betraying a mixture of regret and longing. Axlan's face hardens, his usual snark replaced by a mask of indifference. Through the bond, he's feeling too many things at once for me to understand. He nods curtly, his guard firmly back in place.

Without another word, I turn on my heels and flee deeper into the woods. The trees become my allies, their outstretched branches shielding me from prying eyes. The forest floor is a mosaic of fallen leaves, muffling my hurried footsteps. I run, not knowing where I'm heading, but the only thing that matters is escaping the god who consistently unravels me.

As the distance between us grows, I allow myself to breathe again, to confront the raw intensity of what almost happened back there. My heart is racing, almost as fast as my mind. What the hell was I thinking? It's one thing to desire him, I've come to terms with that. It's impossible to ignore how alluring he is. But what happened back there would only be a bloody disaster. And I have enough of those to deal with right now.

I only slow down my pace when it starts to drizzle, but even the crisp rain doesn't cool me down. I can still feel his desire through the bond, a few whips of hurt and confusion. The wild magic is back again, threatening to boil me over. Everything is so heavy, I could scream. I find a rock big enough to lay on and fall against it as I try to think of anything besides Axlan. It doesn't work, the stupid god is constantly running around my brain.

I'm still consumed by what just happened—my legs wrapped around the king, the way his voice sounds when he says my name. But the bigger part of me can't ignore the fiery past between us. No matter how *physically* attracted I may be to him, there's too much conflict. Too much deception. And worse, I'm to blame. What I did for Mother…

If I could go back and change it—I would.

But I can't, and grasping false hope will only drown me. Been there, done that.

The only way forward is through. And first things first, I have to get this bond under control. It's no use to have more power if it's going to consume me. Maybe that's what happens when you mix magic from a witch and a god. It molds into…chaos.

If only kissing him would get it out of my system. I know we're wearing armor from the other's wounds, but would it be so bad to drop our knives? I'll let him wave his fingers through my white hair in surrender.

Wait a minute—

Maybe that's the key to this bond. Not kissing, though I'm sure that would create its own form of magic. Maybe we just have to let it in. We've spent the day trying to pull the magic out, desperate for the wild feeling to leave. Perhaps accepting the magic would ease it. To lower my internal guard and *stop fighting*. I close my eyes and breathe.

It's subtle at first—a light humming and a feeling of freedom. The doubts and insecurities that once plagued my mind begin to wash away, replaced with something warm. Something powerful. It engulfs me, I'm no longer a bystander in the realm—instead, I'm an integral part of it. The magic settles inside of me, obeying my will as I shape it with every breath.

I raise my hands to the sky, surrendering myself to the energy that surrounds me. I feel the currents of magic converge upon me, wrapping me in a comforting embrace. The warmth spreads through my body, suffusing my every fiber with a renewed energy. My heart rate is higher than when I was atop the king, everything seems brighter.

I am no longer caged by who I once was, but by the limitless potential of who I can become. Forget Mother, and the witches, and every awful thing that's ever happened to me. These things don't define me. This power flooding through me, this is defining.

Thundering dragons. I have to tell Axlan. It's not full solution but it's a start.

Without a second thought, I turn on my heels and go back towards our training ground. The trees blend together as I pick up my pace, eager to get back to Axlan and show him that we're going to conquer this—and that *I'm* the one who solved it. Not him.

Before I can think of where to find the king, I hear something dart through the foliage. One moment, I'm running, the next, I'm soaring through the air.

My back cracks against a solid tree, sending me down into the soil and gasping for air. My vision goes black, and my left arm breaks my fall. Pain sears my bones as I struggle to breathe, begging my body to recover. Immediately, I'm sending out a mental plea to Axlan for help.

When my sight starts to return, I see a group of shapes emerge, barreling toward me. I summon what strength I can, willing my magic to surface. But I feel too weak, too busy begging my lungs to fill with air. I can't move, whatever threw me into the tree had enough strength to break my bones. And it'll take minutes for them to heal enough for me to roll over, let alone run.

The shapes are faster than I anticipated, closing in on me with a certain hunger. One of them makes a grueling sound, halfway between a hiss and a roar. Still unable to do anything but gasp for air, I mentally beg Axlan to find me. There's always been nasty creatures roaming within these woods, and I think I've just encountered one.

Or four. Maybe even five, now that I can see again.

Covered in warts, oozing with some vile smelling puss, massive ugly monsters approach me, slower now that they've realized I'm too weak to fight back. I almost gag, pushing back a wave of nausea. My stare travels up to one of their faces, revealing rows of sharp pointed teeth and four white cloudy eyes.

I'm going to die in the woods, at the hands of these awful creatures.

My heart pounds quicker as my thoughts take form. I've read about these things before—somewhere, somehow. But while I lack oxygen, the only thing I can do is scramble backwards.

It does nothing, and they begin to circle around me, making grueling noises. All at once, the monsters start slashing at me with long sharp nails, momentarily sending me back to the Isle while I stood before my coven as they cut through me.

The memory almost hurts more than the creatures' nasty gashes. My arm is definitely broken and my ribs cracked. Excitement fills their frenzied swipes, and I wonder if this is how I'm going to die. I must be bleeding. *Again.* If there was an award for most blood lost on this realm, I think I would get it. But it's a bad joke in a desperate time because I'm feeling faint—and scared. It would be a shame to go out by a bunch of backwoods foul-smelling forest dwellers.

But suddenly I'm furious—the type of anger that means certain consequences. And certain death for those around me.

The pain stops as quickly as it started, the nasty smell whisked away and replaced by something sweet and sharp. Something that smells an awful lot like the brooding king. Now the excitement in the air is my own, along with relief. I turn my neck, trying to see what all the commotion is about while the creatures hiss nearby.

It wasn't my anger that I was feeling. It was Axlan's. And he's wearing a look of fury. A look of vicious undoing. A cruel, wicked promise.

One of the creature steps towards him, hissing. "You're out-numbered and unarmed." The words are barely audible, but I'm still shocked it can speak it all. Maybe it's not an animal after all.

Axlan doesn't care. In fact, there's a tinge of amusement flowing through me now. He's excited for the challenge; the chance to let his anger explode. To test out his new magic on a living target.

He fixes the cuff of his jacket nonchalantly, though his eyes are still unhinged, patiently waiting. "And you're out of luck—thinking I need a weapon." His smile sends chills down my spine. He cocks his head, "I'd kill you with my bare hands, except I despise bloody fingernails. Don't worry, though—you'll still die."

Silver and gold mist seizes the area, threatening to devour everything in its path.

Axlan delivers on that promise with a single flick of his wrist, unleashing his magic. They don't get a chance to scream. Or to blink. They're not even afforded a glance to each other before they become…nothing. I'm stuck rapidly looking between the metallic magic and Axlan. The magic is so complex, a moving thing of its own. It's like nothing I've ever seen or heard of before. Something entirely new.

But Axlan, he's the embodiment of power. And soaking this up like a maniac, watching his magic in awe. His eyes are glowing, shining bright enough I can distinctly make out the strike of silver. It's not just his eyes, but his entire body. It's the most divine and terrifying I've ever seen him, radiating a vibration that sets my nerves on fire. His broad frame, his always perfectly ravished hair—with that damn drooping ringlet. And those otherworldly lips—

Ah, great. Maybe I hit my head harder than I thought.

He stalks toward me. "I've figured it out. Naturally, acceptance seems to be key. It's a sick and twisted joke."

I pull myself up on my elbows, feeling my wounds start to mend. "What were those?"

He extends a curt hand out, helping me up but avoiding my eyes. "Trolls. Let's go."

I ignore the pain as he gently pulls me up. I barely regain my balance before he snatches his hand away, turning on his heels and heading towards the clearing. He's in no mood to talk about what's happened. No mood to even look at me.

"Ax—" I start to say.

"No." He cuts me off, not bothering to turn around as he keeps walking. "Forget it, Dove. Let's just get back—"

He doesn't get to finish speaking; another troll comes barreling out of the trees with a blood-curdling scream. It must have been hiding in the woods, watching Axlan slaughter the others. Except it doesn't go for Axlan—it comes for me. Maybe because I'm weaker, which proves true when I'm back on my ass a second later.

Axlan doesn't save me. I mean, I'm sure he would, despite being upset. But he doesn't have time to react before another sound fills the sky.

A booming, threatening roar that sounds dangerous enough it can only belong to one creature.

A winged, fire-breathing creature. In a white flash of fury and dominance, it swoops down low, grabbing the troll with a single claw. A *white* flash. I blink twice, making sure it's not just my vision or broken bones. But it isn't—the dragon isn't Saoirse. He's shining white, with pearly reflective scales that even the moon would envy.

The white dragon flings the troll into the air, catching it inside his mouth in a swift motion. I can vaguely hear the troll's bones crack, its hissing pleas vanish as it disappears down the dragon's throat. I get back up to my feet, my heart seems to pound even faster as I watch the dragon come closer. He's flying low, readying himself to land in the grass. I back up for him, not thinking about how he could also chomp *me* down in a single bite, if he wished.

He's bigger than Saoirse, but has similar sharp horns, the same elongated teeth, and smoking nostrils.

And he's staring right at me. Into me. Through me. With bright blue eyes, rivaling the crisp clear sky.

I don't move. And from behind me, neither does Axlan. We're both holding our breath, waiting to see what the dragon will do. I can feel Axlan reach into his magic, just in case. He won't hesitate, even if it would hurt him to kill this beautiful creature. But the dragon isn't concerned with Axlan. Only me, as we stare into each other. There's a buzz between us, a hum in the air. I don't feel the pain from my broken bones or the cuts up my arms. Only the light air that makes me feel weightless.

The dragon breaks our stare first. But not before giving a small huff that sounds more like *stay out of trouble until I see you again* than anything animal. I don't know how I know, but I do. He turns and pushes himself up into the sky. As quickly as he came, he's left. Leaving me exhilarated and terrified.

I sense Axlan come stand behind me, oozing bewilderment.

He clears his throat. "Well, I wasn't expecting that."

Agreed.

CHAPTER 39

I think I'll have to make a run for it, through the castle and past the guards—if I want to get away from Fawn's dress. I'm holding it between my fingers, an hour before the ball is set to begin. All that time I spent hoping she wouldn't pick orange seemed to pay off. Because the dress isn't orange.

Instead, it's yellow. Bright, bold yellow. And it's round enough to resemble an actual lemon. There are more layers than I could have imagined. And it has ruffles for sleeves.

It's how I know I'm paying for my actions. My consequences are shaped as a redheaded librarian.

I pace the room, debating what to do next. If I put on the dress, I'll be forced to attend Wailing Moon in it for the entire night. If I refuse…

A knock on the door saves me in more ways than one. I answer, still in my robe, coming face to face with the same maid that scolded me into an early morning excursion with the king weeks ago. She keeps her face even, handing me a large box before shutting the door behind her. I don't even have a chance to thank her before she's gone.

I move to the table, setting it down to rip it open. With breathless anticipation, I lift the lid, revealing a creation of dark elegance that leaves me momentarily speechless.

It's a dress, but it's not just a dress. It's the prettiest gown I've ever seen, something that looks like it's from both the heavens and the hells—somehow both elegant and daring. My heart pounds as I hold it up.

The fabric, a cascade of silken obsidian, flows like liquid night, caressing the floor in a simple silk pool of shadows. But it's the top of the gown that has me breathless.

I swear the sleeves have been pulled from the night sky and sewn onto this dress. Delicate moons and stars are stitched within the sheer, black billowy sleeves, small diamonds glistening over them. Hesitantly, I run my fingers over the fabric in awe. With how gentle the stitchwork is, I can tell each tiny moon or star was done by hand—this must have taken *weeks* to complete.

The sleeves cap at the wrists, adorned with more of those tiny black diamonds. The rest of the gown is pure silk, looking as if it knows exactly which of my curves to hug. I glance back to the box, which isn't empty. Instead, there's a black corset within, but unlike any corset I've ever worn before, looking like a diamond ribcage to wear over my own. When I put it on the dress and corset, the two items look made for one another, and I look like death herself. Now, I think I'm ready to go.

Though I've been practicing dance lessons and listening to the distant music, I've never actually been inside the ballroom. My lessons have been locked inside Fawn's office and usually turned into card games rather than waltzes. Tea and snorting laughter instead of instructions and twirls. Going there now, surrounded by nobles and the Realm Bound, I can't help but feel nervous. I don't have a great track record of keeping it cool, of not making a scene. The thought reminds me—I should grab a knife. Quickly, I strap one to my thigh, just in case, before slipping into my black shoes and walking out my door.

I meet Fawn in the hallway, and for a moment, she's speechless. The librarian's own emerald dress is simpler than I thought, making her look even more youthful, more beautiful. Her hair is up and covered in flowers, she has ivory gloves that go past her elbows. When I approach her, Fawn extends an arm, shaking her head in approval.

"It's…perfect!" she whistles. "Ax always has such an eye for these things."

I stop walking, and not just because she used a nickname for the realm's most powerful being. "Axlan sent this?"

She laughs. "Well, who else? He has a knack for the finer things, you know. And this is exactly his style. I'm sure he wanted to make sure you looked your very best."

I don't respond, I'm too shocked.

But why would Axlan do this for me? Especially after everything that happened in the forest. One minute we were intertwined, the next I'm fleeing from him and getting attacked by trolls. And that was *before* the mysterious dragon. And our awkward fight. I'm surprised he didn't keep me in the yellow dress out of spite. Besides, he hasn't spoken to me since that day in the woods, he couldn't possibly have sent this.

Fawn looks to me as we approach the ballroom entrance, her doe brown eyes are laced with nerves. I'm guessing she's thinking of how distracted I was during our sessions, how often I would convince her to have fun with me instead.

She bites her lip. "Just…try not to dance with anyone. Don't curtsy too often and if Axlan shows up don't make a scene." *If* he shows up? I thought this Wailing Moon thing was important. Surely, the people expect to see the king. I hesitate, wondering if I should pull on our bond again.

Fawn doesn't notice my pause, pulling me through the arched entryway, our heels clicking against the floor. I dig through the bond one last time, searching for any trace of the annoying king.

Nothing. And I don't feel him near, which pinches me with worry. *For realmsake, at least let me know you're okay.* But he can't hear me. Or at least, I think he can't. I don't really know.

I shake it away, focusing on the breathtaking ball unfolding in front of me. The rainbow obsidian walls glisten and bounce with shadows from all the flickering candles. Either Axlan, Viska, or a light summoner lit the chandeliers with warm colored orbs. There are people everywhere, all dressed impeccably and covered in riches. The windows are open, and the balconies have a canvas roof, so the partygoers can watch the rain and lights outside when it's time. The night sky is already starting to light up, goddess green light threatening to peek through. Beyond the open space to dance is a lavish area to lounge, where a few fae are smoking and laughing.

It only takes Fawn a moment to slide off my hip and disappear into the crowd, leaving me alone in a room full of sharks. I nod my head and smile at everyone I pass, a perfect picture of polite manners as I mentally shuffle through different court members. Viska is standing by a balcony, her dark hair pulled up into a crown and braids of purple weaving throughout.

She sneers as I approach, crossing her arms in dismay over her silky violet gown.

"Shouldn't you be flirting with the nobles? Or is my brother around? I would hate to send him into a rage."

I ignore her jab. "Can we just be civil for one night? People are watching."

She rolls her eyes. "Well, it's not as fun when you don't bite back."

I shake my head. "I'm too nervous to bite. Tons of prying eyes picking me apart."

A rare flicker of a smile crosses her features. "You're telling me. It seems like every time I attend any sort of party, I learn some new and improved rumors about myself. Like, did you know that the last girl I dated, I apparently locked in my cellar? Yeah, I 'wouldn't let her out' until she agreed to keep seeing me. Oh! Or that I have an army of baby dragons growing underneath my castle? And that they eat the noblemen who disrespect me?" I choke back a laugh. "Okay, that second one would actually be badass."

"Right?" she crosses her arms. "Unfortunately, I've never fed anyone to the dragons—that was Ax. He gets to have all the fun!" The mention of the king speeds up my heart. "Have you seen him?"

Her smile falters. "No. He's not usually thrilled with big crowds. My guess is he's lurking somewhere no one can find him." Just as I assumed. He's avoiding, as usual.

I nod. "Fawn's hiding, too. I swear she just vanished."

Viska frowns. "She's here already?" The air around her grows panicked, she glances over the room again.

I furrow my brows. "Of course, she's my watchguard, remember? Should we find her?"

She pulls on my arm in desperation, holding me in place. "No!"

I plant my feet back down, so she doesn't knock me over. "Okay! Gods, what's with the two of you anyways? Did something happen?" This isn't the first time she's gone all psycho when someone mentions Fawn.

Her cheeks turn bright red. "Mind your own business and focus on your role. The least you can do is be a convincing actress. Especially after the distractions you've caused."

Without giving me a chance to respond, Viska shoves her glass into my hand, storming away without another word. Still not friendly, got it.

Wondering what I'm supposed to do at this thing (I mean really, what's the point of standing around and chatting with people you don't like?), I move to the other side of the room near the fruit trays. After a few strawberries, I spot a flash of gold from across the room, taller than the others.

Kier wears a suit of deep green, loosely buttoned and well kept. His smile promises trouble, his glass already half empty. Just like he said, he's back from the scouting party. The king's presence is flocked by other nobles, and he's kind enough to greet them all. He seems relaxed, which is a good thing. Maybe he has news, something that can help.

I ditch my strawberry stem and push through the crowd to approach him, stumbling in his path when a young noble girl bumps into me. Kier moves his golden eyes all over me, taking in the dress, the hair, my glossed smile.

He gives a slight bow. "The moon witch, herself."

"How was your trip?" I ask.

He extends a hand. "I'll tell you about it over a dance."

It's the last thing I want to do, but I can't refuse the god. Not in front of everyone like this. Not when I need to know what he's discovered. I flash him a hesitant smile, moving to the dance floor. Anyone in our path quickly departs, making room for us to pass. I try not to notice the whispers that follow. Kier pulls me close to him when the music begins. "We didn't find anything useful. Just a bunch of dead ends. And tons of mud," he makes a disgusted face.

"At least you tried," I offer. We sway back and forth; I'm trying to remember every step Fawn taught me. Luckily, Kier seems to know the dance, and he's picking up my slack, making us both look decent.

"And you cleaned up nice while I was gone." His face reddens, like he knows he shouldn't say it, but does anyway. "You look good."

Now my cheeks heat. "Thanks, I, uh—didn't pick any of it out." *It was your brother.*

"Oh, I know. That dress screams Axlan, no doubt. It's like he has this sixth sense, I mean—it does compliment the gold in your eye." He leans against my ear. "I think it makes you even prettier, Dove."

I scoff to hide my surprise. "You're shamelessly flirting with me in front of the crowd."

He sighs. "Oh, come on, Axlan isn't here right now."

I blink. "That's ridiculous. I don't care what Axlan thinks."

He raises his eyebrows. "Really?"

"Yes, really." I remind him, "Axlan hates me."

Kier laughs, soft and sweet. "You're forgetting, I grew up with Ax. I know just how deadly he can be. Don't get me wrong, you seem like a decent threat yourself. But there's no way in hell you should have gotten out of that window."

I flinch at the truth. "Would you believe me if I said I kicked him really hard?"

A glimmer of amusement lingers in his eyes. "No. Not even a little."

"Maybe I'm just a better fighter than you think," I deflect.

He chuckles, and I can tell he's definitely laughing *at* me. "No one's as good as Axlan, Dove. Not even you."

Kier dips me towards the ground, cutting off any answer I could've come up with. Axlan didn't let me go that night, Kier is right about that. And something tells me he has his own suspicions about how I escaped that tower alive. For the rest of our dance, my heart pounds. Onlookers whisper and stare, and after what Viska said, I can only imagine the rumors being spread about the scholar and the king's brother. The song ends, giving me the chance to escape before another starts up. No way will I be grilled about Axlan all night. Or let these people watch every breath I take.

Kier bends down to my ear one more time before letting me go. "He's probably outside, staring at the stars."

I swallow. "Goodnight, Kier."

I take off before he has the chance to utter another word about his brother. Dealing with the Realm Bound makes my head hurt, especially when they seem to have their own opinions on my being here. Gods, for a moment I can see why Axlan gets frustrated with these two. They're…trouble.

I make my way to the other side of the ballroom, putting space between myself and the Realm Bound.

Until I spot Sebastian, drunk over a tobacco pipe and a few women. If he sees me, I'll likely never get out of here. Not without a headache. Or blood on my hands. The sleazy man looks up and for a moment, I think he's spotted me until another young girl captures his attention. Suddenly, this party feels suffocating. The people seem to be closing in, the music is getting louder than I can handle. Growing up on a secluded Isle can't be good for social skills. And I'm seconds away from losing my sanity.

Clicking my heels against the floor, I sneak out of an opened door and into the back garden. On my way out, I stop a butler with a tray of sparkling spirits, opting for the bottle rather than a glass. He doesn't stop me, taking note of my attire which very clearly screams *belonging to the king*. I can't tell if it nauseates or excites me.

Either way, I've decided to drink for the night. I think one evening off from constant worry and anxiety won't kill me—unless it does. Regardless, bottoms up. I pop the cork, taking deep swigs as I slip further into the garden and away from the ball. As I get further away, I feel more like myself. Eventually, the stone path ends, and I'm met with mushy grass.

While I've put enough alcohol in my system during my walk to ignore the obstacle, the still sober portion of my brain makes me untie my shoes and slip them off. No shoes, no problem. I take another swig, thinking of my life back home. Of my new one here. Of how *good* this bubbly drink tastes.

I wander the yard, heading to the palace's backside. There's a hill somewhere around here, a good place to sit away from the crowd, away from the Realm Bound. The first time I saw it, the hill reminded me of the one Calix, Althea, and I would waste time on back home. With them being so far away, it seems like the only way I'll feel close to them. And I will find it, despite the constant swigs I keep taking.

Not entirely sure if it's the same hill I was after, I spot a decent sized green lump. Good enough, especially if it means I'll get to be alone. But as I get closer, there's a speck of black staining it. A tall speck of black. Broad and *very* annoying. With big golden eyes and full lips, looking like he fell from the heavens.

Because he did.

Axlan's already laying against the hillside, decked out in royal formalwear, staring up at the stars.

Taking deep drinks from a tall bottle of something.

CHAPTER 36

"Something's got you all pissed off," he slurs. **"Though I guess**
I don't really feel it anymore. I don't feel anything now." He's got a
bottle in his hand, too. I guess violent minds really do think alike.

I hold up my own sparkling spirits, clearly showing him that I
share his mood. "Me neither. I think drinking numbs the bond."

Axlan raises his eyebrows, storing that piece of information
under the "relevant" part of his brain. He's wearing his signature
color in a crisp suit, a crown adorning his curls. I'm too drunk
to really notice, but I can tell it's stunning—full of golden leaves
and vines—much like his tattoos. His cuffs are the only part of
his outfit that strays from usual, and gods be damned they're
covered in the same gems clinging to my very dress. It brings
him together, sharp and royal.

And he's looking at me. I mean, *really* looking at me. With
greedy eyes and golden hunger.

"You got my dress," he says.

I uncomfortably shift my feet, hiding the flush creeping up
my neck. "I think I have to thank you for it. You saved me from
looking like a pastel popsicle."

His cheeks turn to dimples. "Fawn's taste has always been
a bit...eccentric. I, on the other hand, like things simple.
Timeless." Axlan's consuming me with his eyes again. Or maybe
it's not me, but the dress. "Though there was nothing simple
about that needlework."

Hold on. My mouth hangs open. "*You* actually made this?" It was one thing to think he picked it out, but to design it? Fawn really wasn't kidding.

He shrugs his shoulders, taking another sip and staring into the sky. "Sure. I make a lot of things."

I raise my eyebrows. The alcohol in my system doesn't care about our current feud. Or how awkward these last few days have been since we almost kissed in the woods. "Well, I assumed those things were corpses and tyrant laws. Not *dresses.*" Axlan with a needle and thread, spending hours over a piece of fabric. Actually…I can picture it with surprising detail. I bet he gets a thrill from tight stitching or impressive knots. Of course, he does. The god is nothing, if not meticulous.

Suddenly, I require another drink from my bottle. A big, massive swig.

It slides down my throat, warming my legs and my fingertips. Instead of walking away like a sane person, I move beside him, plopping onto the ground close enough for our legs to touch.

"What else?" I ask, curious to know what he can make.

He swallows, just as surprised by my bold behavior. "All the paintings throughout the castle. And in my studio, obviously." He stops to think, pressing his lips together. "The plants in the greenhouse, though I didn't technically *make* those. I just take care of them. Sometimes I renovate the castle when I'm feeling restless. Even though I designed the original architecture and layout." He's too drunk for humility. "Oh, and the stained glass ceilings. Took half a bloody century."

Axlan frowns. "That was hard. Almost impossible, actually. Really difficult. Kinda like you."

I shoot him a nasty glare. "I'm not the one skipping my own party."

He waves a hand through the air. "It's the same every year. And the crowd can be…stuffy."

I shiver, thinking of my encounters with both Viska and Kier. And the whirlwind that came with them.

"It's not the worst hiding place in the world," I admit. "But what's your plan for when it starts to rain?"

He shrugs again. "Drown."

I choke back laughter. "Not a bad idea."

He leans back, propping himself up on his elbows. "I've had worse. Like visiting Mavis and asking her for a simple favor."

Granted, it wasn't his *best* idea, maybe it wasn't the worst. "We'll find a way out of it."

Axlan chuckles, holding up his bottle. "We just did, remember?"

He's kidding, but I still playfully hit his arm. "Numbing is temporary."

He clicks his tongue. "Only if you stop."

I whack him again, he grins.

"I'm only kidding." The moon is reflecting against his curls. "We'll figure it out. You were right the other day. Letting the magic in is a good first step."

I bring my bottle to my mouth. "This better not have as many steps as Dragoncliff."

He takes another drink, too. "Finally, we agree."

I lean back into the grass. "Maybe Mavis was onto something."

He scoffs. "Or just *on* something. Did you see all those drying herbs?"

I'm choking on laughter, thinking of Mavis lighting up before having visitors. Axlan's probably right, the witch is crazy. He begins to laugh, too, and we're both caught up in the mental image. Stretched out, half drunk and giggling on the grass, everything seems…easy. I can feel my defenses lowering no matter how much I fight it.

Here goes nothing. "When I took the Bloodjewel…I didn't know how important it was to you. Hell, I didn't even know what it really was. I thought I was doing right by my coven, my people. I just wanted to protect them…and myself. But it wasn't right; it was wrong. I screwed up. And I'm sorry." The confession hangs in the air, my heart beats through my ears, everything is fuzzy.

Axlan moves onto his side, looking over at me. "We do what we must to survive. You'll make it right—you already are."

I nod, swallowing down the tears that threaten to spill out. "I will, I promise you."

He doesn't say anything for a moment, but I can feel him watching me. Something slips through the bond, something light and eased. "What, no 'you're a brute with bad aim, Ax' jabs tonight?"

I nudge him. "You're a brute with bad aim, Ax."

We lock eyes, both of us wearing a soft smile and heated cheeks. Booze and bizarre feelings.

Axlan hesitates. "Listen, about the other day in the woods—"

A delicate flapping of wings and a musical little *coo* cuts him off. We both look back into the sky, searching for the interruption. From the night clouds, a dove flies towards us, as white as my own hair. It's the first time I've ever seen one in person, and I can understand now why the bird is my namesake. Our shining pearl color—hair and wings—is identical.

This *can't* be good.

The bird lands directly in front of us, its big black eyes screaming *here you go!* while it waits for us to take the tiny scroll attached to its leg. I glance at Ax, who's looking at the bird with confusion, a battle between his wits and the alcohol.

Curiosity wins and I untie the scroll from its leg. As soon as I do, the dove takes off into the night with one final *coo*. While it flies away, the bird makes a grueling screech, piercing my ears.

And then it combusts into a mist of blood, exploding into nothing. It sinks my stomach, dries my throat. Sobers me up. We both stand, hastily coming to our feet. Axlan's holding his breath as I open the note.

Immediately, a piece of long golden hair falls from the inside. Before I panic, I read.

Dearest Dove,

I think it's time we dine again, wouldn't you agree? So much has happened over these weeks, and who better to share it with than my only daughter. If my motherly love isn't enough to steer you home, maybe your cousin will be. If you want Althea to live through the night, you'll come back to the manor for a family meal.

And don't bother bringing the Realm Bound king, though I hear you two have gotten quite cozy. If the god comes along, I'll kill your cousin before you step a pathetic foot on the Isle. We're having lamb and our finest bottle of red.

Warmest Regards,
Mother

I read it over once. And then again. My heart isn't pumping blood, my airways have closed. *No.* It can't be. I knew it.

Too engrossed in the letter, I didn't realize Axlan was standing over my shoulder, silently reading the note. His panic fills my skin.

"Dove, no." He sounds desperate. More sober than he was moments ago.

"Althea," I whisper.

He touches my arm, bending down to meet my gaze. There's splattered blood from the bird against his cheek. "Dove, it's a trap. My men have constant tabs on the Isle and it's been empty this entire time. Whatever Malvolia has planned for you there, it *isn't good.*"

I blink, snapping back into it. "She has my cousin."

"But—"

I grab onto his arm, energy flows under our touch. "What would you do if she had your siblings? If Viska were in trouble? Kier? Don't tell me you wouldn't go." He would. The same way I know myself, I know he would.

And he knows it, too. But he clenches his jaw. "Dove, it's not—"

I shake his hand off my shoulder, pulling myself away. "*Don't tell me you wouldn't go, Ax. Because you would.*" My voice cracks. "I know you would."

He's grasping for reason, bending down to look me straight in the eyes. "Listen to me—she'll kill you."

I take a step back. "She has Althea."

He grabs my hand, stopping me. "Think about this, Dove. Don't be stupid. Please, don't be stupid." I can't tug my hand away, I can't look away from his eyes. "Not when—" whatever he was going to say, he reconsiders. "Just, please. Don't do this, Dove."

It's too late, I've already made up my mind. "I have to."

He senses my determination, perhaps he feels it himself. Maybe it inspires his own.

"No." It's a decision, from the tone if it.

Axlan starts pooling into his magic, doing whatever it takes to stop me. Golden flecks surround him, I feel the energy through our bond.

I don't think, I just act. Which seems to be a pattern with us, now. But this time, instead of kissing his lips or wrapping my legs around his waist, I take a very different approach.

I punch him.

Hard.

Right in the nose.

I knew it wouldn't be enough to knock him out. It's not like there's a guidebook on how much force it takes to take down a god. Fortunately, this isn't my first time throwing fists. He doesn't go down, but he's shocked. And he staggers back, losing his footing—and probably what little trust he had in me. I don't have time to think about that now, he needs to stay behind. I hit him once more before he bounces back. The impact makes me flinch, another betrayal. But I smack him right where I know he'll lose consciousness.

The bond goes numb as he goes down.

Good—I'm sure it'll fill with rage when he wakes up.

Which could be anytime at all, considering he's an immortal god. I take off running, feet slamming against the grass. I don't have time to find my shoes, or to feel guilty. I can't even be impressed that it only took two blows to knock him out. I don't have time to do anything besides run.

To save Althea.

Swimming will take too long. The last trip took me more than a couple hours, and I don't know what Malvolia has planned for Althea. Gods, Althea—it's all my fault. I should have stopped them from going with my mother. I should have forced them into hiding, or even brought them back to the castle with me. I could have saved her. Instead, I left her with Malvolia. I forced my friends to stay back and work from the inside. I did this.

She will not die for me.

BLOODJEWELS

I'm tearing through the woods, trying to remember exactly where the crooked path ends. Whether it's just his lingering scent, or the piece of him that lives through me in the bond, I'm guided straight to Dragoncliff.

The sky rumbles once, followed by a *crack*. Then it begins to pour.

I'm instantly soaked, my dress clinging to my body. There's no caution in the way I move down the cliff stairs. Not this time. I don't have Axlan's judgmental glare watching me struggle. Instead, I'm surrounded by the pouring rain. And the sky, as it lights up green and dances in different shades of color.

"Saoirse!" I scream, still on the stairs. The water sloshes against my steps, I'm using every muscle to keep my feet from slipping.

"Saoirse, please!" I shout again. The rain is coming down in heavy sheets, making it impossible to see more than a few feet in front of me. Even the green night sky disappears. I make it down the last stair out of sheer luck, but still don't see the dragon.

Gods beyond, this was my only plan. I need her if I want to make it to Althea before anything awful happens. Oh, gods—if she dies because of me.

But the entrance to the cave begins to glow and an incandescent pair of stony grey eyes blink at me. The dragon.

"Saoirse, please. It's my mother—she's taken my cousin. My only family. Please, I need to get to the Isle," I sob. My dress is clinging to my drenched frame, my soaked hair sticks to the hot tears on my cheeks. She can shoo me away, she can burn me to ash, if she wanted. I just need her to see how important this is—

Saoirse emerges, towering over me with annoyance. Her nostrils twirl bits of smoke, her pupil is in a threatening slit.

I stare into her eyes, hoping that she'll remember the strike of gold in mine. I'm counting on the blood bond to reason with her. Technically, I'm Axlan's. Maybe she can sense something. If she trusts him, maybe she'll trust me.

Saoirse roars, and for a moment I think she'll scorch me to ash. But she doesn't, instead lowering her wing.

Relief floods me. I climb on her slick back, hoisting up on the saddle.

"Thank you, Saoirse." I wonder how angry she'll be when she learns I knocked Axlan out cold before coming here.

The huff she gives me in return says she already knows. And that she'll deal with me later.

I can handle that.

I grip her scales tight enough to whiten my knuckles, climbing up her back and strapping myself into the saddle. My hands are shaking so badly it takes me a few precious seconds to get everything tightened down. And then I hear it—her wings begin to flap.

CHAPTER 37

Dragon-back has got to be the most efficient mode of transportation. Saoirse soars through the sky, landing us in front of the Isle mere minutes later. Everything is still wet, but the rain is easing up. Thank the gods, because even a mighty beast like Saoirse can't go up against the violent weather.

I slide down her back, catching sand on my dress skirt. Saoirse landed in the same spot my mother claimed to find my father's head. I can't tell if it's ironic or sadistic, but I don't have an extra moment to think. Not when my cousin's life is on the line. I take off, up the sand and into the town square.

Usually, it would be lit up with life, witches drinking into the night, people milling about. Instead, it's eerily empty, wagons and stands are still half full. House doors are open, the muddy paths littered with tin mugs, broken hairbrushes, empty sacks, or whatever else the coven couldn't carry.

She didn't even give them time. A proper warning. She just brainwashed them into blindly following whatever she said.

Just like she did to me.

I let the rage boil over as I sprint through the streets and up the hill. Both manors—Malvolia's and my aunt's—appear empty. The windows are dark and I don't hear any noise, but it's hard to see through all the rain. Regardless, no Althea. No Mother. No sign of any life at all. I'm beginning to think she was just testing how quickly I would come.

Until I smell the metallic tinge of blood.

There's movement near my mother's manor, causing me to look closer. On the doorstep, a small frail frame is croaking something out. I rush forward. Althea is bruised badly, large gashes line her arms and legs. She's bent awkwardly in front of the manor door, her swollen eyes are shut. I dive to her side.

"Thea!" I shake her.

Her chest rises and falls in shallow motions. Thank the gods, she's alive. But she's not moving, and she's pretty banged up. I need to move her, get her away from this place before—

A shrilling voice comes through the open door. The same one that haunts my nightmares. My dreams. "Oh, don't be so dramatic. She's fine."

Knowing there isn't anywhere to hide, I step inside, breathing in the all too familiar air. It still smells like her. In fact, nothing is out of place. Unlike the rest of the Isle around us, the manor is completely untouched. The entryway chairs still shine. The table in the dining hall is still set, candles lit, and utensils out. The pitchers are full of wine and the lamb is still steaming.

Malvolia sits in the head chair. She looks…different. But then again, so do I.

She's wearing hunting leathers, much like the ones I own. Her red hair is streaked with onyx, making her look both younger and older at the same time. And the whites of her eyes…aren't white. They're black.

Completely, utterly black.

Just like the veins beneath her ivory skin, twitching and flowing like they're pumping poison throughout her. All around her eyes, her cheeks, her mouth, dark spidery webs are overtaking her face. While witches aren't human, we're supposed to look like them. And she resembles a beast more than a witch. She looks fine, physically. Her muscles aren't deformed, and her stature is still strong, but her appearance…it's evil.

She frowns. "You look overdressed. And wet. Did I interrupt your date with the king?" she plays surprised. "I don't even want to know what kind of things the two of you are into, given your violent history."

I snap. "Shut the hell up, Malvolia."

She claps her hands together, looking at me with amusement. "Oh, you *have* changed! The daughter I raised would never speak to her mother that way."

"You gutted your daughter on that altar," I say. And for once, I truly believe it. "Now I'm just another name on the scroll of people who you have wronged."

"At least join me," Malvolia gestures to the chair.

I take a seat, knowing what's on the line. I won't toy with Althea's life. I'll do what she asks of me, no matter the price.

Malvolia cuts into the lamb. "Are you having fun playing dress up with the false gods?"

I won't dignify a response; she doesn't need to know anything about the Realm Bound. "Althea is leaving with me."

Malvolia waves me off.

"The death god is pleased you've returned." She sounds convinced of it. "He's thrilled to meet you."

I scowl. "If gods could die, I'd kill him myself."

Malvolia scoffs, rolling her eyes while she hacks at the meat. "You're a vulgar girl." She stares at me with such intensity I almost shriek back. *Almost.* But I am not a girl. And I am not afraid of her. Not anymore. I put my fist on the table, meeting her gaze with equal hatred and threat.

"Let the witches go." I'll try to reason with her. "At least give them the choice. Tell them about your deal with the death god.

It's not fair to keep them in the dark, you owe them the truth."

"Oh, plenty know the truth—thanks to your little friends." She puts a slice of lamb on my plate, pushing it in front of me. "Did you really think I wouldn't be watching their every move? You can't erase a hundred years of loyalty, Dovey. I thought you knew better than that."

I keep an even face. "Malvolia, let them go."

She clicks her tongue. "No."

Someone screams, echoing down the marbled halls. It's a desperate scream. A deep, grumpy, very familiar scream. Every bone in my body freezes.

Malvolia chuckles like a child caught with chocolate as I take off in the direction of the noise. I bust through the back door, barreling towards the hill where Calix is laying. The same hill I'd just been yearning for an hour ago while I laughed with Axlan.

He's bleeding against the grass, cut and bruised just like Althea. I dive down, pulling him into my arms. This is all my fault—

"Calix! Calix, wake up," I sob, screaming with sheer desperation.

He coughs, a heavy sound with liquid beneath it. Oh gods, what if it's his lungs? I grab onto my magic, onto Axlan's, trying to shove anything I can into healing him.

His eyes crack open. "Dove?" His wounds aren't healing as quickly as they should, but Calix begins to take in his surroundings, growing more and more panicked. The rain is falling so fast I can't tell how badly his cuts are bleeding or how deep his injures go.

"What are you doing here?" he demands in a weak voice.

"We have to go, Cal," I sob.

He shoves my arm with weak fingers. "No, you have to run! It's a trap!"

Malvolia appears behind us, climbing the hill in big powerful strides. The rain beats down and the wind is violently howling. "I have to thank you, Dove. Really! Leaving your friends was a bold, ingenious move on your part. It made my life so much easier when I was ready to retrieve you." She cackles. "Just slice them up a little and you'll come running." What the hell is wrong with her? She's always been absolutely insane, but this is next level. She almost murdered my friends. *She did murder my father.* She's done nothing but hurt me and the coven.

I start reaching for my magic, letting the anger take over. Her first mistake was not poking a laced needle through my skin this time. Despite being drenched, my senses are perfectly intact. Her second mistake? Forgetting that I am the daughter she raised—violent and vengeful. She took my friends. She killed my family. Now, I want her dead. I whip whatever I can find first at her, a golden arrow that reminds me of Axlan. Of course, his magic was brimming the surface, eager to fight. A second one follows, fast and silver. Malvolia ducks, missing the arrow. Instead of her usual scowl, she finds it funny, laughing harder. But I'm not done yet. Not even close.

"You really have become his!" she babbles.

I lash out again—now, it's a silver flame. "For the first time in my life, I'm completely my own."

Malvolia dives to the side, but not before the flame catches on her thigh, burning her leg. Within seconds, I step away from Calix and approach her. This time, I let the magic flames run up and down my arms, hissing at my fingertips—shining both silver and gold. The rain doesn't touch them, and maybe it's the rage, but I finally feel in control of the power.

And I'll use it to obliterate her.

I heave the flames towards my mother, pouring years of

heartbreak into them. My entire life, I've done what she's asked, played the role she's given me. Without question, without hesitation. When she needed me—I was there. I tore myself to shreds just to see if she'd notice, uncaring of the consequences.

Not anymore.

Malvolia screams, the flames climbing up her body. She tries to fight them off but they're relentless, melting into her. She isn't screaming loud enough for my liking, so I throw another flame near her shoulder, watching as it eats away at her skin. Now, she's shrieking, begging for her life.

That's more like it.

Through the fire, I can see fear fill her eyes. For the first time, she thinks I'm going to kill her. And she's right. To prove my point, I raise the flames up, burning more of her body. She's grasping the grass in sheer agony, counting her final moments.

Malvolia looks to me in pain, her words like sharp glass. "Foolish girl. You've just signed your death sentence."

Before I can tell her to save me a spot in hell, the rain around us suddenly stops and the air becomes instantly chilled. For a moment, everything is silent except for the popping flames. Until Malvolia chuckles again, as if it no longer hurts.

A sickening crack echoes through the air, and I watch in sheer horror as her jaw begins to unhinge, bones and muscles stretching beyond their limits. On all fours, she crawls out of the flames, and they don't follow her. Time seems to slow as her mouth opens wider and wider, a horrid crunching sound melting with a shriek. It's as if some dark power has taken hold of her, twisting her body and breaking the rules of our reality.

It's hard to tell what happens next.

Malvolia takes an eerie exhale. A dense mist, impossibly black and swirling with otherworldly energy, billows forth from within her unhinged jaw. It pours out like an unstoppable force, a manifestation of her pain, fear, and the unfathomable depths of her hidden evil.

The mist dances and writhes, a tangible embodiment of darkness that has lain dormant within my mother. It swirls and curls, whispering secrets of forgotten realms and ancient powers. I can feel its weight, its malevolence, filling the sky and permeating my very being. Somehow, my mother is even worse than I thought, which doesn't seem possible.

I've seen this before. *Somewhere.* In nightmares or picture books, I can't remember. The mist lumps together, twisting and swirling and taking form. Eyes, more than on any creature. Limbs on its side and back and everywhere they shouldn't be. It grows taller, double the size of me. Double the size of Saoirse.

The Olcar.

CHAPTER 38

The Olcar's fingers turn to claws, slashing the front of my gown. I'm instantly down. Blood leaks out of the long gashes, my insides burn. For a moment, I'm on my back looking at the aurora lights as they dance across the sky. I can see why the folk celebrate this—it's jaw dropping. My breath is shallow, I hear wings flap away in the distance.

I can't blame Saoirse. What's happening here is a losing battle. One strike and the Olcar has me clutching my wounds and gasping for air.

"Get up, Dove! Get up," Calix screams. I twist my head, he's up now. Good. The magic must have healed him decently enough. He raises a ring of fire, creating distance between us and the beast that just emerged from my mother's unhinged jaw.

Talk about family drama.

In the distance, I see Malvolia sag against the dirt and wonder if she's dead. Except, I don't have time to wonder, since she just sent a creature from death after me. My hands push against the ground, and I struggle on my knees. The front of my beautiful gown is stained with blood and when I touch my hand to the wounds, my fingers are soaked. Somehow, the ribbed corset is still intact—with how it's placed against my chest, it's probably the only reason I'm not dead right now.

While Calix keeps up the fire ring, I reach for my magic but everything is wobbly. The death god is full of tricks, and I swear

I remember reading something about beasts with poisonous talons. It's just a guess, but judging how my blood feels like it's boiling, it's a pretty accurate one. Relying on instinct and delusion, I whip out a lash of silver, hitting the creature through the flames. It was a lucky shot, but it barely pierces the beast's skin.

The Olcar presses through the fire, unscathed by the ring of flames. Calix tries to raise another, but the Olcar doesn't care. It's barreling towards us on animal legs, reaching for us with human arms attached to bird-like claws. Every time I think I know what it looks like, the Olcar shifts into something else. By the time it's close enough to kill us, Calix has helped me to my feet and he shoves me behind him, fully exposing himself.

With an earsplitting roar, the Olcar lashes out again, and this time its claw sinks right into Calix's torso.

Calix goes down in front of me with a scream. I don't have time to help him, because its black eyes turn to me. Another claw reaches out, going through my shoulder. I hit the unforgiving ground again. My vision blurs, but I can feel the creature getting closer to me, pressing down on my leg with a hand, paw, claw—whatever.

Looking back now, I realize it was stupid to assume I wasn't going to die when I came here. But honestly, I didn't think I would. Until now, as the Olcar closes in, and my blood boils so hot I can barely feel my bleeding wounds. Calix is breathing heavy next to me, his eyes fluttering open and shut. Between his beating from Malvolia and now the Olcar, neither of us are going to make it out of this alive.

The Olcar moves from my leg to my neck, pressing down with a talon, bearing its teeth and dripping hot saliva on my cheek. I pray to whatever gods might be listening and think about the years I wasted. Until I feel something distinctly angry. Something distinctly…arrogant. Suddenly, my neck feels light again, and the Olcar is blasted away.

Axlan appears from the ring of fire, his eyes blazing, his nose bruised and crooked. I was right about the rage, he's furious. But more than that, he's…scared. I feel it pulsating through the bond, coursing through both our veins.

The king is scared.

But he doesn't show it. In fact, I wonder if he's even admitted it to himself. He slashes at the Olcar as Saoirse roars in the distance, flying a few feet above ground. "We're going. Now." He says it with authority. I allow him to pull me up, grabbing his arms to steady myself. My wounds are dripping and he's looking at them like they're bad. *Really* bad. Bad enough that he puts his hand on my chest, allowing the warm magic to flow through me. They slightly close, enough to stop the bleeding.

But that's all he can afford if we're going to make it out of here alive. Once I'm able to move, I pull on his arm. "I'm not going without Calix and Althea," I say pulling Calix up.

Axlan narrows his eyes in debate but decidedly says nothing, like he knows this is an argument he can't win. Instead, he curtly nods his head, realizing I just made this rescue mission a million times harder.

Saoirse is blowing fire on the Olcar, slowly burning it down. Axlan whistles, grabbing her attention. The dragon swoops down, immediately extending her wing as a stepping stool. Behind her, the Olcar is still recovering from her attack. You can see the urgency in the dragon's eyes, like she, too, needs us to pick up the pace.

"We'll get on quickly, fly around front to grab Althea, and get the hell out of here," Axlan says.

Calix doesn't question the dragon so much as he does Axlan. The hunter looks all over the king, searching for a reason to trust whoever he is. Calix doesn't know Axlan's a Realm Bound god, and telling him that right now would not help the situation.

I meet his brown eyes. "Calix, please." He needs to get on the dragon. We have to move.

He nods, deciding my trust is good enough. We all run to Saoirse as fast as we can, which is a light hobble given the way my insides are still spilling out. Just as we're nearing her wing, a voice echo's out in a small, delicate scream.

Malvolia is holding Althea against her, a knife pressed to my cousin's neck. I stop moving completely, holding my breath, Althea is conscious, swaying back and forth with fluttering eyes. Now that the rain stopped, I can tell her injuries look severe and she looks terrified. But her fear does stop her from shouting "Run!" over and over again, begging us to leave. Calix stops, too. Axlan turns to see them. Instantly, his hands begin to swirl with golden magic. He's aiming to take her down—

"Ah, I wouldn't if I were you!" Malvolia exclaims. She presses the knife harder against Althea's neck, a drop of blood spills down her throat. "Don't move again, Realm Bound."

I frantically turn to him. "Don't, Ax!"

He doesn't move, lowering the magic back down. "Dove," Calix whispers in sheer desperation.

My heart pounds through my chest, my body temperature is climbing.

"Dove, she'll kill her."

Gods, I know, Calix. I know.

I turn to Axlan, whose eyes are darting back and forth for a solution. But I can feel the bond again, and I know he doesn't see a way to get Althea away from my mother. Next to me, Calix is wearing a look of pure fear. He hasn't moved at all; I don't even think he's blinked. I can tell his mind is moving in a hundred different directions, like he's trying to find a way to save her, too. "Dove, we have to do something," Calix says, his finger finally twitching.

He's right, but I don't know what I'm supposed to do. Just a bit ago, I had Malvolia near death, and now she has me right where she wants me. I won't leave now, not without Althea. And I don't doubt my mother will kill her if I don't act fast. Malvolia pushes the knife against Althea even harder, causing more blood to seep from her neck. I've never felt so helpless, so—

"She's going to kill her," Calix's tone is urgent.

I don't know how many seconds pass, maybe a few, perhaps a full minute. Time moves differently when it's about to take everything from you.

Before I can save Althea, Calix sends a lightning bolt hurling towards my mother. It's fast, but not fast enough. Nothing could ever be quick enough to stop her. Calix should have known Malvolia would see it coming. Of course she would, she's triple our age and channeling a vicious death god.

Malvolia sticks the knife into Althea's neck before the lightning can even strike.

My cousin's eyes are locked with mine, and in that small second, a lifetime of memories pass between us. I remember her at eight, picking flowers in the field and daring me to eat the bright colored ones. I see her at twelve, stealing dresses from her mother and staying up all night in my room trying them on. Then again, a few years ago, when she told me the word family meant me and Calix, forever. In this small second, I see her laugh, and the way her voice would instantly melt away my worries. How bright she looked under the sun.

And then I see it all drift away.

Althea's eyes go wide in genuine surprise before she goes limp, like she didn't expect my mother to actually do it. But she did, and the knife is completely sunk inside my cousin's neck. She sags down into Malvolia's arms, lifeless. Her cheeks immediately lose the little flush they had left, her green eyes becoming vacant.

I don't exactly know what happens next. Everything seems to stop and start all at once.

I'm maybe lunging towards Malvolia, out of instinct alone. I don't see anything but her blackened spider face. And I'm going to rip it off her skeleton. Big arms wrap around me, holding me back. I expect to smell lavender or a crisp mint, but instead it's leather and fresh rain. Calix is caging me from my target. And he has approximately three seconds before he becomes my new one.

I'm screaming. Wailing. My voice cracks and shrivels in mania. I try to mold it into words.

"Let go, Calix!" It's savage, violently, utterly hysterical.

He doesn't loosen his grip; my magic starts to simmer—

Malvolia throws Althea's crippled frame aside, like she was nothing. She doesn't bother to look at us, instead turning to the Olcar. I didn't notice before, but Saoirse is in the air again, hovering near the Olcar as they go back and forth, both trying to slash the other. The Olcar is faster, and it manages to tear at Saoirse's wing. The dragon cries out and dips down, three slashes in her left wing. Just like the mark across my own chest.

Once she falls, the Olcar turns its attention back to us. I'm struggling against Calix's grip as it lunges, claws extended. Axlan takes the first hit, slicing open his arm. It moves to swing again when Saoirse cries out and suddenly, another set of wings enter the airspace.

Big, sleek, leathery white wings.

The dragon who saved us from the woods circles the Isle, landing in front of the Olcar. Up close, it's even bigger than Saoirse, making the Olcar look like a nuisance rather than a threat. The dragon inhales, quickly releasing fire. The Olcar screeches, boiling back down. Malvolia cries out, but the dragon lifts it's head up at the sound, breathing the fire toward her.

She scurries out of the way, erratically sobbing out of concern for the Olcar as it screams. The dragon's tail slashes the Olcar, and it melts into a black boiling pile on the ground. Faintly, I make out a glimmer of magic around the dragon, something I haven't seen before. But before I can process that, my mother moves. Malvolia tries to run. *Not a chance.* I flail against Calix, hitting and biting to get him off.

Calix doesn't budge. "Althea's dead! She's dead, Dove. It's no use! She'll just kill you, too!"

Just as I'm about to blow Calix's head off, Axlan comes into my vision, bending down to look me in the eye. I'm not leaving without Malvolia's head on a platter. I won't go without my cousin's body. But he knows that already, so he takes my hand and reasons with me. "Dove, we have to move. The Olcar won't stay down for long." Axlan points to the boiling black puddle, already starting to morph into something else again. "See? We have to go. We can't save her. But you can save Calix. And me. If you just get on the dragon. Please Dove, get on the dragon."

Maybe it's the bond, or maybe it's just his voice, but the rage lessens and my senses return. Oh gods, Althea—

All I feel is grief. Cold, hard grief. It consumes me more than the magic. More than Axlan.

The Olcar rises up again, racing towards us.

Axlan looks to Calix and nods. The hunter picks me up, I kick and scream once again, fighting him off. He throws me over his shoulder, but I'm not going without Althea. I swear to the gods I'm not going without my cousin. They'll have to drag me away, if I don't manage to kill them first.

"Dove," Axlan's voice sounds different, more…magical. Like it has authority that I know I'm supposed to follow. Honestly, it's kinda nice. Maybe I should listen to him. Even though another part of me knows I would never blindly listen to Axlan. That part seems small, unreasonable.

Something isn't right.

I realize my mistake a moment too late, after I look into his eyes. He's compelling me. Well—maybe not full-blown compulsion, but he's using our bond to influence my emotions. He's making his words sound like the only answers. Like I should just get on the dragon and leave this all behind. For once, he's right. Calix's grip never lightens. Axlan's still holding my mind, I can feel it clearly now. But I'm not as upset as I was, not yet. Somewhere inside I know I will be when he lets go. But for now, I'm numb enough to let my tears fall freely as they throw me on the white dragon.

The Olcar is gaining on us, but the dragon is already off, leaving my cousin's body behind.

Calix knows better than to let me go as we fly back. He has his back to Axlan, keeping his grip on me instead. I don't feel anything at all, but as I watch Calix I wonder if he doesn't feel anything, either. His face is void, his eyes hollow. I watch the Isle become a speck, and Althea with it. I see nothing but the sky and Calix's helpless eyes, feel nothing, but the knife entering Althea's neck.

The white dragon has us back in Morbida within a few minutes.

When we land, it's the same place I punched Axlan in the nose earlier. If I had feelings, I might be sorry about that punch. But I don't feel anything. Because Axlan has my emotions locked in a chain around his neck. Can he even do that—compel another compulsion user? Maybe it's the bond. I don't really know, and I'm too numb to care.

Axlan's down first, reaching up to help me off the dragon's back. Calix hands me off and I put my arms around Axlan's neck. For a moment, his face is close to mine and there's heat crackling between us. His warm hand snakes around my waist. My feet hit the ground, but he doesn't move away. Instead, he leans in closer.

"I'm going to pull my magic back," he says, his voice heavy.

I swallow. "Okay."

He tightens his grip. "And when I do, you might feel a little… upset. So, I'm going to need you to promise that you'll remain calm."

I nod. "I promise." What's the big deal?

Calix warily gazes at me, unconvinced.

Axlan nods back. "Okay."

He pulls back, letting the emotions flood back inside of me.

Big. Mistake.

My arms are covered in silver flames, specks of gold infused throughout. I use them to throw Axlan against the castle wall, though it's quite a distance. He hits it with a crack. *That's for compelling me.*

I turn to Calix, rage simmering inside my every step. "You killed Althea."

He staggers back. "I didn't know—"

The flames crawl up his leg. He's flinching as he heaves over, trying to grab at his calf. "Dove!"

I pool into my magic, diving deeper than I've ever dared. Every ocean has a floor, even if it's beneath the dark nasty hollows inside. The flames rise up his legs. His hip.

In my peripheral, Axlan staggers down, clutching his chest. My flames become more golden than silver, the rush of magic bordering euphoric.

The action of Axlan hitting the castle attracted the party, and court members start pouring onto the balcony. At first they're whispering, but once they see the dragon it turns to shouting and screaming. Viska shoves through them, looking bewildered as she reaches the front.

Calix is screaming. Althea didn't get to scream. She didn't get to do anything but wait to die under Malvolia's blade. Because he had to provoke my mother. She told us not to move. She told us that she would kill Althea. He had to strike her down and risk the worst-case scenario. Which happened anyways.

My heart feels like an open wound, my anger is raw and blistering.

"Dove! You're hurting *him!*" Calix pleads, pointing a shaky finger at Axlan as he gasps on the ground. His eyes meet mine, and he looks afraid again, but not like on the Isle. This time, he looks scared of me. He's sending out pleas through the bond, but I numb it out. I only have room for rage.

White hot, blinding rage.

I start the fire on Calix's other leg. Slowly, like how time was moving when the knife plunged through Althea's skin. I want this to hurt, and I want it to hurt for a while. People are shouting all around us. Some are moving closer to the hill for a better view. Good. I'll give them a show. The witches are back, anyways. Might as well let them know. I dive deeper inside myself, finding more power. I feel unstoppable, incontrollable.

Until I see a flash of purple, so fast I couldn't respond.

And then everything goes black. Everything, except for my rage, which claws at consciousness for an extra moment.

CHAPTER 39

Axlan's sitting with a romance novel, legs crossed while he turns the pages in deep concentration. The sun is hitting the side of his face, soaking into him and reflecting back a true god. I've been watching him for a few minutes, hoping that he spends the day engrossed in the chapters rather than looking up to see me awake.

Everything's sore, down to my very teeth. Somehow, I've ended up back in my designated rooms, neatly tucked under a thick blanket. I don't know how many days have passed, or what happened after Viska knocked me out.

I do know that I've calmed down. And while the rage still lives in the back of my muscles, it's agreed to subside.

"That's what I've been waiting for," Axlan says. He flips a page, not looking up from the story. Well, I got half my wish. At least he isn't making me meet his eyes. I don't know what to say after almost killing him. *Again.*

"How long?" I ask. Judging by the pounding from my skull, at least a day.

He flips another page. "Three days."

I blink away the shock. Three days. So much could happen in three days. What of my mother? Or of the coven? Is she truly close to unleashing the death god? How—

"The Isle was empty by morning," Axlan says, reading my mind. He gives a sneaky glance up, hoping I don't see. "There's no sign of anyone. Not your mother. Not…Althea. I'm sorry, Dove." I can tell he means it, and that he knows how deeply Althea's death will affect me.

"Three days, huh?" I evade talking about her. "Viska got me good."

He understands my avoidance, glancing up again. "If you ask me, she'd been waiting for an opportunity."

I imagine she was. I touch my face to be sure—yep, definitely waiting for it.

I almost don't dare ask my next question. "Where's Calix?"

Axlan's gaze grows weary. "He's…here. He's been helping us while you've been out. Information on the witches, weather magic, setting snares."

"Great," I grumble.

"Dove, try not to blame him." Axlan shuts the book, setting it on the table. "Calix told me about your family, about the Isle and the coven. There's nothing more you could have done for Althea. He didn't kill her. Knowing Malvolia, she would have killed Althea either way."

I shake my head. "Maybe he didn't kill her, but he's still responsible. Just as much as Malvolia." My own mother stabbed her niece in the neck, clutching her innocent frame as she bled to death. Deep down, I know it isn't Calix's fault that my cousin is dead. He was just another pawn in Malvolia's game. But he knew better than to play. If he would've stayed still, Althea could be alive. It was his rash behavior that provoked my mother. "He wasn't thinking clearly," Axlan gently says, moving to sit on the end of my bed.

"I know," I say. And I do know. Which almost makes it hurt more. Calix wouldn't get Althea hurt on purpose. But that doesn't change that she's dead. I look at Axlan again. "She'll pay for this."

He nods, putting a hand on my leg. "With her life."

It's my mother who must die.

"I have a lead." Axlan stands up from the chair, pulling on his shirt. "It's across the realm, a place even *I* rarely travel. It's… dangerous. I won't send my men out there."

Just the thought of hunting down Malvolia ignites a new passion under my skin. "Send me."

He meets my eyes, his face serious. "We'll go together."

My stomach flips. "The two of us?"

Alone. On a life-threatening mission. Nothing but undercover travel and the open sky between us. With the fate of Emeraldis in our hands.

Right.

Axlan sits at the end of my bed, touching my knee. "Viska is going to stay and oversee Morbida. She's so organized that her continent practically runs itself. And it's best if we travel unaccompanied—we'll be harder to follow. Harder to gossip about. No one will slow us down. The other night…you almost took me out by summoning all that magic. We need to do more than just let it in. We need to control it."

He's right—I know it. With everything that happened, I almost forgot the magic affected him, too. I really did almost kill him the other night—by accident this time. But the idea of me and him in such close quarters, working together when our lives really do depend on it. When we'll be forced to depend on each other…it could be a disaster.

I meet his eyes. "When do we leave?"

A flicker of a smile crosses his face. "Not until you're healed up. The journey itself will be brutal, and that's before we get to my siblings. The twins can be…theatrical."

Whoa. "Twins?" He nods. "Celeste and Sterling. The youngest

Realm Bound." Axlan gets up from the bed, heading towards the door. "I'll make the preparations. And Dove—talk to Calix. We could use him here, but he needs to be on our side. Really on our side."

I press my lips together. "I'll talk to him."

He nods again. "Oh, and one more thing. I think you have a dragon now."

I suck in a breath. "What?"

"The white dragon from the woods, he's been hovering around Dragoncliff since you went down. He won't let me near him, but I have a feeling he'll be sticking around." Axlan begins to grumble. "Much to Saoirse's delight."

I'm still stuck on the *dragon* part of it all. A million questions, for another time.

"A dragon-riding witch," I say with a goofy grin.

Ax rolls his eyes. "What has the realm come to?"

With a soft smile and a final worried glance, Axlan stalks out the room. I can tell he's still anxious over my injuries, but knows we have more important things to fuss over. After everything that happened, we both deserve some rest. But who else is going to save the realm?

Hours pass, I nap on and off. I let the magic come over me a few times, practicing acceptance. I think of everything other than Althea, of my mother. When I let the pain in, it'll consume me. And I don't have time for that. Not now. Instead, I listen to footsteps pass by, hoping a pair of them will belong to Calix.

Finally, he comes. Well, he lingers in the doorway—arms crossed, hesitating. And he looks awful. Bags are under his brown eyes, his brown hair is messy, there's scruff on his face. He's tired. And hurting. I see bandages peeking under his shirt, bruises line his face.

I sit up, motioning him in. "I guess we've both seen better days."

He blinks at the irony. "Better months. Better years."

For a moment, I don't think he's going to come inside. But then he takes a single step in, followed by another. He doesn't come sit on the bed like Axlan did, though he stations himself in the cushioned chair. I understand, given I tried to kill him a few days ago.

"I'll never forgive you." My voice cracks. I will away the tears. "You didn't kill her, but I'll never forgive you."

He looks at me, but I can tell that he only sees her. And I think he wants to look away, but he can't. His sunken eyes fill with water, even his fingers shake.

"Did you know I loved her?" it's barely a whisper, the first time he's confessed it out loud.

I nod, a teardrop falls. "So did I." And how could he not? Althea is—*was*—everything good about us. She brought light into a terrifying house. She made family more than a sour word in my throat. She patched my wounds and never skipped sugar in her tea. Life without her won't be living at all—just surviving.

And Calix…all those years of stolen glances and purposeful bickering. He's never not loved her, never once gave up on her. I'm certain she took over half of his heart with her when she took her last breath.

He takes a shake inhale. "Axlan told me everything. About the death god, the bloodjewels. The fate of the realm. Your… bond. I don't know what is going on here, Dove. But…I'm on your side. No matter what, I'm on your side. You can hate me, you can blame me. I know I blame myself, too. But I'll still be here, for you. For Althea—it's what she would have wanted. Even if we're teaming up with our captors."

It floods me with grief, knowing things will never be the same. "We have to kill her, Calix."

He nods. "I know. Trust me, it's what I'm living for. But you need to be careful, Dove. Whatever's going on with you and the king…just be careful. Even half conscious—knocked out by his own sister—you were mumbling his name. Things could get messy."

I hide the flush on my cheeks. "We need them to win. We need Axlan." I meet his brown eyes. "But more than anything, we need each other."

He moves from the chair, sitting at the end of my bed. "I'll stay here and work with Viska. I hear she's pretty talented with the elements. Maybe together, we can get some additional defenses up. Just in case. Go with the king, find a bloodjewel. Just—"

"Be careful," I finish for him. "Yeah, I know."

He gives me a weak smile. "Some things never change."

And sometimes, they do.

CHAPTER 40

The sun hits my face when I open the door, breathing in the warm summer air. My left side still aches a little, but it's nothing I can't handle. Still, I take my time on the path to Dragoncliff. Better safe than sorry, especially for what's to come. I've even spent my normal hours training these past couple weeks, building my strength back up for this very moment.

Axlan's leaning against his dragon, his arms crossed over his leather jacket. They're both brooding—Saoirse and the king. But he can't hide how he's feeling, at least not to me.

The cocky bastard is excited.

"It'll get cold, you know." Axlan bounces off the black dragon, digging for something in her packed-up satchel. I do already know. We've gone over it more than once. Along with our travel paths, our backup plans, and anything else we could bicker about.

I roll my eyes. "I'll be fine. Besides, I think Lark's wings are almost double the size of Saoirse's. More wing, less wind to the face."

Axlan scrunches his nose while I mention my dragon—he's still not used to another dragon rider. But honestly, I'm not used to Lark yet, either. Ax was right about the white dragon sticking around. Once I was up and walking, it didn't take him very long to track me down. There wasn't any awkwardness or hesitation. I looked at him and knew—he wanted in on whatever adventure was going to happen.

Ax spent the week fitting him with a saddle much like Saoirse's and spent every spare second teaching me basic dragon riding. Apparently, stealing one in the middle of the night during a torrential downpour doesn't exactly count.

Six days ago, when I woke up from a dream knowing my dragon's name, it felt…right. Sweat dripped down my forehead, my heart was beating so fast that Axlan came rushing through the door, thinking something was terribly wrong. Except it wasn't. Instead, it was perfectly right. The king with his midnight dragon.

And me, with my moon dragon.

Malvolia doesn't stand a chance in hell.

"Wind or no wind—it's going to get cold. And we're in for a long ride." Axlan throws something my way—a sleek black leather jacket, much like his own.

I raise my eyebrows, slipping it on. "Is this your waving white flag of surrender?"

His smile is smug, arrogant, and straight up maddening. "Not even a little bit, Hexen."

ACKNOWLEDGEMENTS

Books make the world a safer place. At least, that's what they've done for me since I was old enough to shove my face inside them. And I hope that's what *Bloodjewels* has done for you, dear reader. Thank you for picking up Dove's story and giving her a chance. Without you, there would be no Isle, no disobedient witches, no brooding gods. May you find a piece of yourself in this realm the same way that I have. May you always chase your dreams, no matter how daunting or far away they seem.

This is my first book, my first acknowledgement, so bear with me while I sob through how lucky I feel to be surrounded by such wonderful people. My father, John, who has taken such loving care of me throughout my life. When I was a child, you'd drive me to the post office and help me mail out handwritten letters to my favorite authors, even if the postage was wicked expensive. Dad, you gave me belief in my passions, a fire that made all of this possible. There were many times I was so wrapped up in the writing process that I wouldn't even hear you come through my door, though you'd smile at me anyways. Thank you for your patience, your tender heart, and your unshakable belief in me, no matter what. I do not know how to fill my car up with fluids or how to put cream on my poorly behaved pug's nose without your help, but I do know how to treat people with kindness. How to love each person who crosses my path. And that is because of you.

There is one singular person who is the reason *Bloodjewels* is on your bookshelves, rather than just a draft in the depths of my computer. Alex, my *amina vestra*, thank you for filling me with your sunshine, with the courage to believe I can be more. The world is brighter with you in it, forever by my side. You're not only the world's best editor, but also the world's best friend. And to Ivy, the other half of me, thank you for never letting me fall down longer than just a moment. It's your steady hand that's kept me upright. To me, you're the entire sky. You both are my coven. The sun, the moon, and the stars.

Thank you to the amazing team at Fractured Mirror for seeing my vision and allowing this book to become what it is. Emily, I'll be forever grateful for the chance you've taken on me. Allison, thank you for bringing the cover and the details to life, and for putting up with my countless novel length emails. I know I can be…a *handful*. FMP is such a special place and I feel honored to be a part of your team.

There aren't enough thank-yous to the rest of my family, notably my mom, who only got a little upset when I would make constant Kindle purchases on her credit card at two AM as a teenager. See? It was all worth it! And to my sister, who spent many hours digging through the manuscript looking for errors (and who found way more than I care to admit), you are becoming such an extraordinary young woman.

And finally, thank you to all of my students, past and present. You've inspired me in every aspect of life. Thank you for picking this up and reading it all the way through. Remember how powerful words and actions are. Remember that you can do anything you set your mind to. Remember that you are important, worthy, and so loved.

ABOUT THE AUTHOR

 **AMBER HANOPHY** is a long-time fantasy lover, cornering teachers and friends into reading her stories once she was old enough to hold a pen. Since then, she's (hopefully) improved her writing abilities while collecting creative degrees and relentlessly studying folklore.

When she isn't obsessing over villains or watching old vampire movies, Amber works with middle school students near her hometown in Western New York, where she lives with her poorly behaved pug. *Bloodjewels* is her debut novel. You can follow Amber on her social media for updates @amberhanophy.